THE LOST QUEEN

THE LOST QUEEN

NORAH LOFTS

LARGE PRINT

Oxford

First published in Great Britain 1968
by
Hutchinson & Co (Publishers) Ltd

Published in Large Print 2008 by ISIS Publishing Ltd.,
7 Centremead, Osney Mead, Oxford OX2 0ES
by arrangement with
the Author's Estate

British Library Cataloguing in Publication Data
Lofts, Norah, 1904–1983
    The lost queen. – Large print ed.
    1. Caroline Mathilde, Queen, consort of Christian
VII, King of Denmark, 1751–1775 – Fiction
    2. Denmark – Kings and rulers – Fiction
    3. Denmark – History – Christian VII,
1766–1808 – Fiction
    4. Historical fiction
    5. Large type books
    I. Title
823.9'12 [F]

ISBN 978–0–7531–8114–0 (hb)
ISBN 978–0–7531–8115–7 (pb)

Printed and bound in Great Britain by
T. J. International Ltd., Padstow, Cornwall

For

*Eleanor Willy who brought this subject
to my notice and died before the story was
told*

*Robert, my husband, and Pearl, my sister,
who made complete concentration possible*

Margery Weiner who did the research

Their Book

Contents

Part One

CHAPTER
ONE

Kew House, January 1765

The Dowager Princess of Wales had long ago learned to control her voice, her facial expression, and her hands; but in anger or distress the pupils of her eyes widened, reducing the blue to a mere rim.

Caroline saw the danger sign and was not deceived when Mamma said, mildly, "But, my dear child." Her mother's most stringent rebukes often began with an expression of endearment. Mamma could say, "My dear George," and then add something which would make even George wince. George was twenty-seven years old and King of England. Caroline was thirteen; and she had just blurted out that she did not wish to be Crown Princess of Denmark.

"But you *knew*," the Princess said. "Negotiations have gone on for a year and you were informed, young as you were. If I remember rightly you taunted Augusta; you told her that she would be a Duchess and you would one day be Queen."

The taunt had been punished; rightly.

"It did not seem real to me then," Caroline said. "I was a child and to a child a year ahead is too far to be understood. It is . . . it is a little like death. We all know that we must die. One day. But nobody worries about it. It never seemed real to me, until yesterday when George announced it in his speech from the throne. And then I knew. I should be so homesick that I should die."

The Princess gave a little laugh, dry but not entirely without sympathy. She had known homesickness herself.

"I have yet to hear of a case of homesickness ending fatally. Princesses are born to be exiled. What is the alternative? Spinsterhood? Think of your aunts."

"Louise could go. Louise would very much like to be . . ."

"And do you imagine that had Louise been suitable *you* would have been chosen? Come, come, Caroline, I credited you with more sense. With Louise there would have been no delay: the marriage could have taken place immediately, which would have been a great advantage. But the climate in Denmark is more rigorous than that of England, and Louise does not enjoy your good health."

The simple, brutal fact was that there were indications that Louise would never bear a child; and princesses were born not only to be exiles, but to be brood mares.

And in the girl now standing before her the Dowager Princess saw every promise and thought to herself that the King of Denmark, and his son, Denmark itself, had been singularly fortunate. Caroline did credit to her mother's unorthodox beliefs as to how children should be brought up; plenty of good plain food, plenty of exercise in the open air, early to bed and early to rise, freedom, simplicity, and behind it all the firm hand, the watchful eye.

At the age of thirty-eight, the Princess of Wales had been widowed, left with eight living children and the ninth, Caroline, due in four months. Not a pleasant or easy situation, but she had made her stand. Her children should have nothing to do with the Court where their grandfather, George II, dallied with his ugly mistresses, and his ugly but clever wife, Caroline, tolerated licentiousness; they should be brought up in purity and innocence in the country at Kew, and told that their father had been a paragon of virtue. Even George, thirteen when his father died, was young enough to be susceptible to references to the dead man — "Your Papa would be much grieved," or "Greatly pleased," or "Would say." She had deluded them all without for a moment ever being deluded herself; Frederick, Prince of Wales, though possessed of a vagrant charm, had been frivolous, a gambler, a lecher, a runner up of debts; his death was timely; a bad influence removed before it had corrupted the children; no more infidelities or extravagances.

The Princess was pleased with her life's work; George was as different from his father and grandfather as a man could be. He was, naturally, her favourite, though she always concealed the fact. Of her daughters she loved Caroline best, partly because she did most credit to the rules under which she had been reared. She glowed with health: there had never been any need to pin a sprig of holly to her breast in order to make her hold her head high. And her spirit was as strong and lively as her frame. She appeared to have realized at quite an early age that strictness did not imply lack of love and sympathy. In her present position Augusta would have sulked, Louise would have wept. Caroline had come along and said in her blunt, forthright way — so oddly pleasing to her autocratic mother — exactly how she felt.

She must, of course, be talked out of this absurd attitude.

"If you think a little, Caroline, you will see that you are very fortunate. Christian is young and, I am told, very handsome. Also, being your cousin, he may well resemble you in disposition and share your love of horses and music and books." The Princess made the last statement in a particularly firm voice, almost defiantly. She had seen enough of marriages between people closely related to doubt their wisdom: but there was no help for it: religion was to blame; Protestant must marry Protestant, Catholic, Catholic, so choice was restricted and inbreeding inevitable. "There is this to remember, too. You are not the daughter of a reigning monarch, only the sister of one. To become Queen of Denmark and Norway is rather more than one would have hoped for for you."

"I know. The truth is, Mamma, I have no particular wish to be a Queen. I know I taunted Augusta, but that was half-teasing. And it was a year ago. All those Ladies-in-Waiting and people fussing round, saying what stockings, even, one should wear; that wouldn't suit me at all. And I know now that the idea of being married does not appeal to me either."

Ha! the Princess Dowager said to herself: now we come to the nub of the matter.

"Have you received a letter from Augusta that I have not seen?"

"From Augusta, Mamma? I have never received a letter from anyone that has not been seen by you." And Augusta's letters — ever since her marriage, a year ago — matter-of-fact epistles with a faint undertone of boasting, how many presents she had been given, how many entertainments had been arranged in her honour, what a wonderful place Brunswick was, had, no matter to which member of the family they were addressed, been intended to be shared by all, and had been so shared.

"I merely wondered whether Augusta had written her bridal letter to you."

"Her bridal letter, Mamma?"

"Sooner or later most brides write one. Often in the first week, to their mothers, asking for pity, which is not forthcoming, since the mother, obviously, has been a bride herself and survived. Others wait a while and then try to frighten some young ignorant girl by warning her of the tortures of the marriage bed. Is that what troubles you? Has some indiscreet, self-pitying female . . ." At the thought the cold, relentless anger of the self-controlled woman moved like a snake in the Princess's vitals. "Who was it?" Whoever it was should pay for this infringement of a mother's rights. In her own time and in her own words she was prepared to

7

give the necessary, the minimum information. Who had forestalled her?

Her eyes had darkened again and her youngest daughter, well trained in every trick of self control, the sneeze which could be prevented by the firm pressure of a little finger to the upper lip, the tremor of the legs, controlled by clenched buttocks, like nutcrackers, the blush defeated by drawing a deep breath and holding it while one counted up to ten, the belch disguised by a discreet small cough, said,

"Mamma, I do not know what you mean."

But she did; because of Alice.

Two years and six months before Caroline was born, the Princess of Wales had wakened in a dark December night, and heard a piteous mewing sound somewhere in or around the house in Leicester Fields where she, her husband and family had moved in to keep Christmas. Search had revealed a baby on the doorstep, newborn, naked, enclosed in the kind of basket used for the delivery of fish. The Princess was not a believer in indiscriminate charity, she thought that most professional beggars were frauds, but, like many other ladies of quality, she was interested in and patronized the properly conducted homes for foundlings. To the one in St. Giles the abandoned baby had been dispatched, given the name of Alice, and reared. The Princess had always shown a special interest in the child who — but for her determination to find the origin of the piteous noise — would have died and when Alice was twelve she had made a place for her in her household. Alice became a run-about maid. Nobody who had not been a member of the royal, or even semi-royal household could understand how much people like Alice contributed to the comfort of their employers. Precedent and protocol had reached the point where the King of England coming back from a theatre, hungry and thirsty, could, lacking an Alice, go hungry and thirsty to bed.

Soon after her arrival in the household Alice was called upon to take a part in some play which the royal children were performing and showed herself to be a natural actress. After that she often took part in their games. The Dowager Princess actually preferred her children to associate with Alice than with those more nearly their equals who tended to be sophisticated before their time, and given to gossip. Alice had been brought up in a good Christian home, had never run the streets, learned bad language or undesirable habits. When they played at charades, as they often did, the children found Alice most useful; she had the gift of invention.

It was Alice who had told Caroline and Louise how babies were begotten and born. Unwittingly she had done so in the best possible way, in the plainest terms without coyness or prurience, making it sound as simple and straightforward as using a tinder box to make a light. Louise said, "I don't believe it, Caro. She made it up. Think how good she is at charades." But Caroline had believed and accepted the facts. It sounded slightly undignified, but after all Mamma must have gone through the whole process nine times and her dignity was unimpaired.

But Alice, before revealing this secret about which such a mystery was made, had sworn them to secrecy — cross my heart and hope to die! It was therefore necessary to deny all knowledge.

Mamma said, "I am glad of that. At the right time I shall tell you all that a girl needs to know. Now, we have agreed that you will be homesick, but that you will outlive. You are not frightened of marriage, not knowing what it means. So what is all this about?"

Outside the windows, in the fading light of the January afternoon, Kew garden lay under snow; the evergreen trees wore snow like a blanket, every leafless twig wore a frill of white. But yesterday, before the snowfall the lilac buds had shone green on the boughs and the tips of the daffodils green in the soil. The snow would melt, the sun would shine, season would follow season. And I not here!

But there was more to it. Fanciful and inexplicable. In the moment when she had realized that her future was decided, that she would be married, be a Queen, be homesick, something else had happened, something for which there were no words. She had been able to come and say to Mamma that she did not wish to go to Denmark, or to be married, or to be a Queen with even her stockings chosen for her; but how could she explain . . . Denmark, not a place on the map, a place where she would be a wife, and if God willed, a mother, and eat and drink, sleep, ride, walk, but a place of threat, of looming, inescapable danger. It had happened inside her head, in less than a moment, between two breaths and it was like a bad dream which had broken away, shown itself in the full light of day and then vanished. A grey sea, a grey sky and between them, darker grey, turrets and cupolas, and a sense of terror and loss. It had no connection with anything, it had a nightmare quality — though she had been wide awake, sitting next to her favourite brother, Edward, Duke of York, admiring George, thinking how well he looked in his robes, how clearly and firmly he spoke, and knowing that presently her name, her betrothal would be mentioned. She'd faced the certainty of homesickness and her distaste for the process that Alice had so succinctly and bluntly described and known that they could both be borne. But this was a different thing altogether.

She had thought about it, all through the evening and the first wakeful night she had known except when suffering from toothache. And now she had appealed to Mamma, giving all reasons except the true one. And, quite rightly and in her usual way of cutting through any obscure or evasive talk, Mamma had asked — What is all this about?

A leaden sea and a leaden sky; an island, with towers, some sharp, some rounded — I saw it as clearly as I see you now — and I was afraid . . .

And fear, in itself, was new to her; she had never been afraid of the dark, or of spiders, of breaking her neck turning somersaults, of heights, bad-tempered dogs or difficult horses. She was not, as most people were, afraid of Mamma; she wished not to displease, but when on occasions displeasure and punishment had fallen upon her she had not been intimidated, looking upon them as part of ordinary daily life.

Nothing like this; a fear that had struck, left its mark, and now defied description. Even as she tried to put it into words it eluded her. She said with what appeared to be wooden obstinacy,

"I don't want to be sent away, or be to married or be a Queen, or go to Denmark."

"And that," Mamma said, "brings us to where we started."

There was a short silence during which they regarded one another steadily. Not only my healthiest daughter, the Princess Dowager thought, and the highest-spirited, but far and away the best looking. Beautiful; a perfect complexion, remarkable eyes, large, vividly blue and dark-lashed, while her hair was so fair, a true silver-gilt, that on formal occasions it would need only the lightest of powdering; the figure not yet fully formed, but very graceful. Wasted on Denmark, really; Empress, Queen of France . . . Staunch Lutheran as she was the Princess regretted for a moment the religious barrier. Then, returning to practical things, she recognized one possible drawback in Caroline's physique; already, at thirteen and a half, she was rather tall for her age. And Christian of Denmark was said to be small.

Caroline braced herself for one last effort.

"Suppose I said I couldn't, wouldn't go?"

The Princess's eyes darkened again, but she spoke amiably.

"You would bring ridicule upon George who has trouble enough already, what with the Whigs and Wilkes and those dreadful colonists in America. You would wreck England's foreign policy. You would break my heart."

"Then I must go?"

"In a year," Mamma said, "you will be so happy, Caroline, that you will look back on this evening and laugh at yourself."

She made that prophecy with complete confidence and sincerity; no young man, in his right senses, could look upon this beautiful girl without loving, and trying to please her.

CHAPTER
TWO

Kew and London, 1765-1766

Time had never flown so fast before; spring had
hardly come with its daffodils and tulips when
summer was there with its roses, then the coloured
autumn, winter again and snow. In part this
acceleration was due to Caroline's feeling that she was
being rushed towards a fate which, though she had
accepted it, still had at odd moments an element of
terror; and in part because with the announcement of
her betrothal and the coming out ball which had
followed, she had become part of the adult,
fashionable world.

Mamma's profound distrust of that world had not
lessened; it was, she felt, if not positively corrupt, shallow
and false; the woman who entertained one lavishly in
the evening was capable of inventing and propagating
the most virulent gossip about you next morning over
the chocolate cups. But it was a world in which Caroline
must live and find her own way; and a girl could not go
direct from a sheltered, simple, informal life with her
family to an important place in a foreign court. There
were, however, signs to be hung out over the most
obvious danger spots.

"It is advisable, my dear, never to listen to gossip. When it starts, change the subject as unobtrusively as possible. And never repeat anything that you hear. And unless you have sound reason to believe it, be sceptical." In a burst of that frankness which her favourite daughter had inherited, the Princess said,

"You will hear it said that Lord Bute is my lover. That is absolutely untrue. He is my friend and advisor. This is the kind of thing that results."

She handed to Caroline a paper so folded as to expose a cartoon. There was George, his appearance, despite the cartoonist's exaggerations, quite unmistakable, Mamma equally easily identified, but wearing an apron to whose strings was attached, and looming over both an enormous boot.

Anger deepened the colour in Caroline's cheeks and flashed in her eyes. "How truly abominable! Who drew it? Who printed it? They should go to gaol!"

Mamma folded the paper smaller and tucked it behind a cushion.

"The English press enjoys great freedom," she said, calmly. But it seemed an opportune moment to bring out another signpost.

"To some extent I have laid myself open to such attacks. Nobody who knows the situation would imagine for a moment that George is led by me; but it is true that he consults me and asks my advice because I am interested in politics. I know *now* that for a woman that is a bad thing. Had I my time over again I should affect not to know a Whig from a Tory."

15

On another occasion she warned Caroline against having favourites.

"Naturally one likes some people more than others, but it is a mistake to allow preferences to show. It can only lead to envy and malice. To be amiable to all and intimate with none is an excellent rule for anyone in high position."

Such advice, most of it sound and good, much of it the fruit of experience, was poured out freely and stored away in Caroline's memory. It was after the remark "intimate with none" that Caroline said to Alice, who was temporarily doing duty as femme-de-chambre, "How I wish that you could come with me, Alice." Everybody, even a Queen, needed somebody to talk to at times, and nobody would be envious of Alice. But it was already arranged that an older woman, named Phyllis, a good hairdresser and needle-woman, would accompany Caroline to Denmark and stay for a time, at least.

As 1765 sped away more and more things were arranged. Her birthday came in June and soon afterwards Mamma began to show for her health the concern previously reserved for delicate Louise. Caroline knew why; she was still not marriageable in the narrowest sense of the word. And she was still growing, which also concerned Mamma, who was herself tall for a woman. "You'll be my height, Caroline, I fear. I was fortunate, your dear Papa was tall."

The theory that Caroline was outgrowing her strength served as an excuse for refusing many invitations in that autumn and winter. Old Doctor

Faversham, somewhat deaf and so long-sighted with age as to be purblind at close range, but trusted Mamma because he had never once disagreed with her, was called in and said "Time" and early to bed, and plenty of red meat and port wine.

By the first week in January 1766, these measures had brought about the desired effect and Caroline was marriageable.

Then unexpectedly Frederick, King of Denmark died and Christian became King. Mamma said, "It is just as well. The position of second lady in the land is never easy." And Mamma should know.

That was in January. By the end of March or the beginning of April, time went so fast that exact dates were difficult to fix, Mamma's whole attitude changed. Caroline, uninformed, sometimes imagined that Mamma, so very clever and resourceful and controlled, had actually taken notice of her protest, made more than a year ago and had been secretly in sympathy with her and biding her time to make a move. For now Mamma appeared to be doing everything possible to delay the wedding.

She said that Caroline would not be fifteen until June and fifteen was full young to be married.

She said that Caroline, marrying not the Crown Prince of Denmark, but the King, should have a dowry of at least £500,000. George said that this was extortionate and the Commons would never grant it. And he was right; while they argued the lilac at Kew bloomed and faded, and then June came with roses and the Commons announced that Princess Caroline would

17

take with her a dowry of £100,000. Mamma said, "That will do; had we asked for that we should have obtained less," and shifted her ground.

Neither Caroline nor Louise had been confirmed, she pointed out; and a girl should be confirmed before she was married. She had always planned that Louise and Caroline should be confirmed together, and Louise had always been too delicate for any extra instruction, for instruction was needed before confirmation.

Instruction took quite a time because Louise had a headache, a backache, and a shocking cough; it was late in August when the two girls knelt before the Bishop of London in the Royal Chapel of St. James and were formally enrolled, two more soldiers for Christ.

And here was another change; for fifteen years God had always seemed to Caroline to be associated with, and very similar to, Mamma, judicial, critical, all-knowing, very ready to mark what was done amiss, to punish if necessary, but fundamentally kind and just. Kneeling, with the Bishop's hand laid in blessing on her head, she recognized God as different, something more, vaster, vaguer, completely disassociated with ordinary things that could be handled and understood. A little like, frighteningly like, that mental vision of Denmark, grey sea and sky and between them darker spires and a cupola. Entirely different but akin, on the same plane of consciousness, of awareness. A spiritual experience?

The Dowager Princess knelt and for once ignoring even George's claim to Providential favour, prayed, "Let her be happy; bless and protect her. I have done what I can, I must leave her, dear God, in Your Almighty hands."

She had done what she could, which was to delay, not to prevent, the marriage. Rumours which might have appalled a woman of less experience had reached her in the early part of the year. Christian, abruptly freed from all control and elevated to complete power, seemed to have gone quite wild.

But then, so had George, who had had what Christian had never known, a good solid, God-fearing background, family ties, a mother's care. George had been twenty-two when he ascended the throne, Christian was only seventeen. George had gone wild; Hannah Lightfoot, Sarah Jennings . . . but he had settled down and now in all England there was not a more uxorious husband, a fonder father. In the end all was well. And the Dowager Princess had convinced herself that all Christian of Denmark needed was a little time, to sow his wild oats and settle down. Yet, in case he should — like her own husband — remain wild after marriage, there was another signpost to be hoisted.

The date of the marriage-by-proxy, which was to take place in London in October, was drawing near and the time had come for what the Princess always thought of as "a little talk". She was incapable even of thinking in the crude terms which Alice had used, yet planning the euphemisms embarrassed her; still she was not the woman to send a girl entirely unprepared for the marriage-bed. Duty before all!

19

Mamma's unusual lack of ease when she began to speak of "physical intimacies, permissible between husband and wife," caused Caroline to become in turn embarrassed, especially as all this obvious effort was a waste. She said, "Yes, Mamma; I know."

At fifteen! So carefully guarded! So innocent-seeming?

"How? Who?"

The darkening of Mamma's eyes warned Caroline that the person named must be beyond reach of recrimination; there was only one, the Queen of England.

"Charlotte, Mamma." A thundering lie!

Surprising, perhaps, but satisfactory. Charlotte was so happily married, she would not have said anything amiss.

"There is one other thing, Caroline. Something that Charlotte, being very fortunate, would not know about. Other women. I think it highly unlikely that Christian will ever see a woman whom he prefers to you for however brief a time. But men are often weak, and women are scheming; and it is the fashion to own a mistress — sometimes merely as a means of displaying jewels and fine clothes. If this should happen, you must not fuss, or sulk, or reproach your husband. You must behave with dignity and on no account must you withdraw your . . . favours. Do you understand what I mean?"

"I think so. I shall try to behave as though Christian had acquired another horse or hound."

20

My poor, innocent darling! Still, there were worse, far more fatal attitudes.

The Princess allowed herself a small sigh. The world outside the reaches of her jurisdiction was full of danger and difficulties and horrible people. Literally one cast pearls before the swine when one reared children carefully. Look at George, who should have been the most popular King England had ever known; attacked on all sides, laughed at because he was a good family man and courteous to all, whatever their estates; called, mockingly "Farmer George" because of his interest in agriculture . . . It was truly disgraceful. And now this beautiful, charming, well-educated child about to be thrown to the wolves. No help for it; rank carried its own penalty.

She took something from the table nearby and said, "Caroline, I don't think that anyone could accuse me of being superstitious; but in every life luck plays its part and I hope that this will be a talisman for you."

She held out a ring, encircled, between two bands of chasing, with a wreath of flowers, the petals enamelled blue, the leaves green, tiny and exquisite.

"Mamma, how beautiful!"

"There is an inscription."

Caroline looked inside the ring and read, "Bring me happiness." Her throat thickened and ached.

"That is my most earnest hope for you, dear child. That you should be happy."

"I shall wear it always." Caroline said; her voice was shaking. She wanted to throw herself into her mother's arms and cry and cry and cry. But that would serve no purpose; it could only distress Mamma, and it would show lamentable lack of self control. So she drew a breath, held it, counted up to fifteen, expelled it, and as usual the trick worked. "I shall look at it and remember your wish for me, Mamma. And I will try to be happy. Resolutely."

"Then you will be, dear Caroline." The Princess put her hands on her daughter's shoulders and kissed her brow.

Go now, before I give evidence of weakness.

I must get away to cry in secret.

Fortunately the Princess, left alone, turned to the fire, gripped the marble overmantel in both hands, almost in the attitude of crucifixion, and wrestled with herself and her emotion. Tears no longer brought the relief that they had done in her youth, her tempestuous, passionate nature had by self-enforced rules become so narrowed and hardened that now to weep gave her positive physical pain. And at fifty-one tears left ravages that remained for hours. And what good could crying do?

So when the door opened behind her she was able to kick a log into place and then turn a calm, undamaged face towards Caroline, whose burst of crying had been checked by the discovery of Alice lurking in the ante-room.

"Mamma, it is Alice. She says there is something of importance . . . She would not tell me."

"Alice?" At loss for a second, then remembering, oh yes, the foundling girl. "Tell her to go to Mrs. Stubbs."

But Alice was already in the room, bobbing deeply so that her starched skirt and apron crackled.

And Alice was in control of the situation.

"Begging pardon, your Royal Highness, Mrs. Stubbs wouldn't do. Lady Mary neither. This is something I thought you ought to know. At once."

Caroline, with a half apologetic glance at her mother, slipped away. Alice closed the door behind her and advanced a few steps, mustering her words as she moved. The trouble with knowing two ways of talking — almost two different languages — was that you had to be so careful. But the H in Highness had come out in the proper, acceptable way and she need not say that again. The rule was to say it once, and then "Ma'am."

"What is it?"

"Phyllis is ill again, Ma'am."

The Princess wanted to say, Oh no! Really, with everything arranged it had been most exasperating to find, two days ago, that Phyllis, the excellent personal maid, had fallen ill in a truly disgusting way. But she was better, she had probably over-eaten.

"She was fully recovered this morning. I gave her her final instructions." They had included the order not to dress Caroline's hair too high should His Majesty of Denmark be of low stature.

"She's worse now, Ma'am. I found her on the stairs, very poorly indeed." Catting her guts out, in fact.

"You informed Mrs. Stubbs?"

"I did indeed, Ma'am. And the apothecary has been sent for."

Then why bother me? Rank carried its penalties, but it also had its privileges, and one of them was that one could delegate, one was buffered, even in this simple household.

"You acted rightly, Alice." And having acted rightly, why was she here? "Mr . . ." she groped for the name and found it, "Simkins' draught was beneficial two days ago. Let us hope that it will be again."

"But suppose it wasn't. Suppose, Ma'am, Phyllis wasn't fit to go." And she certainly would not be, Alice would see to that. "Time being so short," Alice said.

Time was very short indeed; forty eight hours. And really reliable body maids so hard to come by these days; girls preferred to hawk milk, lavender, water, fish or watercress though the streets.

"I was wondering," Alice said, "Whether I couldn't go."

"You are far too young and inexperienced, Alice."

"I can dress 'air," the Cockney slipped aspirate betrayed her. "Hair. I truly can dress hair. If you doubt me, try me, Ma'am. I can take you down and do you up again, any fashion you care to say. To be honest I did Princess Caroline for her first ball when everybody said she looked so lovely. That night Musser Raymond burnt his hand on the tongs and Phyllis had a comb-over, shaking like a jelly she was. So I did it."

The things that went on, even in the most closely supervised household.

"Indeed." The Princess looked searchingly at the foundling girl. Neat, plain, satisfactory in her work and

24

behaviour; youth the only drawback. But here, willing to go, and known to Caroline.

"What about mending?"

"Oh, I can mend, Ma'am. If you would allow me. It's on my leg." She came forward, hitched up her skirt and with a steadiness, indeed a grace that any dancing master might have approved, stood on one leg, the other extended at right angle to it. She wore a neat buckled shoe and a white stocking. All the Princess Dowager's maids received white stockings at Christmas — she bought them, thriftily, by the gross from a hosier in the Midlands.

On this white stocking, just above the ankle, there was a darn, so exquisitely made, so like the original fabric that she was obliged to look closely to see it at all. Old age enroaching? Sight failing? God forbid!

"Very creditable."

That Alice could also wash and iron delicate fabrics might be taken for granted; the Foundling Home helped to support itself by laundering for ladies.

"It is a possible solution," the Princess conceded. "Your youth is the only drawback."

"I shall be eighteen this winter," Alice said. "And being young is a thing orphans get over early, Ma'am."

The words were said without bitterness; a plain statement of a fact which the Princess recognized. At an age when more fortunate children were being led by the hand, foundlings were put in charge of their juniors.

"Do you wish to go to Denmark, Alice?"

"Not particularly, Ma'am." Never reveal a motive.

"Then why do you offer?" Phyllis had been most unwilling and it had needed exhortation and something perilously near a bribe to make her agree to try it for six months. Indeed the Princess still cherished a doubt that Phyllis' indisposition could be a form of malingering.

"Princess Caroline was always good to me, Ma'am: and I thought it would be better for her. Somebody she knew and somebody who knew your rules, Ma'am; such as not gossiping about, and not doing her hair too high and changing wet stockings and underclothes being well-aired."

Behind the Princess's controlled face the tension eased a little. She was not superstitious, as she had said, and certainly no one would expect a reward in this world for a simple act of charity: but the thought occurred and remained — Had I gone back to bed that night, after finding all my own children sound asleep, and told myself, as most women would, that cats often make the noise of children crying, this girl would not be here today, making her offer and somehow seeming, despite her youth, so thoroughly dependable. In her day the Princess had cast a good deal of bread into a variety of waters; never before had she had such a clear example of it being returned.

She said, "Very well, Alice. You had better hold yourself in readiness, in case Phyllis is not fit to travel. But I shall send for Doctor Faversham."

Alice knew no qualm; if the sharp-eyed young apothecary believed that Phyllis had over-eaten and was bilious, the old half-blind doctor would never suspect . . .

"Very well, Alice; you may go."

Bobbing again, Alice said, "Thank you, Ma'am."

"And Alice . . . Thank you for offering to step into the breach. I still hope that it will not be necessary; but I shall not forget that you offered."

Two of the most inscrutable faces in England confronted one another.

"Thank *you*, Ma'am," Alice said.

Caroline, emerging from the small drawing-room, and just about to cry, had met Alice, controlled herself, and then walked upstairs, dry-eyed. It was like checking a sneeze or a cough; you still wanted to, but you couldn't and you were left with a funny unfinished feeling. But it was as well that she had not come upstairs howling, as Alice described it, because in the room which had once been the schoolroom but had been transformed into a pretty parlour, shared by Caroline and Louise, Edward stood warming his hands by the fire.

He was her favourite brother; to be honest, the person she loved best in the world. He was extremely handsome, gay, witty, brave, and he had never treated her with condescension because she was female and twelve years his junior. George and Mamma thought that he had a tendency to be frivolous — but that did not prevent their enjoying his company. For the two years between George's accession and the birth of the new Prince of Wales, Edward had been heir presumptive, a fact which had worried them both. "Charles II all over again, that's what Edward would be, if anything happened to me." "If anything should happen to George, I should abdicate," Edward said. He had no ambition and had many friends whom Mamma called raffish.

But lately Edward had changed; his spirits were less exuberant and sometimes his face wore a clouded, sombre look. Caroline was egoistic enough to imagine that the thought of her imminent departure might have something to do with it — he had once expressed vehement disapproval of the whole system of royal marriages. She was glad that she had not entered the room in tears, and she greeted him with forced cheerfulness in her face and voice.

He had brought her a present; a miniature chest made of red Chinese lacquer, decorated in black and gold; long-legged birds standing amongst reeds, strange looking trees and flowers, mountains as precise as sugar cones. It amused him to show her the secret ways of opening it; press on a certain point and the lid flew open to reveal a complete cosmetic set; close it, press another point and the same lid opened, this time to show needles, scissors, everything needed for needlework and embroidery.

"It works on a tumbler system," Edward said. He pressed a third point and out from the base sprang a secret drawer. "For jewels, or letters," he said. It was an entrancing toy and after she had opened and closed it several times she fetched the magnificent parure of diamonds and sapphires which George had given her. George was, for a man of such simple taste, surprisingly knowledgeable about precious stones — laid it in the drawer and closed the chest.

Then she remembered Mamma's gift, and showed it to Edward and told him what was engraved inside.

He said, "I wish that for you too, Caro. With all my heart. I hope and pray that when you see Christian you may fall in love with him."

"He will be my husband. Naturally I shall love him. I intend to."

She was so young, so innocent, so completely uninformed. He hesitated for a moment and then said, carefully measuring his words,

"I think you should be warned. There is a difference between the will to love, involved with a sense of duty, and falling in love, which is a completely different thing. I'll not deny that a good relationship can be built on affection, consideration, respect ... and people seem to get along. But I'd like more than that, for you. Real happiness. And to fall in love with Christian is your only way out of the trap in which we were all born."

He spoke so gravely and looked so solemn that she was taken aback. It all sounded so portentous; he'd used the word *warn*, as though he saw some danger ahead; he had said he would *pray* — Edward who avoided church, read books by a wicked man named Voltaire and once, at least, to Mamma's great distress, had been seen in company with Francis Dashwood. It was as though Edward knew something, something more ... As of course he did, being a man, a man of the world.

To the business of being in love she had not given much thought — a story book thing, like Romeo and

Juliet; not for people like herself, betrothed at thirteen. She had hoped that she would find Christian agreeable, that he would find her agreeable, and then they would love one another, as husband and wife should. Christian's portrait showed that he resembled Edward to a marked degree and if, as Mamma had once suggested, he shared the same tastes, then, in course of time, when she knew him well, she would love him as she loved Edward. Now here was Edward almost saying that that was not enough.

She said, with considerably less confidence, "Well, then I hope I do. But if will and duty don't serve . . ."

He reached out and took both her hands.

"Don't look so worried," he said. "I was only trying to tell you . . . You see you are so very like me, and I've only just . . . Caro we were reared wrongly. Mamma meant well, that I grant, but she always pretended that we should inhabit the Garden of Eden. Virtue its own reward, truth will out, duty before self. It isn't enough. There's so much for which one is unprepared . . ."

Like falling — as he had done, hopelessly, madly in love with a most unsuitable and unlikely person. He'd loved several women in his light-hearted way; all safely married, well-bred, fair full-fleshed, and gay; three months ago he had fallen in love with a bone thin, sallow, bitter-tongued girl who had been a prostitute since she was eleven years old.

He said, in a different voice, "Anyway, Caro, when we say good-bye it will not be for long. I shall come and see you next year."

"Oh. How wonderful. Is it really arranged."

"I never made the Grand Tour," he said. "And when George asked me to stand proxy for Christian at your wedding — which I did not much wish to do — I bargained. Time and money and leave to go abroad strictly as a private gentleman. Italy, France and then Denmark . . ."

Felicity would go with him; and they would never return. He'd screw out the last penny and live cheaply, in Russia, or Turkey where, when funds ran out, he could always take service as a mercenary.

"Before the year is out, I shall come to see you," he said. "And I hope," he reverted to the theme foremost in his mind, "to find you, not only happily married, but in love with Christian."

"And how shall I know the difference?"

"It strikes, like lightning," he said. Still holding her hands he pulled her towards him and kissed her, "Bless you. God send you happy." He both hoped and feared for her. He knew her better than anyone else did; knew that under the Mamma-imposed, self-imposed shell, she was impetuous, and headstrong and reckless, pathetically anxious to please those of whom she was fond, but at heart, like himself, a rebel, born out of time, or out of place. He had seen her through several crises, most of which, he had realized at the time, would never have arisen had she had the good fortune to be born a boy. She had always accepted Mamma's edicts — no more actual work in the garden, it roughened the hands; no more riding astride, it was unladylike; the necessity of wearing stays, laced tight.

Caroline had always said, in these and a dozen other situations, "Yes, Mamma," "No, Mamma," and then at the first opportunity given vent to her feelings, her real feelings, to him. And he, only too well aware that in her place he would have felt exactly the same, had done his best to soothe, to explain, and while sympathizing, never to run counter to Mamma. And, despite his own present, intense preoccupation with his own problem, he would never forget the night when, having accepted what was her destiny and said "Yes Mamma," "No, Mamma" she had sought him out and become completely hysterical, saying that she would die, like an uprooted tree, that she could not live as an exile. And he had wished, just for one moment, that he were in George's place. By God, he would make some alterations!

But he wasn't George; poor George sat in his own trap, Mamma in hers, plainly labelled. An iniquitous system, about which nothing could be done, except make one's own escape.

And there was one thought that brought comfort. Whether Caroline achieved happiness in the only way possible, by falling in love with Christian, or missed it by falling in love with somebody else, *he* could hardly avoid being fond enough of her to treat her kindly. Many reigning monarchs, forced into marriage with ugly, dull princesses often took out their spite on the unfortunate girl. Wife-beating was as common in palaces as in hovels. Even if Christian failed to fall in love with Caroline, he must surely realize that he was extremely fortunate.

32

★   ★   ★

Alice said, "I'm to get you ready, Princess Caroline. Phyllis is worse."

"Oh dear. And we leave the day after tomorrow, very early, to catch the Harwich tide . . ." Alice hugged her delicious secret and waited until Caroline, dressed for the family supper and wearing the loose protective dressing gown, was seated on the stool before the looking glass. Then Alice dipped the thumb and finger of her left hand into the solution of gum arabic, moistened a strand of hair and with a deft movement of the comb transferred a soft natural curl into a coil, resilient enough to resist heat, humidity and movement.

"There's no need for you to fret. I found her and I went straight to Her Royal Highness; I told her I did your hair for that Ball when you did your coming out and showed her a darn. So it looks as though you'll get your wish. If Phyllis can't travel, and she can't, time being so short, I'm to take her place. *I'm to go with you.*"

In the glass they eyed one another. Alice, expecting to see a look of delight, to hear expressions of pleasure, was surprised and greatly disappointed to see Caroline's face take on a look that could only be called funny. Caroline, looking at the reflection of Alice with triumph glinting through the usually stolid cast, saw behind the leaden sea and sky, the black hump of island. And the looming threat. You too!

Lately she had put the fancy away; it was ridiculous, it must be dismissed. She thought she had overcome it, now here it was, strong and lively as ever.

33

"I thought you'd be glad. You said you wished I could go with you. And now, due to Phyllis being taken bad, I can. I thought you'd be pleased."

"I am. I mean I should be if only I could feel certain that it was the right thing for you. There's the language, Alice. And I'm afraid you'd be lonely."

"I'm used to that." It was true; whenever one caught sight of Alice, even taking the air in her scant free time, she was alone. "And the language I can pick up. Who do you want to take?"

"How can I answer that? Until this moment I thought Phyllis . . . And I shall still hope that she will recover in time."

"And me," Alice said reproachfully, "going to all that trouble to talk Her Royal Highness round. Making a special darn . . ."

After exercising so much self control with Mamma, and with Edward . . .

"Of course I wish you could come, Alice; nothing would please me more and it is only concern for you that makes me hesitate. The truth is . . . I know this sounds too silly to be true and if you ever mention it, even to me, I shall be extremely angry. Now and then, when I think of Denmark I feel that something there threatens me. And just now I felt that if you came you'd be threatened too. On an island, with a kind of castle . . ." Putting it into words made it sound more absurd than ever. "And a tower, in a grey sea."

"Elsinore," Alice said. "And no wonder! That was Denmark." Amlet, Prince of Denmark. Don't you remember? You was Ophelia, drownded dead, so you didn't 'ave any words to learn, all covered with 'yacinths and the tower — it was a ladder wrapped in cloth — tipped over and could've killed you if I 'adn't caught it and sprained my wrist."

One of Mamma's carefully chosen little scenes from Shakespeare, performed before an equally carefully chosen audience. "To be presented by . . ." And then all their names and titles in the gilt edged programmes. The whole thing saying clearly — We may avoid the Court, but we are alive, we are being educated, we are capable of making our own entertainment.

"I had forgotten it entirely. Alice, I think you may . . . I'm sure you are . . . right. I failed to make the connection; Denmark, Elsinore and something dangerous. Now I see. Oh, bless you Alice. And here I've been, all this time, worrying away, thinking I had a premonition."

"Like me, that time. I knew from the minute the Prince of Wales . . . well, as he then was, rigged it up, it'd fall, sooner or later, that ladder. So I kept my eye on it all the while I was being the Clown." People, even the best of them, tended to be ungrateful; here was Princess Caroline, completely forgetful of the fact that Alice's watchfulness and swift intervention had saved her from injury, possibly from death. But my word, how cunningly Alice had twisted that round, all in a minute; offering explanation and reminder, in one.

"So you will take me?"

"Very willingly, if it can be arranged. Nobody has so light a hand with a brush as you, Alice."

So far as it could be it was already arranged. Alice had realized very early in life that what you wanted you must get for yourself. Even her being taken into the Princess Dowager's household had not been luck, but the reward of a diligent, sustained campaign to bring herself to her patroness' notice, in some favourable light, on her visits to the Foundling Home.

The explanation of her irrational fear put the seal upon Caroline's mood. Rebellion, impotence, acceptance, resignation had been steps leading up to the level of fortitude; she would be cheerful at tonight's supper party, dignified at tomorrow's wedding ceremony, brave when the moment of departure came. Common felons, it was often reported, went merrily to execution at Tyburn.

CHAPTER
THREE

Harwich, October 2nd 1766

They had travelled, with only the briefest halts, since half past six in the morning and it was now four o'clock and Caroline was tired and cold. In London a still misty daybreak had promised another day of mild weather, but with every mile eastward the wind had grown colder and rougher and long before they reached Harwich Caroline had thought longingly of the fine sable cloak, Queen Charlotte's gift, packed deep in a trunk in the rearmost carriage. It must be disinterred before she embarked.

But they were not to sail this afternoon; they were on time and the tide was right, but the ship could not put out with this wind blowing. Count Bothmar, the Danish Ambassador who had accompanied his new Queen on this first stage of her journey, came and stood, bareheaded in the gale beside her carriage, to give her this information and to tell her that, since the local inn was a poor place, the Customs Officer, a Mr. Davies, had offered her accommodation in his house where there was room for one only.

Count Bothmar was disgusted. Room for one! In Denmark any family, from highest to lowest, would gladly have vacated their whole house, slept in a stable or cowhouse, or in the open in order that their Queen and her nearest attendants should be properly lodged. But the English were peculiar people, lacking all sense of occasion or decorum. He had been much affronted by the attitude of the crowds which gathered in London and along the route. One would have imagined that the Princess was being shipped off to the Cannibal Islands. They cheered and waved and shouted, and some of the things they shouted were most offensive. "If they don't treat you right, dearie, we'll fetch you back," "If he don't live up to his name, we'll soon have you home." And though far be it from him to criticize his Queen, Her Majesty's demeanour had fallen short of perfection. Last evening, at her proxy marriage in the Great Council Chamber, she had been the personification of dignity, but this morning, on parting with her family, especially her mother, she had clung and cried; her response to the cheering crowds had been too exuberant, and when there was no crowd before whom to perform, she had been gloomy and silent. Well, she was young; she would learn. She was not to blame, her upbringing had been faulty, her mother plainly eccentric.

"I will accompany Your Majesty to this man's house." The man, an oaf, said,

"There's no need, sir. 'Tisn't far, but in this wind . . ." He had then, incredibly, edged Count Bothmar aside, taken a look at the Queen of Denmark, shuffled off his top-coat and wrapped it around her, saying, "the wind is cruel, Your Majesty. You'd best hold on to me, don't you'll be blown away."

And she, abandoning her suite, her state, her dignity, had said, "Oh, thank you Mr. Davies; you are very kind," and gone off, huddled into a Custom's Officer's coat, clutching his arm, across the wet planks of the jetty.

"It was a bit rough by mid-morning, but nothing like this," Mr. Davies said, "till about three. Don't we'd have halted you at Colchester. By the time they'd decided not to sail, it was too late. So Martha said . . . And we'd have opened the front door, but in all the time we've been here it never was opened and short of taking it off the hinges . . . And we tried the parlour fire, but in this wind all we get is smoke, no heat. So it's the back door and the kitchen, Your Majesty."

With the opening of the door he released a great flood of warmth which battled with the wind, embraced her, drew her in. A huge fire on an open hearth, with a black pot on the hook. A good cooking smell and a woman, mulberry silk gown behind a white apron, narrow face, somewhat flushed, earbobs, coming forward, borne on the wave of heat and curtseying and saying, "I bid you welcome, Your Majesty. We're honoured. Come to the fire."

Incongruous by the homely hearth stood a velvet covered chair, digging its clawed feet into the typical cottage rug made by pushing strips of cloth through sacking. Mr. Davies lifted the heavy coat from her shoulders and said, "That's right, get to the fire." For a second or two she basked in the heat, holding her hands out to it. Lovely, delicious.

"It is immensely kind of you, Mrs. Davies, to take me in like this, at such short notice."

"It was the least we could do. If I'd known . . . but it was a plain beef pudding, already on when we knew. I'd have had something fancier, more to your taste, if there'd been more warning."

"Beef pudding is one of my favourite dishes."

"It'll be a bit overdone; as a rule we eat at three . . . So as soon as you're warmed through and Tom has seen to his horse . . ."

There was trenchancy about the last words. Mr. Davies took himself off and his wife offered Caroline a choice between the necessary house, a few steps from the back door and the chamberpot in the bedroom; she apologized for having no better arrangement and Caroline thought of Windsor and St. James Palace where, when there were large gatherings, ladies were accommodated behind screens set up in corners and by the end of the evening there was another odour added to that of powder, scent and pomade. She chose to take the few steps.

When she was back in the kitchen, Mrs. Davies, unaware of the rule that royalty directed the conversation, said,

"I expect that, for all the to-do, this has been a saddish sort of day for you. I remember when I came out of Norfolk to marry Tom I was that cast down, I cried every day for a week." And she had known and loved Tom, promised to marry him as soon as he had promotion, and had only moved from Norfolk to Suffolk. This poor child . . .

"Taking leave of my family was very painful," Caroline said. To her dismay the tears against which she had been battling all day won a near victory, thickened her throat and made the candles which Mrs. Davies was lighting, one after another swim and dazzle.

"You get over it, you know. In the end home is where your baby is born. A bit like birds, women. Not so much the nest they're born in as the one they help to make."

Good, sensible woman; busy with her candles and saying such a comforting thing.

"I'm sure you are right, Mrs. Davies. You have children?"

"One, a boy," Martha Davies said, brushing away — no need to discourage — the memory of the three who had died, one at birth, one of measles, one of croup. "He's over at Bury St. Edmund's, at the Grammar School; that's how we have a bed to spare. He's clever; could be a lawyer one day."

She placed the most recently lighted candle on the table, spread with a stiffly starched cloth and set for three, and then cocked her head, looking towards the door and listening. There was a sound of feet, of voices, soon torn away by the screech of the wind; then the door opened and Mr. Davies edged in, a trunk on his shoulder and in his wake Alice. The fire flared, the candles flickered.

"This poor wench," Mr. Davies said, pushing the door shut and slipping the trunk from his shoulder.

41

Alice gave him no chance to finish.

"Your Majesty, I knew you'd want your warm cloak; and between them they've lost the keys. I said break it open but nobody dared. So I brought it along."

"That was very sensible, and very thoughtful, Alice. Thank you. I shall certainly need my cloak tomorrow."

There was a short, awkward little silence.

Why bring her *in*, Mrs. Davies demanded silently of her husband; if you'd sent her straight back to wherever the others are . . . I've set for three, and the bed for one and I know you. You'll think you should walk her back in case she gets blown off the jetty. And the pudding'll be ruined.

Mr. Davies wordlessly addressed his wife — Well, what could I do? She was nearly here, battling along, and it is a heavy trunk; and with this wind nobody with half a heart would wish a dog out in it for more than a moment.

Alice knew where but for the mislaying of the keys and her own decision to take matters into her own hands she would be spending the night; her waiflike posture was not entirely assumed.

Caroline said, "Mrs. Davies, if it were aggreable to you, I should like Alice to stay. I'm not very hungry, she could eat some of my share and sleep on the hearth, with my cloak for cover."

"Whatever you wish, Your Majesty," Mrs. Davies said.

"That's settled then," said her husband, with hearty relief. He set, in careless man-fashion, a fourth place at the table and handed Alice a plate, "Warm that for yourself, and your hands as well, my dear." Alice was in, merging with her background, unobtrusive as a partridge in a stubble field, as was her habit.

Caroline's pudding was served on a plate of such quality and beauty as to deserve comment anywhere, fine porcelain, clear apple green in colour, painted with bright birds and flowers. Mr. Davies told how he had picked it up on the beach, not a hundred yards from the house, the sole survivor, he reckoned, of a crate from China. It was so like a picture, Mrs. Davies said, that usually it hung on the wall in the parlour. "And we don't use these as a rule, either. They were my grandfather's."

She pointed as she spoke to the wine-glasses, sturdy rather than elegant, and again her husband responded to something in her voice.

"The wine," he exclaimed, jumping up. "A lot of people, Your Majesty, seeing a wine like this on *my* table might think it ill-come-by, but the truth is, wine merchants know what we save them and are generous, some of them, at Christmas." That led the talk to the subject of smuggling — Mr. Davies had some lively little tales. Then Caroline complimented Mr. Davies on his wine, and Mrs. Davies upon her pudding. "The best I ever had." That sounded such an obvious thing to say in the circumstances, that she added, "I honestly mean that, the very best."

Alice had once eaten a better one. There was a butcher who sometimes sent the orphanage a basket of odds and ends. One such offering had been made into a pudding which was put to boil in the wash-house copper, and Alice was told to see that the fire below was kept burning. And an elm had fallen, as elms often did, without any warning, clean across the door, barring her in, denying access to the woodpile. The copper had a wooden lid which she had broken by jumping on it; she had wrenched the legs off the old ricketty benches on which the wash tubs stood; the tops of the benches and the tubs themselves defeated her; so she had fed her apron, her dress and her shoes into the fire. *That* was the best pudding she had ever tasted, but she did not mention it. One of her varied reasons for going to Denmark was to get away from her foundling past; in a strange land no one could note and remark that she had no family, nowhere to visit, even on Mothering Sunday.

The amiable, easy, aimless talk, helped by the wine, ran about the table where a Queen, a Customs Officer and his wife and a foundling serving maid sat. Intimate with none, Mamma had said; but here in this warm kitchen, with the wind howling outside, there was an intimacy of a kind which Mamma could not have disapproved; just Alice, faithful and unassuming, and two kind people who had offered her their best and whom she would never see again. My last night in England, she thought, when Mr. Davies said, as the blast struck and the whole house seemed to shudder, "Ah, that's the last of it. It'll turn now and Your Majesty will have smooth, swift passage."

Alice and Mrs. Davies cleared the table. Caroline said to Mr. Davies, "Would it be possible for me to write a letter?" He looked pleased, "I always told Martha it'd come in handy sometime. I'll fetch it."

It was a box, which, opened out, made a writing desk; its sloping surface, covered with red leather, unmarred by ink or a dropped blob of sealing wax. Silver topped ink pot and sand shaker and a little plaque, "To Thomas Davies, from his friends and colleagues in the Customs Service at Lynn upon the occasion of his Marriage, 3rd July, 1749."

"Martha said a chair would have been more useful. And what writing I do I do at the office. So you'll be the first to use it, and the last. I'll have," he said, with the first sign of diffidence he had shown so far, "another little plate done. And it'll be a heirloom."

She wrote to Edward; "I have just time to write you these few lines from England," she began and paused. Had the wind served she should by now have been well out to sea, the last wrench over. It was still to come, the misery of severance from all she loved and knew and liked. Resolution and calm and the courage she had enforced upon herself, fell away and the tears crowded as she wrote that if patriotism consisted of love of one's country then she could claim that virtue.

They had left her alone long enough to write a much longer letter, and when they returned they ignored her emotional state. She said, on impulse to Alice, "You know, for *you*, Alice, it is not yet too late. I can manage if you decide to go back to London tomorrow."

Alice said, "If you go, I want to go. And if you're a Dane now, so am I."

★ ★ ★

When the Davies reminisced, as they often did, for despite their unruffled demeanour this was the highlight of their lives, never to be forgotten, when they said how pretty, how grateful, how gracious, and how easily she'd fitted in, the Queen of Denmark, one or the other was certain to say, "And her serving girl was so fond of her, it shows what a nice, proper lady she was." Mr. Davies said that Alice's words had called to mind something he'd heard somewhere; could be out of the Bible.

Part Two

CHAPTER
ONE

Roskilde, November 1st 1766

Denmark began at Altona and thereafter the inns grew worse and even the establishments of local nobles where she and her suite received hospitality overnight seemed dark, bleak, cheerless.

This inn, ten miles away from Copenhagen, was the last stop for a change of horses and other necessary purposes, and it was a poor place indeed. Caroline washed her hands in a cracked basin and dried them on a threadbare towel and looked around for a glass. There was none. She reminded herself that she must not make comparisons; plainly Denmark was a poor country; therefore the welcome accorded her all along the road was the more creditable and touching. In places there had been red cloth laid down in the streets, girls dancing and scattering flowers, deputations of burghers bringing gifts. And almost everybody was very handsome in the same kind of way, as though all related; fair hair, blue eyes, often offset by weather-darkened skin, and almost everybody seemed tall.

Frau von Plessen, the Danish Mistress of the Robes, who had assumed office at Altona when her own suite bade farewell and turned back, said,

"Had I but known, Your Majesty, that this place would be so ill-provided, I would have kept out a glass. But there is no time now. We have just received a message. His Majesty intends to ride out to meet you at Roskilde. Six miles away. But you look very well, Your Majesty; very well indeed."

Frau von Plessen ran a cool, horse-dealer's eye over her Queen and was satisfied that with this pretty, amiable, healthy young creature in his bed, His Majesty would no longer seek his pleasures in dubious ways and dubious places. Frau von Plessen was a patriot who would unhesitatingly have given her own life and that of any number of other people for the good of Denmark and the welfare of its King; austere and puritanical herself she doggedly excused the excesses and scandals of the last ten months; Christian was young, his upbringing had been faulty, his friends were ill-chosen; at a time of life when even the steadiest and most carefully reared young men kicked over the traces a bit, he had come into supreme power; naturally it had gone to his head. Like many of her stamp, Frau von Plessen had a firm, somewhat romantic, somewhat exaggerated belief in the influence which a "good" woman could exercise if she chose, but she was realist enough to know that there must first — especially with a seventeen-year-old — be an appeal to the eye and the senses. As she had made her first curtsey before her Queen at Altona she had thanked God, and at the same time felt that had the business of choosing Christian's bride been left to her she could hardly have done better. Frau von Plessen's relationship with her God was occasionally subject to such blurring of identity.

"I had hoped," Caroline said, "for an opportunity to change my clothes and have my hair redone before meeting His Majesty." Before facing what must surely be the most crucial moment of her life. She had already in her mind selected the gown she would wear, the most beautiful one in her wardrobe, the bodice and panniers of white silk embroidered with roses and peonies in their natural colours, the underskirt the colour of the palest of the roses; in that dress, bejewelled, her complexion enhanced by the cosmetics from Edward's box and her hair fresh from Alice's hands, she would have felt something of the necessary confidence.

"His Majesty," Frau von Plessen said, "is sometimes sudden in his actions." Immediately, as though in excuse, she added, "Roskilde is, for us, a place of significance. Our Kings are buried there. Since the tenth century."

Like Westminster, Caroline thought; and reflected that she should be pleased and flattered by Christian's decision to receive her there; it was silly to rely too much upon clothes.

She would have been surprised, and disconcerted, could she have known that her doubts about her clothes and general appearance were shared by Baron von Dehn, the Viceroy of the Duchies, who had received her at Altona and was escorting her to Copenhagen. Baron von Dehn was an honest upright soldier who every night of his life thanked God — his commanding officer — for having posted him to Schleswig-Holstein, well away from the capital, the Court and the King. At such distance the Baron could be far more loyal than was possible when he came into contact with Christian and was visited by such shocking thoughts as — If he'd been my son, I'd have knocked the nonsense out of him; or — If he were under my command I'd order fifty lashes. Baron von Dehn was not unaware that Christian's governor, Count Reventlow, was said to have used the strap freely; if indeed he had, then he had not, in Baron von Dehn's opinion, laid it on hard enough.

The King's decision to meet and to greet his bride at Roskilde was typical of his vagrant and inconsiderate fancies; naturally he was anxious to see her, but it would not have hurt him to have waited three hours and given the poor child a chance to rest a little, to change her clothes and compose herself. The Baron thought his new Queen very pretty and her simple good manners and cheerfulness in the face of weariness and discomfort had endeared her more to him every day; but she was very young and Baron von Dehn was man of the world enough to realize that youth in itself was not a thing to appeal to a seventeen-year-old; he had decided to have a private word with her Mistress of the Robes, who was an old friend of his, and to tell her to choose a dress, a way of doing the hair, of using every possible aid to beauty that would make Caroline look older, more sophisticated, more . . . It was difficult to find the exact word, but women understood these things; a hint would have sufficed. The truth was that an old reprobate would have been enchanted by Caroline because she was young, a young reprobate would probably need something more . . . subtle. It was a pity that at their first meeting the Queen should be wearing a severe — and now somewhat creased travelling outfit and a little hat which made her look even younger than she was. But there was no help for it. He devoted himself, as the carriage rattled and bumped along, to allaying the nervousness of which he recognized the signs. He saw her as a young conscript about to face fire for the first time.

Caroline was nervous; she was also extremely cold. Mamma had been right about the climate; only just November and as cold as England in mid-winter. And Frau von Plessen, in the most respectful terms, had advised against the wearing of the sable cloak; people all along the route, she said, were waiting to see Her Majesty and this they could not well do if she were huddled in furs. Also, she begged leave to point out, the groups of young girls who welcomed their Queen with songs and dances were wearing their white summer dresses. Caroline thought rebelliously that the girls were moving about; singing alone could be a warming exercise, and they were used to the Danish weather; but she had caught the veiled rebuke and decided to yield gracefully. This hardly seemed the moment to put into practice her secret determination not to be dictated to by the Mistress of the Robes; nor was she blind to the fact that Frau von Plessen was an intimidating personality, somewhat resembling Mamma in her confident manner, her aura of rectitude. So Alice, in the rearmost carriage, rode warm and snug, obedient to Caroline's order, "Wear it yourself, Alice," an order which Frau von Plessen deeply deplored but hardly dared to countermand: and Caroline shivered as apprehension and chill exacerbated one another.

At the last moment something, long training in the art of self-control, a natural ebullience of spirit, the mere certainty that there was no escape, came to her rescue and she became calm in a very curious, indeed interesting fashion. One moment there she was thinking herself into composure and courage, reminding herself of other ordeals safely survived, recalling Mamma's panacea for shyness and self-consciousness — Think of other people, not of yourself; and the next she was completely calm and composed, outside herself, watching herself, as though from a considerable distance and as little concerned as though what was happening was happening to another person.

There was an open square, with red cloth in the roadway, hushing the hooves and the sound of wheels; there were crowds of people, and many soldiers. There was a dark, ancient-looking building, its steps laid with the same red cloth, an ante-room hung with faded tapestries and lighted by candles. Frau von Plessen, wearing an anxious expression, tweaked the little hat, spread the skirt, stepped backward. There was a high double doorway, a soldier in charge of each half of the door and beyond a huge room into which the cold winter daylight streamed through tall windows upon a group of men ranged in a semi-circle behind two who

54

stood a little to the fore. His Majesty of Denmark and a short, somewhat deformed youth beside whom the King looked taller than he actually was.

Caroline made the most profound curtsey. Shivering in the carriage over the last mile she had wondered whether, on her shaking legs, she could perform creditably. Now, watching herself, she knew it well done, the heavy cloth skirt in a perfect circle, knees steady, face parallel with the floor; a daffodil bowing to the wind and then rising to stand and await the reciprocal bow, the approach, the words of greeting. Caroline had been ten years old when she had witnessed her brother George's reception of his bride, so disappointingly plain of face, so Caroline, watching Caroline, knew what to expect.

Christian came towards her, moving with something of the wariness with which a dog will approach another. Only those closest to him knew that he was extremely short-sighted; it was a defect, like his lack of height, which he did his best to conceal. When he was almost within arm's reach of her he said loudly and in a tone of surprise, "Oh, but you're pretty. How pretty you are! How lucky I am!" He took both her hands and pulled her towards him and kissed her with a kind of violence, on her cheek, on her mouth, just below her ear. His mouth, like his hands, was very hot and the kisses were wet and slobbery. And his breath was foetid. But it was a warmer and more enthusiastic welcome than she had dared count upon and she was gratified.

"That Your Majesty should approve of me gives me great happiness," she said. It was true; to be approved, to be pleasing, that was all that mattered for the moment. Relief flooded in; the worst was over now and she was in sufficient control of her wits to note that Christian's German was different from that of her mother; she must adjust. She smiled at him.

Still holding her hands he leaned back so that she was obliged to brace herself against his weight; then he leaned forward again and peered into her face, turned her to left and to right and laughed a little and said again, "Very pretty."

The feeling of detachment which had enabled her to make her entrance with calm dignity left her; she was no longer watching herself from outside; she was within herself and beginning to feel an odd discomfort, a sense of something gone wrong. Christian swung on her hands again and as she yielded to the pull she caught a glimpse of Baron von Dehn's face; he stared straight ahead of him, as though on parade, his profile stony with disapproval.

"Am I not to be congratulated?" Christian demanded. "I have the prettiest Queen in Europe."

Baron von Dehn, who had bowed deeply as he led Caroline in, bowed again and said,

"Your Majesty, permit me to congratulate you and to wish you happiness."

Now surely Christian would release one of her hands and either lead her forward and present her to the half circle of men, or stand beside her while they approached, one by one, to be presented. But he still held her hands and said again, "Yes; the prettiest Queen in Europe." Everyone was aware that this was carrying things a little too far; the sense of something amiss filled the whole room. A swift glance past the side of Christian's head — exactly level with her own — informed her that all but two faces at the far end of the room wore exactly the expression of Baron von Dehn's. The exceptions were those of a young man to the extreme left of the group, who looked amused, and of the hunch-backed boy who now stood in isolation to the fore. He looked sick? angry? sick-and-angry? She had hardly time to notice for, almost as though he had caught some signal, he moved forward, three precise steps and brought his heels together with an audible click. And as though that were another signal which Christian recognized, he said,

"Oh yes. Yes. My half-brother, Frederick, Hereditary Prince of Denmark . . . My brother-in-law, Prince Charles of Hesse . . . Count Bernstorff . . . Count von Molkte . . . Count von Thott, Count Bantzau, Count Brandt, Count Holmstruppe . . ." It seemed to be, could it be? a parody of a presentation; the line of men, set in motion by Prince Frederick's action, hurried past her so fast that there was no chance at all of doing what was absolutely incumbent upon royalty, pairing a name and a face and remembering them together forever. It was like running a stick along a row of railings. All she could do was to smile without ceasing and by the end the smile felt like a mask, stiff, suspended from her ears.

"And that's that," Christian said. "And you do not wish to see a lot of stuffy old burghers in their best clothes, do you?"

"I wish to do whatever Your Majesty wishes me to do."

"Well spoken," he said. "They're so rich they lay their best clothes away in pepper to frighten off the moths. And with this cold upon me I can sneeze without *that*!"

She had noticed that his eyelids were red and puffy and his complexion blotchy, but she had attributed it to his having ridden in the wind. A cold would explain the hot hands, the tainted breath and the something-not-quite-usual in his manner. He was probably feverish.

With swift compunction, she said,

"It was very good of Your Majesty to ride to meet me while suffering from a cold. I trust you have not worsened it. I hope it will soon be better."

Louise suffered frequently from heavy, quite incapacitating colds and Caroline knew many homely, comforting remedies, but perhaps this was not the moment . . . After the real marriage she would take good care of his health.

"I shall be well for the wedding," he said. "If I take care now." His voice had gone flat, his manner preoccupied as though mention of his indisposition had depressed him. "I will take leave of you now." He lifted her hand and brushed his lips against it and turned and walked away. All the men bowed and then followed him out in the exact order in which they had been presented to her, except for the young, amused-looking man in the mulberry coat who broke line and fell into step beside the King and said something of which Caroline caught only the phrase, ". . . back to bed."

His doctor?

It could have been worse, Baron von Dehn supposed. The King's behaviour was so unpredictable that almost anything might have happened. As it was, however, it was far from correct. His Majesty had behaved not like a man meeting his bride but like a child presented with a new toy. How long would the hiatus have lasted had Prince Frederick not stepped in? That abrupt departure, too, leaving the Queen and her party virtually discarded. Grant that he had risen from his sickbed to come here — the kindest thing to think was that he was still unwell — another five minutes, to see the Queen to her carriage and on her way, wouldn't have harmed him. Failing that he should have detailed half his suite to ride as escort. Bernstorff, von Molkte, Rantzau, all the real counts, members of the old nobility, must have known that as well as he did; but nobody dare say anything or make suggestions. In God's name what had come over them all in a mere ten months? Scared to death; incredible as it sounded, it was true. Solid statesmen like Bernstorff, brave soldiers like von Molkte, frightened of a half-grown boy!

You, too, von Dehn? You have Her Majesty in charge; you have not lost your voice; you would have given no real grounds for offence by suggesting . . . There was the rub, no real grounds; yet offence might have been taken and next week another man would be viceroy of Schleswig-Holstein and von Dehn in the Blue Tower languishing for so long as it was His Majesty's pleasure to keep him there. Autocracy in the wrong hands was a very terrible thing.

"Your Majesty will be glad to reach Frederiksberg," he said. "We will leave immediately."

CHAPTER
TWO

Christiansborg,
November 1st 1766

"Well, is she pretty?" Juliana, the Queen Mother, asked.

"I would say more than pretty; quite beautiful," Prince Frederick said, "despite the cold and the travelling dress which included an unbecoming little hat. I felt sorry for her. Christian behaved execrably. He fell on her, slobbering and pawing, pulling her this way and that, and I believe, but for me, he would never have made any presentations. When he did, he did it like a peasant chasing sheep through a gateway and then he said he must get back to bed."

Juliana looked at her son and knew once again the sickening, maddening sense of the injustice in the world and of her own failure to right it. If his father had lived a bare three years more. She had been obliged to move so cautiously. No man was easily convinced that his son by his first wife was a simpleton, unfit to rule, but she had worked away and only a month before he died Frederick V had said, "I will consider the appointment of Frederick as Regent, King in all but name, when he is sixteen. To move before then would be folly since the

Senate would see little to choose between a King who was simple-minded and a Regent who was a minor. He'd given his sour little smile and added, "In the event of my untimely death."

She had said, "I was thinking of the far future. Do not speak of your death. I pray God you may survive me, for without you I could not live."

It was completely false; his infidelities shamed and angered her; she blamed her son's malformation upon his excesses; she detested him; she wished him to live long enough to decree that Christian, his heir, was unfit to rule and should be shuffled away somewhere with a keeper and that her son should be Regent. Then he could die and she would know nothing but relief.

But he had died, to use his own words, "untimely" and Christian was King. For Frederick, so clever, so phenomenally mentally precocious, so dignified — despite his poor physique — so tactful, so royal, the future held little, except as some reigning monarch's brother-in-law, another Prince Charles of Hesse. And the courts of Europe were full of handsome, well-set-up young men from whom Kings' younger daughters and sisters were free to choose since their marriages were not of dynastic importance. Who would choose Frederick?

All her plans had come to nothing and now it looked as though her one remaining hope — that Christian should die young and childless — was about to be wrecked; the English girl came of a prolific family; she would be pregnant almost before Christian had his breeches off.

"How did he look? In health, I mean."

"Not well; very red-eyed and his skin very mottled."

"He could never recover from a cold in less than a fortnight and his colds were always disgusting," Juliana said.

"He spoke with some confidence of being well for his wedding," Frederick said, giving the words an undertone. He wondered whether she had heard the rumour concerning Christian's indisposition; probably not since she always made a great show of being Christian's friend. Only when she and Frederick were alone together did she allow her bitter enmity to show. She had conducted her long campaign against her stepson with masterly duplicity, saying, "for his own good," "in his best interests." She had organized punishments for him while never administering more than a mild verbal rebuke herself; and occasionally, when he had been punished, she would sympathize with him, so that Christian believed that his woes were due to his father and his governor; she had managed to retain Christian's confidence and even her enemies — of whom she had her share — never accused her of anything more positive than mild neglect of her stepson and a preference for her own child, human, almost inevitable behaviour.

The whole business had borne a result which she had not foreseen and did not suspect; Frederick, sharply observant from a very early age, distrusted her profoundly. He was fond of her — she was pretty, entertaining and indulgent and she always appeared to be his champion — but when she said, "You should have been King," or "If only your father had lived long enough to make you Regent," he suspected her of regretting the loss of opportunity of being the power behind the power. This suspicion had been confirmed since Christian's accession; a woman who made a pretence of consulting and of advising one whom in private she called "that imbecile" was capable of being deceptive in other spheres. He had fully made up his mind that in the unlikely but not completely impossible event of his ever having any power at all, she would have no share in it. He would love and cherish her — she was his mother — but he would see to it that she had no influence either on him or anyone else.

"I must go down and visit him again tomorrow," Juliana said. "The last two times that Holmstrupp fellow was on guard and said he was asleep, which I did not believe. I must find out when Brandt is on duty." Of Christian's three favourites and boon companions Brandt was her favourite; he was well-born and he cherished political ambitions which he looked to her to forward; they would come to nothing, she would see to that, but while he had hopes he could be used.

There was a slight commotion outside the door and Juliana said, "This will be your grandmother, all agog for news."

A little bit of news, a crumb of gossip, a sweetly-acrimonious exchange of words with her daughter-in-law were about the only pleasures, except those of the table, left to the elder Queen Mother these days. She was sixty-six and growing stiffer in the joints every day.

She creaked in, leaning heavily upon the shoulder of a little Senegalese boy who wore a silver collar around his neck and full court costume in peacock colours. He was the third to wear the collar, to serve the old woman as a substitute for a stick, and to bear the name, Peppo. She lowered herself into a chair and the boy took his place behind it, his arms folded.

"Well?" she said.

"Her Majesty arrived safely. We met her at Roskilde and Christian appeared to be delighted with her," Frederick said.

"So he should be; if she is anything like poor Louise."

During the lifetime of Christian's mother Sophia-Magdalene had shown no great affection for her, but to praise her, to refer to her always as "poor Louise" or "dear Louise" was a certain way of planting a barb in the hide of Juliana, who had taken her place. In Sophia-Magdalene's opinion there had been absolutely no necessity for her son to marry a second time. Denmark had an heir — a very silly little boy, but proper handling would improve him — and it had, if not a Queen Regent, a lively and active Queen Mother. And Frederick, Heaven only knew, had mistresses enough. However, Frederick had chosen to marry again and his new wife had displaced his mother, and never been forgiven.

"On the contrary," Juliana said, "Frederick says this child is very pretty." Which no one could say of Louise.

"Louise's portraits do not do her justice. She had a very sweet nature, a heart of gold. So Christian was pleased? Good. Well, well, I may yet see my great-grandchild." Another life between your hunchback and the throne! The old woman, clear-sighted from hatred, was one of the few whom Juliana had never deceived. She blamed her, almost entirely, for the way in which Christian had turned out. He was a very silly, backward little boy and the proper thing to do was to admit it and make allowances, mark time a little, postpone formal lessons, let him, at six, learn what was ordinarily learned by a child of four, and so on. That, left in control, was what the grandmother would have done. But the stepmother, pretending concern, had urged earlier lessons, longer lessons, "He is so slow . . . It is essential that his French should be fluent . . . How will he ever sign a document? . . . A King must know something of history and geography . . . Imagine a King who cannot add or multiply." It had all *sounded* very well; tutor, lessons, punishments had proliferated; Christian's backwardness had daily become more exposed, and more genuine because each failure to perform satisfactorily had eroded hope and confidence and damaged the boy's character. For, after all, he was not a peasant, to take shame and failure as part of his lot; in his veins ran the royal blood of Denmark and of England; naturally it had asserted itself and made him rebellious and difficult, and, once he was on the throne, intensely autocratic.

She said, knowing that it would annoy Juliana,

"Next thing we know we shall be looking for a pretty bride for you, Frederick." Her voice made it sound as though the search would be long, hard and probably unsuccessful.

"He is not yet fourteen," Juliana said sharply.

Frederick said, with good-humour and dignity,

"When your hopes are fulfilled, Grandmamma, my marriage will concern no one but myself. I shall do my own looking." He excused himself, mentioning an appointment, and went away.

His mother said, "Whether Frederick marries as heir prospective or not, I should favour his choosing for himself. These pre-arranged marriages are seldom successful."

"My son was very happy with Louise."

"She died young; before he tired of her," Juliana said cryptically. "The strain tells later, as you know."

In Sophia-Magdalene's case the strain had become so severe that she was rumoured to have poisoned her husband, the grandfather of Christian and Frederick. She had never been openly accused and the rumour was now almost forgotten, except by Juliana.

The old woman winced, but inwardly. She said.

"I hope that Frederick, when the time comes, looks far afield. In-breeding can be carried to extremes. I have two grandsons; one had great difficulty with his lessons, the other is crooked as a corkscrew."

They could keep up this kind of conversation for hours. They had been at it for years. Both enjoyed it.

CHAPTER
THREE

Christiansborg,
November 1st 1766

In another part of the palace which was as high and wide and populous as a town, Count Holmstrupp, First Gentleman of the Bedchamber, wrapped His Majesty in a robe and said.

"Back into the bakehouse." He opened the door of the adjoining dressing-room and a blast of fierce heat emerged. Christian looked towards the wide bed, spread with fresh cool linen and piled with pillows and said, almost whiningly,

"Oh Knut! After all that . . ."

"Come along," Knut said speaking in a roughly encouraging, father-to-fractious-child manner which sat oddly on his youth, "we've done pretty well so far. Though I say it myself, riding out to meet her was a stroke of genius."

"And I played — did I play? — my part well."

"You gave a most impressive performance. But it was an interruption and the time must be made up."

He hustled Christian into the small apartment where the stove was almost red hot, sat him in a chair covered with towels, wrapped other towels about him and handed him two pills and a glass of water.

"They make me feel sick," Christian said, having gulped the pills down. "The cure is worse than the disease."

"Not in the long run. You can lose your nose."

Already the white islands in Christian's mottled face were disappearing as the crimson ones spread. Perspiration broke out on his forehead. Knut's face was moist, too, and he mopped at it.

"Plain water in the blue jug, salt in the yellow," he said indicating the two receptacles on a handy table.

"Don't go, Knut. Time goes so much more quickly if we talk."

"I have to show myself occasionally — if you want your secret kept. And I shall lock the door behind me. Then Enevold can't admit even Juliana. We want no more interruptions."

Only Count Knut Holmstrupp and Count Enevold Brandt knew what ailed His Majesty and what was being done about it. They took turns to be in charge and repelled visitors by saying that the King had just dropped into a doze. When this was impossible the rule was to say, "I will see if His Majesty feels well enough to receive you," and hustle Christian out of his towels and into bed; a pinch of snuff, to which Christian was not addicted, set him sneezing, and there he was, a man with a very severe cold.

"I don't want to be locked in and left alone," Christian said. "Suppose I had a turn."

69

"You will not, unless you excite yourself. Sit and think of the good you're doing yourself. I shall be back."

"Soon," Christian said, pitiably.

"Very soon."

He went out briskly, closing the door behind him. He crossed the empty bedroom, locked its door and put the key in his pocket; went through the King's private sitting room and into the one beyond where Brandt, Holcke and a couple of cronies were throwing dice at a table.

Brandt said, "Ha, Knut! Off the chain? Being first favourite has its disadvantages." It was genially said but it had its sting.

"Tomorrow," Knut said, "yours may be the only face he can bear the look of."

"God forbid!"

Holcke said, "Valet, nurse, page. It must be exhausting."

Knut smiled. "Being page comes easily after seven years' experience. The other roles, I admit, are more trying. But I am learning."

Really the well-born were so stupid. After almost a year Conrad Holcke still believed that he could provoke Knut by a reminder of his humble origin, which was in fact his pride.

"I thought you should know," he said, looking straight at Brandt, "that he has locked his door and intends to sleep until ten. He will then eat — I trust that I remember this correctly — a steak of venison, two partridges and a marinade of shell-fish. Will you see to the ordering or shall I?"

"I will," Brandt said in a subdued voice. He would have recalled if he could, the acid remark about being first favourite. This peasant's son, this promoted, ennobled page-of-the-backstairs was too clever. He thought of everything. Much of the new treatment of syphilis was unknown, but a diet of slops was as old as the complaint; and only Knut would have thought of ordering, loudly and in public a meal which in itself could kill a creeping rumour.

Knut, seeming to stroll, actually moving swiftly on unobserved stretches of corridor and stairways, covered a good deal of ground and drew attention to himself wherever he went. This behaviour was not solely in Christian's interest, confirmation of the only-a-cold-in-the-head theory. Knut was only too well aware of the reason which stupid people believed to lie behind the favour the King showed him and he was very careful about being alone with Christian for any length of time, careful to encourage other favourites, to leave doors open, to be one of a group.

Within twenty minutes he was in his own apartments. He took an armful of firewood from the supply stacked by his stove, opened a window, stepped out on to the terrace overlooking the garden, walked along and by another window entered Christian's bedroom. There he put the wood down by the door of the dressing room, dipped a small towel into an ewer of cold water, carried it, dripping, into the stifling place and clapped it on to Christian's head.

It was a moment or two before Christian could speak. When he could he said in a faint, complaining voice,

"I thought you were never coming."

"So many people needed to be assured that the ride had not worsened your condition."

"My head was about to burst. I thought I should die . . ." His face was swollen and purple, his eyes bulging.

"You could have gone into the bedroom," Knut said.

"Could I? The slightest movement . . . look!" He moved one foot slightly and the great toe sprang out at right-angles, deformed by cramp: he gave a little scream. Knut went down on his knees, pressed the toe back into alignment and the whole foot firmly against the floor.

"You should have drunk the salt water," he said. "The salt water was to guard against cramp. Here . . ." He lifted the yellow jug and it came up, light and empty in his hand.

"What happened? Did you drink it?" The new, the wonderfully clever doctor in Altona who had advised the salvation cure had laid stress on the necessity of replacing the salt lost by sweating.

"My head," Christian said. "You didn't come. My head was bursting. I poured water on it. The wrong jug . . ."

Knut fell back upon the patience of his peasant blood, the heritage bequeathed him from unnumbered ancestors who had matched their pace to that of the plodding oxen, scattered the seed and waited through

72

bad weather and good, for harvest, mated their beasts and waited for the increase. He mixed some fresh salt water and Christian drank it; he brought in the wood, threw two logs into the stove and laid the others handy. Keeping the little room at this heat without exciting comment was in itself a problem. He removed the sodden towels and wrapped Christian in fresh ones. Christian, realizing from these actions that his discomfort was to continue, muttered and mumbled until Knut said,

"Less than an hour and the whole is wasted. I didn't risk my neck riding through the dark to Altona to get advice that is not to be followed." The hardship and risk of the long ride had hurt him far less than the moment when he sat face to face with the doctor and claimed that he had contracted the pox, like a clumsy sailor on leave, or that other moment when the man had said coolly, — I suppose you have some good reason for lying to me.

Christian said, "Very well. An hour then. But don't go away. I have something for you. I wanted you to have them to wear this morning; but they didn't arrive until we were about to leave. A blue case, on the table by my bed. Fetch it."

When it was brought Christian took it into his damp hands, held it for a few seconds and then handed it back.

"Open it," he said, and waited, with something eager and childlike in his bulging reddened eyes while Knut revealed a set of eight gold buttons, each set with an emerald about the size and much the colour of a pea, ringed with small diamonds. A costly and very acceptable present.

"Very beautiful. Very splendid," Knut said as though commenting upon something impersonal, a sunset, a piece of scenery.

"You like them?"

"Very much. It is a munificent reward for a very small service." He still spoke as though the whole business hardly concerned him. The strength of this attitude lay in the fact that it was not completely false, not a mere pose; Knut was incapable of feeling real gratitude because he always saw himself as the bestower of favours, not as the recipient. Had Christian been able to take the crown from his head, place it on Knut's and say — Henceforth you are King! there would have been no gratitude in Knut's response, he would have been too much concerned with the upwelling of the inward certainty that he would be the best King Denmark ever had.

"They were made to order," Christian said. "Be pleased, Knut, please! Would you have preferred rubies? I couldn't ask. I wanted it to be a surprise. But if you would rather have rubies . . ."

"These please me very well." He closed the case. He had not lifted one of the trinkets, held it to the light to watch its sparkle or done anything that any other man would have done. Christian felt — and it was far from the first time — a sense of disappointment and failure. Knut was his friend, his one true friend in all the world.

The true friend fetched and applied a fresh cold cloth and under its stimulus the King said, still in that rather pitiable manner,

74

"Knut, I am truly sorry about the Order of Danneborg. There is no man living to whom I would rather give it."

"The rules were made before you were born," Knut said. He grinned suddenly, "Even you couldn't dig up my old grandfather and ennoble him in order to qualify me!"

Christian, pleased because Knut had grinned, gave his high-pitched, rather cackling laugh.

"No, I couldn't, could I? That's the sensible way to look at it."

"I'm never anything but sensible."

"Yes, you are, Knut. Always, you are different . . ."

He had always been different. The first to realize it were his parents, humble members of the serf class which recent laws had robbed of all rights and forced back into the mud. By what trick of nature had their coupling produced such a beautiful baby, who grew into such a handsome, fastidious, clever boy with elegant hands and feet, a boy who could not pour pig-swill, or handle a muck-fork, or witness a pig-killing without being sick? They grumbled to one another, their only child and quite useless, and at the same time they competed with one another to spare him the heavy or dirty work; and they worried about his future; there was no place in the world for such as he. Once, and not so long ago, there had been a primary school in every village in Denmark and any peasant's son with brains in his head and ambition in his heart was offered the chance to advance, to become a petty official or even a professional man. Then had come the bad times and the new laws and the government had withdrawn its support from the schools. In the little village in Zeeland where Knut was born, Heer Thaarup, the school master had died of a broken heart when the one-room school was turned into a bullock shed; but his daughter, unmarried at forty and without resources, lived on in the two rooms that adjoined the shed. She had entertained a stubborn thought — If it were a good thing for children to be taught when the government paid for the teaching, it was still a good thing. She had also entertained an imaginative thought; she imagined that if she were prepared to impart the knowledge which she had absorbed effortlessly, through the pores of her skin, the parents of her pupils would contribute enough food to keep her alive. She needed very little; firewood was there to be gathered and what clothes she had would last her time.

She had miscalculated. The new laws decreed that a peasant belonged to the owner of the land he tilled and that every male, at the age of fourteen must start on twelve years' service with the army; if he did not die in battle, or of disease or hard usage, he would come back, an old man of twenty-six and resume work on the holding. In the circumstances it seemed a pointless waste to give a handful of meal, six eggs, a pig's foot in return for having a boy taught to read and write and count. In the end she had one pupil, Knut Bagger, whose parents were glad to have him out of the way and happily, if not usefully, employed. Fräulein Thaarup crammed him mercilessly, feeling that if only she could pass on all the things, useful, interesting and strange, that she knew, her death would be no more than the breaking of a vessel whose contents had been emptied into another. That she would die, and quite soon, was certain, for the Baggers' contribution was inadequate and her attempts to keep herself all came to nothing. Her hens laid away or were taken by foxes; she tried keeping goats and making goat cheese, she tried bees. But Holland banned the import of bullocks and men who could not sell their bullocks, and must still pay their dues, had no money to spend on cheese or honey. Dying the long-drawn-out death of slow starvation, Fräulein Thaarup taught Knut with passion. His education was superior in scope and depth to that being received by the young Crown Prince in Copenhagen.

But he was almost fourteen. Military service loomed and he knew he could not face it. No army sergeant would see the difference between him and the rest of the year's recruits; no army sergeant would spare him, as his parents did from what was hard, dirty or distasteful. *And no army sergeant would want a recruit with only half a hand*. It was the only way out. Dozens of times Knut went out to cut firewood and with the axe in his right hand, looked at his left; a thumb? Two fingers? All fingers, clean across the knuckles? He could never bring himself to do it. The very difference which enabled him to contemplate the deed rendered him incapable of performing it. When he left the little holding he was still unmaimed and his parents had firewood for three winters.

For someone else had seen the difference. No less a person than the King, Frederick V, King of Denmark and Norway, Duke of Schleswig-Holstein. He came to Zeeland for the shooting and said, idly, to the owner of Knut, "That's a handsome boy; he would look well in the household livery." It was enough. His father and mother felt justified in having treated this different boy differently; they saw him as butler, steward, chamberlain, personal attendant upon the King, free from hunger and hard toil, sheltered from bad weather forever, freed of serfdom's yoke.

For Knut the next years were bitterly frustrating. There were two kinds of pages, the well-born, pages of the presence, and the others, pages of the backstairs. Between them there was an impassable gulf. And between a page of the backstairs, however personable and clever, and any advancement, lay the Bad Times. More and more often posts which in former, prosperous years, had been open to young men of humble birth who had ability, tact and application, were being taken by the younger sons of good family.

He had escaped military service — occasionally he looked at his left hand with interest; he was fed, somewhat indifferently by home standards, he was sheltered from the weather, clothed and paid a regular wage, most of which he sent home, from pride rather than gratitude. He occasionally earned a coin or two by writing a letter for some illiterate who wished to communicate with another who would in turn pay someone to read the communication, or by totting up some lazy superiors' accounts in order that they might be falsified within reason. He answered bells, carried wood, emptied chamberpots and in his free time became familiar with the low haunts in the dock area. It was enough, but not enough for someone who had been different all his life and knew it.

He was almost seventeen on the evening when it fell to his duty to carry a basket of logs into the room where the Crown Prince was confined. Christian, on the verge of being fourteen, had two days earlier failed to do four simple sums involved with multiplication and Heer Reventil, reporting this fact to Count Reventlow, Christian's governor, had said, "Your Excellency, it is hopeless. Beating his buttocks black and blue cannot put into his head what God left out. He is with numbers as I am with music. I cannot tell one note from another. Permit me to say that I am sorry for the boy and wish to resign."

"We will try another tack," Count Reventlow said. "One must not give up too easily. He will be confined to his room and given nothing but bread and water, bread and water, until he has worked out those sums and given the right answers."

Reventil said, "Your Excellency, you could confine me in the Blue Tower and starve me to death and I still could not tell one tune from another . . ."

"And that would matter little. We are not talking about *you*, Heer Reventil. We speak of the one who will be King of Denmark and Norway and cannot multiply — or for that matter, add or subtract."

"Because he lacks ability."

"Go tell his father that," Count Reventlow said. "Go on, go over my head. Say that you pity the boy who is incapable of learning and wish to resign. Tell the King that his son is unteachable; an idiot."

"My wish to resign is because I cannot bear . . . Your Excellency some dogs can walk on their hind legs, they are so made, some are not and I would grieve to see one who could not . . . How much more so a boy, who tries and is defeated and has been beaten and still cannot. And I cannot see the necessity; he will be King, one day. He can hire people — like me, like you — who can multiply, add and subtract. To make his life — he will only be young once, you know — such complete misery . . . For two days, Your Excellency, he had been unable to sit down and the sums are still wrong."

"Then, as I said, we will try the bread and water treatment; and you, Heer Reventil, can try to make it work or go to His Majesty and tender your resignation. You will, I imagine, find it somewhat difficult to obtain another post."

This Heer Reventil admitted; so he had given in and he sat in the ante-room, doing his turn as watchman when Knut Bagger carried a basket of logs into the room where Christian lay on his bed, his face turned to the wall. The day's ration of bread, untouched, and the jug from which he had taken only a few sips, stood on the table beside him. He was willing himself to die and believed that by tomorrow if he could resist the temptation — not yet very strong — to gnaw on the dry bread, he would die, and everybody would be sorry.

It was not pity that made Knut pause and look at the boy who would one day be his King; he was congenitally incapable of feeling pity for anyone who was not a peasant, unable to sell his bullocks, behind with his rent. He felt contemptuous of a creature with so few resources, so few wits and so little spirit. He said abruptly,

"I could get you something proper to eat if you like."

The curt way of speaking, the lack of address pierced Christian's apathy; even Count Reventlow, running the strap through his fingers, would say, "I am obliged to beat Your Royal Highness." He turned from the wall, showing a face on which tears had dried and hopelessness had stamped a look which might be mistaken for sullenness.

"How? I'm watched."

Knut made a grimace and still holding the basket turned back, opened the door and said, speaking to himself, "Wet logs again."

Within minutes he was back, and under the upmost logs was the carcase of a fowl, complete save for one wing and a slice from the breast. He handed it to Christian and went to the stove, unloading the logs with rather more noise than was necessary.

"Be ready to throw it under the bed," he said.

The determination to starve to death, so stalwart in resisting dry bread, weakened when faced with cold chicken. Christian sat up and began cramming the meat into his mouth.

"Was this your supper?" he asked in a muted voice.

"No. Ours was boiled carthorse, as usual."

"Danes don't eat horses."

"No? Then it was its harness!" Knut said and gave his wry, lop-sided grin. Christian gave a splutter of laughter, hastily checked as he glanced at the door. Knut felt a great uprush of self-esteem. He was nothing, a mere carrier of wood, an emptier of chamber pots, but he had fed the heir to the throne; and made him laugh.

Stirring the logs about noisily he asked,

"What is the trouble this time?"

"Sums," Christian said, with his mouth full. He nodded towards the table where the paper lay. Knut rattled the ashpan, skipped to the table and saw four simple multiplication sums of the kind that old Fräulein Thaarup had set him as mental exercise when he was seven. Paperwork, since paper was expensive, had played little part in his education. He went back to the stove and said, "The answers are 48, 66, 148 and 900."

Christian scrambled from the bed.

"Say it again. Tell me . . ."

"Wipe your hands," Knut said, clanking the lid of the stove. "If you make greasy marks they will know."

"Tell me again, please."

Knut told him the answers again and Christian scribbled them in.

"When I am King," he said, "I shall give you a bag full of gold."

"If you remember," Knut said, sceptically.

"There are some things I never forget," Christian said, "I shall never forget this."

"Put the bones in the stove," Knut said, "when you've done." Carrying the empty log basket he went away.

It was a mere incident; a page-of-the-backstairs giving tiny proof of his inborn superiority; the heir to the throne grateful for an offhand kindness; but it had results altogether disproportionate.

"You see," Count Reventlow said to Heer Reventil, "it worked. Bread and water until these sums are correctly done, and they are correctly done." The bread and water treatment was, after that, frequently applied, with varying results; and if Heer Reventil saw a certain rhythm in the business, the Crown Prince locked in with an exercise and his bread and water and producing a satisfactory answer, and the Crown Prince locked in with his exercise and bread and water and producing nonsense, or even nothing at all, he never made the connection between these contradictory performances and the rota of duty of the pages-of-the-backstairs. He thought it was the moon. He believed Christian to be a lunatic; and that was why he was glad that he was no longer beaten.

And Christian, with his promise to Knut, had taken a step forward towards a positive attitude with regard to his Kingship, one day. He had entertained thoughts — When I am King I will put Count Reventlow in the Blue Tower and have him beaten, every day — but such thoughts were not sufficient to sustain him in moments of misery. The thought that Knut was his friend who must one day be rewarded, was far more heartening.

"Knut, when I am King you shall be a Count. You shall be First Gentleman of my Bedchamber. Knut, when I am sixteen I shall have my own household and you shall be the head of it. Knut, look at this map . . . London, Paris . . . *which* is Vienna?

For Knut the whole business became a game, a fascinating pitting of his wits against authority and entrenched power. Every move he made — introducing Christian to the pleasures of alcohol and then of sex, served a double purpose; it increased Knut's confidence in his own superiority and it strengthened his hold on the Prince who would one day be sixteen, and have his own household and have appointments in his gift.

Christian never attained the semi-independent state of which he and his one true friend so often talked. Juliana, working away like a mole, convinced Frederick V that the boy was still too immature to have his own establishment, that he must be kept in the background for another year or two. At the same time, and for the same reason, she advised that his formal education should cease; she had been alarmed by Count Reventlow's occasional mention of slight improvement; it served her purpose to say that what learning a boy had failed to acquire by the time he was sixteen was unlikely ever to be attained.

There was a little space during which Knut found escapades too easily planned to be exciting and he focused his attention on the provision of funds for more and more expensive pleasures. He found a Jew in a waterfront hovel who would buy anything and ask no questions: easily portable treasures were removed from cabinets and tables, and never missed. "All will be yours one day," Knut said, "and a man cannot steal from himself."

And then, without preparation or warning, Christian was King.

He had been kept so resolutely in the background and Juliana's propaganda — disguised as concern — had been so successful that most people were pleasantly surprised to find that their new young King was not only normal-looking but handsome; that he had dignity and enough good sense to realize that he was a novice in affairs and would sit in Council, apparently listening and saying little. He enjoyed considerable popularity for a brief time. Then the rumours began, concerned now not with inability to learn or to behave, but with bad company, undesirable influences, midnight orgies in the palace, excursions to low dives on the waterfront. And even if rumour could be discounted, it was a fact that Knut Bagger, a serf's son, a page-of-the-backstairs had been ennobled, created Count Holmstrupp, given an estate of rather over a thousand acres to the south-west of Copenhagen and made First Gentleman of the Bedchamber. Between four and five hundred peasant families went with the land, and a great stone house, where Knut's mother sat with her workworn hands restless in the lap of the first silk dress she had ever owned, directing others in the tasks that had been hers: his father, believing that the master's foot is the best manure, was still out of doors from dawn to dusk, making certain that if his serfs failed to produce enough to pay their dues it would not be through lack of advice and exhortation; but now he rode on a fine horse. Every now and then one of them would say, "I always said, did I not, that the boy was different?" They were decent people, and had they known by what devious ways their son had advanced himself they would have been shocked; but they would have wished nothing undone. Security was very sweet.

Had the great ones, members of the old nobility, been able to bring themselves to accept the new count, even with the coolest civility, Knut would have continued to exercise the restraint upon Christian to which his two-months' impeccable behaviour was so largely due. Knut was practical; he did not expect Count Bernstorff to greet him as a brother, or ask him to dinner; he was without social ambition and there was no profit in dining at Count Bernstorff's table. But their attitude towards him, often verging upon the positively rude, instead of invoking resentment that could be worked off in a burst of temper and an insistence upon his rights, invited another, far more dangerous game of wits. Christian was now accepted and secure, nothing short of revolution could unseat him; Knut had his patent of nobility and the title deeds to his estate, nothing short of the loss of favour could reduce him. So, how far could Christian be pushed or coaxed in the business of reducing the pride of the proud? Already a long way; everybody must bow before speaking to his Majesty, even when answering a question; everybody must bow when he entered, and when he left. The words, "Your Majesty" must be included in every sentence, silly as it sounded in a prolonged conversation. And this was only a beginning; presently there would be dismissals, sudden and arbitrary.

He changed the cloth on Christian's head twice, spoke of this and that, told Christian about the meal he had ordered.

"But you're not to eat a mouthful. I will dispose of it."

Christian groaned.

"It is essential," Knut said, "that you should be completely well by your wedding. Only a week more to work in. It could hardly have happened at a more awkward time."

For that was another aim he had set himself — to see that Christian's marriage was conspicuously successful; another blow at dirty rumour. He intended to establish himself with the Queen and to use his influence on Christian to her advantage. One day — not too soon — but one day, he was going to need a wife, and if all went well the Queen would appear to choose that wife for him.

He looked at his watch, one of Christian's gifts, and said,

"That is near enough to an hour." He pulled aside the sodden towels and offered his arm, knowing that after every treatment Christian turned dizzy when he stood up.

Christian, in the cool smooth bed, revived a little.

"She is pretty, isn't she?"

87

"Very pretty. I told you; I think you are enviable."

"*Now*," Christian said with some emphasis. "I sometimes think . . ." He hesitated; thought took many forms; of Knut's manner of thinking, inventive, shrewd, purposeful, he knew himself to be incapable, whenever he tried to think in that fashion a kind of fog closed in; but sometimes through the dim, hazy, passive mind there were flashes; it was like the sun shining out from the edge of a cloud. "I sometimes think, there is a balance, Knut. A year ago. Who envied me then? And even now . . . Knut this I would not say to anyone but you. The truth is that sometimes I feel like a man with two heads. One says one thing, one another. It's been worse lately, with the sweating and the pills. It is most unpleasant. Because which am I? You're so clever. You tell me. Which am I?"

Knut was at the table where there were decanters of wine, red Spanish wine, forbidden to sufferers from syphilis, part of the deceptive show, and one full of fruit juice, which looked like wine and which Christian could drink with impunity. He carried a glassful of this and put it into Christian's still clammy hand. Then he sat down on the foot of the bed and looked at his King sharply. He knew him to be stupid, slow-witted, dull and slow of apprehension — and thanked God for it; had he been otherwise Knut would still be Knut Bagger, page-of-the-backstairs, his third livery outgrown, his beard, however closely shaved, obvious; too big, too old, out into the street with him . . . Christian's stupidity and his wretched situation had been Knut Bagger's life-buoy — combined with his own talent.

But the earnest and repeated question "Which am I?" sounded like raving. Like fever talk. "Which am I?" What did he mean?

"And there's a question," Christian said, "to fox you, my dear friend. When my two heads get to work . . . But nobody could have guessed, could they? You were there. You saw me. And she is pretty. It wasn't difficult. I . . . I behaved as you told me, Knut. You said yourself, an impressive performance. But there are two jugs, you know . . . I mean two heads. And one ached, all the time because there was a cannon ball in it, thumping about. It is melted now in the heat of the stove. That at least is something to be thankful for. But there again, what is good for the one is bad for the other . . ."

There was no point in trying to follow such talk; probably Christian was slightly fevered.

"At Vidborg," Knut said, "there are, as you know, the hot-houses where my father hopes to grow flowers for market all through the winter. I will send Axel, very early in the morning to fetch what he has. That should please her; women like flowers. And I think it would be a good idea if you sent a poem, too. In the old style."

Christian looked blank.

"I don't know any poems. Worse than sums."

"That need not worry you," said Knut who had learned from Fräulein Thaarup at least two hundred of the measured, rhymeless, repetitive verses that told of Denmark's long history and the exploits of such heroes as Harold Bluetooth. He thought for a moment. "How is this?

The wind from the sea is a cold wind,

The sky in the west is clouded,
But the cold wind from the sea and the clouds from the west
Brought me a rose.
Pink-petalled, sweet scented, the dew fresh upon it,
The rose came to me, out of the west.
Out of the wind and the cloud of the west
Came my bride."

Not bad, he thought, for the spur of the moment; worthy of a more appreciative audience. Christian looked baffled, but he said,

"Oh, very good Knut; very good. Yes, I see. England is west isn't it, and the wind was certainly cold."

"I made it. But you must write it out and sign it; as though you had made it yourself."

"Couldn't you write it and just let me sign?"

"It must all be in your hand. Look, it is not so much to do. She's young and homesick, and she'll be lonely at Fredericksberg, with you laid up here. You want to please her and make her happy, don't you?"

"Yes; she is pretty." Then from the dull bafflement light struck and Christian said with an air of triumph,

"It must be written in German, you realize."

Everybody else was so very clever, and Knut the cleverest of all, but every now and then, even in Council, Christian saw something that everyone else had missed.

"That I hadn't thought of," Knut admitted. "It wouldn't sound so well, though. We'll send it in Danish with a request that Frau von Plessen reads it as it is and then translates."

Frau von Plessen was one of those who highly disapproved of Count Holmstrupp and regarded him as a bad influence; but she was not a stupid woman and even if she could so far delude herself as to imagine that the verse was of Christian's making she would know that only from Vidborg could come a bunch of roses in November. That would show her. Between favourites in the sense that many people regarded Knut as a favourite, and wives there was never anything but bitter animosity.

"I shall now unlock the door and leave," he said. "You would be wise to say that the cold ride put you back a bit. I'll look in later and dispose of your supper for you."

CHAPTER
FOUR

Fredericksberg,
November 2nd 1766

When the flowers and the verses were delivered Caroline was entertaining the two Queen Mothers who, to their chagrin, had arrived together, and the diversion was welcome for the visit had struck, and sustained, a note of awkwardness, neither formal nor intimate, and both ladies had said things, outwardly smooth and courteous, which revealed their antagonism and seemed to be inviting Caroline to side with one or the other.

Caroline herself was ill-prepared; Frau von Plessen had said that it was unlikely that any callers would come before afternoon; so she faced the pair both painted and powdered, splendidly attired and much bejewelled, in her loose morning sac and with her hair tied back with a blue ribbon and spilling haphazard curls. Also, despite her exhaustion, she had not slept well.

They had exchanged the ritual curtseys; then the old woman had let go of the shoulder of the little black boy, stretched out her claw-like, ring-laden hands and embraced Caroline and kissed her. She had a curious dry dead smell about her.

"You are so like dear Louise," she said. "It is as Louise's niece that I welcome you to Denmark, and hold you dear."

The other one — Juliana — gave a little laugh, a pleasant tinkle. "You must not think that a dubious compliment. No portrait ever did your aunt justice — or so we are told. And naturally one forgets . . ."

"My memory is excellent," the old woman said.

Caroline was much the youngest, but she was a reigning Queen and therefore responsible for the direction of the conversation; but no matter what she tried, sooner or later the veiled bickering broke through. Both were to blame, she decided; and by the strict standard of her own upbringing, both were rude; the purpose of this visit was surely to make her welcome, to make her feel at home; it was having the opposite effect. She cast round in her mind for a subject new enough not to be riddled with old enmity and said,

"I should be very pleased if you would call me by my name." It seemed silly for three woman to sit about addressing one another as "Your Majesty."

"I will most gladly," Juliana said. "I so well remember when I arrived in Denmark. Nobody called me by my name. My husband, of course, used endearments, but I longed for someone to say Juliana."

Sophia-Magdalene said, "Humph," in a very disbelieving way and added, "I always called Louise by her name. But she was a King's daughter and had no need to stand on her dignity."

"Caroline is a very pretty name," Juliana said.

"If you use it you will make confusion; she is to be called Matilda."

"Oh, am I? Nobody informed me." She had always disliked her second name thinking it had an elderly sound.

"The person most nearly concerned is always the last to be told anything — or that is my experience," Sophia said. Her voice and the look she cast in Juliana's direction told Caroline plainly that there had been some occasion in the past when something had been concealed by the younger woman.

"Why am I to be known by my second name?"

"As I understood it, some nonsense which I shall ignore about Caroline being derived from the French. Popular feeling in Denmark at the moment is anti-French. And Matilda is a good old English name. In the old times the English and Danes were good friends," Juliana said.

"So good," Sophia said, "that the English used to pray in churches to be delivered from the Danes. They're very conservative; perhaps they still do." It was not exactly the most tactful thing to say, but as she spoke the painted, monkeyish mask of her face creased and shifted into a delightful smile which said that if they did it would be rather comic, wouldn't it?

"I shall call you — if I may — Caroline," Juliana said.

At this point Frau von Plessen entered, followed by a page who bore a bunch of roses. They were yellow and white, the pink one was only just in bud and Knut had changed "pink-petalled" to "soft-petalled". He had an eye for detail.

Frau von Plessen, rather self consciously, read Knut's effusion in Danish, then as requested, in German. She knew where the flowers had come from, she knew who had composed the verse, but she was, none the less elated. The influence of a good woman was already making itself felt and His Majesty was making use of that clever mercenary little rogue who had so often used him.

Caroline said, "That is beautiful. So are the flowers. How exceedingly kind of . . . His Majesty." Alone with his grandmother and his stepmother she would have used his name, but he was His Majesty to Frau von Plessen and the blank-faced page.

Almost reverently Frau von Plessen laid the sheet of paper on the table by Caroline's chair and said that she would fetch a bowl. Caroline lowered her face to the flowers; they had no scent; no that was not quite true; they did not smell like roses, they smelt, very faintly of the manure which had warmed and nurtured their roots.

"Christian," his grandmother said, rather heavily, "is kind, at heart. And good; and anxious to please." There had been a period when he had spent some time with her; regularly and she had indulged in some grandmaternal spoiling, of which the silly little boy had taken advantage and given Juliana good reason to say

95

that after a visit to his grandmother Christian was always more unruly than ever. It was to this that she had referred when speaking of being the last to know anything — she had been obliged to send to ask if the boy was ill that he had not come on the usual day. He was stupid, but not bad; it was Juliana who had made him bad.

Juliana said, "Christian is kind at heart; and good and anxious to please. I entirely agree. But I should hate Caroline to be deluded into thinking he is a poet."

"How would you know?" the old woman said with sudden savagery. "So far he's had no reason to be. He was delighted when he saw ... Matilda, you heard what Frederick said; he thought she looked like a rose and she did come from the west, so he simply wrote down what was in his heart and it turned into a poem."

"Perhaps he grew the roses, too," Juliana said, satirically.

"So he did, in a manner of speaking. Vidborg was his property until that rapscallion talked his way to it. And in my opinion it still is, with everything that grows in it and on it."

Suddenly all their differences were forgotten, the moss-grown grievances pushed aside as they allied together to attack Holmstrupp, taking turns to warm Caroline against him. Much of what they said was libellous and would have been more so but that both women stopped a little short of complete frankness out of respect for Caroline's youth and innocence. As it was, they managed to convey a picture of someone without honesty, or honour, with no respect for himself or anyone else, a self-seeking, immoral liar and cheat who had such ascendancy over the King that as the grandmother said, "he'd sign his own death warrant if Holmstrupp wrote it out and told him to."

This was rather worse than when they were launching little darts at one another and Caroline couldn't help thinking that there must be some truth in what they said, their sudden unity was impressive. The pleasure that the flowers and the verse — and the thought which had gone to them — had aroused in her slowly dwindled. This attack on Holmstrupp — she connected the name with the handsome young man in the mulberry jacket who had walked out of the Roskilde hall by Christian's side — had the effect of making Christian, her husband, the King, somehow ludicrous and pitiable, hardly a man, and certainly less than a person.

She tried to interrupt, tactfully. She asked where Vidborg was, and that evoked a description of the beautiful old house now in the possession of two old peasants who were using even the hothouses for profit and would have had pigs in the hall and fowls in the long gallery had their son not forbidden such practices.

It was the more embarrassing because of the presence of the little African behind Sophia's chair. He stood still and upright as a statue, his eyes fixed on the far wall; but he had ears.

In any case, Caroline disapproved of silver collar boys who were becoming fashionable in England too. Mamma deplored the custom of acquiring them young, treating them as pets and then when they were too big to be decorative any longer turning them into the street to starve or take to crime. Lord Bute also disapproved the fashion and his friend, Lord Mansfield, went further and said that the keeping of slaves was illegal in England, and one day he would prove it.

As the antiphonal castigation of Count Holmstrupp went on, Caroline glanced uneasily at the child behind the chair and the old woman, intercepting one of these glances, paused and laughed and said,

"Oh, you need not worry about Peppo. He is from Senegal and understands nothing but French. I've had him almost two years and he knows that if I ever caught him learning anything else I'd have his tongue cut out." As she said this she craned her head round and looked at the boy with possessive affection. Then she leaned forward and broke one of the pastries which had been served with hot chocolate as soon as she and Juliana had arrived. She popped it into his mouth, exactly as one would give a dog a tit-bit.

But at least the subject had changed. Sophia said, grumbling, that no matter what you did they would *grow*. Schnapps was supposed to check growth, so was sleeping in a cupboard where it was impossible to stretch out at full length; but these were myths; all her Peppos had drunk up to a pint of schnapps a day and slept in a cupboard; this one grew a little more slowly than the others but he was growing and would soon have to be replaced.

"If you would like one, I'll see to it for you. My merchant is very reliable; they're all guaranteed to be sound and without vice."

The alliance had broken down with the change of subject and Juliana said that she, for one, didn't care much for black boys, they all stank.

Peppo stood, so immobile that he seemed not even to blink.

The pastry that had been pushed into his mouth lay wadded between his upper teeth and his tongue; he would remove it when he was no longer the subject of talk and had been forgotten.

He understood Danish and German and in the last year had picked up a working knowledge of English from a god called Smith who was in charge of Count Bernstorff's stables. Something rather more than a year ago Peppo had carried a message and taking a short cut across a pasture had fallen in with Smith who had a horse on a long rein. He'd stopped and stared; he loved horses and this was a particularly handsome one. The man looked at him, not very kindly, but Peppo was not disturbed by that; nothing much could happen to him while he wore the Queen Mother's collar. The man said something in a completely unknown tongue; then he spoke in Danish, "Who're you spying for?" Peppo was not supposed to know any Danish, so he went on staring at the beautiful horse, so much more beautiful than the man whose face was all puckers and whose legs were very bowed. Then the man laughed, picked Peppo up and threw him on to the horse's back, saying something in that unknown tongue, half laughing, half jeering; Peppo recognized the tone, he was accustomed to having jokes played on him — sooner or late *She* always punished the jokers; and she would punish this

99

one, if Peppo lived to tell, and for a second or two he was not sure if he would. For the man with a word and a jerk on the rein set the horse in motion. Peppo grabbed with both hands at the animal's mane and put his head down, at the same time clenching his small legs against the smoothly groomed, terribly slippery, bare hide. It was like clinging to the side of a moving mountain; terrifying at first, and then, as he found that he could maintain his grip with hands and knees, suddenly enjoyable. But, Mon Dieu, when *She* heard about this joke the man would be punished.

She was never told about it; for when the man halted the horse and lifted Peppo down, his whole manner had changed; he patted Peppo on the back, started to speak in the strange tongue, switched to Danish, telling Peppo that he was a natural born rider and he'd like to see him in a saddle. Come back any time. Peppo maintained his blank, uncomprehending face, patted the horse which was sweating lightly and walked away. He did not even say, "Merci, Monsieur," lest the man should guess that he had understood the invitation.

But he went back, again and again. The Queen Mother, his mistress, always slept from two in the afternoon to four and sometimes there were whole days when the stiffness in her joints kept her in bed and she did not need Peppo to lean upon. All his free time he spent with the man Smith, learning about horses, learning English. He now knew that there was a place called England — from which Smith had come — and in England a place called Newmarket, and in Newmarket a man called Sir William Craven who had servants, specially privileged, called jockeys. Being black did not matter, if you could ride and didn't weigh too much. One day, when he had learned all that the god Smith had to teach, and didn't weigh too much, Peppo would be a jockey in Newmarket.

Cake was bad. They were talking about something else now and not looking at him, so he slipped the moist wad into the palm of his hand and put it into the pocket of the peacock blue breeches. It would leave a mark and *She* would scold but it hardly mattered; one lived for the future.

Frau von Plessen came back, bearing in her hands a silver bowl for the roses. She looked, rather diffidently at the two Queen Mothers and said that Madame Brisson had arrived to make the first fitting.

"A fitting for what?" Caroline said.

There was a little, stunned silence. Sophia, reaching for the shoulder of her little black boy, said,

"What did I say? Nobody tells anyone anything. It is always the way. Your wedding dress, Matilda, your wedding dress."

"I brought it. The one I wore in London. It is quite beautiful, satin and lace and pearls. It cost a great deal. I wore it only once. Would it not serve again?"

She had already started, in her mind, a letter to Edward, describing the country as she saw it, the cottages mere mud huts, the great houses in decay, the cattle emaciated, inns on the main road, post houses, without so much as a looking-glass. And as she planned this honest, but not critical letter she had thought, with complacency that she had brought a good dowry, and had clothes, and jewels enough. She would not be an expense to them. Christian's remark that burghers could afford to lay up their clothes in pepper seemed to contradict her observations; so had the palace of Fredericksberg, so much more up to date and ornate than any royal residence in England; so had the clothes and the jewels of the two Queen Mothers, but the impression she had gained along the road had not been entirely erased.

Juliana laughed and said, "We are so nationalistic these days that you would hardly be regarded as legally married unless you wore a dress of silk, woven in Milan certainly, but bought by a Danish merchant, shipped in a Danish ship to a Danish mercer and sewn by Danish hands."

"Madame Brisson is not a Dane," Sophia said promptly. "She is a religious refugee from France. She has suffered for her religion. *And* she has worked for Madame de Pompadour."

They took their leave and went away. Both had been amiable to her but they had spoiled her pleasure in Christian's tribute and they left her feeling the mental equivalent of having stroked velvet the wrong way, a prickling unease. They would be, naturally, her closest associates; they were, strange to think!, her family now, but she felt that to please one would be to displease the other; or she might, like that unfortunate young man, displease both and then they would combine against her. A frightening prospect.

And that, she thought, as she picked up her poem and went into her bedroom to submit herself to

Madame Brisson's hands, was a silly way to think. How could they harm her? One elderly, and one old woman neither of whom had the benefit of Mamma's upbringing — "I will not tolerate bickering and innuendoes are detestable; if you have a grudge say so, openly." Mamma had also said, "Friendly to all, intimate with none." That rule must be applied to the two Dowager Queens.

Deliberately she switched her mind from the subject. She would send, in verse, a reply to Christian; something hinged on the contrast between the cold of yesterday and the warmth of his welcome and the hope that the wind from the west was blowing his illness away. Verse writing had been very prevalent at Kew; at Christmas and on birthdays. Edward's were best; his lines "To my Brother upon the Occasion of His Coronation," likening George to a Colossus with one foot in the Far East and one in the Far West and at the same time likening him to Atlas who bore the world on his shoulders, had moved George almost to tears.

She must write some verse for Christian; she must write to Edward while her impressions of Denmark were still sharp and fresh; she must be busy and not brood . . .

CHAPTER
FIVE

Christiansborg,
November 8th 1766

She had kept busy and she had not brooded. The week which might have been a lagging vacuum, passed in no time. The fittings alone took vast tracts of time because every now and then Madame Brisson would retreat to the farthest distance the room allowed and there sit down on the floor, cupping her chin in her hands and studying Caroline who stood in a garment that seemed to be made completely of pins, as though she were some strange animal. Finally, in her yellowish face her purplish lips would move and give an order and one or the other of the two young women who always came with her would adjust a pin or two. It seemed to Caroline that the dress, when completed would not be so pretty or so becoming as her first wedding dress; but when she said so, obeying Mamma's command to speak out openly, Madame Brisson went into a kind of convulsion and presently gasped out that the aim of this dress was not to be pretty, it was to be splendid; Her Majesty would go to her wedding in a gown of unsurpassed splendour. It would also be, Caroline felt, as fitting followed fitting, of unsurpassed weight; padded, wadded, boned, embroidered and bejewelled, it assumed every day more and more the quality of a suit of armour. It could have stood alone.

Christian's sister, the Princess of Hesse, came to visit her; her manner was rather chill and formal, but her conversation was amiable. Caroline had tried at various times to recall Christian's features, but at Roskilde she had not been calm enough to observe very exactly and whenever she visualized him she seemed to be able to recall only the red-rimmed eyes, the heavy-lipped mouth: now confronted by his sister who closely resembled him, she remembered what she seemed not to have noticed, the high, squarish forehead, the straight eyebrows, the aquiline nose — all of which could be handsome on a man, but were less kind to a female. Both brother and sister had inherited the famous so-called "white eyes" of their mother's family, eyes of so pale a blue yet opaque that they might have been made from moonstones.

After the Princess came other ladies, the wives and daughters of the great families; they welcomed her to Denmark, expressed their wishes that she would be happy, and, if they were old enough, spoke fondly of her aunt, Queen Louise. Then, in every case, conversation languished, almost every topic dying on the block of the monosyllabic reply. Offered refreshment a great many of them chose tea — a gesture to her nationality: and she discovered, to her dismay, that none of them rode. "No, Your Majesty," "Never, Your Majesty." Finally she asked why not and Countess

105

Rantzau said apologetically, "In Denmark it has not been considered correct for ladies to ride horseback." She added hastily, "For Your Majesty, naturally, it will be different; whatever the Queen does will be correct. And as you will be honorary colonel of the Holstein Guards and probably other regiments, there will be occasions when it will be necessary for you to sit on a horse."

"I wish to do more than sit. Riding is one of my greatest pleasures."

Countess von Moltke, a lady of great dignity and splendour contrived to look quite timid and shy as she said that her husband, Commander-in-Chief, would have great pleasure in providing a suitable mount and an escort for Her Majesty. How large an escort would Her Majesty wish? Two, Caroline said, choosing the minimum possible. Countess von Moltke's neck reddened, a sure sign that behind the paint and powder of her face, she was blushing.

"If I may be permitted, Your Majesty . . . so great an honour should not be so much restricted. Dare I suggest six?"

The timidity, the constant repetition of "may I be permitted," "dare I," "if Your Majesty would allow" contributed to an uneasy atmosphere; as though, Caroline reflected, she were a very large dog of uncertain temper, constantly to be placated. In England people in close contact with George and Charlotte behaved with respect, but nobody acted as though they were expected to bite. Manners were different here; or perhaps the extreme stiffness was because she was strange and would wear off when they knew her better. She sincerely hoped so.

Her brother Henry, Duke of Cumberland, had given her as his parting present a fine new saddle of chestnut-coloured leather, mounted with silver. Her riding habit was of dark green cloth and with it she wore a little hat, turned up at one side and on the other trimmed with a swoop of cock's feathers, tawny, green and blue which curved down over her ear. It was, of all the outfits she owned, or was to own, the most basically becoming; and the prospect of riding again, of trying her fine new saddle for the first time, of being out in the winter sunshine — it was a mild still day, "a weather-breeder", Frau von Plessen said, and snow would soon fall, God send not before the 8th, the wedding day — gave a sparkle to her eyes and a spring to her step. As she came down the steps and smiled at the six young men who saluted her, two of them fell romantically and irrevocably in love.

Seven grooms held the heads of seven horses. Six were matched, all black, shining like ebony, restless and lively. The seventh was a kind of muted strawberry roan, heavy, thick, immobile, old. It lacked only the rockers and the nailed on red-felt saddle to be the replica of the horse in the Kew nursery — Good Dobbin.

It wore her fine new saddle.

She stopped on the lowest step and said, "Oh no," in English, and then in German, looking at the horse with distaste.

One of the brilliantly uniformed young men stepped forward and bowed.

"Allow me to assure Your Majesty, it is a good, safe horse. It is the horse of the drum major. It has a gentle pace and is impervious to noise or any other sudden disturbance such as rabbits."

She remembered Countess von Moltke's word, "a suitable mount". This was what they deemed suitable for her — one of the best horsewomen, if not *the* best in England. It was an insult — not intended, she realized that; their motives were of the best; but it simply would not do; they must learn.

"I don't want a good safe hobby horse." She ran her eye over the six matched blacks and chose the most restive. "I want that one."

Young Baron de Schimmelman, who was in charge of the party, and whose horse it was, turned pale. Sweyn was not easily handled, he himself had fought him, daily, before gaining mastery, and with a woman on his back, he'd be up to his old tricks again. He'd throw her, or run away, break her neck.

He said, "Your Majesty, that is an evil horse. Permit me to say that I dare not . . ."

"Trust me with him? No ill will come to him. See . . ."

She walked down the last step, went to the horse, pushed the groom away and put her face close to, but not touching the horse's muzzle. She breathed out, puffing into the distended, twitching nostrils. A trick of great antiquity, a carefully guarded secret known to few. In England she would have said, softly, "I am your

108

friend. Do you accept me?" for that was part of the ritual. But this was a Danish horse. So she merely breathed on him and he stood still, without a finger on the bridle, while the saddles were changed.

The management of horses she had learned in a curious way, from an old man who had once been one of her father's coachmen. He was actually the man who, years before Caroline's birth, had driven the horses on that mad ride from Hampton Court to St. James's Palace, the Princess of Wales — Mamma — already in labour with Augusta and Papa determined that the child, whom he expected to be a boy, the heir, should be born at St. James's. There were trimmings to the story; there had been no sheets to put on the beds and Augusta had been born between two starched table cloths; there were only six candles in the whole establishment, and so on. Of what must have been a hideous experience Mamma never spoke, but she certainly cherished old Edgar, though by the time Caroline became aware of him he was quite useless and often tipsy. He lived somewhere in the lofts over the stables and was fed from the kitchen once a day and when the weather was fine used to creep down and sit with his back to a sun-warmed wall and watch the comings and goings in the stable yard.

One afternoon — it was just before George's accession, and Caroline was nine, three or four of them had been riding together and were returning to the house, Caroline lagging, unwilling, as usual to exchange out-of-doors for indoors and the dancing lesson presently due. As she passed the old man he

109

reached out and took hold of a fold of her skirt, with, considering his dead-leaf frailty, a clutch of considerable force.

"Wait a minute," he said, "I got something to tell you and something to give you; but it's a secret. It's something money can't buy." She was not frightened exactly, but disconcerted; old Edgar was tipsy again and talking nonsense, and indoors Signor Sarti would be waiting, and she must change her clothes.

"Tell me tomorrow," she said, pulling at her skirt.

"That'll be too late," he said. "I've had my tomorrows and my boy being killed at Portobello, there's nobody for me to pass the word to. So take this, and listen, listen hard." He pushed into her hand a piece of bleached bone which could have been rather more than half of the wishbone of a very small fowl. "Keep that on you," he said, "when you're near enough, blow in their noses and talk to them as though they was people and any horse'll do just what you say. *Any* horse. The savagest'll eat out of your hand and a dying one'll run five miles to please you."

It sounded like nonsense, but later in the day old Edgar was found dead, there where he sat, in the sun, so she kept the bone for sentiment's sake. And then, one day, George came back from a visit to Euston in Suffolk with some peculiar tale about the secret eastern association of horsemen whose members had an uncanny power over horses; it smacked of witchcraft, said the practical George, and in earlier days would have led to trouble.

Caroline had no idea whether the bit of bone held any virtue, but she had tucked it into the ribbon or the feathers that had decorated a succession of riding hats and no horse had ever given her any trouble. As for talking to them as though they were people, she had always done that, but as time went on the words had become stylized, a routine, rather as prayers did.

She and the five young officers clattered away and presently young Schimmelman, mounted on another black horse, joined them, harried and anxious still, until he realized that the evil horse was behaving impeccably.

Caroline greatly enjoyed her ride; the young men seemed to shed some of their formality, there were fewer monosyllabic replies and apologetic prefaces to remarks; there were smiles, and even now and again some laughter.

She was their Queen, she was young and pretty and friendly, and she certainly could manage a horse; their talk afterwards was tinged with inevitable exaggeration and by evening Christian, in his sweat-box for an hour, knew that his bride was a horsewoman of superb quality. His own experience with horses had been unhappy; he'd been timid to start with and Juliana had said — with some truth — that for a King to be deficient in the management of horses was a great disadvantage. Her suggestions as to how this deficiency could be remedied and her talks on the subject with his tough old riding master, had all been prompted by the hope that the clumsy young fool might have a fall and break his neck. This had not happened, but he was still

111

not entirely happy on horseback and his mounts were always carefully chosen.

That one of his two heads which did not wish to be married and thought that life as he had led it for the last ten months was so good that any change could only detract from it, that head which had noticed at Roskilde that Caroline looked not only pretty, but proud, and at least three inches too tall, took temporary charge and knew a pang of jealousy. It also associated his present discomfort with the need to be well by a certain date. Nature cured — given time, and the number of noses lost in the process was small; look at sailors, they lacked legs, arms, eyes and ears, but he could not remember seeing one without a nose, and they had syphilis practically all the time. In fact the brutes carried and spread it; they came ashore, their pockets full of money and they weren't content to frequent places and drabs that any man with sense would take care to avoid; no, they must force their way into places like the Golden Crown. With this result.

He said abruptly.

"Knut; what happened to that coffee-coloured little bitch?"

"She is in a sack at the bottom of the Sound, anchored down with stones and old iron."

"Good. And Madam?"

"She had a most unfortunate accident. The banisters gave way. As you may imagine she fell very heavily; she is unlikely to walk again. And almost as bad, from her point of view, while she lay downstairs — I understand that it was impossible to get her up to bed — somebody raided her rooms and found her hoard."

Christian wiped his streaming face on the end of a towel and looked at his one true friend with profound respect and admiration and gratitude.

With what appeared to be a change of subject but was actually a logical follow-on, he said,

"One day I shall institute a new Order without any nonsense about two generations of noble birth as a qualification."

"Not yet," Knut said. "That way it would look like a consolation to me; I should dislike that. It contents me to think that my grandson will qualify for the Danneborg. He looked at his watch, changed the cloth on Christian's head and said, "Another twenty minutes."

"There's one thing." Christian said, "I don't intend to have any of this English nonsense about politics. Her mother, so they say, rules George and her grandmother was a busybody. Juliana told me that this afternoon."

"She's far too pretty to bother about such things."

With a pang of pain Christian's other head took over.

"Yes," he said, "she's very pretty; and . . . and well-disposed. She wanted to come and see me, but Frau von Plessen said she might catch this cold. She has sent a message though, every day, hasn't she?"

"And the family recipe for onion gruel."

"All the same I'm not sure about this riding — for a Queen. Who's her Master of Horse?"

"So far I know he has not yet been appointed."

The other head, with a stab and a tremor set to work.

"Baron de Bulow," Christian said, and his two heads, coming together with an agonizing clang, knew once again that he was cleverest of all. For de Bulow had Hanoverian origins, Hanover and England were one. The Queen would never suspect de Bulow of wishing to thwart her . . . as thwart he would, obedient to his King's order.

"Here are your pills," Knut said; proffering the flattened globes of mercury and bismuth.

"They make me feel very sick you know. If I were allowed proper food, I doubt if I could get it down."

"They work," Knut said, "and so does this . . ." He indicated the overheated little room. "Your lip has healed, the rash has almost disappeared . . . and the other symptoms."

He did not mention them. The limitations of his own squeamishness staggered him, and in any other person would have provoked derision. He could organize, perfectly and without a qualm the death of the little half-caste girl whose embrace had infected the King, and the ruin, physical and financial of the old woman who ran the Golden Crown and had not been careful enough, but there were things that he could not bring himself to mention.

"Yes," Christian said, gulping the pills. "I am better. All but my head. My head is sore. And there are two of them. Sometimes they work together and sometimes they pull away from one another. It is very painful. Because which am I?"

Knut recognized the question, asked, on another occasion, in exactly these circumstances. It probably had something to do with the heat.

"Come along," he said, unwadding the towels. "Ten minutes short, but you are better. Come to bed."

"There was just one thing," Christian said, putting his hands to his head and pressing his two heads together. "That doctor . . . The treatment was cruel . . . but it has worked. I shall be well for my wedding — thanks to you. But thanks to him, also. Especially for the salt water. I think he should be rewarded."

"I paid him," Knut said, remembering the big, easy-mannered, disbelieving man who had done what nobody else had ever done, looked through him as though he were a pane of glass, made him feel — if only for a moment — that he was non-existent. "I paid him well."

"I know," said Christian, who prided himself on never forgetting a favour or an injury, "but I feel that something more . . . Knut, you know how to punish people . . . think of a reward for this man. What was his name?"

"I don't think I ever heard it. I was told that he was very clever and had studied in Germany where medical knowledge is the best in the world. I was told how to find his house. I addressed him as Doctor and to him I was a nameless man."

And he as good as called me a liar.

Out of the bake-house, into the cool bedroom and the smooth welcoming bed, Christian could say,

"One day we must find him out and reward him. For except for my head, Knut, except for my head, I am cured. And I shall be well for my wedding . . ."

Part Three

CHAPTER
ONE

Christiansborg,
November 10th 1766

The footfall of the sentry in the courtyard came up to her, muted by distance; an owl loosed its lonely, eerie cry: somewhere a clock struck and another answered it. Four o'clock in the morning. It had been the longest day in her life and here she was, still awake, two hours after Christian had rolled over and gone to sleep. Did all brides lie awake in the night, looking back on the events of the most splendid day of their lives as though through a thick mist, or across a wide moat. That was I — going cheerfully, even eagerly, to my proper wedding, and this is I — lying here in the dark; no connection between the two; there can never be any connection. Yet she had heard women speak, heard Mamma speak, and only this morning, yesterday morning, heard prim Frau von Plessen speak, sentimentally, with a fond backward look to the day of their wedding. Was something wrong with her?

Mamma had always counselled her children to examine themselves, to ask, in any crisis — Am I myself to blame?

Everything had gone so well; the ceremony, long and solemn and quite beautiful; music and the clear pure voices of boys, fountains of sound, springing upwards to the arched roof. White roses on the altar. Christian, all in white and gold, immensely handsome and supremely dignified. There she had not failed. She had even mastered what responses were required of her in the Danish tongue, mispronounced perhaps, but clearly audible. And inside the rigid dress, with the heavy train dragging on her shoulders, she had born herself upright, and moved with grace. No fault there.

Then the feast — too late in the day to be called dinner, too early to be supper; a long table, everything on it, even the salt cellars, of gold and a hundred and fifty people sitting down, all the very highest of the Danish nobility and the Ministers from other countries — the British Minister's name was Tetley . . . She and Christian seated midway along one of the long table's sides; the two Queen Mothers opposite. There were other tables in the rooms to left, to right.

After the feast — interminably prolonged — the creation, admission and robing of the twelve new Knights of the Order of Dannesborg in honour of the occasion. In that she had no part to play, except, when it was over, to extend her hand to be kissed.

And finally the ball. Before this Frau von Plessen, with a tiny pair of silver scissors, cut away the dragging train and Caroline had felt like a bird let out of a cage.

Despite her preference for outdoor exercise and her reluctance to go in and subject herself to Signor Sarti's tuition, she danced well. With Christian she led the first

120

Minuet; there were Gavottes, Cotillions, Passepieds. And then quite suddenly Christian clapped his hands and shouted to his brother-in-law, "Charles, lead the Kehraus through all the apartments."

"Now?"

"Now. Begin."

With that, suddenly, something happened; everybody seemed to go crazy; one moment so prim, touching finger tips, measuring steps, bowing, advancing, retreating, the next forming up into a long line, hands on the hips of whoever chanced to be in front and clutched by the one who followed, to the sound of music — no longer the known tunes of Purcell, Handel, Bach and Haydn, but something strange and wild, with a compulsive rhythm, the long column, like a snake made its way through room after room, upstairs, downstairs, through a cavernous kitchen with firelight twinkling on copper pans and pots, and at one point out for a few seconds on to a torch-lit terrace and in again.

It was a strange thing to see this staid company so completely abandoned, moving with something between a skip and a shuffle, the men reinforcing the music's rhythm with shouts that sounded like hunting cries, the women's headdresses and sometimes their hair, tumbling into disarray. It would have been understandable had more alcohol been consumed. Wine had flown freely at the beginning of the feast, but about half-way through Count Holmstrupp had come out of one of the side rooms — the one known as the Rose because of the colour of its windows and hangings, and leaned over Christian and said something in his ear. Christian looked displeased for a second, then smiled and touched the Count on the arm and nodded. As Holmstrupp went away, Christian reached for his glass, but not to drink. He moved it about two inches nearer the centre of the table and did not touch it again. Abstention had run like a whisper outwards towards the ends of the table and soon no one was drinking. So the Kehraus, whatever it was, was not a drunken dance; it was more as though long hours of over-controlled behaviour must be compensated for and strictly curbed spirits allowed some outlet.

Then, except for the havoc that it had worked on hair and clothes, it might never have been. Formality closed in like ice upon the taking of leave. It was well after midnight; there was now nothing but the disrobing between her and her bridal bed, the "physical intimacies" of Mamma, the crude down-to-earth act described by Alice. Standing there beside Christian, so handsome in satin and gold lace, Caroline was grateful for the Kehraus; hers was not the only flushed face, not the only heart beating too fast and too hard and too high above the edge of her bodice.

The old Queen Mother, having made her painful curtsey, embraced them both. The same dry, dead smell emanated from her. She said to Caroline, "I wish you every happiness." Whatever she said to Christian made him give a little yelping laugh. Juliana embraced neither of them, but she smiled as she wished them long years of happiness. (She knew Christian very well; for years she had studied him through the magnifying glass of hatred and jealousy and although her view was distorted, minimizing the good or the potential good and emphasizing the follies and failings it was a penetrating view. Two days earlier she had made one of her visits; he was better and in his private sitting-room, wearing a furred robe over his shirt and breeches. Into the casual talk about his health and the imminent wedding she inserted a sentence which any loving mother, on good terms with her son, might have said with the best intention. "You must remember Christian, that she is a Princess, not one of your hired women." She knew her step-son very well.)

The King's bedchamber and the Queen's adjoined, with a communicating door. Caroline's room was very fine, all white and gold and rose. The walls were lined with the rose-coloured silk and in every panel there was a white and gold framed looking glass in which reflections answered one another, so that when, at last she was installed in the vast bed, and waiting, she could see to her left and to her right, an infinite number of candles and Carolines and rose-hung beds with white and gold posters, growing smaller with distance, finally diminished to nothing.

She assured herself that she was not frightened. On the surface of it Mamma's "intimacies" and Alice's blunt statements hinted alike at something undignified; but every married woman in the world had borne it and emerged undamaged. And there was that term, "one flesh", which she understood, the wishing to be part of, to be one with. She had experienced it once, with a spray of lilac on a May morning in Kew gardens; not enough to look at it, to smell it, something more was needed; she'd taken a great bite out of it, lilac a part of me, all one, the morning, the birdsong, the dew and the sunshine, everything.

It had tasted horrid, sharp and peppery, and she had spat it out and the next day passed, with averted eyes, the bush where one spray hung maimed. But it had been an experience of a sort and she had thought of it . . . sometimes . . .

She was prepared for the act that would make her one with Christian; and hoped that in its performance the love, the lightning that Edward had spoken of, might strike. It hadn't at Roskilde because everything had been so hurried and confused — but there she had felt kindly towards him; today, restored to health and definitely handsome, he had been impressive. And there had been all the kind messages and inquiries — sent from his sickbed — and the gifts . . . The lightning had not struck yet, but perhaps soon, in the next half hour it would, in the act of making two people into one.

He came in and hovered, portrait of a young man, framed in the white and gold of the posts and canopy of the bed. It occurred to her that he, also, might feel a trifle shy, a little apprehensive about those intimacies. She offered him a tentative smile.

"You're very pretty," he said as he had said it at Roskilde.

"And you are very handsome."

"The snow held off," he said.

124

"Yes; it was a beautiful day. And in every respect, a splendid wedding."

He appeared to swallow something and with jerky movements went about quenching candles until only one was left, on his side of the bed.

Then the fog closed in.

Louise had been quite right to disbelieve Alice. Mamma had been nearer the mark though *indignities* would have been a more accurate word. He fell upon her rather as a starving dog might fall upon a hunk of meat; he used his teeth on her and his ruthless hands. One might have imagined that she had in some way angered him; but how? She bore it without a word or sound of protest, though there was some hurt involved. But not what Alice had said. Then all at once he made what seemed to be a sound of disgust and flung himself away from her, rolled over, said nothing when she wished him good night, and within two minutes was asleep; she knew by the change in his breathing.

So now, here she was, a married woman, in bed with her husband, with a fog and a moat between what she had been and what she was, and would in future be. Her mind was confused and her body felt as though it had been involved in an accident. Not one kind word, after the compliment to her looks; not a gentle touch. And most troubling of all, she felt that she had in some way displeased him. Of the oneness, of the one flesh there was no sign at all, except that hers was his in the sense that he could do what he liked to it.

The sentry's boots sounded again on the stones, and presently the clock struck five.

★   ★   ★

"It is," Christian said, "a lump of frozen codfish and I'll be thrice damned if I go near her again." There had been another feast — there were to be four in all — and more dancing, of shorter duration and it was not yet midnight.

Knut had already deduced that all was not quite well. Christian had strutted and boasted just a shade too much, used coarse gloating expressions a little too deliberately when talking to him, Brandt and Holcke, yet been short and irritable with everyone else; and the Queen, though more thickly painted and powdered than yesterday, and with that translucent look about the eyes which women wore after an almost sleepless night, lacked the inwardly satisfied, indolent, triumphant air which all but the most hardened old prostitutes wore afterwards — for a short time, at least. Once or twice during the evening's festivities he had seen an almost pensive look on her face.

He said, quite sternly, "It is far too soon to judge. Virginity is an over-rated condition. You took that hurdle?"

"I was superb. Never better. A dead woman would have responded," Christian said untruthfully.

It was possible; Straight from a period of abstention, almost — thanks to Knut — dead sober, and the girl so delectable, Christian *might* have performed well. But Knut could not be sure; he had shared most of Christian's jaunts and talk in bawdy-houses was free and brutally frank; there had been rumours of . . . oddities which because they affronted Knut's peasant-normality and his unpeasant-squeamishness, he chose not to think of much.

126

"You must make allowances," he said. "She is very young, and ignorant. Within a month . . ."

"Don't talk like a fool! How should you know? I know. And I know what's wrong with her. She has the spleen — that English disease that comes of drinking too much tea."

That was brilliant; one of the flashes that proved how clever he was. Knut's suspicions deepened.

"Spleen, whatever that may be, and cold blood may go together for all I know," he said in his most agreeable manner. "In that case you have my commiserations." He then used a phrase which he had only used in private to Christian three or four times in the course of their long association, and when he did it always gave Christian a jolt. "Your Majesty should remember that this marriage was not made for pleasure. You need, Denmark needs, an heir."

And I need, my reputation needs, that this should be a successful marriage, outwardly, at least.

Christian's memory of last night's failure, of other failures, gnawed away. "A Princess, not one of your hired women . . ." Juliana couldn't know, of course, nobody knew; but hired women did what they were hired to do. And one maddening aspect of the situation was that he had not been deterred by her being a Princess, he had deliberately ignored that, done his best to humiliate her. In that, also, he knew he had failed; she had wished him Good night as sweetly and composedly as though . . . He realized suddenly that he hated her.

127

"Denmark," he said sullenly, "can make do with Frederick."

"That I had overlooked," Knut said.

"I don't care about Denmark," Christian said. "I am not going to bed down with a lump of cold codfish for the sake of Denmark. I shall be dead anyway."

"That is true. But there are the years between. No child yet? Her mother bore nine; her brother's wife was pregnant within three months and has been pregnant, at due intervals, ever since. The Queen of Denmark, one of this prolific family has no child — she has the spleen instead. Oh, the pity of it. And the gossip and the speculation. And in the end, that sad little comment, Christian VII died without issue."

Christian who had been pacing about his bedroom, sat down in a chair and looked at his one true friend with a defeated expression. Both his heads had been troublesome all day, but they had been together. Now one, with a wrench, leaned away.

"Knut, if I didn't know that you were my friend, my oldest, my one true friend, I should think you were the Devil."

"How old-fashioned," Knut said, lightly. "On a par," he said, "with the idea that a man should love his wife, whereas every reasonable man knows that a man's duty is to get his wife with child, to be civil to her in public and in private avoid any scandal which might cause her distress."

One head said, "Absolutely right. Trust Knut to put the matter into a nutshell." The other said, "Oh God! Oh God!"

128

CHAPTER
TWO

Copenhagen,
November 1766-June 1767

It was, or so everybody said, the coldest winter in eighty years. Even the sea froze, and it was possible to go on foot, or by sledge, over the ice to Sweden. It was a wonderfully gay winter, too. The previous winter season had been curtailed by the death, in January, of Christian's father, so this one must make up for it.

Clustered around the Amalienborg Plads were the houses, the palaces in which the families of Schack and von Molkte Brockdorff and Leventzau entertained like princes; balls, elaborate dinners, musical receptions, operas competed with one another. Count Bernstorff's mansion lay a little farther out from the palace, but his entertainment was unique — an indoor horse-race in a great enclosure, the floor of it made of hammered-down peat.

Caroline had set herself to please those who sought to please her. She had said that she would try resolutely to be happy, and to that she held. Between her and Christian something was wrong, she recognized, though she could not name the failure. Christian

129

recognized it, too, and was spiteful about it; she had two proofs of that. One was the order, out of the blue with no warning or preliminary, that she was to speak nothing but Danish, not even to her femme-de-chambre.

Caroline had always been a little puzzled by Mamma's decision that it was not necessary for her to learn Danish. "Everyone of standing, everyone who came into contact with you, will speak German, or French, both of which you yourself speak fluently." The Dowager Princess, when she said that, had just been made aware of the ugly rumours about her future son-in-law and was extending a frail, futile protection to her daughter; by not knowing Danish Caroline would be spared servants' gossip. Her own most shattering, because first, disenchantment had come about in that manner, hearing herself called "Poor lady . . ."

Christian's order seemed to aim a blow at one of the small pleasures with which she had tried to fortify her determination to be happy. Every evening, when all the others had gone, Alice took a brush and applied the gentle, regular strokes which removed the pomade and the rice-powder and the gum-arabic, and soothed the nerves. And as Alice brushed, or tidied the room, they had talked in the old easy way, the kind of talk possible only to those with enough common background to make explanations and identifications unnecessary.

Just occasionally Alice had something of interest to report. Undeterred by the strange city, the strange language and the weather — snow had begun to fall

130

two days after the wedding, she had ventured out, exploring and shopping. One day, in a shop where she was endeavouring to attain her object by pointing and speaking English in a loud clear voice, she had been accosted —

"Little man, bow-legged. He said to me. 'You English? Bless your heart. So'm I. How did you get here?' So I told him and he told me how he came. We had quite a talk. It's a funny thing about foreign parts; I shouldn't have looked at him twice in London, little bow-legged, dried-up thing. But here . . . well there's the feeling; you've got to stick together."

Eventually, adding piece to piece, Caroline knew a great deal about this stray Englishman whose name was Smith and who had come to Denmark to deliver two horses which Count Bernstorff had bought from Sir William Craven. Despite the vile crossing the horses had arrived in wonderful condition and the Count had offered Smith a post of master of his stables, so Smith had stayed, highly paid, deferred to, but homesick for an English voice. He had made himself a fireplace on which a kettle could be boiled; he had a teapot; he brewed tea three or four times a day. He invited Alice to drink tea with him.

"Will you go, Alice?"

"I went. I had the best cup of tea I've had in this place. What is it that they do to it? It always tastes so *thick*. Had you noticed that?" Between two strokes of the brush Alice realized that she had put a foot wrong again; never, never, not even over so simple a matter as the making of tea, did Princess Caroline, pardon me,

Queen of Denmark, criticize her new country. Loyal to the core, poor dear. And to what?

To what? Alice asked herself. At Roskilde the long line of waiting carriages had gone round and round and she, shrouded in sable, holding the red lacquer box in her lap, had gone round and round in the last of them and had chanced to see His Majesty emerge from the hall and come down the steps, laughing. He looked reasonably handsome, he appeared to be amiable, he was certainly young. Alice's first impression had been favourable; but immediately after the wedding she had been aware of something wrong, and gossiping with Smith, who had no respect for any man, had brought her a good deal of enlightenment.

One evening Caroline asked Alice if she intended to marry Smith.

"No fear," Alice said. "He's not the marrying kind, nor'm I. And no funny business either; I made that plain before I ever set foot in his place. It's just the tea and the talk and the sticking together in a foreign land."

Informed of the order, direct from the King, that Danish was to be spoken even during this comfortable hour, Alice said,

"Did they say how that was to be managed? If you talk Danish to me I shan't understand a word."

"Alice, you once said that you could pick up the language."

"So I have, enough words to get along with, but not what you could call talk. That'll take years. So I'm afraid we shall have just to go on as we are."

132

"It was a definite order," Caroline said. "And the thing is that I'm afraid . . ." She stopped; that was giving too much away. "It is just possible that if His Majesty thought that speaking English to you delayed my learning the language thoroughly . . . he might order you to be replaced. Then where should we be?"

"We just mustn't be caught at it, that's all," Alice said, lowering her voice. "When anybody's around you jabber to me and if I know the answer in jabber I'll use it."

He'd only given the order to be awkward: Smith said the King of Denmark was the most awkward man in the world, didn't know his own mind for two minutes together, sacked anybody who argued or didn't bow low enough and in a tantrum could scare even Count Bernstorff. He didn't scare Alice, she believed that he had no power over her; she wasn't his servant, she wasn't a Dane, even by marriage — but her mistress was, God pity her. So in future English would be spoken very softly, very secretly.

The next spite-inspired order concerned Caroline's riding. Count Bernstorff had invited her to ride — while the snow and frost continued — in his great, peat-floored riding school. It was nothing like riding in the open but much better than not riding at all. The information that His Majesty considered the continuance of the practice inadvisable, was a great blow, and there was no way of getting round it.

For this order Frau von Plessen had an explanation which was new to Caroline. Plainly embarrassed by the

133

delicacy of the subject but firm in the performance of duty, she said, primly,

"Riding on horses is not good for women who . . . wish to become mothers."

Caroline laughed; there was sometimes a new note in her laughter, these days.

"If that were true, Frau von Plessen, England would be depopulated. My mother rode regularly and had nine children."

"It is now March," Frau von Plessen said.

Four months. She had never mentioned the matter to anyone, but she had reverted to thinking that Alice had, after all, been right. It took more than some kisses that turned into bites and rough handling — it was difficult sometimes to hide the bruises — to beget a child, otherwise she would have been pregnant by Christmas, or early in the New Year. Christian was either incapable, or he disliked her so much that he was unwilling. She was still not very clear on the subject but she had come to the conclusion that he had expected the lightning to strike and when it had not, blamed her. He might have some reason, though she had as days became weeks and weeks added into months, observed that reason did not govern all his doings. There was — so far as anyone could see — absolutely no reason why Prince Charles of Hesse should have been dismissed and banished; he was an amiable, compliant man, always willing to represent Christian on any occasion that threatened to be boring.

Nor was there any reason behind much of Christian's public behaviour; he'd start dancing a

Cotillion and in the second or third figure, walk away, leaving seven other dancers at a loss. He'd talk and laugh at a concert or a play, or get up and leave noisily, bringing even an *opera seria* to a standstill. He insisted upon the most rigorous formality; the bow before speaking, the deadly "Yes, Your Majesty," "No, Your Majesty," yet often he would withdraw to a corner or an alcove with his cronies, Holmstrupp, Brandt, Holcke and laugh and slap them on their shoulders, He was occasionally very rude, to his guests; to his hosts and hostesses.

She had done what she could; danced indefatigably, clapped until her hands stung, launched intrepidly upon the Danish language, the first to laugh at her own mistakes: she had deliberately asked questions which could not be answered in the dead-end monosyllabic way. As a wife, for some mysterious reason, she had failed, but as a Queen she was a success — a credit to Mamma. It was sometimes easy enough; she could momentarily lose herself in a dance, a play, a musical evening, a conversation. If the lightning about which Edward had spoken had fallen on her, but missed Christian, she would, she realized, have been in far worse case; it would be terrible to be in love with a man who never once talked to you as a fellow human being, whose only real contact with you, apart from the sitting, the standing side by side, His Majesty, Her Majesty, was when he came through the communicating door and punished you for a fault that you were not aware that you had committed. And who issued orders, obviously malicious in intent.

★ ★ ★

"It is now March," Frau von Plessen had said to Caroline.

Knut said to Christian "Four months. Look, am I your friend or not? Don't you trust me? What is wrong?"

"She has the English spleen. I said so from the first."

"The English breed in considerable numbers."

"I got one who didn't; or hasn't so far. And I am tired of hearing about it. There are enough old women prying." His old grandmother saying that she had little longer to live and hoped to see her great-grandchild; his stepmother, not quite so outspoken but on the same theme, remarking that she thought the Queen looked thinner, which was true. The whole situation was beyond him; one of his heads wanted to confide in Knut, tell him everything, ask his advice, beg his help. The other counselled caution, secrecy and the pretence that all was well.

Knut said, "If you could spare me for a day or two I'd like to go to Vidborg. My father has been laid up for a few days and he frets."

"You are angry with me," Christian said, like a child. "Because I said you were an old woman. I take it back, Knut. I didn't mean it. I'm short-tempered these days, You must bear with me."

"I took no offence," Knut said, recoiling a little, as he always did when Christian verged upon the sentimental. "My visit to Vidborg is necessary; the old man thinks the place will go to ruin if he neglects it for one day. As for being an old woman — maybe I am in the sense that I like to see a marriage work."

He had so set himself to see that this marriage should appear to work, that he was prepared to go again to Altona and face again that clever, arrogant bastard of a doctor who had seen through his first pretence and been tactless enough to mention it. But the seeing-through had, in itself, been proof of the man's ability; and the cure had worked. And this time, anyway, there would be no sudden disconcerting exposure of pretence; he could say, simply and truly, "The friend on whose behalf I asked your advice last October, is cured; but I think he is having a little trouble . . ."

"Come back as soon as you can," Christian said. "Enevold and Conrad are good company . . . but I shall miss you. Oh, and another thing. Tell your father — this will comfort him — that all the taxes on Vidborg are remitted . . ." One head said that ten years would be a generous concession, the other suggested a grand gesture . . . "for the next hundred years."

"That should make him lie easy in his bed," Knut said. "He never has — as my agent — ceased to worry himself about the tax and the dues. At heart he is a peasant; and *so am I*. He sees, as I do, that the landowner can only pay his tax if his peasants pay their dues; but he feels for a man who must sell his ox or the bed his grandfather died in, or the loom on which the stuff that clothed four generations was woven . . ."

He was breaking his given word, verging upon the political; and he had promised, when the gift of Vidborg teetered in the balance, property of the Crown, needing the consent of the Council for its sequestration . . . they

137

had come, three of them and said we will not delay the transfer if you will promise to refrain from any political activity. Clear proof that they feared his influence. And politics held no interest for him; straight from the back stairs, the young King's favour shining on him like the sun, what did politics mean? When he learned — as he did with the ease with which he had learned everything else, he had kept the promise given so blindly. He had never once mentioned taxes, or peasants' dues until now, and that had come about by accident. He had his own kind of pride. Also he was shrewd enough to see that politics bored Christian. And now he had remission of taxes for a hundred years — which was something none of those who were always groaning about their taxes had ever attained. It was in fact a gift without precedent, but not more than he deserved.

He set off for Altona by way of Vidborg in good heart.

"The man is, in fact my brother-in-law and my exertions on his behalf, in the autumn and again now, are because I am fond of my sister who is very anxious for a child."

"She could take a lover. In fact that is what I should advise. The child would stand a better chance of being born healthy."

"In her case that is impossible. He is older than she is and very suspicious. What urges me to desperate action is the fact that he blames her — he chose a young wife, he has property and wishes for an heir. He uses her unkindly."

Absolute inspiration; he had enlisted the man's sympathy.

"I suppose he has tried highly spiced foods, oysters, hard-boiled eggs. They are popularly believed to be effective."

"I should not have bothered you again — or ridden all the way from Meldorf . . ." Another brilliant touch. "Your advice in October was so good . . . And I hate to see my sister unhappy and ill-used, through no fault of her own."

"Strictly speaking it is outside my province. There are drugs, most of them very dangerous." He left the word in the air and his bright eyes shot a glance that asked — Is that what you have in mind?

"Nothing dangerous," Knut said and his sincerity was convincing. "Everything is willed to a nephew — unless my sister has a child."

"This," the doctor said, writing one word on a piece of paper, "rightly handled, is not dangerous. As much as can be lifted between the thumb and middle finger, no more, twice a day. You will have to go to Hamburg to obtain it." He wrote again and handed the paper to Knut. "There is a stuffed crocodile over the door," he said.

"It means a woman's happiness," Knut said; and again the sincerity shone through. The Queen would be happier; the marriage might mend. "And the charge?"

"The same as before." Those who could pay must, because there were so many who could not, and the doctor was sentimental about the poor.

139

"And with it a thousand thanks," Knut said, laying down the gold. He hurried away to take a boat across the Elbe to the great German port where everything from East and West was to be bought and sold.

Alice had been absolutely right; it happened in all four times, and in April Caroline's link with the moon was broken. She and Christian had been one flesh, without attaining any one-ness or any joy, but she would — if God were kind — have her baby.

Frau von Plessen begged leave to point out that the abandoning of horse-back riding had brought about the desired result.

The old Queen Mother said that once having seen and held her great-grandchild she would say "Nunc Dimittis" and gladly lay her aching bones to rest. She also offered an abundance of hoary old-wives' advice and at the end of it a caution that had the smack of reality.

"Whatever you do, keep the child, boy or girl, out of Juliana's reach. You'll see — she'll act the grandmother to perfection. You must not be deluded. She has ruined two. Christian a child at seventeen, and her own, Frederick, an old man at thirteen. I speak frankly because my time is short; and watching you these last months I have come to see that you respond too easily to what looks like kindness."

Christian's reaction to the news was a wild jubilation. One used the term "jump for joy" but whoever saw it happen? Christian jumped, five or six times. "Done it by God, done it." He then abandoned his apartments that adjoined hers and went back to the rooms on the ground floor, overlooking the garden which he had occupied before his marriage. The rooms next to hers, he said, would be needed for nurseries. That was in June for she had not told anyone until she was *sure*. The baby would not be born until January and there was no need for Christian to move yet. But she accepted the significance of the "Done it by God, done it", and of his removal. He had, to all intents and purposes, finished with her. The marriage had failed in the sense that it had not made either of them happy, but it had succeeded so far as it gave prospect of an heir. If the child should be female most likely the whole dreary business would have to be gone through again. But it might be a boy; she clung to that hope; and in the meantime she had something else, not so far in the future, to look forward to. In September Edward, ending his Grand Tour, was to come and spend two weeks in Denmark.

Christian said to Knut, to Enevold and Conrad, "We'll have a holiday in the Duchies; get away from it all, be free men for a while." The suggestion was greeted with enthusiasm.

To Knut, alone, Chrstian said, "We might go to Altona, and, incognito of course, across to Hamburg for an evening. Altona, Altona, that strikes a note. Isn't that the place where the doctor . . . the salt water and the pills . . ."

And — did you but know it — the powder, as much as a thumb and finger can lift.

141

"He lives — or lived — in Altona. But the place itself is not worth a visit."

"He is worth a visit." Christian said. "I'd like to call incognito and give him the surprise of his life. I never forget, as you know, an injury or a favour. I should like to go in, consult him about some trivial ailment, then reveal myself and tell him that he was to be my personal physician, and see his face."

"Do you want him as your personal physician, or is it a joke?"

"I never joke about serious things, Knut, as you should know. I owe him something; he is clever. And the post of my personal physician is the highest honour any doctor could wish for."

It was a warm day but Knut was conscious of a chill starting at the nape of his neck, running downwards.

"He was well paid for his services. And — I have seen him, remember — clever, certainly, but not an amenable man. I think you would regret the appointment, once it was made. Difficult to explain . . ." And it was difficult even for Knut, to whom words came so easily. "He is clever and so well aware of it that he is . . . arrogant. What you say he questions, in words or a look which asks a question. I was not easy with him and I venture to think that you would not be, either."

"We shall see," Christian said. "I'd like to see him and judge for myself. What was his name?"

"I never knew it. I was told how to find him and that he knew the latest cure for the Sailors Pox. As he had.

But his name I never knew and I very much doubt if I could find his house again."

He could have found the house blindfold and the name was Struensee, Johan Frederick Struensee . . .

CHAPTER
THREE

Fredericksborg; Copenhagen, June 1767-January 1768

The King and his friends went holidaying in Schleswig-Holstein and Caroline retired to Fredericksborg, one of the royal residences for summer use. Here in the heart of the country — and taking advantage of her condition — she was able to institute something of the easy, informal life of Kew. The country around was beautiful and far more prosperous than some areas she had seen. Christian's father had used the castle as a place of entertainment for visiting royalties and other important persons and had realized the importance of show. A system of subsidies had resulted in snug cottages replacing clod hovels, sleek oxen at work in the fields, some large houses in a good state of repair. Sometimes by carriage, often by foot, she moved about, watching the hay and presently the harvest being gathered in, and practising her rapidly-improving Danish on the peasants who regarded her at first with awe and then with affection.

In all that she did now she had the support and approval of Frau von Plessen. In the early part of the year — a period to which she looked back with distaste, wondering how on earth she had borne it — she had emerged from the night with vivid bruises, a puncture of the skin on the upper half of her left breast. She had concealed it, as she had concealed other marks, during the process of being dressed, but when she stood before her glass she realized that just above the edge of her bodice the extreme fringe of the bruise showed, looking like a dirty mark. Wondering to herself, a lace scarf perhaps, or a brooch so pinned as to lessen the decolletage, or a different dress altogether, she fumbled at her bodice, pulling it up.

Frau von Plessen, who was present said,

"It is not a perfect fit, it needs . . ." Before Caroline could stop her she had both hands on the dress, ready to show what it needed; she was inclined to be critical of Madame Brisson, whom she regarded as an exhibitionist. What the gown needed was never told; Frau von Plessen's words ended in a little gasp. She turned herself about and said to Alice,

"Bridgit. Here." Alice knew Bridgit, who occupied much the same position in relationship with Frau von Plessen as she did with the Queen, and the gesture explained the errand. Alice went away, moving at the leisurely pace she always adopted when she obeyed an order from anyone but her own mistress.

"Who else has seen?" Frau von Plessen demanded.

"Nobody. It is nothing. As I have told you, I bruise very easily. And this I did by being clumsy. I ran into . . ." What could even a clumsy woman run into to make a bruise at that particular point?

Their eyes met.

"As Your Majesty wishes," Frau von Plessen said. "But in this case the skin is broken. It could fester. I have, however, some ointment which Bridgit shall fetch."

Self-control and reticence were qualities which Frau von Plessen valued highly. She had been inclined lately to think that in some respects Caroline lacked the ultimate dignity incumbent to her position; she sometimes invited people to sit when Court protocol demanded that they should stand; there had been the horse-back riding, the slightly too-exuberant dancing, the slightly over-enthusiastic reception of any entertainment; and there had been the remark, "It is not necessary to address me as Your Majesty every time you speak."

But now Frau von Plessen recognized the true dignity which repudiated the sympathy almost any woman would have sought, and the fortitude which could make light of a painful situation. From that moment Frau von Plessen's manner and her whole attitude towards Caroline changed, took on a new and real respect and became maternal; and as far as she was capable of making it, indulgent.

So it had been a good summer, and before the end of it, some time early in September, Edward would arrive. He had chosen the time well; she would not yet be ungainly, and the Danish summer would not yet have suffered its sudden collapse. In Denmark there was hardly any spring or autumn; there were just a few days in late April or early May when winter loosed its hold and retreated — she had seen that for herself, and Frau von Plessen said that autumn was about ten or twelve days in mid-October when the woods blazed and then were stripped by the wind and the night frosts.

She looked forward to Edward's visit with an intensity that surprised herself. She had written regularly to her mother, less regularly to Louise; cheerful letters, as regularly answered; but there were a thousand small things, too trivial to merit mention on paper; and a few too large. It would be possible to tell Edward that the lightning had not fallen, either on her or on Christian, but that she had survived. It might even be possible to discuss with Edward the business of favourites and mistresses. Why not? She was a married woman and Edward was a man of the world. To whom else could she speak frankly? In ten months she had not had a real talk to anyone. Also she was curious. Edward had written to her twice since he started his tour and although he was so responsive to scenery, to architecture, to anything old and beautiful and strange, he had described nothing, made hardly any mention of where he had been, what he had seen. His letters were indeed short and stilted; but perhaps he was saving up everything to *tell* her. In fact the last one, saying that he would be with her early in September — the exact date he would let her know — said, "I have much to tell you," and she had some things to tell him, and to ask him.

She had hoped that Edward would be in Denmark before Christian returned and the formal reception of His Royal Highness, the Duke of York, by his Majesty of Denmark started on its arid, crowded, formal course. She would have liked to have received Edward alone, at Fredericksborg, where the last of the harvest was being brought in. But Christian returned in the third week of August, went to Christiansborg and sent her an order couched in civil terms, to join him, "In order to receive Your Majesty's brother, His Royal Highness, the Duke of York."

Edward liked flowers and was fond of fruit. Every day, the step a little heavier, the breath coming a little shorter on the stairs, she went to look over the apartments where Edward would be housed. Momentarily she expected the arrival of a courier. Daily she went into the rooms that Edward would occupy to see that all was in readiness. Daily — or so it seemed — she increased in girth; and among all the other things that she had to ask Edward was that he would be the child's godfather.

One morning, coming back to her own apartments she found the younger Queen Mother awaiting her. Juliana had a country home, Fredensborg, where she spent the summer, but now she was back.

The chocolate and the pastries were served.

"You must excuse me, Juliana. Anything rich or sweet . . . I live, these days on bread and apples and cheese."

"My dear Caroline; there is no need to explain to me, For four months, before Frederick was born I could eat nothing but rye-bread and the sausage they make in Wolfstein-Buttel. What we suffer in order to attain motherhood!"

148

"I tell myself it is worth it."

"We all do." The talk ran hither and thither for a while; how well Christian looked, having benefited from his holiday; how well Caroline looked, and the small but special party which Juliana and Frederick planned to give in Edward's honour.

"Do you know the day of his arrival?"

"I expect a letter hourly. Unless it comes soon he will arrive first. Edward is not usually . . ." At that moment the door opened and there was an attendant with a letter on a silver salver. Taking no notice of the seal or the superscription, Caroline snatched it up, crying, "Here it is! At last. Now I can tell you . . ." She broke the letter open.

It was from George. Heart-broken himself, he informed her, in the gentlest and most sympathetic terms that Edward had died in Monaco.

She said, in feeble protest, "Oh no! No!" and fell huddled to the floor.

Juliana picked up and read the letter which had fallen from Caroline's flaccid hand. She reflected that such a shock, in the fifth month, might well bring about a miscarriage. And the girl herself might die.

She did nothing. She carried, as most ladies did, a pretty toy of gold filigree full of grated hartshorn in her reticle, she did not reach for it, nor for the bell rope. Caroline lay rather as though she had been kneeling and been pushed over sideways. A bad position and the longer she stayed in it the better. On the side table a clock ticked away; five minutes, ten, fifteen. For a mere swooning fit, a long time. Eventually Juliana moved unstoppered her hartshorn bottle, wetted her handkerchief in one of the flower bowls, disarranged her hair a little and pushed the letter under Caroline's skirt, and called help.

"It was a letter," she said to Fraulein von Ebhn, the first to arrive. "She read it, cried out and fell. I did my best to revive her."

Caroline was unconscious for four hours. When she came back to herself she was in her bed and knew a moment of confusion; then she remembered and turning her head on the pillow began to weep for Edward whom she would never see again; twenty-eight years old; the dearest, the most positively alive person. A voice silenced forever; a smile gone from the world.

Crying, Frau von Plessen allowed, was good, it brought relief; she handed one dry handkerchief after another, replaced a soaked pillow and made sympathetic noises when Caroline's misery threw up such disconnected sentences as "Poor George, he will miss Edward so much," and "I intended to ask him to be godfather," and "How does one catch a chill in Monaco at the end of August?" and "He said he had something to tell me; now I shall never know."

But when, well on into the evening, Caroline who had eaten nothing since breakfast, refused to take a sip of wine or a spoonful of nourishing broth, Frau von Plessen said, "Your Majesty, you *must* think of the child. Loved ones die, and it is like losing a limb; but life goes on. There is life in the unborn and it must be nourished. Refusing food," Frau von Plessen said, "cannot avail the dead and could injure the child in the making."

There was truth there, and Caroline acknowledged it. There was such a link between unborn children and their need for nourishment that any gravid woman was advised to indulge her fancies, to ask for foods out of season and get them if she could. Her unborn child had so far made no demands, she had craved nothing out of the ordinary.

She forced down a few spoonfuls of the broth and then Frau von Plessen presented her with an apple. She looked at it, remembered the bowl put ready for Edward, the apples they had eaten together, the small apples Edward had carried in his pocket and given to horses.

"Not that," she said. "I shall never eat an apple again."

"Never mind," Frau von Plessen said. "You took your broth bravely. Now drink this and you will sleep."

Frau von Plessen — off duty for the day — had been entertaining a few close friends in her own apartments. From this small corner of private life which a Mistress of the Robes could hope to maintain, she had been rudely jerked and brought to confront Juliana the Queen Mother, almost hysterical, Fraulein von Ebhn, on the point of collapse, Her Majesty huddled on the floor and a number of people running about and saying "What to do?"

Her Majesty had her own physician, but his house was some little distance away: it was possible however

that the King's new physician — and favourite — Dr.
Struensee, would be in the palace. His post did not
entitle him to have rooms under its roof, but he was
there every day and often spent the night in a borrowed
bed. Frau von Plessen sent a servant running to fetch
him and another to bring back Caroline's own doctor.

Struensee arrived first and apart from ordering that
the Queen should be put to bed, and all restrictive
clothes loosened and heated bricks put to her feet, he
had done nothing, made no attempt to restore her to
consciousness. "It's the most merciful thing that could
have happened," he said. Frau von Plessen thought his
manner casual, his attitude unprofessional — but it
matched all that she had heard about him — and she
was glad when the proper doctor arrived and began to
apply — ineffectually — all the tried methods of
restoration. The room still reeked of ammonia, vinegar
and burnt feathers, and Caroline's hands had been
slapped until they were scarlet.

As soon as the Queen's own physician arrived
Struensee had retired; but perhaps he was less casual
than he seemed, for much later, when Caroline was
conscious and crying wildly, he had come to inquire
how she was, and then, diving into one of his sagging
pockets, produced a small phial.

"It's a harmless, mild sedative," he said, "If she can
sleep for twelve hours, time will have begun its healing
work."

This was, Frau von Plessen realized, unorthodox
behaviour, the Queen not being his patient, and she
was for a time in two minds about administering the

dose; but Her Majesty was so greatly distressed, and then, reminded of her duty, had been so amenable and tried so hard with the broth; and there was something in what Dr. Struensee had said about time and its work. Twelve hours sleep would act as a buffer.

The King had not come near, though he had sent a message saying that he commiserated with his wife's grief and shared her distress. The crack in Frau von Plessen's loyalty widened a little more.

That night she spent uneasily on a sofa in the next room with the door open, dozing off for a few minutes, waking with a jolt, listening, tiptoeing in. Waking, twelve hours later to a sense of misery and loss, not immediately identified, and when it was, falling like a blow, Caroline found her Mistress of the Robes seated near the bed; her face a little drawn, her eyes hollowed.

She began to cry again, but less violently, and what she said was sensible. "I know it has happened. I must bear it. Crying does no good . . ." but she began to cry again. In the next moment of calm she said, "I must write to Mamma. And to George. Edward could always make them laugh." Edward would never laugh again.

"Your brother," Frau von Plessen said presently, "would be grieved by your grief. And he would wish you to have a strong healthy baby. The baby may resemble him; and Edward could be one of his names."

Thus patiently, adding word to word, she tried to direct Caroline's attention to the future, to the baby. She trotted out all old beliefs about pre-natal influences on birth-marks — the strawberry coloured disfiguration which showed that the mother had craved strawberries out of season and not been able to obtain them, the mouse-shaped, mouse-coloured mole that resulted from the mother having been frightened by a mouse — and on disposition; a mother who cried and was sad would bear a querulous, ill-thriving baby, and vice-versa.

It had a cumulative effect and time began its work and her condition helped; the placidity and euphoria of advancing pregnancy muffled her mind and emotions, just as its physical manifestations slowed her step and shortened her breath. When Christian finally braced himself to visit her and indulge in the fantastic pretence that nothing had happened except that she had fainted and fallen, she was conscious only of the mildest irritation and could even see something faintly comic in the fact that the King of Denmark and all the Court were in mourning for the King's brother-in-law whose name, whose demise, were not mentioned once during a half-hour visit. A loving husband would have made some effort to share her grief, even though he had never met the man she grieved for; a loving wife would have been stricken to the heart by the not-sharing; but partners in a marriage such as theirs, though they missed some joy escaped some forms of misery as well.

And she had Frau von Plessen; and she had Alice — much more of Alice than formerly; for on the day after the news came when Frau von Plessen said that she must change her clothes and have her hair re-arranged, and would send Fraulein von Ebhn to sit with Her Majesty, Caroline said, "I would much prefer Alice. She knew him."

154

By Frau von Plessen's strict standard of etiquette there had always been something not quite correct in the relationship between Her Majesty and her femme-de-chambre; typically English, she supposed, but to be regretted and contravened as much as possible; but to her now completely compassionate heart the last three words made a certain appeal.

She said, "If you are sure that she will not upset you further. If she begins to cry . . ."

"I have never," Caroline said truthfully, "seen Alice cry over anything. She was reared in a hard school and I believe the whole world could drop dead . . ." Dead. Dead. A word used often enough, its meaning only just realized . . . "and Alice would not shed a tear."

Before Alice was admitted — not to act as handmaid at the dressing table, but to take Frau von Plessen's place, the Mistress of the Robes tried to talk to her, strictly. It was very difficult because the girl was so stupid and in almost a year had acquired hardly any Danish at all. And her strictness broke down when one must communicate in single words and gestures.

"Not to cry," Frau von Plessen said, shaking her head and making the motions of a woman weeping, "No. No. Not to cry."

Silly old hen!

Alice alone of all the people in the Palace — perhaps of all the people in the world — understood what His Royal Highness's death meant to the Queen. Despite the difference in their ages they'd always been a pair, a little set apart from the rest of the family; within the family bond, another, closer; within the family resemblance another likeness more exact.

"No cry," she said. "No. No." In her turn she gestured moving her skinny hands about her lean body, shaped and tempered by early privation, so that later good feeding had no effect at all. "Baby," she said. "Cry. Bad. Baby."

Frau von Plessen's almost exhausted mind managed the reflection that there were occasions when communication could be achieved with the minimum of words.

"You may go in," she said.

Alice had her own contribution to make. She said,

"It's worse for you than him. You should bear that in mind. It's sudden and it's shocking, but I reckon it suited him, dying like that, in the middle of a happy holiday. Pretty soon they'd have been marrying him off; he wouldn't have taken kindly to that. Being told what to do always set his back up, didn't it? And there's another way of looking at it; getting old is no joke, a lot of aches and pains, going deaf, or silly. It is sad for you — the rooms ready and everything, but for him maybe it's what he would have chosen, a short life and a merry one."

Where did grief and self-pity merge? I had so much to tell him, to ask him. And he had something to tell me. He's dead. The world is the poorer, denuded of the good-humoured wit, the handsome face and splendid body. I am bereft.

156

"And you don't want, do you," Alice said, "a poor grizzling little baby . . .?"

The drawer in the bottom of the red lacquer box, much too small now to serve as a jewel case, held Edward's letters. She took them out and read them again and noticed sentences that she had skipped over — "Life is more complicated than we were led to believe." "My visit to you will defer my return to England and give me a chance to think." About what? "I hope to stay for a fortnight, but I must yield to circumstances."

It was over. Edward was dead; and propped up by Frau von Plessen on the one side, Alice on the other, she went down the ever narrowing path that led to January and her delivery.

Even Juliana failed to disturb her calm. She made frequent visits — she and Frederick occupied the whole second floor of the Christiansborg Palace and could visit without setting a foot out of doors where, once again the snow lay deep.

"I completely lost my temper with Christian, yesterday," Juliana said, "You will probably hear about it, so I may as well tell you myself, so that you may know the truth." Under the flick of blinked eyelid she took in the smooth, steadily ripening bulge which, coming to fruition, would end — this time finally — her hopes for her son. There had been so many ends; her husband saying, "We must wait until Frederick is sixteen," her husband's death, Christian's accession, his marriage the plan for which she had opposed and been forced to accept, when her husband said, "Yes, he is a *silly* boy, but it is a political alliance, and sometimes marriage is a steadying influence." Then there had been her secret campaign to wreck the marriage; "Christian, have you ever looked closely at this portrait of your mother? Your bride may resemble her." And then the remark — calculated to paralyse, about the difference between a Princess and a hired woman.

All come to nothing. Pregnant within five months; how? why? Holmstrupp in ascendancy still and nothing changed; then the fall, the long swoon — Juliana when she rang the bell had thought that Caroline was dead . . . But she was not; she was here, resilient, bulky. And it was late in November, the seventh month.

"I really gave him a thorough scolding," Juliana said. "It passed all bounds. To appear with that woman, in public."

"What woman?"

Juliana widened her eyes and put her hand in front of her mouth.

"I thought you knew. Oh, what have I done?" She dropped her hand. "Between us, I trust, there is no room for hypocrisy. Steifelette Kathrine, so called on account of her beautiful feet. Dear Caroline, I *have* shocked you. Pray forgive me. I shall hold it against Christian that in my anger with *him* I let slip something that hurt *you*."

For the shot appeared to have gone home. Caroline's face gave evidence of shock; not enough, but some. Juliana mistook its cause. This was in fact the first direct evidence Caroline had met with of what Mamma had so delicately called "other women", but with things

158

as they were between her and Christian, it was to be expected. What darkened her eyes and made a little patch of pallor around the nostrils was the sudden and complete realization that Juliana had deliberately planned this revelation, had come here with the intention of making it, was, in short, not her friend, but her enemy. And if now . . . perhaps all along . . . since the beginning . . . responsible perhaps . . . no, no, that was dramatic nonsense. None the less, she remembered that on Juliana's very first visit, she had, under a pretended frankness, tried to spoil the poem. Nothing in her relatively sheltered life had prepared her for quite such malice or duplicity; but she kept her word about treating the thing lightly — as though Christian had acquired a new horse or hound. She threw her head back slightly and said,

"Shock? Hurt? Look at my ankles." She lifted her skirt to show their swollen state. "Could any man be blamed for preferring a woman with beautiful feet?"

The letter came in the Queen's personal post from England which the Queen's Secretary had learned was to be handed to her just as it arrived, and the moment it arrived.

It was written on poor coarse paper, sealed with the smoke-tinged wax from a dripping candle, pressed down by a thimble. It read —"

"Madam, Your Majesty of Denmark — I thort you would want to know that he thort of you a lot and was sorry at the end that he never got there to tell you our plans. We was going to Rushia and get married but it was not to be. I've got the baby now and am up and about again. He is a luvly boy that will be like his farther one day and I mean to do my best for him. We never got to Rushia so he carnt have what he shoold, but I shall do my best. I thort you would like to know. I hope you get a luvly boy two, and just as easy.

Yours respectfully, Felicity."

Caroline read it twice, filling in the gaps. Then she sent for Mr. Gunning who had succeeded Mr. Tetly as Minister to Denmark.

When he arrived she asked him to be seated and said,

"I wish to discuss with you a matter of some importance."

He thought — Steifelette Kathrine! And what can I do?

She handed him the letter and he read it without comment. The essence of diplomacy was to let the other party get into position.

Her Majesty, lacking all finesse, said,

"I think that the child referred to is that of my brother, the Duke of York."

"With all due respect, Your Majesty, I would suggest that that is an unwarranted assumption. Unless you have some reason, other than this . . . er . . . missive." He looked at it with distaste. "His Royal Highness is not mentioned."

"Not by name. But I feel that the woman who wrote this knew that I should understand. And she wrote out of good-will. She asks for nothing. She gives no address and signs only her christian name."

"So I observed. My first thought was that it could be a begging letter: or some form of blackmail. But that can hardly . . ."

"Mr. Gunning, I want your help in finding her. I can think of no one else to ask."

"Your Majesty knows that I am always at her service. But with nothing to go upon except the one name . . ."

"But you see," Caroline said eagerly, "she mentions being with my brother at the end, so she was in Monaco in September. Now she writes from England. So she must have returned. She is not . . . not the kind of woman who travels abroad except in a menial capacity, and she was pregnant. Someone, at Harwich or some other port may have noticed her. A Customs Officer perhaps or some other official who might remember her. I think she is poor; a sempstress perhaps. They work long hours for very little. However well she means, the child would be reared in unfavourable circumstances. I should like to help her."

"If it is your wish I will set some inquiries on foot."

But they would not be very vigorous or very searching. There were enough scandals about His Majesty's younger brothers, borne with remarkable patience, or could it be indifference, by the King. And in fact, Mr. Gunning reflected, the Queen of Denmark's attitude was unusual. No shock, no disapproval. Bastards were plentiful, but young women, correctly brought up felt, or pretended to feel, some recoil . . . Tolerance and laxity could be confused. Then he withdrew that thought. Sentiment, that was what dictated her behaviour; she was pregnant herself and so

161

felt akin with any woman who was, had been, or claimed to be. It occurred to him that the writer of the letter might be very cunning, as frauds so often were. One letter, asking for nothing, giving no name and address, could induce confidence.

"I want her found, if possible," Caroline said.

"One thing I would ask, Your Majesty. Should another letter from the same source arrive, please do nothing until you have conferred with me." He paused and then said, "The wish with which the letter concludes, is the wish of us all and one with which I should like to be the first to associate myself."

An easy, safe delivery; and an heir to the throne of Denmark.

CHAPTER
FOUR

Copenhagen; Fredericksborg, January-May 1768

The chief midwife, and her assistant, the Queen's own physician and two others — called in to provide moral support on this portentous occasion — all assured Caroline that it would be an easy birth; she was in splendid health, and young, and there was, the older midwife said, a tradition of easy childbirth in the Royal Family, because of their narrow heads. She had assisted at the birth of His Majesty, and of the Hereditary Crown Prince; just a pain or two and a grunt and it would be over.

Frau von Plessen also took a resolutely cheerful view and Alice, having taken the double precaution of hiding a knife *and* a pair of scissors under the bed "to cut the pain" was equally confident.

All were wrong.

It went on and on; through one day, and a night, and a second day, relentless, mounting torture which battered all the barriers of fortitude and pride and finally broke them down.

163

On the first day Frau von Plessen thought that Caroline was being a little too brave.

"It sometimes helps," she said, "to cry out."

The chief midwife agreed; she'd known several instances of a good yell doing the trick. Some hours later she remembered cases where a sniff of pepper and a sneeze had served. This was not one such case.

Beyond the suggestion that some warm, spiced wine would keep up the Queen's strength, the doctors were not helpful. Childbirth was regarded as a woman's work and too close an association with it beneath a doctor's dignity — no real doctor was anxious to earn the name of man-midwife. Comfortably installed in the ante-room they looked in at intervals to see how things were going. As time went on some concern was felt, but no positive alarm. A first labour could last forty-eight hours; interference often did more harm than good; God who had laid this ordeal upon women, had made them very tough.

Alice, quite early on, began to cry; every pang that wrenched at Caroline seemed to communicate itself to her in a shuddering rigour. Presently, when Caroline moaned, Alice put her hands over her ears and made noises like an animal in a trap.

"If you cannot control yourself," Frau von Plessen hissed at her, "go away." After that Alice put her hands not to her ears but to her mouth.

Caroline lost all sense of time and occasionally of identity as well; a bit of her floated away and up and from somewhere near the cornice looked down upon

164

the writhing, moaning figure on the bed. Poor Caroline; she is going to die . . .

When the candles were lit at the second sunset she did not see them as candles, just blurs of light; she could not tell one face from another, but voices were still recognizable; her sense of hearing seemed to have sharpened; people were talking very loudly, the shift of a log in the stove was an explosion, the tick of the clock a heavy hammer.

The pain stopped quite abruptly and at the same time she began to leave herself again, not this time for the ceiling but for a soft, engulfing darkness that lay waiting under the bed. The child had been born, she thought, on that last pain, and she was dying.

She said, in what sounded to her a loud voice, but was in fact the faintest whisper, "Frau von Plessen . . ."

"I am here." Others might need food and sleep but she had been out of the room only for the briefest moment on the most necessary errand. The bones of her hands were bruised, perhaps broken, because Caroline had clutched at them so fiercely, seeming to draw some slight comfort from the touch. But the grasp had slackened suddenly.

"I am going to die. I want you to take charge of him. Nobody else, *you*. And . . . send . . . Alice . . . home."

She would have liked to entrust Alice with a message to Mamma, but it was too much effort, with the pain over, the baby born and the soft dark closing in.

"If you give up now," Frau von Plessen said, "you will die, and the child with you. Rouse yourself. Here, drink this. Drink it. Now, try again. You're not to give up, you're not . . ." She lifted Caroline's shoulders from the bed and shook her fiercely. That started the pain again and Caroline screamed; the heir to the throne of Denmark slipped, feet first, into the midwife's waiting hands. She took him, in the approved style, by the heels and holding him upside down slapped his buttocks until he gave a desolate kittenish cry.

"It is a boy," she said.

"Well, there you are," Christian said, accepting congratulations. "Nobody can say that I have not done my duty by Denmark. In a year and a half, a fine boy."

It was not a fine boy; nothing like the solid, pink and white baby of which Caroline had dreamed. Even the narrow Royal-Danish head seemed too heavy for the frail neck, at the ends of his arms and legs the hands and feet hung straight and limp; a rag doll badly stuffed. And all over, even to the eyelids, a funny colour, like the plums that fall early from an overladen tree.

But he was hers and the lightning struck the moment she was able to see him clearly. It seemed strange that all that bulk, so carefully carried, all that food, all that exercise in the fresh air had not produced something more thriving, with more apparent hold on life; but because he was so puny — five pounds, the midwife said, and it was incomprehensible that the birth had been so hard — and so, well, face it, ugly, she loved him all the more. She was determined to feed him herself. To devote the rest of her life to him. He was hers and she was his. He was the one good thing she had salvaged from a foundered marriage; he was the product of thirty hours of agony; to get him born she had repudiated death.

She decided to feed him herself though it was not a fashionable thing to do. The social activities of a nursing mother were restricted, and the process was held to be detrimental to one's shape. Her bosom had always been much admired, so white and well-formed; now it proved its usefulness: within a week the child's colour had improved; at the end of two the flaccid neck had strengthened and the limp, fin-like hands and feet were altering. Every day he became more and more like the baby of her dreams.

Self-and-child-involved, happily fulfilling the function for which she had been born, cherished by Frau von Plessen who, if not actually proud of herself was conscious of duty well and truly done, and by Alice, she was hardly aware of the outside world at all. She was the most popular person in Denmark and Norway and the Duchies, the recipient of many messages of congratulation and gifts, but they all seemed to come from a different world from the one which she inhabited. And Christian's two visits did not ruffle the calm. On the first occasion he said that he had not realized that new-born babies were so ugly, so closely resembling skinned rabbits; on the second he said that the child's name had been chosen — it was to be Frederick. She accepted that, it was her father's name, too; and nothing was worth making a fuss about, now. Whether the child bore Edward's name or not, he would be like him, because the death and the new life

— the anticipation of which had made the death just bearable — had a mystical link: and naturally she would bring him up by Mamma's rules.

Frau von Plessen, in her own apartments, which had seen so little of her of late, looked at her reflection in the glass and was satisfied that she was attired and coiffured with the utmost correctitude. Earlier in the day she had requested and been granted an audience with His Majesty. At the appointed time she made her stately way down stairs and along corridors — a walk of almost a mile; was announced and admitted and made her curtsey to Christian who — to give him his due — had forgotten the appointment. Knut had recently introduced a new game of cards, less dependent on skill — of which Christian had little, or upon luck — of which he also had little, than upon the ability to pretend that the cards one held, or drew, were more valuable than the ones held, or drawn, by the other players. It was in fact a game that anyone could win simply by sitting tight and from time to time adding money to the "pot" in the centre of the table. He, Knut, Evenold and Conrad had been playing for three hours; and he was winning. In the excitement and the heat he had removed his coat and slung it over a chair, he had unbuttoned his waistcoat and completely forgotten his wife's Mistress of the Robes. He had also been drinking fairly steadily, taking advantage of Struensee's absence. Struensee was a wonderful fellow, after Knut the best fellow in the world, but he held some most uncomfortable views about eating and drinking.

Christian said, "Lay them down, just as they are. We can continue later." He laid his own cards on the table, buttoned his waistcoat and indicated to Brandt, who was nearest, to bring and hold his coat.

"Go away," he said, "but not too far. This will not take long."

Properly dressed, or almost, for in buttoning his waistcoat he had misjudged, he sat down, and left Frau von Plessen standing.

"Well? What is it?"

"I have taken upon myself, Your Majesty, to intercept an order. I have never done such a thing before and I trust that my breaking of a rule may be taken as proof of my seriousness."

What order? He'd issued several that day; with the Russian Grand Duke and his woman — not quite wife, not quite mistress — arriving tomorrow, and Bernstorff's agitation about the old Russian claim to the Duchies, the need for conciliation . . . he had been obliged to give a good many orders.

"It concerns Her Majesty, Your Majesty," Frau von Plessen said helpfully; Christian looked blank; the long session at cards and the wine had blurred his memory, at no time very strong. "The command that she should attend the banquet for the Grand Duke Alexis."

"Oh yes. Did you say intercepted?"

"I was afraid that Her Majesty would attempt it."

"She must manage it. Whatever happens we must not offend the Grand Duke."

"Her Majesty is not yet in a fit state of health. It was a very hard birth and only fifteen days have elapsed, Your Majesty."

Christian had one of his brilliant flashes.

"I did not know, Frau von Plessen, that you had qualified as a physician." He must remember that to tell the others; meanwhile he cackled at his own wit. And the old woman looked as though she had been slapped across the chops.

Frau von Plessen was momentarily stricken and silent — not by the sarcasm, but by what was happening inside her. The loyalty to her King, part of her blood's heritage and overlaid by a lifetime of rigid orthodoxy, of two years of making excuses for this latest occupant of the throne, crumbled into nothing as she realized that not only did she disapprove of, she positively disliked His Majesty.

"I took the liberty," she said, "of consulting Dr. Imer. He is of my opinion."

"He's an old woman; and you're another! All this fuss about having a baby." He laughed again. "I forestalled you. I consulted the Queen Mother Juliana and she assured me that unless there were complications any woman could be up and about in a fortnight. I'm not asking her to dance a polka." A thought flashed, another brilliant one, but it was gone before he could catch it and put it into words; that angered him and to be angry always made his head ache.

He said — waiting for the brilliant idea to return.

"It's because everybody went about saying how wonderful you were. Anyone would think you'd had the

170

baby! You've got above yourself, Frau von Plessen. I will not tolerate presumption. And there is another thing . . ." the clever thought had returned. He levelled a finger at her and said furiously, "Don't think I don't see through you. There's this quibble about whether they're legally married, or even married at all; but let me tell you, Madame is received at the Russian Court and what is good enough for the Empress Catherine should be good enough for Queen Matilda."

"I assure Your Majesty that that aspect of the affair had never once occurred to me. Her Majesty's health is my only concern. She is not yet strong enough to stand to receive, or to sit through a banquet."

He'd had enough of this.

"Her Majesty no longer concerns you in any way. You are summarily dismissed, Frau von Plessen."

Now she looked as though someone had punched her in the belly. The dismay on her face, the sudden droop of her upright figure merely spurred his anger and malice.

"And banished," he said with delight. "You will be on your way out of Denmark tomorrow morning or on your way into the Blue Tower."

The pride and conscious rectitude of a lifetime enabled her to pull herself together and to say with dignity,

"I beg leave to say, Your Majesty, that my whereabouts makes no difference to my contention. Have I leave to withdraw?"

"Go to Hell," Christian said.

She managed a perfect curtsey.

★　★　★

Christian, resuming the game, found first that he had forgotten the very elementary rules, and then that his luck had changed. He demanded that his friends sympathize with him for his lack of privacy, for the fantastic state of affairs where an old woman could not only intercept his order, but come pushing into his private apartments and scold him. His temper was not improved when Struensee arrived and said that he was fully in agreement with Frau von Plessen; women did get up and about — sometimes within a few days — but often enough they suffered for it later.

Struensee had now occupied the post as the King's personal physician for six months; during that time he had minded his business, kept his eyes and ears opened and studied carefully the relationship between Christian and his boon companions; Holmstrupp, the least amenable of them, the least grateful, often the least sympathetic, stood highest in Christian's esteem; Holmstrupp, if he had wanted it, could have attained a seat on the Council, Brandt and Holcke, both politically ambitious, anxious for that honour, would never get it in a hundred years; Christian regarded them as playfellows and no more. When Christian spoke, as he did to Struensee, in confidence, about this troublesome business about the two heads, Struensee saw in it more than the complaint of a naturally indecisive person constantly called upon to make decisions, and often of two minds about them. He saw deeper. He saw that Christian was completely divided; between his wish to dominate and his wish to be dominated; just as he was divided between his latent homosexuality — Knut its immediate object — and his desire to be a devil with the women, a desire inculcated and fostered by Knut. He was, in his own words, "a man with two heads," and Struensee, in whom pity sprang easily — pitied him, but not to the extent of losing sight of the thousands whose case was more pitiable; the poor amongst whom, as pastor's son and as doctor he had lived, and whose cause he could serve by gaining control of the King. For that reason alone he had accepted the appointment: he had set himself a term of two years. If by the end of that time he had not, as doctor, gained the King's confidence, and as a man attained some influence over this so-easily-influenced young man, and persuaded him to think about justice and reform, then he would resign and resume his real work.

He was naturally a blunt, outspoken man and within a week had realized that where formality and ceremony and exaggerated respect were concerned, Christian had a split mind; in public he revelled in the exacting of servility; in private, with his friends he permitted and even encouraged great freedom of conduct; though here again he was unpredictable, quite capable of calling Brandt or Holcke sharply to order. Never Holmstrupp. Struensee realized that he lacked four assets possessed by the ex-page: he was no longer in his first youth, thirty-one, he was not conspicuously handsome, he made no appeal — Thank God! — to Christian's streak of perversity, and he was without Knut's single-minded, deadly self-interest. But he could

173

serve the King as Knut could not, by promoting his health and alleviating his ills and he could offer a domination, warmer in tone, wider in scope, less frustrating than that exercised by the younger man.

On this evening, when Struensee made his remark about women being up and doing, Christian repeated his sarcasm to Frau von Plessen.

"I did not know, Johann, that you had been appointed as physician to the Queen."

"Nor did I," Struensee said with a look of bright interest. "Since when?"

Christian's ill-humour fled; he cackled.

"If the old woman had said that, I might have forgiven her. As it is I sacked her."

Any dismissal of the high and mighty was pleasing to Knut; Struensee thought — Another injustice! But I am not yet in a position to make effective protest. Brandt and Holcke, the one with a great friend, the other with a sister in need of a near-sinecure, well-paid were all attention. Brandt — with years of leisurely good-breeding behind him was about to ask if Christian had a replacement in mind and then steer talk around to *his* candidate. Holcke jumped in ahead and said, "My sister would make an admirable Mistress of the Robes. She's quite stupid." He spoke as though it were a joke.

They all laughed. Holcke said,

"It is a better recommendation than it sounds. Frau von Plessen was clever. Her salon was a hot-bed of political talk."

"If I'd known that she'd gone sooner. Very well Conrad. Let my chamberlain have her name and I'll make the appointment official tomorrow."

With a couple of laughs and one of those instant decisions which so delighted him, between him and his annoyance Christian felt better and the game went on, Struensee now taking a hand. Christian began to win again. Nobody took much notice when, Holcke having made an error in tactics, Brandt said, "Stupidity must be a family failing." Raillery, an exchange of insults just made inoffensive by a grin, were common coinage in this closed circle. Presently Brandt said something in so soft a voice that only Holcke heard; he said "That I will take from no man," and jumped up and aimed a blow at Brandt, a blow that fell short because Brandt leaned so far sideways that his chair overturned. He was on his feet in a second and attacking Holcke. In a moment it was clear that this was not one of those playful scuffles in which Christian — but never Knut — sometimes indulged. There was some blood. Knut, feeling sick, averted his eyes and sedulously gathered the scattered cards.

Christian said, "Stop it!" in a voice of genuine authority, but neither man heard him. Struensee got up, took them, one in the right hand, one in the left, by their collars, pulled them apart and held them so, like a couple of puppies, calmed by the cutting off of breath which the pressure on their windpipes provoked. Holcke struggled and kicked, then gave in; Brandt raised his hands, tore away his shirt and neckcloth, wriggled free of his coat and hit Struensee in the mouth. Struensee threw Holcke away and with his right hand thus freed and with blood streaming over his chin, fended Brandt off.

The evening, begun with an old woman who said frankly that she had taken upon herself to intercept an order, had ended with this disgraceful exhibition; in his presence. He had said "Stop it", and they had taken no notice. On every side his authority was being thwarted. This was intolerable.

Of the fight itself he had only a blurred, imperfect view; the far edge of the card table was the limit of his clear vision, and sometimes even to see that was a strain.

He said, "Stop it, or I shall call the guard. Now, line up in front of me. This behaviour I will not tolerate; who struck the first blow?" Nobody answered. Which was the first blow? The one that missed its mark or the one that went home?

Both Christian's heads were at work and one of them was concerned with the necessity of hiding the fact that he did not see well. He knew that Struensee had ended the scrimmage; and Struensee was dabbing at his mouth with a blood-stained handkerchief.

"Who hit Johann?"

There was a little silence. Then Brandt said,

"I did. Conrad cheated, I told him so and he aimed a blow at me. I hit him back. The doctor fellow interfered and I hit him."

"I did not cheat," Holcke protested in a very peculiar voice; the pressure on his windpipe had affected it. "Enevold accused me and I resented it."

"It was," Christian said, "a Brawl in my Presence." He looked at the two men; Holcke a bit ruffled but still properly dressed and trying to excuse himself; Brandt in a torn shirt, no coat and still defiant, calling Johann the doctor fellow . . .

Christian drew himself to his full height and in his most official voice sentenced Count Enevold Brandt to banishment . . .

It had been, in a way, a quite exciting and satisfactory evening.

Frau von Plessen walked back, every stairway, every corridor a narrowing tunnel, leading to the one end, penurious exile. Go to Germany and teach French; or to France and teach German?

She went back to the apartments, so loved, so carefully ordered, hers no more. Whose? Bridgit was still tidying the bedroom. So little time it took for a way of life to be destroyed; a walk, a few sentences exchanged and all was over.

"Begin to pack," she said to the startled girl. "Call the others and set them to work. Everything in these rooms that belongs to *me* must be packed and ready to be removed by seven o'clock tomorrow morning."

Under Bridgit's puzzled gaze, Frau von Plessen thought of transport — no more carriages available, summoned by a mere word. With a sickening little jolt as she realized the significance of the order, she told Bridgit also to send a page to bespeak a hired carriage.

But under it all she was concerned for the Queen. Their friendship, born of a bruise, matured by a year of

177

mutual respect, and sealed over the childbed, had never been one of ostentatious manifestations. Caroline had given her a brooch to celebrate the birth of the Crown Prince, and she had said, "If my own mother had been with me she could not have done more." Frau von Plessen had replied, "It was Your Majesty's example that inspired my fortitude." But there was a bond, and the breaking of it — particularly when she heard of the circumstances — would pain the Queen. Women in lactation should not be upset. She could think of no way of guarding Caroline from the blow, but she might delay it for a little and she could evade the perilous business of saying a permanent farewell. She went in search of Countess Hotstein and Frau von Ebhn.

"I have been dismissed — and banished," she told them simply. "The reason we need not discuss, you will know all tomorrow. But if her Majesty were not told, for as long as it is possible for a secret to be kept in this place, I think it would be as well. I propose to tell her that I am about to take a short holiday. When the truth reaches her — if you are careful — I shall be far away. A *fait accompli*," said Frau von Plessen, "is always easier to accept. And now, where are the keys?"

The key to the jewel coffer was immediately available; those of the clothes closets which lined the Queen's Wardrobe were never used, and had to be hunted. But they were found, and holding them in her hand Frau von Plessen went to Caroline and asked leave to absent herself for a few days on a small holiday.

"You need it," Caroline said. "You look quite exhausted, Frau von Plessen. Look, his hands are beginning to curl; like little shells; like rose petals."

She has the child, Frau von Plessen reflected; and although God's will had in the last hour become difficult to understand, she thanked Him that this had happened after and not before the birth.

"I trust that Your Majesty and His Royal Highness have a good night," Frau von Plessen said. "I will now go into the Wardrobe and see that all is in order."

The keys, the keys, where were the keys?

What a beginning for Frau von de Luhe, the new Mistress of the Robes, appointed in the morning, on duty within an hour, faced with blank incomprehension from Her Majesty, who had not, it seemed, been told that she was expected to receive the Grand Duke or to take her place at the banquet table; faced with sullen inertia from the two Ladies-in-Waiting, both of whom resented her appointment over their heads; and every closet door, every chest and coffer in the Wardrobe locked. And no keys.

The keys lay at the bottom of the Sound, tossed out by Frau von Plessen as she rattled by in the hired carriage. She had lost her post, her pension, her right to live in her own country because she had said what she believed to be true — that the Queen was not yet strong enough to take part in a public function. Neither dismissal nor banishment had changed her mind.

Of course, she realized, as the ill-sprung carriage bumped along, they would use axes.

They used axes. It all took time and time was in short supply because even when Her Majesty understood the order — so mysteriously mislaid, she said that the baby came first and must be fed. She said she could be dressed in ten minutes, and her hair took only another ten, Alice was quick and clever.

Caroline had not, since the birth of her baby, been fully and formally dressed; and for one shattering moment it seemed that she could not be so on this important evening, for when the axes had done their work the character of Frau von Plessen's final duty was revealed. Not one garment was fit for immediate wear. The damage was not vast, nor malicious, seams neatly split, frills and flounces removed, gathers loosened. And from every pair of stays the laces had been removed.

After a long day of uncomfortable travel and an almost inedible meal at a public table, Frau von Plessen went to a hard bed in an inferior room in what was, at best, a poor inn. Caroline sat beside Christian at the banqueting table and he eyed her with distaste. The puffiness of pregnancy had not yet wholly receded from her face and neck; her gown — borrowed from Frau von Ebhn who was nearest in size, was not grand enough to befit a Queen on such an occasion, nor did it fit its present wearer, slightly too short, slightly too large everywhere except across the bosom, where it was too tight.

He believed that she had been just a trifle late and arrived with some signs of haste upon her, in this unbecoming gown, her face badly arranged, on purpose, to shame him, or to show how much of her earlier, impeccable appearances had been due to the overseeing of Frau von Plessen. Or perhaps it was all some typically female rebuke to Madame who was so perfect that she did not seem to be flesh and blood at all; she could easily have been one of those porcelain figures which the Copenhagen factory was beginning to produce from models made in Dresden. (Her toilette, from first to last, had taken three hours.)

He wanted to hurt her and presently that head of his which was cleverest of all heads, suggested the perfect way.

He said, "I have today decided to make a visit to England. In May. An agreeable month, I am told."

Even the blurred, puffy features could not conceal the expression of sheer joy. She said,

"Of all the loveliest month! And I can show Frederick to Mamma. I have longed to do that. He improves every day. By May he will be so beautiful . . ."

Christian took and chewed a mouthful before replying.

"I do not propose," he said, "to take you with me."

On top of the rush and confusion, the consciousness of looking her worst, the standing to receive, the effort to understand the Grand Duke's German, Madame's French, the shock of joy, this was too much. She could not even ask "Why" because to draw a deep breath and count to fifteen, twenty in order to maintain self-control, precluded speech.

"It would be unwise," Christian said, quite reasonably, "for the monarch and the heir to the throne to be absent from the country at the same time. There are accidents, by sea and by land. And you *chose* to act as milch-cow."

In control of herself again she said, quite calmly,

"I had taken neither fact into consideration. He will not be weaned until June . . ."

She leaned forward and began to talk to Madame in her near-perfect French. Madame discovered that Her Majesty of Denmark — not so pretty as she was said to be, and not at all well-dressed — had some merit as a conversationalist. Presently Madame exercised the wit which was as famous as her beauty and her ambiguous status and Caroline responded with a burst of laughter. Christian should not see that his manner of breaking the news had hurt her.

But in the privacy of the bedchamber, Madame said to the Archduke, "That is not a happy woman. One can always tell by the laughter . . ."

CHAPTER
FIVE

London, October 1768

The Dowager Princess of Wales was planning one of the only gatherings that she positively enjoyed, a strictly family party. She talked it over with George, head of the family;

"I have never yet had a proper talk to him; and I must. With just the family, in my own house, he can hardly evade me."

George showed a lamentable lack of enthusiasm.

"He may consider it a dull way to spend an evening."

"It is one way to detach him from Count Holcke and even from Count Bernstorff. Of course *he* is in a different category altogether, but if he is present, Christian affects not to understand my German and calls upon him to translate. That makes intimate talk impossible."

"I can't talk to my brother of Denmark at all," George said, with a plaintive note in his voice. "I've never found any subject that interests him; he looks at nothing. And his laugh goes through my head. I've treated him," George said, truthfully, "as I would expect to be treated were I fool enough to visit him. But talk to him I cannot. I sometimes wonder how Caro manages. There's nothing *there*. Nothing I can lay hold on, anyway."

How Caroline was managing was what concerned the Princess. She had the maternal ability to read between the lines and once or twice even the lines themselves had been eloquent. There was this Frau von Plessen who had been "very stately and correct", then "kinder than I thought at first," then "very kind indeed" and finally "wonderful." Wonderful in January; and Caroline's first letter after the birth of her child had told exactly how wonderful Frau von Plessen had been: in February dismissed and banished. Why? She had been replaced by Frau von de Luhe, and though Caroline had written, bravely, "I may come to like her . . ." no later letter had recorded a change of mind; and Frau von de Luhe was a sister of Count Holcke whom the Princess Dowager had summed up, at first sight as a sycophant and a rake.

And there was further evidence of something wrong somewhere. At her first meeting with Christian, as soon as the formal ritual was done the Princess Dowager had asked all the questions natural to a mother who had not seen her daughter for seventeen months, during which the daughter had borne a child; Christian's answers had been perfunctory; Matilda was well, the child was well; he had then turned aside and said, quite audibly, "This doting Mamma bores me."

That was very offensive; but the Dowager Princess was not a woman easily deterred.

So, here Christian was, seated between his mother-in-law and an aunt-by-marriage, two hundred years old by the look of her, and very hard of hearing and, from the way she fell upon her food, starving as well. One of his heads said "Trapped! How much can you remember? What sort of birth was it? How much did the baby weigh? These are questions that any husband and father would answer, easily, and with pleasure. I am a husband; I am a father. I should be able to answer . . . but I can't. A boy, ugly and puny at first, improving now. And naturally the birth of an heir pleased everybody. *My* chief feeling was relief."

The other head, at the cost of a little pang, suggested a way out of this family talk. I'm King, it is for me to choose the subject for conversation. I shall talk, continuously, and fast, so that she cannot bother me with her questions.

He began to talk about himself and his stay in England which he had so much enjoyed. How he had been to Oxford and been given an honorary degree in some subject that he had never heard of and now forgotten. His physician, Dr. Struensee had been similarly honoured, given a degree in medicine. He spoke of Cambridge, Leeds, Manchester, York and the rousing welcome he had received in these places; of the noble houses of Ditchley, Blenheim, Stowe where he had been entertained in princely fashion. He remembered practically nothing of what he had seen, he had gone so fast from place to place and the range of his vision was so limited, so he fell back upon the word splendid. Everything he had seen was splendid, the hospitality he had received was splendid, the English crowds were splendid. As well they might seem, the

Princess Dowager reflected sourly, since everywhere he went he threw gold pieces about as though he were scattering pebbles.

He could not speak — to his mother-in-law — of the place which had impressed him most and where he had enjoyed himself, Mrs. Cornelis' establishment in Soho Square. Mrs. Cornelis had been one of Casanova's paramours. Nor could he mention the other haunts of vice and dissipation which he and Holcke had frequented whenever they could slip away. So his talk about England began to dwindle and he switched to his imminent visit to France and how greatly he was looking forward to it. The effort of keeping up this flow of talk was a strain and the pull between his clever head and his other one resulted in the usual pain.

Quite early on the Princess Dowager had decided that he was drunk; only that could account for the gabble, the jerky way of speaking, the shallowness of the talk and the repetition. She looked at him closely and decided that his appearance had deteriorated while he had been in England: Caroline had written that he was handsome; she herself had thought him not unhandsome, if rather small, when she first saw him and his looks had been the subject of much favourable comment. But now his complexion was not merely pale, it had a leaden tinge, there were purplish pouches under his eyes and a twitch at one side of his mouth; his eyes had a wild and sometimes an unfocused look. She was inclined to discount scandalous gossip about royal personages — look what was said about George, about herself; but seeing this old face upon a young man of twenty she was inclined to credit some of the rumours of his dissipation.

George — placed at his own request at the farthest point of the table — had ceased to eat, he was very abstemious about food as well as wine, and had begun to fidget. He would not, at this family table, exercise his right to end the meal when he chose, but she could not keep him waiting forever. And she had not, so far, brought the conversation around to the subject so near to her heart; every time, before she could complete a sentence, Christian had interrupted, most rudely, and resumed his monologue.

Now he was talking about Versailles, of his wish to see that fabulous, ruinously expensive building where even the orange trees grew in silver tubs.

"Our own palace at Hirscholme is said to be a copy. Miniature, but in a more beautiful situation. It is on an island. The name means the Isle of Stags."

Well, at least they were now speaking of Denmark.

"Caroline," the Princess Dowager said firmly, "has often mentioned its beauty."

"Matilda," Christian said. "In Denmark she is known as Queen Matilda. And so I think of her."

"My daughter," said the Princess Dowager, who was capable of detecting and administering a subtle verbal rebuke. "There are so many things which a mother naturally wishes to know, things which letters do not tell."

Christian offered no help at all; he did not even ask what she wished to know, or offer to tell her what he could. His attitude made her questions sound very trivial, very feminine; but she asked them resolutely and was answered grudgingly. Then she said the thing that she had made up her mind to say.

"I have a feeling that Matilda . . ." a sop . . . "very much misses Frau von Plessen whom she seemed to regard as a friend. I was most distressed to hear that she had . . . resigned."

"She was dismissed."

"That increases my distress. I had hoped that I might persuade you to persuade Frau von Plessen to withdraw her resignation." Really life was very difficult; one deplored lies, avoided them when possible, taught one's children to avoid them; but where did untruthfulness and tact overlap? "You see, I understood that in the crisis Frau von Plessen behaved most admirably. And Matilda is very young, even now, a reliable, mature woman, of whom she was fond . . . Was her fault too grave to be overlooked?"

She was an interfering, pig-headed old harridan — very much like you, Madam!

"She disobeyed a direct order — from me!"

"How tiresome." She braced herself. "Could it possibly have been a misunderstanding? Or if deliberate, could you not bring yourself to forgive her?" She was pleading now, because time was so short. "I ask this clemency because I have felt, almost from the first, that Frau von Plessen contributed a great deal to Caro . . . Matilda's comfort and happiness."

Christian said, "I always find it difficult to refuse any request from a lady — a beautiful lady." He added the last words with deliberate malice and was pleased to see that she swallowed the flattery and looked relieved. "I could recall her and reinstate her tomorrow: but it would make things awkward." He paused, gloating over his clever head. "The trouble is, the moment she returns to Court I should be obliged to leave. I will not share a roof, a doorway or a staircase with her. You see, she is mad. On one occasion she slashed the Queen's clothes to ribbons. Matilda was forced to attend a banquet in a borrowed dress that fitted badly." His shrill laugh rang out and George flinched.

It was at times like this that the Princess Dowager missed Edward. She felt unable to bother George over what seemed a trivial matter, he already had worries enough to drive any man mad. William and Henry would not understand, and might even take any criticism of Christian as a maternal rebuke to themselves, since they had turned out to be giddy and pleasure-loving. She admitted to herself that there was nothing that anyone could *do*, but it would have been a relief to talk to someone who sympathized.

Christian was missing Knut as sharply as the Princess Dowager missed Edward. Knut had had an excellent reason for not coming on this trip. His old father had died in his saddle and the horse had carried the corpse home to the usual door where Knut's mother was waiting to greet her husband. She gave a scream and fell down. "My father," Knut explained, "did not even keep tallies; he told everything to my mother, who stored everything in her head. I feel that I am needed at Vidborg."

Plausible enough, but the shrewd side of Christian's brain offered another explanation. Knut resented Struensee. He had been opposed, from the first, to this choice of personal physician, and although the two men never quarrelled openly, there had been a sense of strain ever since Struensee had come to Copenhagen. Knut called him, behind his back, "the Lutheran pastor," and sometimes to his face, "Honest Johann" in no flattering manner. He made mock of the measures which Struensee had advised for the improvement of Christian's health, saying that if abstinence over food and drink, and going to bed early made for health no peasant would ever die. Christian would have liked to think that Knut was jealous of Struensee; but if so the subject of the jealousy was power, not affection; Knut knew that Christian loved him as he had never loved and would never love anyone else. Yet here again came the divided mind; Christian sensed in his new doctor a kindness, a warmth, a lack of self interest unknown to his first favourite.

Still, he missed Knut at every turn: how Knut would have laughed, for example, over his clever retort to his mother-in-law. Whenever Christian ordered presents for great English lords, and he was very lavish with rings and gold snuff-boxes, he ordered something similar for Knut, knowing in advance how they would be received. When he presented one of the gold snuff-boxes to Garrick, the great actor knelt and kissed his hand. Knut would probably say, "A pretty toy. Thank you," with no real gratitude. Yet, because the unattainable is always the most sought after, Christian must go on striving.

One day, when he was thinking along these lines he decided that in addition to all the gifts, he would, upon his return, give Knut really startling proof of his generosity and good will. Making the muddled dues an excuse he would remit the taxes on Vidborg for a year.

To this decision he adhered though in January 1769, when he returned to Denmark finances were in a poor way. Nobody on the Council dared to suggest that the £200,000 that Christian had spent in England, and the slightly larger sum he had flung away in France, was profligate. What they did say, with maddening monotony, was that the Exchequer was empty and that the harvest had been exceptionally poor.

Even Knut, distantly admiring Christian's gifts, informed of the greatest concession any King of Denmark ever made to a subject, surely, said, "That will be most welcome. The harvest was so poor . . ."

CHAPTER
SIX

Copenhagen, January 1769

Supported on one side by his mother, on the other by Alice, the Crown Prince of Denmark bounced and stamped, enjoying the touch of his feet on the floor, and making joyous noises. In a few days he would walk. He already prattled freely, if unintelligibly and had a distinctive way of greeting his mother and Alice, his two favourite people. Soon he would talk.

Fräulein von Ebhn rustled in and handed to Caroline a roll of stiff paper, bound by a ribbon with a dangling seal.

"From His Majesty, Your Majesty."

Christian had come back from England and France in a more inimical state of mind towards her than ever. He had proffered no information about her family, and answered the questions which she felt compelled to ask in a brusque, deterrent manner. Now he was communicating with her by this official-looking document. What about?

The scroll opened unwillingly, as though reluctant to reveal its message. She stared at it with disbelief and then with horror. It informed her that from tomorrow, his first birthday, the Crown Prince of Denmark was to be given his own establishment. He would live at Fredericksborg and be attended by —

There followed a list of governors, governesses, ladies, gentlemen, names over which her eye ran, taking in nothing. Skipping these, she read that His Royal Highness' Household would be controlled by Her Majesty, Juliana the Queen Mother, and that Her Majesty of Denmark could visit His Royal Highness every fortnight.

She said, in a muted voice, "Alice, they plan to take him away from me." Then she said, "This I will *not* tolerate. See to him . . ."

She let the offensive document spring back into its cylindrical shape and holding it in one hand and her skirt in the other, sped away.

She covered the ground between the two apartments far more quickly than poor Frau von Plessen had done, but bursting in to Christian's apartments found herself confronted by much the same scene. Cards and money on the table, her husband and some other men — she never knew who they were — sitting around the table in unbuttoned ease. Everything that was violent and passionate in her nature had mounted as she ran and at the sight of Christian, sitting there, playing some silly game, rebellious rage took charge.

She said in a loud voice, "You can't do this to me!"

She had made the worst possible approach, and by ill luck hit upon the worst possible moment. Neither Knut, the old favourite, nor Struensee, the new one, happened to be present; either, the one from preconceived design, the other from sympathy, would have intervened. As it was there was no one except sycophantic hangers-on and when Christian said,

"What can't I do?" there was, behind the question the menacing hint of the autocrat's unlimited power. She heard it and recognized the threat. In Denmark this man's word was law.

She said, "I am sorry. I should not have said that. May I begin again and beg you, beg you, not to hand the child over to hirelings?"

The other card players stirred uneasily; one even pushed back his chair, very quietly and stood up.

"Sit down," Christian said roughly. "This will not take long. When I issue an order it is an order."

"He is so young," she said. "I had hoped to have him with me, until he was six. Please reconsider. Please rescind this one order."

It was unfortunate that in distress her face took on a resemblance to her mother's: God protect men from such women! It was unfortunate that in the short time since his return from France several things had combined to ruffle Christian's temper. It even angered him to find that everything had run smoothly in his absence — and then he was angry with himself for being so unreasonably angry. His head, despite all the remedies tried by Struensee, grew steadily worse; alcohol no longer cheered him. And in his absence Caroline had grown two inches.

"I have nothing more to say on this subject," he said. "You are disturbing our play."

She began to cry, dropping on her knees beside his chair and putting her hand on the arm which he had moved to pick up his cards.

"It will break my heart," she said. "And he'll miss me. He knows me now. Christian please, listen to me. Over this one thing . . ."

Anger clanged in his head.

"Get out! Leave me alone," he shouted. He pulled his arm free and jabbed his elbow at her. It could have been no more than a gesture of repudiation, but it hit her on the cheekbone, jolted her teeth, and rocked her as she knelt.

"Call Axel," Christian said, "and tell him to conduct Her Majesty back to her apartments."

"Don't bother," Caroline said. "I can make my way back. Go on with this important game!"

She tried to hurry; to get back to the child; not to waste a moment of what little time was left. How long would it be? Fredericksborg, a summer palace, disused since September, would take some little time to make ready. The Household with all their high-sounding titles would require some time to assemble. A week? Ten days? Hurry! Hurry! But such a stitch in her side had developed and her heart was beating so rapidly and so unevenly that she was obliged to stop to catch her breath and to bend down to touch her toes — an infallible cure for stitch in the side. Tonight it did not work. She had said that her heart would break and it seemed that it had, in reality; that a part, sharp as a fragment of shattered glass, had fallen and lodged

195

behind her lower ribs and that the maimed part remained, working at double speed. And it was true what Mamma had said — self-control, once lost, was difficult to regain. Tears were still streaming down her face when she stumbled into the nursery, where Alice sat sewing by the cot.

She jumped up and asked what was the matter.

"In a moment . . . I'll tell you everything," Caroline gasped. She took a self-punishing look at the child who slept with his dimpled hands thrown up on each side of his head. His hair was like Edward's, true gold; so were the eyelashes that lay in crescents against the cheeks, still flushed from his last exercise. Who, at Fredericksborg would look on him with love? The hirelings, concerned with their office and salary? His step-grandmother?

"Here," said Alice, "lean on me." She put her arm, meagrely flesh but strong as iron, around Caroline and helped her into the bedroom and to a chair.

"What happened?"

Caroline told her — not mentioning the jab of the elbow but ending, "This I cannot bear, I've borne a lot, but this is unbearable."

It all fitted in with what Smith had said only yesterday. "Come back in a rare funny temper by all accounts. Sackings right and left; even old Bernstorff is expecting the order of the boot any day. Everybody useful, out!"

And Princess Caroline had been useful; she'd made the poorest specimen of baby that even Alice had ever seen, into one of the best. So she had, virtually, got the sack.

196

"He might think it over and change his mind," Alice said.

"He won't. He is determined to hurt me. Why? What did I ever do? God, what did I ever do to make him hate me so?"

"They'll look after him well," Alice said, determined on comfort. "He's *their* Crown Prince." She was sorry for Caroline, a doting mother; but she had no concern for the child. Children, she knew from first-hand experience, were tough as nettles, they'd flourish anywhere given the minimum of nourishment.

Then Alice saw on Caroline's white, stricken face the red mark which tomorrow would be a bruise; it was already slightly swollen as well as discoloured and Alice in her day had seen its like many times.

"What happened to your face?" she asked in a tight voice.

"Oh that? Nothing. I managed, as I told you, badly. And I . . . well, I clutched at his arm and he thrust me away and his elbow hit me. It's nothing. Nothing compared to the blow he dealt my heart."

You may think so, I don't, Alice thought to herself. Hearts were luxuries, very nice if you could afford them. But a clout in the face was a clout in the face; and that little runt had dared!

"I wasn't counting on your company again, so soon," Smith said, pouring boiling water into the chipped brown teapot.

"It must be the weather," Alice said. "I felt kind of low. Very low. I got a glimpse of the King the other day

197

and thought he looked poorly. And, you know what, I found myself wondering what'd happen if he *died*."

"You was low," Smith said. "Don't you fret about that." He put a blunt dirty finger to the side of his head and made a screwing motion. "Live to be a 'undred. Look at Bedlam."

"But if he did. What'd happen to her?"

"She'd be all right. Top dog I reckon, till the boy was old enough to take over."

He decided not to mention the alternative, because it was only the echo of an echo, one of the stories he'd heard his grandfather tell. The old boy had had a rare memory for tales, he could make a thing that happened long ago sound like yesterday. Something about some little Prince who should have been King of England being killed and buried by his wicked uncle.

And the wicked uncle was a hunchback. So was Prince Frederick.

"Blimey!" Smith said, feeling the heritage of the illiterate and seeing the possible repetition of a pattern.

"Blimey what?" Alice asked.

"The things women can think up. To worry theirselves with. Beats me. You must a been low."

"I feel better now. There's nothing like a good cuppa tea. I'd look better too if I could get some of the stuff I used to put on my face when I was in London."

Smith studied her face; nothing'd alter it much, and in his opinion it was all right as it was; but women were always fussing and prinking.

"You could send for it."

198

"*And* pay customs. Not to mention the nosiness. You don't know how we live. Twenty people pawing everything over. Vot is dat? Parcel vrom England?" Heartlessly she mimicked the one or two people who had tried to communicate with her in her own tongue.

"Well, if that's your only worry," Smith said. "I could get you anything you wanted, within reason. No questions, no customs. I get stuff in, for the horses. So long as it wasn't bulky."

Even in England a true member of the horseman's association would go to five different apothecaries' shops, on five different occasions, to get what was needed, lest anyone should guess; and some items were unobtainable in Denmark. So he had established his contacts. "It ain't bulky," Alice said. "A very little of it'll go a long way."

Part Four

CHAPTER
ONE

Copenhagen; Hirscholm, January-September 1769

In the grief of separation pride came to her rescue and enabled her to put up a show of not caring. There were some men about the Court who had seen her kneeling, weeping and being repulsed. They would have talked, she felt and probably within forty-eight hours everyone knew. Juliana made no attempt to conceal her triumph, and though she took her duties as head of the new Household very lightly she mentioned them often and was always ready to volunteer to Caroline the latest information about the child. It was necessary, therefore, not to go about with lowered head, sagging shoulders and a gloomy face, admitting that one had been hurt. It was necessary to appear to be on good terms with Christian.

Christian was almost equally anxious to appear to be on good terms with her. Knut had been furious and very outspoken; an interrupted card game and the onset of a headache were no excuse, he said, for behaving like a drayman and hitting your wife in the face. "I did not *hit* her, Knut. She clawed at me and I pushed her away. That is all."

Knut asked who had witnessed this pretty scene, and as soon as he knew the men's names he sought them out. The King, he told them, deeply regretted that he had spoken and acted impatiently to the Queen; it was because he had been suffering from a blinding headache and hardly knew what he was doing or saying. But if a word was spoken about the matter reprisals would be instant and ruthless. The King was King and the Blue Tower waited.

Doctor Struensee disapproved of taking a child from his mother. Children needed their mothers and the Queen had proved herself to be a mother in a million. "Had you consulted me," he said, "I should most strongly have advised against it. Is it too late to cancel the arrangement?"

That Christian was unwilling to do; but he was anxious to show that the arrangement had caused no permanent breach and that the Queen was resigned to it. So, when they appeared in public together and she smiled at him, he smiled back; when she tried to engage him in animated conversation he did his best to listen and respond. Until one day a very strange thought struck him.

He had taken away her child, put a deliberately malicious limit to her visits, rejected her pleas and struck her in the face. Yet she seemed to bear him no grudge, why? Trying to get him back into her bed? Anxious for another baby? The thought alarmed him. Not for anything, not for anybody, would he go through *that* again.

204

Four months passed. Caroline made her visits; trying not to betray to those who now had charge of her child anything of her constant misery and growing consternation. Usually, in the carriage coming back to Copenhagen, she cried, and then, in order to face the cruel world and deceive it, was careful to repair the damage the tears had done. Only Alice knew. Only Alice understood.

On a lovely day in May, she made her heart-wrenching visit, and returned to the capital, where, in the evening, behind a false face, and splendidly robed and bejewelled, she sat beside Christian at a performance of an opera in the private theatre. She was now so near hating him that his little mannerisms jarred almost unbearably. Every time he gave that stupid cackling laugh she had to grip her hands together and draw and hold her breath. Yet during one of the intervals she leaned towards him and said, with deliberate sweetness.

"Afterwards, may I have ten minutes' private conversation with you?"

"Afterwards there will be presentations. And supper. Late. Could it wait till tomorrow?"

She compelled herself to speak amiably; not pleadingly, she had seen where pleading led, but amiably.

"It is of some urgency — and it concerns us both."

"After supper, then," he said, unwilling but a little curious. In a previous interval he had seen her talking to the British Minister, Mr. Gunning, and it was possible that something had been said about a visit from one of her brothers. George would not stir from England; Edward was dead, but there were two others whom he had not liked at all when he met them in England, but to whom he would be bound to make hospitable gestures.

However, at the supper table, his earlier suspicion revived. Later he said to Knut, forgetting or ignoring the one true friend's uncompromising attitude towards the marriage,

"I think she has designs upon me, Knut: at table she was flirtatious." He giggled. "I shall receive her here and I want you to stay in the next room and save me if she becomes too demanding."

"She can't please you, can she?" Knut said musingly. "Once you complained of her coldness."

Christian made an effort to explain.

"When you don't like a person the more often you see her the more you dislike her. You don't know; you've never been in my position. It's seeing two sides to everything that is the trouble."

"And what other side is there to being married to a lady who is beautiful and amiable and well-disposed towards you?"

"It's the other side of me," Christian said cryptically.

This time Caroline was properly dressed and calm and whatever happened she was determined not to lose her self-control.

"It concerns our son," she began. "I visited him today."

"I saw him, not long ago. He looked well. He has gained in weight."

"Because he has no exercise and is overfed. Apart from getting fatter, Christian, he makes no progress at all. You would not notice on one visit, but nobody talks to him, or plays with him. They treat him like an idol, and he is turning into one. A fat torpid idol, made of tallow. It frightens me. That is why — at the risk of displeasing you — I must ask once more will you not make some different arrangements?"

"We've had this all out before. I thought he looked well. Every report has been satisfactory."

"It may seem so. But listen to me, please. When he was moved he was on the verge of walking and trying to talk. Now he makes no attempt at either. On my first visit, and my second, he roused himself and stirred a little: on my third visit he seemed not to know me. He leads a vegetable existence and he is becoming a vegetable. I am terrified that if something is not done he will become a simpleton."

The word was ill-chosen. It had been used in the past, with reference to the man who had the cleverest head in Denmark.

"You say that, of your own child?"

She pressed on. "When he lived with me he had a name and knew it. Now nobody calls him by his name. His Royal Highness means nothing to a child of that age; nor do the bowings and curtseys. The constant change of attendants, and the number of them, confuse him. There is no personal touch at all. So he is slipping backwards."

Christian's clever head had an answer for that.

207

"You say all this because you and all your family were brought up like wild ponies. My son is being reared and treated as a Prince should be."

"A Prince is a child, like any other child."

"Ha! You've been talking to Struensee. And Struensee read a book. French." He wished he could recall the name, but that was too much to ask, even of his clever head.

"I have never discussed our child with Doctor Struensee. But Christian, I am trying to discuss him now, with you, his father. He is now sixteen months old, and he was a lively child. Now he sits there, sunk in apathy and if he shows a sign of life at all they say he is hungry and cram in more food as though they were fattening a goose. Do believe me. He is slipping backwards all the time."

"I am quite satisfied with the way he is handled; so is Juliana."

"She has seen him twice in four months," Caroline said bitterly.

The clever head was very active this evening.

"I think your complaint is that he did not remember you. A fortnight is a long time to a child."

She knew that she was making no progress. She changed her plea.

"Then may I go more often? Once a week?"

There was a perfect answer to that.

"Then he might miss you and pine."

"Would you permit me to reside at Fredericksborg? Just for the summer?"

"You are Queen of Denmark. You have other duties."

She looked at him, at the set stubborn face and the moonstone eyes — now a little wild because the effort to keep up with the clever head was a strain. She had made no impression at all; she never had: she never would.

"Nothing I have said has made any impression at all, has it? I am his mother. I know. I can see what is happening. My child is being ruined. I try to explain and you take no notice. You treat me as nothing. What did I ever do to you that you should treat me so spitefully? In every respect I have served you as well as any woman could do, God be my judge. As for my duties as you call them, I repudiate them absolutely. If I am to be nothing, nothing I will be. I will not make another appearance, I will not stand . . ."

The door to the inner room opened and Count Holmstrupp came in. Christian's back was towards him, and over the King's head the favourite made a warning, silencing sign. She was so taken aback at the realization that this, a prearranged and private talk had, like the other one been overheard, that she stopped, the final threat unspoken.

"Your Majesty will permit me to conduct Her Majesty back to her apartments?"

"Yes," Christian said, very loudly and definitely. Thank God for Knut who had never failed him, except in the one and most important way.

The red rage boiling up in her had been momentarily stemmed by that warning gesture. But what had she to lose now? Rage, reinforced by the certainty that

209

Christian had arranged for a private conversation to be overheard, choked her,

"You will be sorry for this . . ." Knut put his left hand on her left arm, his right behind her waist and literally ran her out of the room. For what he seemed — a pretty boy — he had amazing strength. But she was strong too, and very angry; she pulled herself free and said, "How dare you? I shall call the guard."

"He could not help with this," Knut said. "I have just saved you from a gross error."

"Acting the spy! Listening to a private conversation? Laying violent hands on me?"

"Forestalling His Majesty's next order, which would almost inevitably have been to forbid you any further visits to the Crown Prince."

She was silent, thinking what that would have meant.

"How well you know him," she said in a low, bitter voice.

"I have been with him now for many years; in one capacity and another. And in *any* man a threat provokes a counter-threat, if the power is there."

"My visits are extremely painful, but I think that without them I should die. I am indeed very grateful to you. Count Holmstrupp."

He offered her his charming, lop-sided smile and said,

"It was nothing. Mere self preservation. When the master is angered, the nearest dog is kicked."

In the early days of her marriage, perhaps influenced by Frau von Plessen, she had been inclined to blame Christian's lapses on his little gang of favourites,

Holmstrupp, Holcke and Brandt; she had therefore, while preserving courtesy, remained aloof from them, faintly disapproving. Very seldom indeed had they found upon their dressing-tables the coveted little invitation to dine at the Royal table. Christian had never grumbled at the omissions: it was as though he were anxious to keep the formal and informal parts of his life separate. She now perceived that Count Holmstrupp had charm and good sense and seemed not to be inimical towards her; and his influence on Christian was evident.

She had just lost another contest with a stubborn, unkind, and unpredictable man and in this moment of loneliness and defeat she clutched at the slightest crumb of comfort.

"You heard it all," she said. "Everything I said — and more — is true. The child is being ruined. Could *you*, perhaps make him see . . ."

Knut took refuge in formality.

"Your Majesty, it is not a subject upon which I could even express an opinion. I never interfere with politics or policies. There is this to be borne in mind; every child, prince or peasant has the handicap of his upbringing. Most survive."

She was aware of being repulsed: but she parted from him cordially, repeating her thanks, saying that she would always remember his timely intervention.

So she should; so she would. At least once a fortnight when she went to Fredericksborg . . .

Left, temporarily alone, Christian congratulated himself on having been firm, articulate and dictatorial. But as

211

always, there was the other side. Some of Caroline's words had left an impression: "Torpid idol," "vegetable," "slipping backwards." Should a child of that age be beginning to walk and talk? Who would know? Whom to ask? Struensee, with his absurd ideas, culled from a Frenchman's book? No. Juliana? She was not doing her duty; she had the title, she drew the salary; she'd made only two visits. She must be reproved. But how, cajolingly? Masterfully? The constantly present conflict between his need to dominate and his desire to be dominated, made his head clang.

There was also the threat to be considered . . . "I will not make another appearance." If she held to that it would be awkward. A breach of etiquette. Husbands and wives, whatever the differences between them, always appeared together when occasion required. On the other hand if she withdrew, what a relief, no more false smiles needed, no more chatter to be listened to.

The gap between his two minds was full of pain and pressure but his hands no longer relieved it. But he had, quite recently, found another method. Take the two heads to the wall and *bang* them together. An extraordinary thing to do, but it worked. It hurt but the physical pain seemed to drive out the other, worse one.

Struensee, although he was a big and heavy man, moved lightly and from experience of sickrooms had a habit of opening and closing doors quietly. So he came in and found his Majesty of Denmark vigorously and rhythmically beating his head against the wall.

He knew then that he had failed; his care, his advice — moderation in all things, had not been effective.

Sympathy and understanding were not enough. Pity remained. Pulling Christian from the wall, hearing him say, "But Johann it helps, it helps," Struensee thought — Poor fellow, and was then immediately led away, in his own mind, by the consideration of the intricate links between mind and body.

He decided to try upon the King, in place of the laudanum which had a soothing effect, but was in itself a deadly thing, a new drug, about which he had only lately heard and which, as a doctor, he had regarded with proper, professional caution. It came from the east; the captain of a Dutch East Indiaman had first mentioned it in Europe. It was derived from a plant and in India it had been used for a thousand years as a cure for melancholy, for moon madness and for split minds. It was called Rauwolfia. The Dutch seaman's wife had gone crazy after losing her baby; the drug had cured her and he, thinking of all the other people in similar straits had brought back a supply, unappreciated, practically unnoticed. The western world had its own methods of dealing with the demented: chain them, whip them. Drive out the devil of madness by making him uncomfortable ... Johann Struensee no longer believed in the devil, nor in God, but he had an open mind: and when a patient was driven to bang his head against the wall experiment was justifiable.

On Christian the stuff had an almost miraculous effect. He ceased to complain about his head, became calm and even, at times, cheerful, not in his former noisy, frenzied manner, but in a way which greatly encouraged Struensee to hope that a cure had been effected. Christian, in gratitude, appointed Struensee to the State Council where, though he would be only one voice — and that a lonely one — Struensee felt that he could make beginning towards the changes he wished to bring about.

The first of these had nothing at all to do with politics. Now that the King was becoming rational, open to argument, Struensee intended to discuss with him again the upbringing of the Crown Prince and urge more modern, liberal measures and the return of the child to his mother. That proposal had to be delayed however, because the Queen herself fell ill.

To Caroline her affliction seemed like a punishment for having made the threat to withdraw from Court. She had begun to tell Christian that she would not stand beside him, and though, in her own mind her burst of temper and her threat had been fully justified, she was punished by being made unfit, and then unable, to stand anywhere at all. First came a recurrence of a disfigurement to which both Edward and George had been prone, and which she herself had suffered once or twice. Raised red weals all over the body accompanied by a slight fever. The marks could vanish as suddenly as they had appeared, within a few hours, in two days at most. Even Mamma had not taken this seriously; George II had suffered from it and at Kew it had come to be known as Grandfather's Stripes.

This attack, however, was accompanied by more feverish symptoms than she remembered, and by a swelling of her feet and legs. "I will not stand . . . I

214

cannot stand; I cannot even force my feet into my slippers."

Doctor Imer said, "Is it possible that Your Majesty is again pregnant?"

"I know I am not."

He advised rest, the feet raised. To himself, with great regret, he murmured the word "dropsy", sad in so young a woman; but it ran in families. A Queen of England, not a direct ancestor, but a relative of Her Majesty, had died of it, grossly swollen.

Tapping, in the early stages could afford some relief; so presently Dr. Imer tapped, Her Majesty bore the making of the puncture with admirable fortitude, but the results were disappointing. "Dropsy", a nasty word, apt to a nasty condition, began to be whispered about.

It helped to establish the King's new serenity of mind. No question now of keeping up appearances. Her Majesty is unwell; she has dropsy. How sad!

The word reached the Dowager Princess and horrified her. She'd borne and reared, past the first dangerous year, nine of the healthiest, most beautiful children; fresh air, plain food, plenty of sleep, every rule applied and with what result? Four in their graves, and now Caroline, dropsical. Another thing handed down from that disagreeable little grandfather. But one must not give up hope. Caroline was so young! Hastily she scribbled down the recipe for every diuretic she had ever heard of. "Take of celery root, well pounded . . ." she wrote, knowing, as she wrote that no celery would have a root worth pounding until September.

★ ★ ★

Caroline insisted upon making her regular visits to Fredericksborg; eager, willing hands, those of Alice and her page, Mantel, aided her heavy, dragging steps into the carriage, and out again. The child did not know her, or Alice who had been one of his favourite people.

"At least he's growing," said Alice, trying to comfort. "They can't grow every way at once." Alice saw the situation clearly; the boy was daft, like his father. But daft or not he was *her* child and she'd suffered for him; she wanted to have charge of him. And so she should have, as soon as Alice, now armed by Smith, had a chance of going into action. She should be top dog. But it wasn't quite as easy as dealing with Phyllis because here she had no access to the kitchen, but she'd manage it somehow. Just let him wait; let him wait . . .

Caroline accepted Doctor Imer's verdict and believed that her days were numbered. Sometimes she could stand away from herself and pity this girl, just eighteen years old, who had started out on life so eagerly, with such good intentions, and who had been disappointed and frustrated at every turn. Often the self-pity brimmed over and melted into a more corrosive flood of feeling, pity for all poor human beings, born, through no choice of their own into a pitiless world. The lame, the halt, the blind, the deaf and dumb, women who longed for a child and never had one, women who bore a child and lost it, and another . . . People worse off than I am; but what is the comfort there? All lost, helpless, doomed. It was a horrid world and since she could be of no use to anyone, she would be glad to be out of it. She decided that she would rather die at Hirscholm than in Copenhagen and Doctor Imer favoured the move. Alice, torn between her intention, which involved contact with the kitchens, where she was just beginning to be accepted and unnoticed, and her need to be wherever Princess Caroline was, went to Hirscholm rather unwillingly. Alice did not believe in the dropsy talk; Princess Caroline was sick from grief.

"You'll get him back, you'll see," Alice said, "And he's *all right*; a bit fat and lazy, that's all. And you should be ready to have him back. If you ask me, pingling at your food is why your legs swell. There's swelling from under eating as well as over. Did you know that? I've seen it. Eat something now. Just try."

"What is the use, Alice? I've nothing to live for. I might as well be dead."

"That's no way to talk," Alice said sturdily. "While the boy's alive and you're alive, there's hope. Mrs. Brewster always said — Put a hard heart against a hard sorrow."

The change of air was beneficial; the dropsical symptom disappeared, but Caroline's spirits remained low and her body languid. She roused herself to make the torturing visit each fortnight and refused to take interest in anything else. Her ladies-in-waiting complained of the dullness of Hirscholm and absented themselves as much as possible.

So far as Caroline had hardened her heart it was against Christian. When she heard that in September he and the Court were coming to Hirscholm she determined to make ill-health an excuse for not participating in anything. If she could avoid it she would not even meet Christian; even pretence was ended now.

Christian was due to arrive on Saturday and there was the usual bustle of preparation. By Friday evening his apartments were polished and ready down to the last detail. But he was not yet in residence and the guards who usually stood, immobile as statues at the head and foot of stairs, and in corridors, had not yet taken their positions. The outside of the palace was patrolled as usual, and if between midnight and one o'clock in the morning any yawning sentry looked up and saw a faint light move inside the tall windows, he thought nothing of it. Hirscholm, like other palaces, had its ghosts.

The move to Hirscholm, where Caroline was already installed had agitated the King. He had not seen her since the interview which Knut had interrupted, but he remembered her threat. All summer the story of dropsy had explained her absence; but she was well again now, and simply sulking. There would soon be — if there were not already — talk of an open breach between them and this he was anxious to avoid. He feared that he would be driven to compromise, an idea repugnant to him. A weekly visit to Fredericksborg perhaps, which would be a triumph to her. He knew that on this subject his one true friend was against him, and so was his other, new true friend, ignorant bachelors both of them, siding with her because they thought she was pretty — pretty, with all that hair like an old man's beard. But he was King of Denmark . . .

218

By the time they arrived and were installed and served with supper he was approaching incoherence, saying that one head ached and the company that was to perform *Le Sorcier* on Monday evening should do so in the Queen's presence if he had to drag her to it by the old man's beard. Knut thought she was pretty, a pretty wife, with no welcome; who asked her to stand, she could sit at table, couldn't she and it was all the fault of Dr. Imer; Johann had better take a look at her . . .

Struensee decided that a dose of Rauwolfia was needed. He proffered it, in the form of a sugar coated pill and Christian washed it down with a draught of water from the carafe that stood on the table by his bed.

"Everything will seem better in the morning," Struensee promised.

"She won't. Not to me. This water is putrid!"

It was September, the end of the summer; wells were low, rivers shallow; nowhere was water at its best.

Early on Sunday morning Christian woke to terrible pain and the same condition which Alice had once used euphemistic terms for. He managed to rouse Axel, who ran for Doctor Struensee; not far to run, because as a Member of the Council the doctor was now entitled to a room in the palace and was not relegated, as he had been before, to a place in a distant annexe.

Neither doctor nor patient knew it, but Struensee saved Christian's life by forbidding him to drink cold water between the bouts of vomiting. Cold drink would

219

only increase the stomach cramps; warm milk was the thing.

Knut, roused by the noise, was obliged to take his squeamishness away; and even Struensee, hardened to unpleasant scenes in insanitary places, gave orders that another room should be made ready so that His Majesty could be carried there as soon as the vomiting and purging ceased.

Struensee blamed the Rauwolfia, partly because there was nothing else to blame and because he had been told that it sometimes had side-effects; as with other drugs, as indeed with certain food, there was in some people a limit of toleration; Struensee knew cases where men had lived on fat for twenty, thirty years, then, unaccountably, been sickened by it and never able to eat it again. It was the same with the rich red wine of Portugal. Hundreds of men drank it in vast quantities and suffered no ill; but there were a few who, after drinking it for years, had a fit of gout, and ever after, if they took so much as a glass, were stricken again.

There would be no more Rauwolfia for Christian.

The room in which the King had been taken sick was thoroughly cleaned next day; one of the nose-wrinkling, irreverent-comment-making servants took the half-empty carafe, poured its contents down the drain and refilled it.

"But I tell you there are nettles," Christian said. "They sting my hands and my feet. It had been so all my life. I always knew, but, of course, I was clever. I always kept away from them, but I do not intend to walk on them. And I shall make no compromise. I've been thinking this over. She's proud. Now *that* I realized from the first. Nobody else did. She said, that day, at Roskilde? Yes, at Roskilde, some burghers and a clock, she said she wished to do whatever I wished her to do. That was a lie. I wanted her to go away. I never took to her, you know. One always can pretend not to care. I've a great deal of practice, one way and another. But I will not walk on nettles."

Struensee, listening to this rambling talk, realized that behind the placid, near rationality imposed by the Rauwolfia, the King's mental condition had been deteriorating. Insanity, seeming to be halted in its creeping advance, had simply turned about and under cover, broken into a gallop.

Poor fellow, Struensee thought, looking down upon his King, relaxed now in the clean bed, the cleansed room, comfortable except for the imaginary nettles that stung his hands and feet.

Pitiable; and at the same time useless; a tool broken in the hand.

His old father, the pastor in Altona, had been given to trite sayings. One was, "When God closes one door He open another." Struensee preferred the word *opportunity*. The door of opportunity towards which he had been making a cautious and rational approach had now slammed in his face. This poor wrecked mind would never back or push through the reforms that Struensee planned. It seemed, indeed, doubtful at the moment, whether he would ever sit in Council again.

Struensee cast about, looking for another door marked opportunity; and he thought of the Queen.

CHAPTER
TWO

Hirscholm, September 1769

Caroline submitted herself to Doctor Struensee's examination with bad grace, proffering the minimum of information, answering his questions in grudging monosyllables. His visit had been forced upon her and she resented it and was suspicious of its purpose.

Finally he pushed back into his pocket the wooden tube which he had held between her chest and his ear and said,

"I am happy to inform Your Majesty that so far as I can tell there is nothing organically wrong."

She had known that he would say that; he had been sent to say it. Her two ladies-in-waiting, standing at the foot of the bed, their hands folded at waist level, exchanged a look — Haven't we always said so?

"Then why do I feel so ill?" There was a sharpness in her voice, a new development. The children of the Princess Dowager had been taught that even rebukes must be administered in a gentle tone.

"It is possible to feel ill, to be ill, even to die from causes not detectable by auscultation." His voice was deep and its tone not unsympathetic. Part of the trick!

223

"Whatever your conclusions, Doctor Struensee, I do not feel well enough to attend the opera this evening."

On account of the King's indisposition the performance had been postponed for three days. She guessed that Christian was anxious to resume the false, outwardly agreeable relationship so abruptly ended on the evening of that other opera in May; he did not believe in her plea of ill-health and had sent his own physician to say that there was nothing wrong with her and that she was keeping to her own apartments, having nothing to do with him, or his Court, simply because she was still sulking. Doctor Struensee would report as he had been told; Christian would order her to take her place beside him, and she would still refuse. Then he would probably say that if she were too ill to lead an ordinary life she was too ill to visit Fredericksborg; and she was now too low in mind and spirit to care very much. The visits had grown worse. They were now dosing him with calomel, which in Mamma's opinion had killed more children than small-pox. Every now and then his apathy gave way to screaming rage, and the fools couldn't see that this was his protest against his unnatural way of life; they thought he needed a dose. She, his mother, had no say in the matter; her visits served no purpose, they merely tortured her. She would relinquish them, cut her last link with this world, lie on this bed and die.

"The pain in your side puzzles me," Struensee said, standing between her and the window and looking down at her. "I cannot account for it."

Or believe in it, she thought; if I had an open wound it would attract more sympathy, though it might not hurt me half so much.

"Then you cannot prescribe?"

"Oh yes," he said easily, "one can always prescribe."

Do it then and go away. Between her and the window he loomed like a great brown bear, brown face and hands, brown clothes, the cloth of good quality and well-cut, but worn wrongly, as though he had dressed in the dark. She had never before been so close to him, for until he was made a member of the King's Council he had not been eligible for admittance to Court circles, and by that time she had retired. She'd seen him, but always at a distance. He was said to be a great womaniser; what women could see in him puzzled her.

"I make it a habit," he said, "when dealing with an adult who is conscious, of treating medical matters as a private thing, between me and the patient. So if you would ask your ladies to withdraw . . ."

His manner lacked respect and for that she blamed Christian. Not that it mattered; nothing mattered now.

When they were alone he turned to the window and looked out towards where the woods blazed in their brief autumn glory.

"It is a beautiful day," he said. "There will not be many more. It would do you good to get up and take a walk in the sun."

How clever! Well enough to walk in the sun in the morning; not well enough to attend the opera in the evening.

"And that is what you prescribe?"

He turned back and propped one of his heavy shoulders against the bedpost. Again not correct!

"Amongst other things. You lack fresh air and exercise. Possibly also your diet is faulty. You are English. When I was in England I noted the wealth of vegetables; at one dinner, ten vegetable dishes. Here we have few and not so good. But these are trivialities. What really ails you — and you know this as well as anyone — is the separation from your child."

Clever again; said sympathetically, to lead her on, make her admit that she was, in effect, sulking.

"That is outside your province, Doctor Struensee."

"Oh no," he said, and smiled. The smile looked kind, and as he moved his head the light caught his eyes and she realized that he was not all brown. His eyes were as blue as cornflowers. "In fact the first thing I shall prescribe will be the return of the child to your keeping."

"That would be a waste of time," she said with quiet bitterness. "His Majesty would never agree."

"I never waste time," Struensee said. "I give you my word the child shall be back with you, completely in your hands, within a week."

Her heart, which had beat with such deceptive steadiness under the wooden tube, began to leap and impede her breath.

"How can you promise such a thing?"

"His Majesty has convinced himself that I saved his life last Saturday night. My stock stands so high with him; whatever I asked he would consent to."

She was still a little cautious.

"And why should you side with me in this . . . this difference of opinion about how a child should be reared?"

"First as a matter of principle. I believe that mothers and children should be together. But that is not all. I need your trust, your goodwill, your co-operation. Don't mistake me; I am not striking a bargain. The boy comes back to you whether you work with me or not."

"Work with you?" she repeated the phrase in a puzzled way. "I don't know what that means. What I do know is that to have him back, to have him until he is . . . six, and is strong and happy and knows right from wrong, I would do, I would give anything."

"I shan't hold you to that, I promise," he smiled again. "If you would just remember that I mean well. How long is it since you were on a horse?"

"Oh, a long time. I hardly remember. His Majesty did not approve; and my Master of Horse was embarrassed. And if I insisted something always happened to the horses, they went lame, or had the staggers."

"They now have me to deal with," he said, and laughed. "In my early days some of my best patients were horses. And cows. If I present myself, with two sound horses, at the south door this afternoon at three o'clock, would you feel able to ride with me for half an hour?"

"If I did that," she said in a burst of frankness, "I should be almost bound to make an appearance this evening."

"Not if I said you were so much exhausted by the exercise. But it might be that having heard what I have to say — things that can not be said here — you may attend the opera this evening, willingly."

"In return for having my child back?"

"But I promised," he said. "I told you there was no bargaining. There is the future to think of and that is what we must discuss, where there is no chance of being overheard."

"Very well," she said. "Three o'clock this afternoon; at the south door."

To Alice, and to Alice alone, she confided the exciting news; trusting that it would cheer her. Alice for the last day or two had been unusually glum.

"Alice, this morning Doctor Struensee promised me, firmly promised that at the end of this week we shall have Freddy back. This afternoon I am going to ride with him to discuss the future."

The future was not shaping itself as Alice had planned. By now the daft little runt who was King of Denmark should have been lying in state, stone dead and Princess Caroline should be top dog. What had happened to the stuff? Did they fob off people at a safe distance with an inferior article? Did the sea-voyage affect it? In that quiet, eerily waiting room, lighted by the single candle, she had put into the water carafe four times as much as had practically killed Phyllis. Alice had failed and she was not accustomed to failure; quietly, working like a mole, she had always hitherto achieved her objective. Now in her biggest enterprise she had failed; so she was glum.

"It's be nice to have him back," she admitted, knowing that this was what Caroline had longed and pined for, poor dear. But when she looked into the future she saw little hope, not so long as the daft fellow could swing things this way, that way, by a word. Alice said, "We shall have to get to work on him, shan't we?"

Doctor Struensee plainly had influence. From some unidentified tack-room where her own saddle had hung gathering dust, it had been unearthed, cleaned and polished and there, on the back of a sound but not very exciting looking horse, it awaited her. Just to be riding again was pure pleasure and it was a wonderful afternoon; still warm and sunny, just touched and crisped by the cold which, at dusk, might harden into frost. Life renewed itself in her.

"Let them walk," Struensee said, after one brisk trot. "Here nobody can listen or spy. I can tell you that, at this moment, the King is dictating an order, carefully worded, for the amalgamation of the Royal Households. Economy is the official reason, so that no one can take offence."

She said, "I can still hardly believe it. And I can never express one tithe of my gratitude to you."

"I don't want gratitude to colour your attitude towards what I am about to propose," he said very seriously. "It concerns the King's mental condition. What I am going to say may be a shock to you. I believe that within a year he will be hopelessly insane."

She said, "Poor man," and then, after a little pause, "I suppose that accounts for his behaviour," She looked back over the years of her marriage; yes, madness accounted for everything.

"Poor man indeed," Struensee said; "but at least he will be humanely treated. We must look at the wide issues. In my opinion he is, even now, unfit to govern; with care that fact can be concealed for a year. But somebody must govern."

"I couldn't do it," she said promptly. "I know nothing of politics or procedures; and I dare not face the responsibility."

"You repudiated that idea very hastily. Have you ever given the matter any thought?"

"No. Well at least . . ." she laughed rather shyly, "when the Crown Prince was removed I did wish that I were Catherine of Russia, and could have my own way. But I know I'm not that kind of woman. I just want to live in peace and watch my child grow, and presently teach him a few simple things."

"And so you shall," he said comfortably. "I'm prepared to take on the government of Denmark; but I shall need your help."

"In what way?"

"By countenancing what I do. You may know nothing of politics but you are Queen. The nobles who regard me as an upstart have a great respect for you. If you appeared to approve of and support me, it would be of inestimable help — especially in the beginning. I hope that you will whole-heartedly support and genuinely approve; naturally I should discuss things with you and

230

take note of your opinions . . . Most of the reforms I plan are based on the English pattern."

"I shall favour them, of course," she said, giving him a bright glance.

What a difference a little happiness made, he reflected rather sadly, remembering the limp surly woman he had examined only a few hours ago. Well, it was his intention to make happy as many people as possible.

He said, "So far as the King is concerned your co-operation is even more essential. He is not yet demonstrably incapable and until he is he and you and I must appear to be in the closest accord, a sort of Trinity."

"You mean that I must sit by him at the opera this evening," she said and laughed. "How oddly things turn out. This morning I felt that you had been sent to force me into doing it. Now I will do it most willingly. Do you realize that they were giving him great doses of calomel — my son, I mean — and charting the results with complacency."

For the rest of the short ride they talked about rearing children. Some of his ideas were extreme; letting children run barefooted, for example. Others called Mamma to mind; and when he suggested that the Crown Prince should be given a little foundling boy of his own age as constant companion and playmate and that absolutely no difference should be made between them, she thought inevitably of Alice. At Kew some differences had been made and Caroline had

231

always resented them and sometimes protested saying
— Alice must have some, too.

When they dismounted he dived into his pocket and
produced a couple of small apples; one for each horse.
She realized then why his clothes sat so badly on him,
he did not mind what he put into his pockets.

"I should have thought of that," she said, taking the
apple that he offered her and holding it to the velvety
muzzle. "I always did, in the old days. Today I forgot."

"I always think — what *dull* lives they have, even in
kind hands. Eating almost the only positive pleasure."

Something within her, too deeply hidden even to
have a name, woke and stirred. She took leave of him
rather hurriedly.

Struensee was well satisfied with his day's work. His
new tool had fitted itself into his hand with surprising
ease. But something about her, a directness, a
simplicity, a sweetness, had made him decide to exploit
her as little as possible. She must be used, but she must
be kept happy, too.

CHAPTER
THREE

Copenhagen,
Winter 1769-Spring 1770

Alice had her own ideas about the treatment of children and if at times these did not coincide exactly with the doting of a fond mother and the theories of a doctor, she still knew that she was right. She had had experience.

She played a game with the Crown Prince of Denmark, a game with a meaning. He sat on her knees and she chanted,

"This is the way the ladies ride — trip, trip, trip.
This is the way the gentlemen ride — trot, trot, trot.
This is the way the farmers ride — jog, jog, jog."

The movement of her knees fitted the word of action and the jogs were quite violent, get some of the fat off him, get his brains working. At the end of the chant she said, "Say Mamma!"

He was so backward that the installation of a young orphan had had to be postponed for a while; orphans of

233

his age walked and talked and had learned the first lessons of survival in a hostile world. The little boy was already chosen; his name was Tammi and it was hoped that he might be brought to the palace in time for Christmas.

As time went on Alice's voice took on a certain astringency. "Say Mamma!" She was determined that that should be the first word spoken by that laggard tongue. It was not. One evening, sitting in Caroline's lap, Freddy said with the utmost clarity, "Jog, jog, jog. Say Mamma!" Caroline hugged him and wept from relief. In a short time he was garrulous. Jogged by Alice, dieted by Struensee, he lost weight and began to walk, not in a tentative way, one step today and two tomorrow, but boldly, confidently, making up for lost time.

Alice, surveying this progress and Princess Caroline's new happiness, now knew that it was all her doing. She had seemed to fail in her effort to remove the tyrant, but she had made him ill enough to put the fear of God, of hell and damnation into the little sod who'd thought he could play fast and loose with Alice's Princess. Alice could well imagine how, waking in the dark, catting his guts up, he'd been terrified into a determination to mend his ways.

Sometimes she woke in the night herself and had uncomfortable thoughts about Judgment Day. But she could always plead that she'd had a bad start and had done what she could. To this were two answers — You tried to commit murder! And — You didn't do so bad, neither! God, when he rebuked her, spoke in the

234

controlled voice of the Princess of Wales; when he approved he spoke like Mrs. Brewster of the Foundling Home in St. Giles.

It was a winter of gaiety, change and gossip. Other people than Alice saw a change in the King; where once he had been amused in the wrong place, by the wrong thing, or the wrong person, now he was amused by nothing at all, he seldom danced, he sat through the most lively entertainment with a look of boredom and generally behaved with an aloofness that gave him an almost portentous dignity.

The change in his demeanour was acceptable; change in policy held an alarming element. In the first year of his reign, when he was tightening the rules of etiquette, demanding monosyllabic replies, the constant use of his title, he had, paradoxically, professed liberal views, and mentioned reforms which he intended to bring about. In five years he had made no changes at all, except in dismissing old ministers, and Count Bernstorff had survived. Now he was dismissed and as though he had been the rock holding back the flood, once he had gone, the spate of reforms came thick and fast.

The first was the liberation of the Press; censorship was abolished; and the chief result of that was a flow of laudatory articles praising the monarch and his Council. Criticism of the government, attack by lampoon and caricature, never having been known in Denmark, took some time to breed.

235

The proposal to re-open the primary schools was understood and accepted, because the dearth of educated poor men was beginning to be felt; everyone knew of Customs Officers who could hardly count, of Police Officers who could barely read or write.

None but the stoniest-hearted could object to a proposal to provide homes for orphaned and abandoned children. And having accepted that, and the need for a school in every village, it would have been irrational to complain about the Stamp Act which would provide the necessary money.

Then came a law which indicated to the weather-wise which way the wind was about to blow. It freed serf's sons from conscription to the army. They were to stay at home and produce instead of scrambling into uniform and eating at public expense. That law sounded reasonable in view of the economic situation; Denmark was at peace and could manage with a smaller army; but it touched a sensitive and wary nerve; serfs were property and if one law concerning them could be forced through, so might others, more destructive.

There were other things to talk about.

One of Struensee's first moves had been to recall from exile Count Enevold Brandt who had been sent into exile for striking Count Conrad Holcke in the King's presence. Holcke left Court, Brandt was re-established and made a member of the Council, where he always sided with the man whom he regarded as responsible for his recall, Struensee.

Struensee had moved into place as first favourite. The King referred everything to him — "Struensee knows what I wish. Struensee knows what he is about. I agree with Struensee." And the Queen, who had always held aloof from the clique of former favourites, treated this one differently.

(And we know why, the critics said. She is English and all the moves so far made have been towards the English pattern!)

Count Holmstrupp was seriously paying court to the Queen's newest lady-in-waiting. She was Amalia von Dennecker whom poverty, age and infirmity had kept from Court for twenty years. He was a violent old man, aghast when he learned that the Queen approved of a possible match, which if it came about would relate a serf's son, a page of the backstairs, to half the noble families in Denmark. All the old Count's children, poor, good-looking and charming, had made advantageous marriages . . .

In Denmark spring was as brief as winter. The snow melted, the icicles dripped and vanished and the trees put out their green. Summer, like winter, could make a great stride in a single day.

The last day of April in the year 1770 was such a day and Caroline went riding with Struensee. They rode often, but seldom alone; Count von Bulow, Baron Schimmelmann, even Prince Frederick were anxious to ride with her, to admire her horsemanship and to display their own. This afternoon, by sheer chance, they were alone; and to both of them the situation was both welcome and unwelcome.

The thing that had moved in her, last September, and said — This is the man with whom I could be one; oh, if only *he* had been King of Denmark, had never slept again. She had reached the point, long ago, before Christmas, when if he entered a crowded room in which she stood with her back to the door, she *knew*, not in any ordinary way, but in the marrow of her bones. She could hear his voice in another room, in a corridor, on a stairway and melt with longing. When, as frequently happened, he stood close to her and talked to her directly, she was afraid to look at him and often had no idea of what he had said or of what she had replied. She was hopelessly, helplessly infatuated.

Struensee was in little better case, but he had put up more resistance; he took a rational stand; a woman was a woman; nature, the life force, intent only upon the business of propagation had arranged — probably on a chemical basis — that this one should attract, this repel. But that was not the whole truth; blood called to blood, bone to bone, mind to mind. Often, when he was obliged to stand by her he was compelled to look away, and afterwards hardly knew what he had said. There was between them — and it was not a romantic simile — the same attraction as that which existed between a magnet and some iron filings. Irresistible; but it must be resisted.

Side by side they trotted through the western allee which bounded the city on one side, and along a suburban road, lined with new houses, the homes of prosperous merchants and then into the woods where leaves, of so clear a green as to be almost transparent, were breaking out on every bough and the cuckoo was calling.

By this time the horses had lost their first friskiness and conversation was possible. He had his subject; the innoculation of the Crown Prince against small-pox. The connection between small-pox, the killer, and cow-pox, the mild inconvenience, had now been well observed, he said. The term, "a skin like a milkmaid's", was eloquent. Milkmaids contracted cow-pox and escaped small-pox; so the procedure was to innoculate, to deliberately infect a child with the harmless complaint and give him immunity for life from the other.

"Would you agree?"

"Everything that you have ever suggested for the child has been of benefit, Doctor Struensee. I am confident that this, too, will be beneficial. Yes, let it be done at the earliest opportunity. Small-pox is rampant in summer."

With other things; many of them the result of accumulated filth and clogged drains. He had in hand a bill that, put into effect, would make Copenhagen the cleanest city in the world. Others would copy. The diseases that flourished in filth and stench would diminish. He intended also to do something drastic about supplies of sound drinking water, the disposal of night soil, the keeping of pigs within the city's boundaries, the regulation of brothels, the setting up of proper abattoirs. He had a thousand plans and he thought about them resolutely as he rode through the woods on this sunny afternoon alone with the woman who attracted him more than any woman had ever done. He refused to be sentimental about his own feelings and sometimes told himself that they were largely due to her inaccessibility; people always craved, with a particular fervour, the thing that was forbidden. The taboo in this case was not moral — he had flung away the old morality that his father preached; nor was it a matter of status — he had a good enough opinion of himself to think he was fit to mate with any woman alive; it was a thing of strategy and expediency; he and Caroline now worked together and a love affair would be an unnecessary, probably a dangerous, complication.

The path along which they rode was wide enough to take three horses abreast; it ended in a belt of larches through which two much narrower paths, hardly more than trails, led off. Always at this point they turned around and went back.

Today Caroline said, "It is such a lovely afternoon, Doctor Struensee; shall we ride on a little and explore? We've never tried either of these paths."

He was aware of reluctance.

"They probably lead nowhere," he said. "And they are very narrow. I have work awaiting me. We might not be able to turn."

She laughed. "I can turn a horse on a dinner plate; and so can you."

He had reached the state — knowing it to be crazy — when he would have given her one of his arms if she asked for it, so he said,

"Very well. Ten minutes only. Which way, right or left? And will you ride ahead or shall I in case of obstructions?"

"This way," she said, and chose the left hand path and rode first. She was to remember for a long time that it was she who chose the way.

As he had supposed, the path led nowhere; it ended quite soon in an abrupt drop down to cultivated land. Between the wood and the tillage great beeches stood on either side of the path, driving their grey roots down as though seeking foothold on the lower level. The spaces between the roots formed a series of caves. In two of them pigs were rooting; in others some scarecrow children, gathering handfuls of something and cramming it into a sack. Her eyes took them in at a glance and then looked across the field towards where something moved. It was a plough. A man leaned upon its antler-like handles, bearing down, guiding the share which turned up the soil, just liberated from frost; and in front of it, supplying the motive power, was a woman. She was tethered to the plough by a rope which went over her left shoulder, across her breast and under her right arm. Both her hands were clenched at the point where, but for her hands, the rope would have bitten into her shoulder. A woman, harnessed to a plough; and to add the last touch of horror, she was very heavily pregnant; as she lunged forward, straining, her swollen belly almost touched her knees.

As Caroline stared, appalled, Struensee forced his horse alongside under the beech boughs, took a glance, reached for her horse's bridle and turned it about.

241

"That," he said in a low fierce voice, "is the kind of thing I mean to do away with."

The horses jostled in the narrow space, their riders as near together as though they shared a sofa. There was the wood with its bright young leaves, the windflowers, the cuckoos. Lovely as ever. Unheeding.

The pent up emotion found its focus. "That *poor* woman," she said, and burst into tears, crying for the woman, harnessed like a donkey, for Edward and Louise who would never know spring again, for the cruel contrast between this scene and that, and for herself, eaten hollow by a passionate hunger that could never be admitted, much less satisfied.

Struensee said, "Don't cry. My dearest, my darling, I can't bear it. Don't cry." He put his arm out and clasped her. She yielded to it and in an awkward posture — one they were to laugh about later — put her head against the edge of his shoulder and cried harder, but with different tears. It was true. The lightning could fall upon two people simultaneously. Oh bliss. Oh joy. Happiness, in love, forever. And Johann would do something about children rooting beech mast and women harnessed to ploughs. He was the most wonderful, the most admirable, the most deserving-to-be-loved, the most loved man who had ever lived.

They said all the things that lovers say. When did you first . . . ? It was intended from the beginning . . . If this, if that hadn't happened . . . But it did; it did! Like all lovers they were transported out of mere human state into something different, they were the chosen, the

242

elect, brought together by forces unimaginable. Even his rooted scepticism yielded a little to the influence of the first physical contact, the first kiss. He felt himself to be singularly blessed — by whom, or by what, he could not say. Singularly blessed, much work to do, the ability and the power, always increasing, to do it; and now to all that this was added.

He was the first to recover his sense of reality. "We must be very careful," he said. And Caroline, feeling that the first kiss had made him her lover forever, was aware of the peril that threatened such as they. "We must indeed be very careful," she said.

CHAPTER
FOUR

Copenhagen, May 1770

Sophia-Magdalena lay high, propped with pillows. One window stood wide to the mild Maytime air, and between it and the bed was a brazier on which stood a small cauldron which bubbled and gave off an aromatic steam. Despite all these attempts to ease it, her breath came with difficulty, making a noise like pebbles being rattled together. Her lips, the tips of her nose, the ends of her fingers were blue.

Two ladies and the ever-attendant Peppo were in the room when Caroline entered. The old Queen Mother, sparing her breath, dismissed them with a slight movement of her hand. The ladies went, glad of the release, Peppo stayed. He could be patient for a few more days; he would soon be released permanently. His mistress was dying and when she drew her last rasping breath he would go the the man Smith and be trained to be this thing called jockey and go to England.

"You too," Sophia-Magdalena said. "Keep the door. Outside."

As soon as they were alone she said to Caroline, with no sign of fear, or distress or self-pity, a plain statement of fact —

244

"I am going to die, my dear."

That was all too plain; she wore Death's colours already; but one never admitted such things; it was the duty of a sickbed visitor to bring cheer.

"Oh no," Caroline said in a false, sick-visiting voice, "you must not talk of dying. With the good weather here and the remedies that Dr. Struensee has suggested . . ." She broke off, seeing the change on the old woman's face; suddenly alert, knowing, sharp. What have I said?

"Aaah! It is true then. You foolish, foolish unfortunate girl . . ." She made an effort and pulled herself a little higher in the bed. "You cannot even say his name without betraying yourself!"

And what might that mean? Surely no one, least of all this old woman, for months immobile from rheumatism and for weeks kept to her bed . . .

Caroline said, "If I speak Dr. Struensee's name in any particular way it is because I have confidence in his skill. He cured me . . ."

The noise that Sophia-Magdalena made could have been a laugh, had there been enough breath for it.

"I'll warrant! Ruin you, too, unless you listen to me. You must listen . . ." She lifted one blue and white hand and hit herself on the chest and made a hawking noise. "No time," she said, "to tell you . . . except that you are a fool. A lover, yes, but far away, not a man you see every day, talk to, look at, speak of. Far away, that is the way to do it and stay safe. Ordinary women commit adultery; Queens commit treason. Do you realize that? And you so guileless! No defence at all, give yourself away by a look, a tone of voice, bound to come to grief."

Agitation had worsened her condition; now her breath sounded not like pebbles rattled together in a sack but like heavy, heavy footsteps walking through pebbles, ankle deep. And what could she know? It was only a month; in fact rather less than a month; in that time they managed, with the utmost carefulness, to be twice together, truly together. What had been done and noticed to bring, to this old woman's death-chamber, such certainty? Dared she ask? Dared she demand to know who started, who carried the tale? Or would that be an admission? How would she take this if she were *innocent*?

The word had a weight and a significance that it had never held before; a word for a condition lost forever. Lost before the first kiss or the first tender word — there was something in the Bible about lust in the heart being as bad as the act itself. Because it *was* lust, not love. Love such as she and Johann knew could never be wrong, whatever the circumstances. Even now, realizing the loss of innocence, she could feel no guilt.

"I've lived just long enough," the old woman said. "I can tell you how such things are managed. The world is full of men, better born, better looking; pick another. Take a dozen, but not here. Not even in Denmark. There! You see, your face betrayed you. Very well, then send him away. And take to travelling . . . never the same place twice, and never the same suite. If he's a true lover he'll go wherever you are."

It was the method she had adopted herself; up and down Europe, once, twice a year, generally to spas, seeking relief from the pretended pains which later had, ironically, become genuine. It had not lasted long, only a little more than six years; but those six years had been her *real* life; now that she was dying she saw that with extreme clarity. Those six years shone with a light which passing time, nor even grief, could blur. He'd been a soldier, so handsome, killed at Minden, and when the news eventually reached her there had been nowhere to cry . . ."

Caroline said, "What my voice or my face conveys this morning puzzles me." That was true; she had determined that not by a glance or a gesture would she give a sign. "I spoke, as I explained, with confidence of Dr. Struensee and perhaps I did look a little . . . taken aback by the mention of a dozen . . ." better not say "lovers", too near, too almost holy, ". . . paramours. In the four years that you have known me have I ever given any indication that I desired one, leave alone a dozen? I know that you have been unwell; I know that as my senior you are entitled to respect from me, but I should be obliged if you would tell me who started this tale and why you are speaking as you do."

Sophia-Magdalena put her hand to her chest again and made that same hawking sound, clearing the clogged voice.

"Open the door," she said. "Not like *that*! Go softly, open it quickly. They tempt that black imp away and listen. All right? Then push this pillow higher. Good. Listen; they have been waiting; they know that Queens under the trappings are women. Von Bulow? Schimmelmann? My grandson, Frederick? One of Christian's pretty boys? As you say, you gave no indication, disappointed, they said English, cold as codfish. *Then*, it must be about a month ago, you rode out with *him* alone and came back; you had been crying, but you looked happy. You allowed him to innoculate the child; you commended him to me. It was enough, more than enough. When a fire is laid, only a spark is needed. I had my doubts," she said, her voice weakening. "You are very young, very foolish . . . but my dear, a man of no breeding, pleasant enough, but not . . ." Not anything like the man I loved, the man who loved me, "Not a man to take such a risk for. I ridiculed the gossip; but when you said his name, I *knew*. Love, if you must, but not here . . ."

But *his* work is here; the aim that brought him from Altona; and *my* work is here, the proper rearing of my child, restored to me, by him.

She looked at what the bed held, some stiff set bones, some flesh, here shrivelled, here bloated; the sparse hair and the hues of death. Did this poor ruined body ever know the rapture? Shall I, will he, ever come to this? God forbid. From this place, where death hovers, as over us all, regardless of our years — Edward lived less than half a life-time — let me go away; let me lose this terrible, terrible feeling of human mortality in the clasp, the look, the voice that is life itself.

She stood up.

"I am afraid that my visit and the subject of this talk has exhausted you. Rest now. I will come again tomorrow. And please, *please* have no concern for me. You know how ill-founded most gossip is. It is true that Dr. Struensee and I rode alone together one day; it just so happened. And I did cry, because I saw a very sad sight. And then having cried I may have looked happy because he promised me that the reforms he planned would do away with such sights forever."

She saw from the look in Sophia-Magdalena's eyes that she did not believe a word.

"You think to put me off, to die in peace. I need no soothing." Even through the rasping, difficult breathing the resentment, the near hostility showed. "I'm less concerned for you — especially if you are going to be foolish and stubborn, than with what may happen to the Queen of Denmark! I bore that title, too. I had enemies; all that gossip about poison . . . It came to nothing because there was no truth in it. It is the gossip that has truth in it that is the danger. So bear in mind what I have been saying; or you'll regret it."

Getting annoyed must be bad for her, too.

Caroline touched the blue-tipped hand.

"Try to rest now. I shall come tomorrow and hope to find you much improved."

She was spending her usual late-afternoon play-hour with the children; a quieter time than it usually was because Freddy after his innoculation had been a little restless, with slight fever. Johann had said he should stay in bed for a day or two and Tammi, upon whom the innoculation had made no impression at all, had taken to his bed, too, emerging every now and then, because he was healthy and therefore restless, to pretend that he was Freddy's doctor, and administer "medicine", a sip of fruit juice and water. All that Caroline was required to do was to ask from time to time, "And how is my poor little boy today, Dr. Tammi?" The answer was always as monotonous; he would be better if he took his medicine. Johann also had great faith in fruit juice.

Presently the Crown Prince, feeling better, tired of his passive role, threw back the covers and announced that it was his turn. "Tammi be poor little boy. Dr. Freddy make well. Tammi take medicine." The switch was made amicably.

Alice, who had been down to oversee the making of more fruit juice, came in with the jug and the news she had just heard. The Queen Mother, Sophia-Magdalena had died that afternoon.

"Oh no!" Caroline said, stricken with guilt. Had the exertion hastened her end? Ridiculous idea; the old woman had been on the verge of death for some time. But the thought stayed, and with it the memory of the way they had taken their last leave of one another. She had hesitated about kissing the ravaged face, feeling that if she did so, after the scolding and the unbelieving look, Sophia-Magdalena would take it as a sign that for her there would be no tomorrow. Oh dear, how very sad.

She felt the tears gather in her eyes and turned away to the window to hide her distress from the children.

"Her time was up," Alice said, not meaning to sound callous; simply wishing to console. "Nothing to fret over, really."

"Drink it," Dr. Freddy said sternly. "Nice medicine." He then added, because he had reached the imitative state and the ability to acquire not merely words, but whole phrases from other people's conversation, "nothing to fret over, really."

Caroline was poised between tears and laughter when Struensee came in to see how his young patient was doing. He solemnly took two pulses, laid a hand on two foreheads, applied his wooden stethoscope to two chests.

"Both doing well," he said. "They can resume normal life tomorrow. There is one thing, though, which I had better not mention here, or *that* will be incorporated in the game."

"If you will come this way, Dr. Struensee," Caroline said, and led the way into her own, adjoining bedroom.

They did not close the door. Alice wished that they had. This game had gone on quite long enough: the children were getting what she called out of hand, as they always did if she was absent for more than ten minutes; and sticky orange juice all over the place! She said in a voice no less dominating for being muted,

"That'll do! Shut up and stand still while I wash you ready for supper." They knew that with Alice there was no argument; meekly Dr. Freddy and Dr. Tammi lifted their faces, held out their hands.

On the other side of the not-quite-closed door Caroline and Johann met in one of those impulsive, compulsive embraces to which the secrecy which might at any second be disturbed lent a particular flavour.

Breathless from the grip and the kiss Caroline said,

251

"Say something. Anything. Alice . . ."

"You looked disturbed — on the verge of tears again, just now. What is it?"

She began to tell him about the death of the old Queen Mother; of her visit that morning; the trend their talk had taken. Then she broke off and said,

"You must speak. This is supposed to be a consultation."

He said, "There is absolutely no reason for you to blame yourself. It is far more likely that her determination to talk to you kept her alive for twenty-four hours. Look at it that way. In any case, her course was run."

"That is exactly what Alice said." As she said that Caroline deliberately raised her voice a little and spoke towards the door.

Alice, on the other side of it, heard, out of the mumbled blur that one distinct reference to herself and hoped that what they were talking about was the folly of spoiling children; unless someone was firm this pair would soon be out of hand.

"But she frightened me too. To think that so soon, with nothing, nothing to go upon . . ."

He was also slightly unnerved; but for years now it had been his part to console and hearten, to make light of the sinister little symptom: and on this afternoon he slipped into the part the more easily because he loved her and had it been possible would have prevented her from ever entertaining another sad or worrying thought as long as she lived.

"It was guesswork," he said, and his voice held its habitual professional assurance. "Guesses are like bets, make enough and sooner or later one comes near the mark. I forbid you to worry."

She looked towards the door and said quietly,

"This has lasted long enough."

"All we have to do, Your Majesty," he said, moving towards the door, "is to be careful."

"I assure you, Dr. Struensee, we shall be very careful."

"In the meantime," he said — and they were now through the door and into the room where Alice waited, with two quelled little boys awaiting their supper — "I think that I am upon the verge of a very important discovery. If my investigations lead to the result that I hope for, I trust that Your Majesty will be pleased."

"Any discovery that you may make, Dr. Struensee, will be of absorbing interest to me."

Alice thought, sceptically, that Dr. Struensee's next discovery would probably be that a child could escape whooping cough by spending a night in a shed with a bullock that suffered from husk. She quite liked him, but she had no patience with his theories; the one thing which he needed to understand and did not was that with children the flat of the hand, applied to the bum worked wonders. He was a fool, but the world was full of them, and he was a harmless fool; he had done Princess Caroline a good turn in getting her boy back; that was his one great meritorious act, in Alice's eyes.

253

Most of his other ideas were rubbish. But he was Princess Caroline's friend; and if nobody else understood that friendship between a man and a woman was possible, Alice did. Look at her and William Smith . . .

CHAPTER
FIVE

Luneberg, August, 1770

The Princess Dowager embraced her daughter and knew that it was true; the rumours were justified. A woman in love, and loved in return carried something about her, indefinable but unmistakable as a flower scent; bones receded, flesh triumphed. With such a feast spread any beggar — even a mother — was welcome to the crumbs, some closeness of embrace, some warmth of kiss . . . Oh dear, it was true!

When the first horrid rumour had reached her the Princess Dowager had discounted it, telling herself that Caroline had perhaps been a little indiscreet and that the world — hating all those too good for it — was putting the worst possible interpretation upon her behaviour.

She had at once written to Augusta, asking her, almost ordering her, to make a visit to Caroline and investigate. Augusta replied that she had no time and that if half of what she heard was true she would prefer not to be involved. The Princess had then considered going herself, but there again, she knew the world; the visit would arouse suspicion; she had not gone when Caroline was pregnant, nor later to see her grandson.

Why now? Nobody would trouble to remember how ill poor Louise had been.

She wrote to Caroline, not very frankly since it was unwise to put much in writing, but Caroline understood and included in her next letter the remark, "You, of all people, should know how poisonous gossip can be."

The Princess then appealed to God, asking him to send some adequate reason for going to Hanover. Many of her prayers in the past had been unanswered, but the response to this one was swift. Under George III, the first of his line to prefer England to Hanover, the Hanoverians were feeling neglected and seized upon the celebration of some old forgotten battle date to invite the King, or some member of the Royal Family, to attend the festivities. "I will go," the Princess volunteered almost before George had finished explaining.

She was fifty-six and no longer in the best of health, but she did not spare herself. There were parades in which it seemed that millions of men marched past; she diverted her mind by thinking that if the threatening trouble in America ever broke, here was a splendid reservoir of armed force; she sat through interminable banquets and attended several balls. Now she was in Luneberg, on her way home, and it was natural enough for Caroline to join her there.

Feeling the dread certainty in her heart she held her child at arms' length and studied her. She looked so well, and so beautiful; every promise of her girlhood had been fulfilled; happiness and fulfilment lay on her

256

like the bloom on a grape. It was hard to know that one must destroy . . . On the other hand, it could not be allowed to go on, and hundreds of women never knew this particular happiness at all. Caroline must do her duty — and live on her memories.

The time and the place for a stern private talk were not easily come by, but she managed it on the second day, choosing a seat in the centre of some formal flowerbeds, so that nothing should be overheard.

Now that the actual moment had come she felt curiously diffident and she began to attack with less decision than she had intended.

"I think you know what I have to say, Caroline. Even allowing for exaggeration, you appear to have been acting with a singular lack of discretion."

"In what way, Mamma?"

"In such a way that everybody is saying that Doctor Struensee is your lover."

"And does that make him so?"

She was prepared to hedge, to lie outright; but the last word sent a warm, weakening current through her bones. He had used it, that first night, in the dark, with tenderness and triumph, "Now I am your lover." He was her lover, the most wonderful, exciting, completely loving lover any woman ever had. The word, even spoke in that cool, denunciatory voice had a magic all its own.

"If he is not," Mamma said, "such talk is dangerous. But I feel, I fear that he is. And you have not even been *careful*." Again the old woman's, world weary voice and cynical attitude, love if you must, but be careful.

And they had been, extremely; neither of them was blind to the risk.

"I do not admit, Mamma, that there is anything to be careful about: but it would interest me to know why you accuse me of lack of discretion."

"On more than one occasion you have allowed Doctor Struensee to sit beside you on a sofa."

"And *that* makes him my lover!" She laughed; not in the way her mother remembered, the innocent, girlish tinkle, nor with the false gaiety which Madame had recognized as misery in disguise; this was a hearty laugh, tinged with mockery. And with relief, too; if that was the most revealing thing she had done . . . But there, turned towards her was her mother's face, graven by time and anxiety, needing comfort.

"Mamma, when Doctor Struensee attends a drawing-room he is often tired. Being Christian's physician is no easy job, but it has not distracted him from other work. He is active politically; he will ride, any day, ten miles to look at an interesting medical case, he is writing a book about the merit of innoculation. Knowing this — and since he is often late — I invite him to sit, and he is glad to do so."

"When he is not on the sofa beside you," Mamma said, "you follow him about with your eyes. Is that correct behaviour?"

"It is sometimes necessary. Christian is . . . in a poor state of health. Doctor Struensee administers palliatives, sometimes effective, sometimes not, and if the room is crowded and I cannot ask, I look and he gives me a sign."

258

"And could you not ascertain your husband's condition for yourself?"

"There are times when the sight of me sends Christian into a frenzy. Mamma, this is not generally known and we hope to conceal it for as long as possible. Christian is mad; and getting worse."

The Princess moved her hand, which in the last year had grown lean and marked with liver-coloured blemishes, and took Caroline by the wrist.

"It has not been easy for you. Christian impressed me most unfavourably. But you have your child. You must think of him. When Christian's state of mind can no longer be concealed you *must* be ready to step forward, a woman in an unassailable position with an unblemished reputation. My dear, *you must give him up*."

Deal with this, here and now, dismiss for the moment the thought that had come and grown and loomed when Caroline said that Christian was mad. Christian and George were first cousins and unlike as they were in every way, there had been times in the last month or two when something in George's quickened speech and the repetition of it reminded her of Christian, talking, talking at her table. Push that thought aside; God could not be so unkind. Who would be a mother? Constantly threatened.

The warm August day was moving towards sunset; from the close set beds of heliotrope and mignonette scent arose. And for Caroline, like every other pleasant scent or sound or touch, it connected itself with

Struensee. Give him up? Never. But here was Mamma with her anxious face.

"Mamma, what am I to give up? Friendship with a man who has befriended me. I was ill, he cured me. Christian and I were at odds, he brought about a reconciliation, superficial, but enough. Are you one of those who believe that friendship between a man and a woman is impossible?" She could ask that with a certain authority, for besides being lovers they were friends; minds as well as bodies attuned. She was convinced that had he been an old woman in a bonnet, she would have loved him; and that he would have loved her had she been an old man on a crutch. That was the beauty of it.

The Princess Dowager had recovered herself. She withdrew her hand.

"You know best what is to be given up, Caroline. But mind this. A woman with a lover cannot afford to fritter away her good name. Reputation is like money; a heavy debt forbids minor extravagances."

Echo after echo of old Sophia's death bed talk. Mamma so prim, so precise, paying the heavy debt, counting pennies in other ways. Lord Bute!

"You may think," the Princess Dowager said, looking straight ahead to where a fountain threw up its rainbow-tinted spray, "that this is something that only happens once in a hundred years, that for this you were born. That is nonsense. Any rutting deer, any cat on the tiles. It is all the same; as you will learn. You may regard me as an interfering old woman, paying too much attention to gossip. But I am your mother; it grieves me

260

beyond words to see you throwing away your good name because of an infatuation."

She was making no progress. She shifted her ground.

"Have you thought of the danger? Suppose these rumours reached Christian's ears — while he is still sane enough to take action?"

"Since they have reached England, they are probably rife in the Christiansborg. Christian trusts Doctor Struensee *absolutely.*"

There was nothing for it but to fall back upon an appeal to sentiment.

"This may well be our last meeting in this world, Caroline. I know you. When this affair has run its course, and I am in my grave you will suffer remorse that, because of your lack of frankness, our last meeting was so unsatisfactory."

That weakened her defences, but only temporarily. It was essential that no one should know, no one. Not even Alice. Even Providence seemed to have conspired to keep their secret. Johann's bedroom was immediately above hers and, judging by the windows, should have been the same size; but it was not, and poking about to discover what accounted for the discrepancy, he had found an old secret stairway, all twists and turns, which ended in Caroline's bedroom. It was full of cobwebs, so old that they were almost as substanial as muslin. A stairway for lovers long since dead. In Johann's room the head of it was hidden behind a silk panel, in hers its foot lay behind one of the mirrors. To Caroline, euphoric with first love, it had seemed like a gift from God.

"It is very difficult to be frank when combating rumour. It is like fighting a breeze. Will it comfort you if I promise not to allow Doctor Struensee to sit beside me on the sofa, and to avoid looking at him?"

"That, at least would be wise." Really, summed up like that the total of offences seemed ridiculously small. But there was something else. Something that had made her think that Caroline had lost all sense of seemliness. Ah, yes . . .

"This riding astride. That also must stop." Riding astride like a man, in leather netherhose, Augusta had said.

"I suffer," Caroline said, "from an almost permanent stitch in the side, which some postures aggravate. Riding side-saddle is one of them. So I changed over. And if whoever told you that mentioned the breeches, there is reason for them too. They are better than bunching up a skirt and exposing an immodest amount of leg. The Holstein Guards gave me a complete uniform when they made me their colonel-in-chief. They are flattered that I wear at least half of it regularly."

By chance she had diverted her mother's attention. How long had she suffered this stitch in the side; where exactly did it lie; had she asked medical advice? The girl appeared to be in such splendid health — but then who could have looked better or seemed more spirited than poor Edward just before his Grand Tour? Trouble upon trouble, worry upon worry.

They parted amiably; and on her tedious journey home the Princess, greatly in need of comfort, took refuge in an unusual self-deception. I talked to Caroline, and she admitted nothing. For every action that had been criticized, she had a most reasonable explanation. The whole thing has been grossly exaggerated.

Once out of sight of Caroline, this was not difficult so to believe, and by the time the Princess Dowager had said it, and written it a dozen times, she had succeeded in convincing herself.

CHAPTER
SIX

Christiansborg,
November 1770-June 1771

Knut said, "If I had coveted a seat on the Council, I could have had it years ago."

It was no longer called the Council, but the Cabinet, and Struensee, as head of it was called Prime Minister; and he had just offered Knut a place in it, and Knut, like an experienced rat shied away from the bait.

Struensee, to Knut's surprise, changed the subject.

"I imagine that you would remember Heer Reventil?"

"He was the only tutor who did not believe boys' brains were in their bums."

"Well put. So I heard. We've reached now the point where *he* needs constant supervision. He once mentioned Heer Reventil to me, with a certain fondness. He would make a good keeper?"

"Up to a point. He's about so high . . . and frail." And they both knew how strong Christian could be when, emerging from apathy, he became violent.

"He could have an assistant. I saw one of the old Queen Mother's discarded blacks begging in the street yesterday."

264

"That sounds sensible," Knut said, and he waited.

"His growing infirmity," Struensee said, "worries me in another way. The boy is strong and healthy, but he is only *one*. Croup, measles, whooping cough carry off hundreds of children every year, and there is no known cure or preventive. I think it would be as well if His Majesty — before he is quite demented — begot another child."

Now we come to it!

"It would be as well. Why not suggest it? You're his doctor."

"Yes. But when I had some hope that his health and sanity could be saved, I did advise continency. And when I some days ago spoke to him of his duty to the Queen and to his dynasty, he reminded me of that advice."

"Yes. I can see, you are in awkward position. The real trouble lies, of course, in his aversion to the Queen. He never liked fair women and she is very fair. He once compared her hair to that of an old man's beard." Knut drew a breath and said, "This prejudice I do not share. The woman I wish to marry is a veritable snow-maiden. But there are difficulties. I am — it is no secret — of low birth. Nothing but an Honour would make me even half acceptable in her father's eyes."

Struensee had already done so much; he might be able to manipulate the statutes of the Order of Danneborg . . . even of the Elephant.

Now we come to it.

"A new Order, very exclusive, twenty-four members only, is about to be instituted," Struensee said, hating

265

himself, and the necessity to cajole. "It is confined to those who deserve particular recognition from Her Majesty."

Knut had earned this and much more by his timely intervention; but his peasant blood assured him that everything must be earned again and again, and his passion for manipulating puppets rose up and clamoured for a chance.

"It could be managed," he said. "Her Majesty would have to wear a wig." He smiled, relishing Struensee's bewilderment. "He might be persuaded to perform, with a dark-headed girl, and if he thought he was getting the better of you all."

"I hate it," Struensee said, "especially the connivance with Holmstrupp. But I see no other way. The gossip goes on and though Holmstrupp has sometimes said that marital relations were normal, he knows, so must many others, that it is not true."

"I more than hate it; it is repulsive."

"It involves being seen in his bed. I will guarantee that he will be asleep almost before he is in the bed. Trust me, darling."

"What I hate is having to push something so splendid and right out of sight as though it were a filthy rag. It comes over me at times, I want to stand up and shout, *this* is the man I love, the man who loves me; and I shall bear his child."

"You'd be run out of Copenhagen on a hurdle."

"I shouldn't mind; if you were run out, too."

"I shouldn't be. They'd have my head."

She said, "Listen, before we go through this masquerade, let us consider an alternative. I've thought of it often, lately. I could take Freddy and go on a pretended visit to Augusta. You could make some excuse about seeing your father and we could meet in Hamburg and disappear. We could go to America; they say that Virginia is a pleasant place . . . Johann, why not? No more lies or subterfuges. Just ourselves."

Her eyes were sparkling and her cheeks were flushed; she looked like a child planning a delightful outing. How could he say to her — *My work here is only just begun*.

"Queens and Crown Princes are not allowed to disappear like that, my love. Think of the hue-and-cry. Think of your brother. Think of Freddy. Even if we succeeded we should be depriving him of his heritage. Equally important we should be robbing Denmark of a King sound in mind and body and *properly trained for his job*." He intended to train young Frederick himself.

"I never wanted to be a Queen," Caroline said. "I am not happy at the thought of Freddy being a King. My brother George would have been far happier as a simple farmer and even poor Christian might have managed better if he had been a cobbler or a chimney sweep."

Sometimes her acumen surprised him.

"That may be true. But here we are, and here, I am afraid, we must stay. There is no escape. We must, if we can, avoid any real cause for scandal."

267

She thought of Edward saying that they were all born into a trap. And the sad little phrase, "We never got to Rusha" ran before her eyes again.

"Very well. If it is the only way, I will wear a black wig and lie in a bed and see that in the morning I am *seen* there, without disguise. What I loathe about it all is the parody . . . Once I even enjoyed bawdy jokes. Can you believe that? Now I *know*; only those who know nothing of love can regard it . . . or anything to do with it lightly. I believe you that Christian will fall asleep. But morning will come and I shall be sickened to be found in a position, justified by law, approved by the Church, and quite meaningless, whereas found in that very same position with you, whom I love, with whom I am one . . . I should be run out on a hurdle. It's wrong, Johann."

"It is one wrong, amongst many. Some, if we are clever and patient, can be put right. A real scandal next July could set back the liberal cause in Denmark for a century. And it is only by freeing *people* that we free manners and habits of thought. Even about love. If once we can free the people, Queens will be enabled to love common people like me. I am convinced of that. But you and I must beat down a path. We must survive July."

Knut said to Christian, "It's the best trick we ever played on Them. Right under Their noses. She's black as a crow and knows every trick in the trade."

Muddle on muddle on muddle. Christian had almost given up; there was a refuge from the head trouble and it was simple. Take no notice. He had discovered that it was possible to go to sleep, standing up, eyes wide open. And in this somnolent state his heads and their diverse intentions did not trouble him any more. No pain at all. Nobody, not even Struensee, knew, of course, because he was too clever for them. Clever enough to have found and taken occupation of a darkish, comfortable kind of cave or a burrow, like rabbits. From time to time he was called out, "Sign here; and here; and here." He always signed, get it over and done with and I trust Struensee completely.

The passive, painless times of retreat were interspersed by others; short but hurtful. I am King of Denmark; I have only to write my name and you're exiled, or in the Blue Tower. I can write my name and if that is not enough I can smash you with anything handy. I can kick and bite, too.

He was still responsive to Knut, to his voice, to his presence; still anxious to please him. He saw no point in this trick, this joke, but if Knut said so . . . And at the back of the muddle on muddle on muddle there was the glimmer of a thought — if the woman they'd given him had been dark instead of so horribly fair, and if she had known every trick in the trade instead of being a lump of codfish things might have been so different; but like the sums and the maps what did it matter now? A man had only to back away into his burrow.

"Yes," he said. "That would be a joke."

He still remembered in a vague broken way other jokes, in another time. When we were young . . . a bag of gold, Knut; I'll make you a Count; you shall be First

Gentleman of the Bedchamber. What went wrong? The one true friend and the two heads; the easy retreat into sleep with your eyes open; the painful emergences — I am King. What I say is law.

Which am I? And what went wrong?

Caroline lay in the King's bed, the black wig, detestable evidence of perfidy, of all that was shameful and disgusting, upon her head, and her face pressed against the pillow, away from the light of the seven-branched candlestick. Christian stumbled in and said, "Black. He was right," and then practically fell into the bed, made some soft rather happy noises and was asleep. Just as Johann had promised.

He had not even had time to blow out the candles, so cunningly and strategically placed. She got out of bed, very quietly and went round to his side of the bed, to retrieve the stand and once she was in bed, blow out the candles. But on Christian's side of the bed she paused and looked down on him. In his drugged slumber he looked young and, like any sleeper, vulnerable.

What went wrong? If only he had been kind, she thought. I was so young and inexperienced, kindness would have been enough. I should never have looked elsewhere. No, that is a shabby, a self-exculpating thought; wherever in whatever circumstances I had met Johann, we should have fallen in love. The lightning would have fallen.

She thought of what life would have been had she never known love, and pitied all the people in the world who had missed it, and they must be the majority,

270

otherwise the rules would not be so harsh and she would not have been forced into this horrid little masquerade in order to justify the birth of a child begotten in love. How odd that one must prove this poor demented boy had been the father and not Johann, so strong and clever and good. What a topsy-turvy world!

She got into bed and blew out the candles. Then she remembered the wig and dragged it off, reaching out and by feel alone finding her robe and pushing the disgusting thing into the pocket.

She slept in little snatches, troubled by dreams. She rode an unruly horse, which was exhilarating until she was thrown and landed back in the bed where Christian moaned softly. She worked in the Copenhagen china factory and made a beautiful vase for Mamma, and just as she was about to present it she let it fall and Mamma began to cry. This time Christian was snoring. Towards morning she fell into a heavy, dreamless slumber out of which she woke abruptly to find Axel drawing back the curtains to let in the leaden morning light. Count Holmstrupp and Count Rantzau stood half-way between the door and the side of the bed where Christian lay; in the doorway itself were Count Brandt and a young officer, dressed for riding.

Count Rantzau begged a thousand pardons for the disturbance; His Majesty's signature was needed on a despatch; November days were so short, the courier was anxious to get started.

Caroline smiled and said, "I am afraid we have overslept."

271

Christian woke, confused by the heavy sedation; but the request for his signature was a familiar one. He wrote it.

It had all gone like a well-rehearsed play; between them Johann and Holstrupp had managed very well. No one would dream of doubting Count Rantzau's word, his family was a byword, "loyal as a Rantzau" people said; and no doubt the courier had been equally well chosen — I saw, with my own eyes, Their Majesties in bed together, some time in November.

There was one small hitch. Christian, having signed his name, turned in the bed and saw her. He looked at her for a long time as though he had never seen her before. Then he said in a loud shrill voice,

"What did I tell you? Knut, Enevold, Axel. Look for yourself. There are two. Two heads! I'd done with it. Now look!"

Black as a crow against the white pillow; silver fair in morning light: and the pain he thought he had done with cleaving his own skull like an axe. He put his hands to his head and moaned.

Caroline slipped away, feeling as though she had been caught in the act of adultery.

Heer Reventil arrived that day. He attributed his sudden recall to a burst of gratitude — belated but welcome — on behalf of ex-pupil. At the sight of him, being an emotional man, he burst into tears; being a man of good heart, he quickly pulled himself together and resolved to do his very best for the boy whom he had always regarded as half-witted. Here also was a first-hand chance for him to prove his theory about the moon's effect on lunacy. He'd make some careful notes.

Christian, completely baffled by the problem of another person's two heads, backed away into his cave. Occasionally, under Heer Reventil's kind handling, he would emerge and sometimes complain about a black crow. Heer Reventil took this is a reference to Peppo, who was very black, but also very strong, a fact for which Heer Reventil was sometimes grateful — especially, he noted, at full moon.

And all through that winter and the spring of the next year, Struensee said in his reliable, firm voice, "Just sign here. There is no need to read it. It is in order and needs only your name."

Sign here; and here; and here; don't bother about the Cabinet meeting if you are tired; it's boring; I can convey your wishes. Just sign here.

Christian had dicovered that it was possible to reach out from the comfortable place to which he had retreated and sign his name. In one of his better moments he had recognized Heer Reventil, the one of his tutors who had been kind, and he had a muddled notion that by signing his name clearly and well, he was pleasing him. Once he said, with heart-breaking pathos, "I write well. Show it to him."

He put his good firm signature to the Statutes governing the Order of Matilda which was to be part of his birthday celebration on January 29th 1771. He put it to the patent of nobility which made Johann Federick

Struensee a count. He would sign anything; his arm
was so long that he could sign his name without
emerging from his retreat.

But there were times when they dragged him out and
dressed him up and pushed him about a bit; on most of
these occasions he found his talent for sleeping with his
eyes wide open, and even standing up, very valuable.

Knut said, "If this becomes law it will be the end of
you. It is nothing but highway robbery and . . ." he
made a significant, jerking gesture with his neckcloth.

Struensee laughed: "But I have already taken the
precaution of abolishing the death penalty for robbery,"
he said.

"Serfs are property." It was a flat statement.

"Serfs are men. Lately, by iniquitous laws they have
been forced back into feudal slavery. I should have
thought that you . . ."

"Being born one! Don't be absurd. Mine are
well-treated, well-housed and I never exact from them
more than is due. But they belong to me. I *earned*
them. How would you feel if everything you had earned
was taken from you by a stroke of a pen? Your title, your
position, your salary, the favour of the King . . . and of
the Queen?"

There was a leer in the last words. Struensee chose to
ignore it. Even Knut knew nothing as a certainty.

He said, "You take entirely the wrong approach to
this problem. England has had no serfs for four
hundred years; the landowners flourish there. Rents are
real money; far more valuable than day-labour,

274

unwillingly performed, or the right to beat a man, or to take away from a moderately prosperous fellow his best beast or to demand, when his daughter marries, a tally of six geese. Holstrupp, it's medieval, a system completely outworn because it is bad for everybody. Peasants fear to look prosperous, fearing exactions, whereas they should be proud. The really energetic ones hide their money under the hearthstones or in their mattresses — money that should be in circulation. It cuts both ways; some eat what they could sell; some sell what they should eat. A system of reasonable rent would benefit all."

"You may be right," Knut said. "I happen to be open minded and some of your arguments hold water, for me. In an academic way. But it will be the end of you."

But it was for this that he had left Altona, Struensee thought. Everything that had happened since had sprung from a wish to help the oppressed, from his seizing the unexpected opportunity. He did not believe in his father's God, but there were times when he felt the finger of destiny.

He went ahead. *Sign here; just your name.* The new laws forbade any Public Office to be bought, sold or bequeathed; such offices were the perquisites of the dwindling middle class and represented money invested. There was resentment about that, and about the policy of retrenchment in both public and private spending.

Madame Brisson wrote to her faithful friend who had always sent her patterns and descriptions of the latest Parisian fashions and whims, "It is hardly worth

275

your trouble to inform me any more. Her Majesty seems to be content with hunting dress in the morning and in the evening a gown a year old. It would seem invidious for any other lady to appear more fashionable. My business is almost at a standstill."

General Gahler, who had succeeded von Molkte as Commander in Chief of the Army, approved the new laws, so far as they affected him. "Clodhoppers, pulled away from their mothers. Give me the volunteer, every time. Volunteers don't chop off their thumbs in order to get back to mother and her apple dumpling."

The bill, making the serfs free, abolishing day labour and any other imposition except reasonable rent and taxes paid direct to the State, was passed. Sign here. And Christian signed, writing the one word that made many of his subjects free men again.

Once it was done Struensee became conscious of the lassitude that followed achievement. But laws must not only be passed, they must be enforced. He recognized his own bone weariness; law-making by day, love-making by night. Had he been his own patient he would have said — Into bed with you; and stay there for forty-eight hours. But there was no rest yet. The law was so revolutionary and so far-reaching that the autocrat who supposedly had passed it must be cajoled into making public appearances; a somnambulist, hedged about by the watchful. Hardly anyone outside the immediate circle realized the King's true condition.

And then there was Caroline. If Struensee missed so trivial a thing as a hunt, or a drawing room, she would say, not with complaint, easy to deal with, but with love — It was not the same without you; or, I should have enjoyed it more had you been there.

There were times, not frequent, but a trifle too often to be comfortable for an idealist, in love, when a voice at the back of his mind asked — Is it possible for a man to have too much of love?

Part Five

CHAPTER
ONE

Copenhagen, June 1771

Alice had never, in all her life, received a letter. Now, on a lovely June morning, she received one from William Smith, in Germany.

It was written in his voice.

"Dear Alice, a nod being as good as a wink to a blind horse, I trust you get my meaning. There is bad weather brewing and why should you go down? If you come here I've changed my mind about marrying. Thursday is the Hamburg ship they'll take you on to pay at this end. But any other would do. Be *quick*. Your sincere friend, W. Smith. It is very comfortable here and I will do right by you."

She had never had a surname, or any family or sweetheart; never anything for herself, but here, laconic and offhand, was a proposal.

She remembered their last meeting; nine months ago, in September last year. She'd gone in for a cup of tea and found Smith sorting out what he considered useful things from the accumulated rubbish of years.

"It's come," he said, "Old Bernie got the sack. Not that he need worry, acres and acres in Germany. And we're taking all the nags."

She said, "I shall miss you."

He grinned. "You mean you'll miss the tea. Cheer up. I'll leave you the pot."

The rest of the visit was occupied by his telling her how he had at last shipped young Peppo off to Sir William Craven, with a label round his neck, with the address and an announcement that all charges would be paid on delivery; he reckoned, he said, that that was the best way of making sure the boy got there; and he reckoned, he said, that once Sir William had seen Peppo up he'd be grateful to W. Smith.

Finally they had shaken hands and parted; and here he was, asking her to marry him.

She got his meaning all right. Bad weather had been brewing ever since it became obvious that the Queen was again pregnant. (Mother of God, don't let it be like last time!) Some people said that it couldn't be the King's; other people said, vehemently, that it was. Bad weather would strike if that poor loony had one of his sensible spells and said — This is none of mine. And if that happened Alice would be there, in the thick of the fight.

She wrote, "Dear William, bad weather is when you stand by, so thanking you, I'll stay here. I'm glad where you are is comfortable. I hope young Peppo worked out all right. Your sincere friend, Alice. I use the teapot every day."

That was a lie; in palaces it seemed that the one thing you couldn't be sure of was a freshly boiled kettle of water. So the brown pot stood on a shelf and only very rarely did it remind Alice of the donor.

The talk that had reached Smith in Germany was loud and acrimonious in Denmark.

Young Axel von Staffeld's mother was a great gossip, and she was listened to because Axel was in a position to know. He said to her, "You are not to say that again, or to allow anyone to say it in your presence. With my own eyes I saw their Majesties in bed together; in November."

Count Rantzau, when he took the trouble, could make himself heard in a large and crowded room. "I deplore the man's politics as much as anybody: but this is calumny. Their Majesties were co-habiting in November, as I can bear witness. I entered the bedroom with a despatch."

"Yes, I did call Karl out," Count Schimmelmann said. "*And* I saw the colour of his blood. Any other *gentleman* who repeats such filth may expect my seconds to call upon *him*."

Juliana said to Prince Frederick, "One is now inclined to wonder who fathered the boy."

"Struensee was then in Altona."

"You know what I mean. Some other obliging friend. Frankly I never believed Christian to be capable."

"Why not? The village idiot usually has a large family."

He was eighteen now and had largely outgrown his deformity. It increased her bitterness to think that between him and the throne stood an idiot and a child of dubious paternity. Perhaps he was beginning to feel the bitterness, too; he had become less and less agreeable lately.

The serfs whom Struensee had freed felt that nothing, not even a Queen's favour, was too good for him; but they were not yet accustomed to freedom and had no way of making their opinion felt.

The great nobles — all landowners, were, with few exceptions, virulently opposed to the man who had come so far and so fast, and done too much too quickly. A man who took other people's property would do anything. But — and here was the difficulty — there was a tradition of fanatical devotion to the Monarchy and one hesitated to believe that the King was a cuckold, the Queen a trollop. Still, one must bear in mind that she was English and that many of Struensee's reforms were on English pattern. Every lady who had been persuasive in bed, every gentleman who had yielded an argument between the sheets, was bound to be a little suspicious.

The most salacious and venomous talk went on at the middle level amongst those who had lost profitable offices and sinecures and monopolies. It pleased them to think that the man who had hurt them, in the name of reform, was badly in need of reformation himself. He'd spent his days making laws and his nights breaking the seventh commandment. He'd ordered the streets of Copenhagen to be cleaned up, what about the Palace?

In Brunswick, Augusta, without much difficulty, believed the worst.

In England the Princess Dowager knew that if she believed it she would simply turn her face to the wall and die. So she refused to believe it; and went out and about more than usual, holding her head high, defying rumour.

Caroline spent the summer at Hirscholm, the prettiest of the Royal residences. Freddy and Tammi, at three-and-a-half, were old enough to begin to ride. They had identical ponies and Caroline, now bulky and slow, conscientiously divided her time between the two, dealing with one while a groom attended the other. She was fond of Tammi, who had charm of his own and who called her Mamma, but she was secretly gratified by Freddy's more fearless attitude. *My son is my son.* This was especially evident when it came to giving the ponies their tit-bits, held out on a flat palm. Tammi was inclined to flinch away; then the pony would nudge him. Once it pushed him over. The Crown Prince of Denmark said, "Freddy do," and offered the crust. Caroline wondered whether it would be against Johann's rule about absolutely equal treatment for both boys if, presently, she gave her son the little cockade with the magical bone in it. Not that there was anything in charms, of course; and she could make Tammi a cockade similar in every respect but one.

Despite the warm weather and her increasing discomfort, to which the stitch in her side contributed, she hoped that this baby would be a little late. The masquerade had been staged in November; *let me hold together until early August and thus defeat them all.*

285

But on July 7th, just as the groom had led the two ponies away and she was walking back towards the steps, at the top of which Alice sat sewing, the first pang struck. She bent over and it passed. When she reached Alice she released her clasp on the two plump, hot, leather scented little hands and said, "See to them . . . I think I . . ." Leaning forward a little she made what speed she could into the cool palace.

"You stay here," Alice said to the little boys, indicating the stretch of terrace. "If you move or get into mischief, I'll give you something to remember."

They knew what that meant. Alice was the most potent person in their lives. Alice openly accepted, for Caroline's sake, all Struensee's rules; some were good, and these she observed, some were daft, and these she ignored. No rewards, no punishments; so how could a child *learn*? Freddy and Tammi had both felt the weight of her thin hard hand and knew what she would give them to remember if they moved, or got into mischief. They began to turn somersaults.

This time it was almost too easy; she was hardly undressed and on to her bed before she was a mother again. This time a daughter; this time a child of love, beautiful from the first, plump compact, pink and white, born with a good head of hair and slatey blue eyes.

Everything now depended upon Christian's attitude.

They came to the mouth of his burrow and said, "Your Majesty is a father again. This time a daughter."

He said, "Indeed, indeed."

286

Heer Reventil shouted into the cave, "Would Your Majesty care to see the child?"

"If you say so." His good head had a whole list of things that could be said without causing any trouble or pain. This was one of them.

Little fragments of memory remained to him like the old brittle leaves of autumns long ago. There had been a baby, ugly; this was different and he granted the difference with the one word, "Pretty".

His Majesty's visit to his daughter and his remark that she was pretty was duly reported in the Press. One paper did venture to print a caricature of the scene, but the thing was a little too subtle to make much impact.

Caroline lay in her bed and made plans for her daughter whose life should be so very different from her own. Any suitor for the hand of the Princess of Denmark would have to come and be inspected; would ride, dance, talk; and the girl herself should say — this one.

Yet she was not wholly emancipated; when she looked into the future she thought of George's first-born, Prince of Wales. He was now nine years old — just the right difference, said to be so handsome that they called him Prince Florizel, and intelligent and high-spirited as well. And what a wonderful thing, it would be if, to the England that she had left so unwillingly and still yearned for, she could one day make the gift of a Queen, beautiful to look at and well brought up, and with a fresh strain of blood in her veins.

She lay there, feeding the child, dreaming her dreams; and this time she was up and well again within a fortnight.

There was still the little hurdle of the christening; and here Heer Reventil came into his own.

"I am well aware," he said to Struensee, "that with the medical men and with the general public, anything that cannot be proved by rule of thumb is dismissed as superstition. But I can say with absolute certainty that if His Majesty is to be present at, and take part in this christening ceremony, the moon *must* be consulted." He produced a little black book.

"This is not a diary in the accepted sense, Count Struensee. It is a chart. See for yourself."

Struensee took it and read, "Moon almost full; bad day"; "Full moon; very bad day. Peppo needed"; "Moon waning, better day; went to concert, seemed to enjoy it. Well behaved"; "Moon at nadir; almost rational; talked of old times."

"There is more in this than meets the eye, Count Struensee," Heer Reventil said. "I first noticed it with his lessons and suspected that lunatic was not a chance word."

"I know that people who plant seeds claim that those planted in the dark of the moon wax with it and outstrip those set a fortnight earlier, when it was on the wane. I always meant to test it out for myself, with radishes . . . but I never had time," Struensee said. He looked again at the little book; the writing was small

288

but clear as print and the pattern emerged; ridiculous, inexplicable by any medical reasoning, but plain.

Heer Reventil said earnestly, "I have thought about this a great deal. Most of us are ruled by the sun: Who is not happier more generous and more cheerful when the sun shines, and more dismal and bad tempered on a dull day? Who is not more timid in the dark? A thought that is only a thought at three in the afternoon can strike a deadly blow to the heart at three o'clock in the morning. You admit that. You are a doctor; did you ever ask yourself why so many people die at or around that hour."

"I never asked myself why, but it is true. Four out of five deaths occur between midnight and sunrise."

"Because," Heer Reventil said earnestly, "most people are ruled by the sun, which has a twenty-four hour cycle. These others, the lost people, subject to the moon, suffer greater variations, the moon being variable and the sun constant. I, personally, am very sorry for these lost ones, the moon people."

Taking a step backwards into the dark ages, Struensee said,

"Could you then, Heer Reventil, suggest a good date for Her Royal Highness' christening? Their Majesties have agreed upon the names. His mother's, Louise, and her mother's Augusta.

And when had that been agreed, Heer Reventil wondered. So far as he knew . . . No matter. What mattered was that he was being consulted, his theory about the moon and lunatics had not been scorned, his importance had not been under-rated.

"May I have back my book? I dated every page. Let me see now." He ruffled the pages and chose the date. The King's behaviour on the occasion appeared to confirm the theory and to justify the choice.

CHAPTER
TWO

Copenhagen,
Winter 1771-1772

Despite the lack of new dressed in the latest Paris styles
and the limitation upon the number of courses to be
served at any one meal, Copenhagen was gay again
that winter. The baby Princess was given a splendid
christening, quite as splendid as her brother's had
been. Some critics carped and said that this was
unusual in the case of a second child, and a female;
was it an attempt to make up to the child for the
suspicion and the talk? This attitude did not, however,
prevent those who held it from enjoying the festivities;
and the King, thanks to Heer Reventil's little book,
was able to appear, not only at the christening of
the child whom he thus accepted as his daughter,
Princess of Denmark, Duchess of Holstein-
Augustembourge, but at two or three immediately
subsequent functions.

Then came the wedding of Amalia von Danneberg to
Count Holmstrupp. Her old father, resigned now to
what he had thought of as a mésalliance, came creaking
into Copenhagen — bringing his own feather bed —

and managed to make an entirely original contribution to the political opinion in the capital.

Hitherto those few landowners who had not been opposed to the liberation of the serfs had been hot-headed young idealists, prone to talk about freedom and liberty and the rights of man: but old von Danneberg struck a practical note.

"The man's a genius," he said, meaning Struensee. "Rent is the answer. Whenever I tried to collect my just dues, the fellow who owed me most had two broken legs or an arm in a sling; he had five starving children and his woman was in the straw with a sixth. The pig was dead, a fox had taken the geese. I could have whipped the fellow, but what would that have put in my pocket? And I am a merciful man. I was steadily being ruined; I've been ruined for twenty years. Day labour — look back on how that was done. I swear that every time my day-labourers turned up, the ox was on three legs, the plough was broken, the scythe without a handle and the men either broken backed or coughing their lungs up. But rent — rent is a different matter; they *like* paying rent. You may laugh, but this is true. There's a widow on my place, six children; she's lived at my expense this last seven years. She never paid so much as a potato — what do the fools do, plant them upside down? I never had the heart . . . being a merciful man. In the ordinary way her oldest would be in the army now; as it was, he came along with the rent, the day before it was due as a matter of fact, but of course they can't count."

He was perhaps the first and most willing welcomer of the new order; but whether one liked it or not, there was proof that a clogged, moribund economy was moving. Struensee's abolition of the laws that snatched a boy into the army as soon as he was big enough to be useful was not without effect. Boys had endless reserves of energy; they would work on the family holding — now rented, and then rush out to work for pay, doing the work formerly done by laggard, grudging serf labour. Also prosperous serfs — and there were some — formerly afraid to show any sign of prosperity, because of the dues, men who had hidden their little hoards under the hearthstone or the mattress, now felt free to take out money which had been out of circulation, sometimes for many years, and buy new tools, better stock animals, and sometimes for their wives real gold rings to replace those of base metal that had served for forty years. Denmark was experiencing a mild, economic boom.

Struensee had always said that his reforms would not be the ruin of the country, but its making. Caroline was so glad for his sake, and for the sake of people like that poor woman harnessed to a plough. He was the saviour, not only of her life and sanity by giving her back her child, by giving her the inestimable gift of love; he was saving Denmark, too.

Juliana the Queen Mother, who had come from Fredensborg for the christening of the baby who was her step-grandchild; stayed on. There was a ballet, an opera, a concert. The re-opening of her salon was warmly welcomed.

Of the day of the Holmstrupp wedding Heer Reventil wrote, "A disastrous day?" And the moon had nothing to do with it; by Heer Reventil's calendar the King should have been as capable on this day as he had been at the christening of his daughter; a bit somnambulant, vacant-looking if you came close, which few people were allowed to do, but well-behaved, quiet, withdrawn.

But by some strange chance it had not been that way at all. And the ridiculous thing was that the day had started rather well. Any uninformed person, seeing his Majesty at breakfast would have believed him to be completely normal, a young man whose slow speech and movement could be attributed to a lethargic nature and gathering weight. But within an hour he proceeded to go mad — if an already demented person could be said to go mad. He became noisy and violent, talking loudly and somewhat incoherently about women as black as crows, women with hair like the beards of old men, and how the two could be confused. "But he should be warned. Hurry, hurry. Send Axel on a good horse. *He must be told*. I loved him — he never loved me — but he was my one true friend. *I am King of Denmark. I will not have him ruined as I was*. All this about two heads, nobody believes me but it is true. I made mine come together; she didn't even try. Is that fair? *Knut must be told*." Christian glared at Heer Reventil and said, "If nobody else will dare to, I will. I'll do it now."

294

In no time at all Peppo's muscular services were required. Then Christian wept and tried to pour into Heer Reventil's shrinking ears an account of his love for that one true friend who had never even been grateful. He seemed to sense that Knut had gone forever and began to speak of him as if he were dead — which, so far as the King and Court and Copenhagen were concerned, he might as well have been. Knut, having obtained exactly what he wanted, wealth, property, the Order of Matilda and a well-connected wife, retired with his spoils. He intended to make Vidborg the most prosperous place in Denmark and to enjoy life. Let Brandt be First Gentleman of the Bedchamber. Something more than a desire for private life activated Knut. Like his forefathers, like William Smith, he could sense bad weather brewing.

Caroline did not sense bad weather, but she sometimes had a little superstitious feeling that such happiness could not last. She had, in effect three children, the two little boys, romping and growing like puppies, the new baby in the grand state cradle thriving, every day more beautiful. The dangerous corner had been safely rounded, and the fact that there had been danger had done the seemingly impossible, welded her and Johann even closer together. Now that his most revolutionary law was passed and seen to be working he was more completely hers. He had only one more major reform to make; something to do with the activities of lawyers: the pressure to which he had been subject, the need to do everything, was easing off; he excused himself from

295

Court functions less frequently; he came down the spiral staircase more often.

When she felt her happiness threatened the thing she feared was that something might happen to him; a collapse from over-working, over-loving; or something deadly caught in the pursuit of his work, half-medical, half-political. His campaign to clean up Copenhagen and make it the healthiest city in Europe took him into some insalubrious places: he had only to hear of some sea-faring man carried from a ship suffering from some exotic disease and off he'd go, dropping everything, in order to investigate, to see for himself that the quarantine rules which he had initiated, were observed.

"You don't know," she once said to him, "what I suffer for fear something might happen to you."

"I do, darling, from the moment that you told me you were pregnant, I went through that mill. Knowing what had happened before. You should have no fear for me. A doctor who has not succumbed to this, that or the other by the time he is thirty is likely to live out his full span. You must not worry."

There had been a time when hurried and busied, and on occasions weary, he had asked himself whether a man could not have too much of love. He had learned the answer to that. There was the work, which must be done; the ends that must be reached; and for a while, a year perhaps, he had in a way grudged the time, the energy which — nobody to blame for this but himself — he had been diverted. He was wiser now; a man however busy, however devoted to crusades, needed the soft, secret place where nothing else mattered, except to

296

be himself, and to be accepted as himself. He had set himself a course and as he ran it, he had been tempted by the forbidden fruit in a weak moment; and found it not as his father would have said, a dead sea apple, but sweet and satisfying and completely his own.

A few days before Christmas Louise-Augusta fell ill and developed a rash. Johann said it was measles and that the boys would certainly catch it; just as well to get it over and done with, since the disease was apt to be accompanied by complications later in life. Neither of the other children, however, showed any sign of indisposition, and this, and the fact that the baby's rash disappeared very suddenly and completely, confirmed Caroline's suspicion that the baby had actually suffered an attack of Grandfather's Stripes. But the illness had already been announced as measles and since no one wished to come into contact with a woman who was suckling and nursing a child with that complaint, Caroline had a completely private and very happy Christmas in the nursery. She also missed, but did not mind missing, the festivities with which the year 1772 was ushered in.

CHAPTER
THREE

Copenhagen, January 1772

Juliana, at forty-two, had come to the point where woman's behaviour often justifies the term "change of life". Where faithful wives take lovers, spinsters and widows make injudicious marriages, careful women indulge in disastrous investments. Now, looking back she believed she saw where her mistake had been made; she had depended too much upon chance and circumstance to come to her aid; she had been passive where she should have been active.

Her apartments on the first floor of the Christiansborg had been, ever since her return to the capital, a rallying ground for malcontents. She moved among them, watchful, calculating. She observed Count Rantzau, he who had been so insistent that there could be no doubt about Princess Louise-Augusta's parentage. About that he had not changed his mind, he was a loyal monarchist, and it was as a loyal monarchist that, sitting in the Cabinet, he had been deeply shocked to learn that a Bill, taken by Struensee to the King for his signature, had been brought back bearing instead of the one word "Christian" the words, "By order of His Majesty the King: Struensee."

298

(Christian now had periods when he could not be bothered to reach out that elongated arm and sign his name; and Struensee, working against time, was impatient.)

Count Rantzau said, in his carrying voice, "In my opinion that is forgery. I would have resigned from the Cabinet there and then except that I feel that my resignation would be welcome."

Heer Guldberg, who was a lawyer, but well enough connected on his mother's side to have access to Juliana's circle, said,

"Technically it is not forgery; no counterfeit signature was involved. It was an undue assumption of power, which, if not checked, could lead to anarchy. It implies," he looked round at the company, every member of whom had great possessions, "that I could sell any property, by order of — and the owner's name, signed Guldberg. That would be anarchy."

Somebody said, "Struensee thinks he is King."

"And why not? Who but a King sleeps with a Queen?"

"That is a remark which I hotly resent," Count Rantzau said, swinging around with his "calling out" face. Nobody wished to be called out by Count Rantzau; nobody had made that remark.

There were other remarks, made and stood by.

General Eichstadt regarded the reduction of the army as deliberate sabotage. "Very shortly England will be at war with her American colonies; France will join in. There will be a situation of which, but for Struensee, Denmark could have taken advantage. It is complete nonsense to say that one volunteer is better than ten pressed men. It takes ten shots to lay ten pressed men low; one shot can dispose of one volunteer, however willing and cheap he may be."

Colonel Knoller agreed.

Juliana had very little difficulty in picking her team and she had no fear of lack of support. Old Count Dannberger might gloat over his rents and praise the new regime, but for one of his opinion there were fifty who differed. There were those who had exacted more than their dues and found rent a poor substitute; there were those who had deliberately made the new way hard to work and seen their freed serfs load up their few possessions and trudge off in search of more accommodating landlords.

Everyone agreed that Struensee must be brought low before he ruined the country absolutely but . . . Even when she had picked her team, and the goal — Struensee's downfall — was sighted and agreed, there was no unanimity with regard to the rules by which the game should be played.

General Eichstadt and Colonel Kneller were soldiers; they accepted the fact that in any engagement there must be casualties; people who simply were in the way and must be mown down in order that the enemy could be reached. Heer Guldberg was indifferent. But Count Rantzau and her own son, Frederick, thought that the Queen should be left out of the whole affair. Plot against Struensee, by all means, chop off his head, have him drawn and quartered; nothing was too bad for him. But why involve the Queen?

"Because it is necessary," said Juliana, who, over Christmas, over New Year, had taken Caroline's place as first lady and meant never, never again to be deposed. "Nothing but a charge of criminal communication with the Queen — which is treason, can bring him down completely. You must see this. To rid ourselves of him we must bring a capital charge."

"And blacken Her Majesty's name?" Count Rantzau asked.

"Could it be blackened more?" Juliana said. She had noted that even in the free-spoken company in her salon, even those who were disposed to believe that Struensee and Caroline were lovers, were inclined to say things like "old enough to be her father", and "taking advantage of youth and innocence", but the guilt was tacitly admitted.

She said, "What I propose will in fact *clear* her name. Both must be arrested, for the sake of formality; he goes to strict confinement, the Queen to a comfortable place. He will deny the charge of criminal communication; then, a little pressed upon, he will admit it. But she will continue to deny it. Then he is guilty of violating Her Majesty, by claiming to be what he never was. Can you see?"

Heer Guldberg had schooled her well.

"There are too many suppositions for my liking," Prince Frederick said. "Suppose he denies and continues to deny. The capital charge will not be proved and the Queen will have been uselessly humiliated." He had no doubt of the guilt; but when he thought of the young, innocent creature who had arrived at Roskilde, found herself married to an idiot and then thrown into close contact with an experienced seducer he could blame her for nothing worse than silliness and lack of judgment.

Count Rantzau said, "I dislike the term "pressed upon". What pressure can be put upon a man to make him admit a crime which will cost him his head?"

"An appeal to his vanity," said Juliana. "He is a very vain man. Skilled lawyers know how to take advantage of weaknesses of character."

She could speak with confidence, for behind her front team she had another, picked men, haters of Struensee, ready to take over the administration, willing to take orders from her.

"I still contend," Prince Frederick said, "that it would be far better to charge Struensee with what he has indubitably done and leave the Queen out of it altogether."

Juliana looked at him with impatience, but of course, dear boy, he did not know all.

She said, "The other charges, peculation of funds, mishandling the Crown Prince — what do they amount to? Not enough to hang him. In gaol or in exile he would be the focus of plots for the next twenty years. With the people who profited by his reforms he is very popular. There will be outcry enough when his policy is reversed without him lingering somewhere waiting for riots and shouts of 'Bring back Struensee'."

"That is a point to be considered," Count Rantzau said.

"And here is another," Prince Frederick was stubborn. "If the Queen is accused, England will not like it."

"England has troubles enough of her own. As for being accused, is she not being accused now, in every coffee house, in every ale-house, in all but a few homes? Isn't the baby known as Little Cuckoo? I'm sure that if the whole situation could be explained to Caroline she would agree that this was the one way to clear her name, for good. Unfortunately . . ."

Unfortunately. Here at least they were in agreement. Even Count Rantzau, who believed, because he must believe, that a Princess of Denmark was the daughter of the King of Denmark, knew that it would not be safe to take the Queen into confidence. She so fully approved of Struensee with all his English-flavoured laws.

Arguments such as these were lengthy and repetitive. Once, when they were alone together, Juliana said to her son,

"Don't you *wish* to be Regent?"

"Of course I do. I wish to save Denmark." He knew Christian to be an idiot; he believed Struensee to be a villain; he felt within himself the ability to make an excellent Regent, capable of undoing the harm already done and of fighting off the threatened anarchy. "I simply wish that I could become Regent without wading through a lot of filth. And there is another thing; this will strike a blow at Royalty everywhere."

"That is nonsense. It will strike a blow against upstarts like Struensee and the Royal person concerned

303

will emerge unscathed — or do you doubt that? Do you believe that they will both confess?"

"I think neither will; and we shall be left exactly where we were."

"No!" she said, "No! With the removal of Struensee you will be Regent. That in itself is enough to justify . . ."

Yes, I shall be Regent — and *you* will be surprised.

At the moment she was dominant and he was but one voice, sometimes half-heartedly backed up by Rantzau. Once he was Regent he would not only save Denmark, but Caroline too. She had been foolish, but excusably foolish, in taking up with that great, clumsy, self-opinionated oaf, but the Prince Regent would rehabilitate her; she would be the first lady in Denmark, he would show her every respect. Denmark had its heir; there would be no need for the Regent to marry.

He looked ahead. He did not believe that Struensee would confess; on minor charges he would go to gaol or into exile. The poor infatuated child — he always thought of her as the fifteen-year-old, a little bewildered, at Roskilde — would grieve for a while; but she would recover. He would lift all these parsimonious rules that Struensee, the Lutheran pastor's son, had imposed, he would argue that when you were poor it was essential to *appear* rich; and on many glittering occasions the Queen of Denmark and the Regent would stand or sit, side by side . . .

CHAPTER
FOUR

Copenhagen,
January 16-17th 1772

A masked ball, the gayest and least formal of functions took place on the evening of January 16th. Heer Reventil had chosen the date, though with rather less assurance than he had shown on former occasions. The King's behaviour on Count Homstrupp's wedding day had slightly shaken his faith in his moon theory, and since then what he called "good" days had become less frequent. It was on what should have been a good day that Christian had refused, absolutely, to sign some document for Count Struensee; he had on that occasion been equally impervious to Heer Reventil's coaxings. He had become violent, too.

Struensee knew exactly what was being said, even by his picked Cabinet, about that signature and he was anxious that the King should make an appearance, looking like a man who could perfectly well sign his name but had not bothered to do so, trusting everything to his Prime Minister; he wanted the King and Queen to be seen in public, and on good terms together, and both on good terms with himself. This crumbling façade needed to be propped up for just a little while longer. He thought, with longing, of the day when he could let it fall, when he could abandon this masquerade — on the political front. He had already drawn up a rough draft of a proposed Constitution of Denmark, based not on universal suffrage, even his progressive ideas did not extend so far, but on a limited vote by responsible citizens who could elect members for a Parliament which would, in its turn, choose and appoint ministers. Once this was done, and he hoped that having forced through so much in so short a time, he might bring it about by Easter, it would no longer matter if Christian's real state of mind were known. The poor mad man could be left in peace. Autocracy in Denmark would be at an end. The Parliament could choose its own figurehead — a Regent. It might propose Caroline, but he would advise her against accepting, she was so completely non-political, so completely a domestic creature. He would opt for Prince Frederick. And if he, himself, were invited to serve as Prime Minister, he would of course accept and do his best to guide the young Parliament's first wobbly steps: if not he would not mind; his job was done. Starting off in 1768 as the King's personal physician he had completely changed Denmark; *and without a drop of blood shed.* That fact particularly gratified him.

When he looked ahead, beyond Easter 1772 when he hoped that his real work would be done, his ideas were somewhat vague. So much depended upon the Parliament he intended to bring about. This year he would be thirty-five, a young man still, by years, but he had — long before he left Altona — always done two men's work in half the time. He thought idly of himself, semi-retired and acting in a consultant capacity; of Caroline rearing the children; the eyes of the world no longer so sharply focused on them; but there would be time to think of that, later. For the moment, because he had in a moment of desperation dispensed with the King's signature; and because his latest reform dealt with the regulation of law-suits and had set every lawyer in the land against him, and even Brandt had said, "Meddling with lawyers is always dangerous," it was necessary for the King to appear and behave well at this masked ball where narrow little bands of black velvet conferred a purely supposititious anonymity.

Arranging it, Caroline said, "Darling, we shall be able to dance together. Just once. Everybody else will be so concerned with partners not available at ordinary balls, nobody will notice us."

As with so much else in a stultified and stylized society, the masked ball had its rules, never broken. Until midnight when everyone unmasked, nobody knew anybody, all were strangers, and when midnight struck and the music stopped and the trumpeter blew a great blast, expressions of surprise, some genuine, many false, were in order . . . Gracious, who would have thought?

Struensee said, "So long as you dance with *him*, too."

"Even masked he would never ask me."

"Then *you* must ask *him*. Darling this is very important. If you could so contrive it that at the moment of unmasking, when everybody is laughing and saying who would have thought, you could be there, beside him, laughing . . . it would make a good impression and be immensely helpful to me."

"I will see to it," she said. "But the Running Steps I wish to dance with you. What with one thing and another I never have, and it is the best dance of all."

Except in a cotillion, as one of eight, she had not dared, since Luneberg, to dance with Johann at all. The new dance, just come from Vienna, called sometimes Running Steps and sometimes the Waltz, she had only tried, being careful, being discreet, with her brother-in-law, Prince Frederick, who, despite his slight physical malformation, was an excellent dancer. The Running Steps was quite different from any other dance where one touched hands, or linked arms at most; in the new dance the partners almost embraced. It was considered very daring and many old-fashioned people refused to try it at all. It was always accompanied by soft, sweet music with a distinctive beat, so that conversation was possible between partners, and unlike many dances it was very easy, nothing to remember, simply the one, two three. It was not running, that was a misnomer; it was gliding, and with Prince Frederick it was delicious; with Johann it would be heaven.

Despite Heer Reventil's fears, the King was co-operative and seemed to understand what was required of him. Brandt took charge of him and for a few moments stood beside him, in a prominent, somewhat isolated position — The King, in converse with a friend, watching his guests enjoy themselves.

Christian had decided to sleep inwardly as he had through so many functions, to stay in his secret cave and let nothing disturb him. But the light of thousands of candles in glittering chandeliers and wall sconces, the sound of the music, the myriad-coloured dresses and uniforms roused and excited him; he began moving his head and tapping his foot, and then, breaking away from Brandt, pushed his way into the nearest group of dancers, then engaged in the third figure of a cotillion. The gentleman thus displaced stood aside; the ladies — considering themselves honoured — made extra and more profound curtseys. Christian blundered through the dance, muddling all the moves as he had often done before, but remembering to bow at the end and to kiss the fingers of the lady whom he had partnered.

Brandt, the watchful, joined him as soon as the last chord sounded and Struensee made his way towards them. Then Christian said in a puzzled way, "Where's Knut? And Conrad?" He repeated the question in a louder, more demanding tone.

"Somewhere about," Brandt said, soothingly, "with the masks it is hard to tell."

There was something wrong with that; I know you, you're Brandt. I know Struensee, too. So where are the others?

At this moment Caroline rustled towards them; partly in pursuance of the usual policy of keeping him, on such occasions, buffered from the uninitiated; partly so that what Johann wished to be seen, should be seen, the three of them together, in accord; and partly so that when the music began again she would be so close to

309

Christian that he must ask her to dance — if he failed to then she would ask him.

He knew her too. He'd wanted Knut and he'd got Matilda! He gave his high, shrill laugh, and moving quickly behind her put his hands to her waist and shouted, "Charles, lead the Kerhaus!" He had himself dismissed Prince Charles of Hesse from Court more than three years before. The Kerhaus was always the last dance, but Brandt, with presence of mind, acted as though the order had been given to him and shouted, "The Kerhaus! The Kerhaus." Anything was better than risking Christian losing his temper; and the Kerhaus always ended in such confusion with the re-arrangement of clothes and hairdresses and the search for cool drinks and ices that it might be able to get the King safely away. Brandt was finding his job as first favourite, first Gentleman of the Bedchamber, a heavy responsibility and he looked forward eagerly to the day when Struensee would have completed his programme and the whole pretence could end. He proceeded to lead a fast and furious Kerhaus, intent upon exhausting everybody, of reducing Christian to a state where he would volunteer to go to bed. On his own hips, where the brocaded jacket flared out, the Queen's hands lay lightly. On Caroline's waist Christian's hands, now full of the lunatic strength which occasionally tested even Peppo's muscles, clenched like an iron girdle, tighter, tighter, harder and harder. His left hand pressed on the site of the pain which was never quite quiescent, but with which she had learned to live. She could no longer wear her stays tightly laced, and all her dresses had been let out at the waist. Certain postures exacerbated the pain, and she had learned to avoid them. The pain also increased in moments of agitation; but it had never been like this. She turned her head and said over her shoulder,

"Christian, please. Don't hold me so tightly. You are hurting me."

He let out one of the whooping calls that accompanied the Kerhaus and squeezed harder. Nobody would have believed that any man, any manual labourer, could have had such strength in his hands.

She said into Brandt's ear, "Shorten it, please. I have no breath."

He pretended not to hear; the more breathlessness, the more dishevelment, the better.

Keeping her right hand in position on Count Brandt's beautiful coat, she released her left and reached for Christian's fingers; they were rigid, cataleptic. The sweat of agony broke out on her face and dripped down, like tears. She set her teeth and endured. But when the Kerhaus ended, what with pain and breathlessness, she was barely conscious and it was her despairing grip — I must hold on, I must hold on — which, growing heavier and more retarding on the flare of his beautiful coat, that eventually brought Brandt to a standstill.

Then in the general confusion, Brandt took Christian away and handed him over to Heer Reventil — Peppo hovering in the background — and said, "Not bad, not good either." And Christian, backing away into his secret burrow thought with satisfaction that anyone

311

who forced him out of it, would be sorry, would be punished, would say "please".

Ladies repaired the ravages of the premature Kerhaus; gentlemen quenched their thirsts. There was still some time to go before midnight and there was one waltz before the unmasking. She danced it with Johann and was restored. He had, she thought, giving her still aching body into his embrace, the truly healing touch.

"Has it gone as you wished?" she asked.

"It could not have gone better."

He sounded satisfied and she decided not to tell him now about what she had suffered in the Kerhaus. Instead she said, in time with the music,

"I *love* you. *I* love you. I love *you*."

After midnight, masks removed, all pretence at anonymity discarded, she danced the second waltz of the evening with Prince Frederick who seemed quite unlike himself. He had what Caroline thought of as a pretty wit; for her he had enlivened dozens of dull functions. They had a silly private joke between themselves — every human being resembled some animal; it was silly, but there was enough truth in it to merit — afterwards — a serious thought. Tonight there were no jokes, no comparisons to pussycats, butterflies carthorses . . .

She said, "That Kerhaus completely exhausted me. Did it tire you, too?"

Juliana had never once, never once admitted that he was not completely physically able and he, from early youth had adopted the same attitude. Let nobody pity me!

"No. It was too early, that was all. But if you are tired . . ."

"Not in the least. I have recovered my breath; and this is my favourite tune."

He felt like Judas Iscariot . . . no, that was a ridiculous comparison. Iscariot had had no power, or come to that, any wish to protect.

One, two, three.

He said, "I should not wish you to be overtired, or *in any way distressed*. Trust me; I am your friend."

She thought that, exhausted by the Kerhaus, he had taken a little too much of the ice-cooled wine. There was a kind of vehemence in the last words, utterly unlike his usual light, almost flippant way of talking.

She said, "Then give the signal. I *am* tired."

It was part of the ritual. The gentleman dancing with the first lady present at any ball had only to lift his hand. The musicians recognized the sign and ceased to play dancing measures. Twenty minutes, at most half an hour of pleasant little tunes, making a background sound for the departures, and then they would be done.

Carriages, in strict order of precedence, lined up and rattled away. The musicians packed their instruments. Yawning pages doused candles and stoked stoves. Window by window the great palace darkened. It was a night of frost, the stars crystal clear and sharp.

The guards, men specially chosen by Colonel Knoller, took the few steps allowed them, this way, that way, not enough to warm their feet, and blew on their fingers, and cursed the cold.

313

★ ★ ★

Caroline listened by the nursery door. For this one evening the cradle had been taken from her bedroom lest her late return should wake the baby.

Anna Peterson was waiting to help her undress and to brush her hair.

"Just take it down Anna. No brushing. I am tired."

She was soon in bed and asleep.

Struensee slept too; he had spent most of the previous night with Caroline, had been busy all day, had danced vigorously.

Christian was the first to be awakened and he took it badly. For inside the comfortable cave, there was yet another sleep; and from this inner sanctum he was dragged, by voices, by lights, by somebody shaking his shoulder. Jerked into the open he recognized the three people by his bedside; his stepmother, his half-brother, Count Rantzau. Waking him, shaking him, by candlelight. He did not speak but he made a gesture of dismissal, brushing them away.

Juliana said, "You must wake up, Christian, and sign some papers."

She was the first woman — the only woman — to whom he had been attracted; dark haired, voluptuously curved, sweet-scented and often seeming to be on his side. But what a wicked thought that was: your father's wife! Wicked, wicked boy. Then Knut; wicked again. But he'd finished with all that. Mentally backing away and taking refuge in his cave, he said, "No".

Juliana said, "Christian you must sign. There is a plot. A plot to kill you. Do you understand me? Unless you sign your name you will be killed."

"Tell Struensee," Christian said and turned into his pillow, away from the lights and the faces and the voices. "Go away."

Heer Reventil who slept in the adjoining room came padding in, his nightcap awry, asking what was the matter; asking it once without ceremony and then with little bows.

"His Majesty must sign these orders," Juliana said. "There is a plot to kill him which we have just discovered."

"To kill . . . ?"

"It is an order for an arrest," Prince Frederick said.

"Come, come, now Your Majesty," Heer Reventil said, upset by this talk of killing but not averse to exercising his power. "You have only to write your name. Just write your name. You do it so well. You write your name very nicely. Write it for me."

Reluctantly Christian came to the opening of his cave and reached out that long arm that he imagined and wrote his name twice. Seeing him do it, without a question or a glance at what he was signing, justified them all in their own eyes. And they felt even more justified when, drawing back into his refuge, Christian remembered that he was King of Denmark.

"Now go away. Leave me to sleep or I'll have all your heads off tomorrow."

Colonel Knoller had not even waited for the order of arrest to be signed. He went, with two soldiers, one

315

carrying a lantern, into the room where Struensee slept, took him by the shoulder and said, "Get up. You are under arrest."

Struensee had the trained doctor's trick of passing from sleep to full consciousness in half a second. Three armed men, and behind them his personal page, Arild, with a newly lighted candle in his shaky hand.

"Arrest?" he said. "Show me your warrant."

"That will be forthcoming. Get up."

"Arrest without warrant is now illegal in Denmark," Struensee said.

"That can be argued about tomorrow. Will you come, or be taken?"

Three of them, armed — even the one with the lantern had his hand on his sword hilt.

"You have the better of me. Allow me to get into my breeches."

Calm began to desert him as he dressed under their hostile eyes. What had happened? What did it mean? What of Caroline? What of the King?

"Can you tell me why I am being arrested?"

"There are several charges; they all amount to the same thing — Treason."

"Ludicrous," he said. "His Majesty has no more loyal . . ."

"That I prefer not to discuss."

Struensee thought he understood it. Knoller and a few other malcontents, upset about the reduction of the army, had staged a *coup*. Kidnap the Prime Minister; show him what a few determined soldiers could do. Such tricks had worked in the past, but this one would not; not in a progressive, properly governed country like Denmark in 1772.

"Where are you proposing to take me?"

"To the Blue Tower."

Many of his recent laws had been designed to take the dread out of that ill-reputed place; it and all the other prisons in the country were now places where men awaited trial or took their just punishment. A man could no longer simply disappear . . . Nevertheless, the name had, from long association, a sinister sound.

"In that case, Arild, I'll need my top coat." He caught sight of the boy's bleached and stricken face and said quickly, "There's no need to look like that, Arild. Law will be back in the saddle by dinner time tomorrow."

Arild doubted it. Armed men didn't take a man out of his bed at three in the morning, and say "Treason" and say "The Blue Tower" in order to turn him loose next morning. He snatched at Struensee's hand and kissed it and gulped out some valedictory words, "The best and kindest master . . ."

"Get out of the way," Colonel Knoller said.

When they had gone, Arild remembered that written words could be dangerous; and Struensee's apartments, even his wardrobe, held many papers. Arild gathered them together quickly and pushed them into the stove which belched and smoked under the load, and had to be poked. Most of them were government papers, but alongside them into the stove went Struensee's almost completed book about innoculation, quoting the Crown Prince of Denmark as an outstanding example of its

317

efficacy; and there were two little notes from Caroline, saved because they were of an uncompromising nature; and there were some minatory letters from Struensee's old father, the pastor in Altona. They had been saved bacause it amused Struensee to see how very wrong the old man had been: "My son, you have not the strength of character to support power;" and "Your ambition has always exceeded your ability." Echoes of his under-rated, repressed and harshly criticized youth, he had preserved them as proof of how wrong even a godly man could be.

They all went into the stove and were consumed. And only just in time. Arild was not alone in realizing the importance of words on paper. When, within an hour, others came searching they found nothing and went away empty-handed.

Caroline was accustomed to wakening suddenly; a child crying, Johann able, after all, to come. So, abruptly disturbed she was instantly alert, not frightened and said "Yes, Alice," as was her custom. Then focusing her eyes, she saw Mantel, her favourite page, lighting candles, and just inside the door Count Rantzau, Colonel Eichstadt and Heer Guldberg. Am I dreaming? No. Three men, one of whom she looked upon as a friend, two known and recognizable, but virtual strangers, in my room. Why?

She raised herself on her elbows, and saw that by the nursery door, Alice stood, barefooted in her nightgown.

She said, "What is the matter? Why are you here?"

January nights were long; January mornings very dark. Have I overslept?

The three men jostled each other; a step this way, a step that. Then Colonel Eichstadt came forward, a paper in his hand and said,

"Madam, we have an order for your arrest."

"Show me," she said. "Mantel, please bring a candle nearer." She was, far inside herself, surprised at her calm; had Alice, from the other side of the room, spoken of a child coughing, wakeful, she would have been out of bed, barefoot, agitated, out of breath. But this was different; she took the paper, read the horrible charge — criminal communication with Count Struensee, and recognized it as the polite, legal term for adultery. She heard again the old Queen Mother's rasping voice — ordinary women commit adultery, Queen's commit treason.

Fear clamped down.

"You will find it in order," Heer Guldberg said. "And it is signed."

As had happened with her before, fear produced its own antidote. It would never do to show her fright. She looked up and said, "*You* are not in order, Heer Guldberg. Until this charge is proved, or I give you permission to do otherwise, you will address me correctly."

In the big bed she looked small; her face, blurred with sleep and surrounded by the unbrushed hair had little beauty, but there was something about her at that moment that roused the first doubt in Count Rantzau's mind. His fanatically royalist blood ran hot, ran cold, ran thorny, recognizing the mystique of divine right. He knew then that he should have sided more firmly with

319

Prince Frederick. It should not have been done this way.

He said, "Your Majesty, this is little more than a formality. I swear that you will suffer no discomfort or indignity."

She was already thinking of Johann.

"Withdraw while I dress," she said. The door had hardly closed behind them when she was out of bed, running to the nursery door. Alice was almost dressed.

"Alice — out the other way. Warn Count Stru . . ."

Alice made a little sound to show that she understood, ran to the outer door, opened it cautiously, closed it noiselessly.

"Guarded."

"This way, then," Caroline gasped, and ran to the mirror panel and worked the catch. "Take a candle . . ."

Alice scuttled up the spiral stairs and almost immediately descended them again, moving at breakneck speed.

"He's gone. There's only Arild, burning papers."

"Thank God!" His room empty and a page burning papers offered a hope that Johann had been warned.

"Did you shut the door at the top?"

"It shut itself; nearly caught me by the skirt."

"Did the boy see you?"

"No. He was by the stove, rattling away with the poker."

Nothing in the girl's face or manner showed that she had just been precipitated into the middle of a secret, or that she had sustained the shock of her life. She'd known what was being said, but she had always argued

320

with herself that it was impossible; miles of corridor, flights of stairs, guards everywhere, how could it have been done? People who spread such tales didn't know what they were talking about. Now she understood and thought — And me in the next-door room!

She gave no sign.

"Help me to dress, please," Caroline said. How much warning had he received? In which direction had he gone?

"Will they be moving you?" Alice asked.

"I suppose so." Where did they lodge Queens accused of treason?

"Better dress warm, then," Alice said, just as though Caroline proposed to take a walk on an inclement day.

She was almost dressed, her own ice-cold fingers fumbling with buttons, Alice's equally cold, pinning her hair into some sort of order, when she thought of the children, especially the baby, not yet weaned. She caught her breath, Alice said,

"What about the children?"

"I do not know. I shall try to insist on taking the baby. Wherever I am will be the best for her. The boys — they might be happier here. And Alice, please make up some tale: you are so good at inventing, and I am so distraught just now, but make up some tale. Whatever anybody else says, tell them I shall be back soon."

As of course she would be; nobody knew; nobody could prove anything. Only Alice knew about the staircase.

"I suppose I must ask about the baby," she said as the last button, the last pin went home.

She went into the next room where the three men waited.

"I assume that you propose to remove me."

"To a safe and comfortable place," Count Rantzau said. "All that Your Majesty could possibly need . . ."

"I must take the Princess with me. Because she was unwell she was not weaned at six months. The process — vital in a child's life — has only just begun."

No plans had been made for the immediate future of the little girl, suspected of being Struensee's daughter. Heer Guldberg resenting his recent snub, said,

"We have no instructions, Your Majesty. His Royal Highness, the Crown Prince, naturally remains in the custody of his father, the King."

Who was himself in charge of a keeper.

"My daughter, the Princess Louise-Augusta, has only just recovered from measles," Caroline said. "If, in her present state a premature weaning is enforced, and anything untoward should happen to her, you will be held responsible." Her steady, level stare included them all. And again Count Rantzau flinched inwardly.

"I am sure," he said hastily, "that in the circumstances nobody would wish . . . Your Majesty may certainly take Her Royal Highness . . ."

And there, as though she had been waiting for the word, was Alice, cloaked and hooded, carrying the baby, warmly wrapped and sound asleep in the crook of her left arm and carrying in her right hand a bulging, bulky valise, its gaping top revealing some of the articles needed by a baby of six months old.

"We're ready," she said, addressing Caroline.

322

"But Alice . . . I thought . . . I wanted you to stay and see to the boys and explain."

"They'll be all right, Your Majesty. I did not come to Denmark to . . ." Blimey, she almost said "to tend brats." ". . . to tend children. I came to serve Your Majesty. His Majesty of England and the Princess Dowager of Wales approved my appointment and if I remained here while you were taken to another place, I should have failed in my trust."

Alice so seldom used titles that when she did they rang like new-minted coins. And behind the words there was the defiance of integrity. Let them hear it. Princess Caroline's brother was King of England; her mother was Dowager Princess of Wales. Let them all remember that.

"So," Alice said, "with Your Majesty's permission, I will carry Her Royal Highness, but the bag . . ." She had intended to hand it to Mantel, but he'd scuttled off. Typical, Alice thought. She ran her sardonic eye over the three men and fixed upon Colonel Eichstadt because he was splendid in his uniform. "If you would be so obliging," she said, and pushed the gaping valise into his hand.

He had never, in all his life, carried anything except a weapon, not even a spray of flowers to a lady. Out of sheer astonishment he took the revolting object and carried it as far as the head of the stairs, where, as was right and proper, a subservient figure slid alongside and murmured, "Allow me, Your Excellency," and relieved him of it.

323

★　　★　　★

Wolfgang Mantel had not slept soundly since his grandmother had sent him a Christmas cake. She lived at Zell, near Hanover, where she kept a poor little inn; and she had seemed quite agreeable when he said that he wanted to see the world. But the cake had called him home. In its centre was a pigeon feather and a sprig of the herb which represented regret — its spotted, bluish-green leaves were perfectly preserved and Mantel recognized it. The old woman could neither read nor write, but to the boy who, until he was twelve and grew ambitious, had been her companion, aide, confederate, the message was loud and clear. It said — *Come home or you will rue it*. He had not obeyed. He had eaten the cake, sharing it with his fellow pages; the feather and the sprig, now rapidly crumbling, he had placed amongst his hose. But since Christmas he had not slept well; waking jerkily and thinking — Is this what she warned me of? Or this? Or this?

On this night he had wakened from his light, uneasy sleep, become aware of a stir, thought, "Ah, she knew!" pulled on a few clothes and with a candle in his hand, gone along to the Queen's room. What was said there, meant only one thing to him — they were taking her away; and hustled out of the room when she dismissed them all in order that she might dress, he had slipped away, bundled his own absolute necessities together and then emerged determined, if possible, to go wherever *she* went, the beautiful, soft-spoken woman who was Queen of Denmark, who always said "please" when giving an order, and smiled.

324

With his own meagre belongings in a little pack, slung over his shoulder, Mantel took the valise from Colonel Eichstadt's hand and holding it fell into the rear of the procession making its way down the grand staircase. Of them all he was the only one who felt no fear, no doubt at all. The old grandmother's message inside the cake meant simply that she wanted him home. "Or you will rue it," was a purely superficial thing. Before he had left the *Sand Krug*, tucked into the edge of the forest, his grandmother had thrown the knuckle-bones for him and foretold, looking a little bewildered, that he would live to be eighty and be remembered in a book. So, in the dead hour of night, he walked confidently towards the waiting carriages, the gaping valise his passport.

They drove through the night, slowly, trusting almost as much to the instinct of the horses as to the pale, uncertain light of the carriage lamps. Day began with a faint grey light in the east; and then, veil by veil, darkness peeled away until all was grey. Grey land, grey sky, grey sea; and presently, in the grey a dark solidity of towers of pinnacles.

Elsinore! Caroline recognized it.

And I am come here. With Alice. I knew it, all along.

The seagulls wheeled and let loose their desolate cries.

CHAPTER
FIVE

Copenhagen, January 1772

The Blue Tower offered accommodation of varying kinds. There were rooms that were tolerably clean and fully furnished. Until Struensee had passed an act forbidding the practice it had been quite customary for fathers to obtain a *cachet* which enabled them to have unruly sons imprisoned there until they promised to mend their ways and be obedient: and nobody wanted his son back lousy and stinking.

Below ground there were other, different places, and as he was hustled down and down, green scum on the walls, steps growing damper and the graveyard smell everywhere, Struensee began to feel genuine alarm. Knoller and his friends must be very sure of themselves to dare treat him so infamously.

He, the law-giver, made one more stand for legality.

"It is against the law to confine even a guilty man in circumstances detrimental to his health," he said.

"Your law no longer runs in Denmark," Colonel Knoller said.

The cell seemed completely dark when he was first pushed into it, and he was obliged to feel his way about it in order to find something to sit upon: there was nothing, no bed, no stool; just an evil smelling, damp-feeling blanket which had been thrust in before the door clanged shut.

Presently he saw that the cell was not quite unlighted; in the centre of the ceiling there was a little grill, about the size of a book, through which the light of a lantern or a candle filtered.

When he dressed he had picked up his watch: he now found that by standing near the little ray of light and holding the watch high towards the grill, he could just see its face. It was four o'clock. The Cabinet was due to meet at ten in the morning and to hearten himself he chose to believe that it still would. He had done so much, in so short a time to put the government of the country on the right lines — not truly constitutional yet, but that would come — that he had faith in the Cabinet meeting, *coup* or no *coup*. Six hours to go.

At four in the morning in January, in Denmark, it was cold everywhere, but the cold in this stone cell was bone-piercing; he was glad of the blanket, despite its smell. And huddled in it, he entertained thoughts of the kind about which Heer Reventil had spoken.

Did you, Johann Frederick Struensee, work so fast and so hard because you sensed that your time might be short?

Did you, by yielding to love, condemn yourself? What other reason could there be for the accusation of treason? Lessening the numbers of the army? Not bothering about the King's signature? My son you have not the strength of character to support power.

As though he were his own patient he prescribed for himself; such thoughts must be opposed. Think cheerfully.

This was an attempt by the army to put the clock back and it would come to nothing. He was known as The Friend of The People; the people, once they knew where he was would pull down the place with their bare hands, stone by stone in order to liberate him. The King, demented as he was, would ask for Struensee. And Caroline . . . Great Heaven, if he failed to present himself, look at Freddy, Tammi and the baby, and drink the usual cup of coffee . . .

Treason! the voice in his head reminded him. Only in the act of love did you commit treason, and if, on that account, you are a traitor so is she! What will they do to her?

These were the standard night thoughts. Look at the time again. Half past four. The hours dragged their caterpillar length, horrible thoughts attacked him and he fended them off, and at the end of the year it was six o'clock in the morning. The first workers would be stirring now, huddling into their clothes, cramming down hasty breakfasts. Apprentices with blue chill fingers would be taking down shop shutters. Would there be in the streets any sign of the coup overnight? Posters? Chalked notices? Would the whisper start and run swiftly around, "Struensee is in the Blue Tower"?

At eight o'clock, after what seemed a lifetime, a light flickered behind the bars of the door and there was the sound of a shuffling step. An ancient man set down a lantern and opened a hatch in the bars and held towards Struensee a bowl of something wet and dark.

He was not hungry yet, but his other need was urgent. He voiced it. The old man seemed not to understand, or not to hear.

"I can make it worth your while to treat me properly," Struensee said. "For the hour or two I shall be here. Do you know who I am? Struensee; Count Struensee. By mid-day I shall be in a position to give you a pension." There was no response at all. The man was deaf. Deliberately chosen for this job?

He regretted that he had no money with him; nothing of value at all, save his watch and a ring which Caroline had given him; he was not yet desperate enough to part with either. Deliverance might come at any moment; it must. He made a motion of rejection towards the bowl; the gaoler withdrew it, slammed the hatch and shuffled away.

Despite the fact that he was not a dandy, and had accustomed himself, as a doctor, to look unmoved on blood and pus and vomit, he was an intensely fastidious man: it was with disgust that presently he used the furthest corner; a disgust not assuaged by the realization that some previous occupant of this dreadful place had been driven to the same extremity.

When I get out of here the first thing I do, the very first thing, will be to appoint prison inspectors. Laws are not enough; they are evaded.

After an eternity it was ten o'clock, and the light from the little grill was grey instead of yellow. Ten o'clock; and in the stately panelled room the Cabinet would be meeting now. His chair empty. He had chosen every member himself; Brandt was a personal friend and Rantzau had been one of the stoutest upholders of the baby's legitimacy. In half an hour now . . .

The time until midday passed so slowly that twice he thought that his watch must have stopped: at last he began to visualize the possibility of the whole Cabinet having been arrested; of Colonel Knoller in the Prime Minister's chair and his minions around the table; of Caroline under strict guard.

A government could be overset; he knew, he had done it himself when he dismissed the old Council and instituted the Cabinet. But I hurt nobody, he thought angrily: Bernstorff, my most rigid opponent, simply went to Germany to lives as a private gentleman on his estates. It was an honourable dismissal.

Treason!

He tried to be calm; he walked about the cell, five paces along each side, avoiding the corner of which he had again been forced to make use; he jumped and slapped his arms across his chest, restoring his circulation. He must keep his health and his sanity; when the next food was offered he must eat, though to do so in this place was a violation of every instinct.

Again and again he reminded himself that nobody could *know*; they'd been so very careful. Again and again he reminded himself that even if Knoller had taken over completely he couldn't simply push the ex-Prime Minister into an *oubliette* like this.

Daylight faded and was replaced by candle or lantern light in the grill overhead. At six o'clock the old man offered what seemed to be the same bowl and Struensee took it. It held some warmish liquid greasy and tasteless, and some bread crusts which had to be fished out with the fingers.

Struensee carefully wound his watch and looked at the time. Fourteen hours. For the first time it occurred to him that he was not going to be liberated. His friends were powerless, his enemies in control, and it was their will that he should stay here, treated as the worst felon should not be treated, until he died.

He took the watch key and made a little scratch on the back of the watch; one day.

On the second day he attempted to bribe the deaf man with a visible reward. He pulled off and held up the ring and then made gestures of sleeping, of spreading a mattress on the floor. It was impossible to sleep on the stone with only that one poor blanket. The old man appeared to understand; he nodded and grinned. And he took the ring. But he brought no bedding and Struensee was left to learn that it was possible to sleep on stone with only one poor blanket.

The watch bore four little scratches when he woke from sleep to aggravated discomfort and realized that he was ill. Every bone in his body; not only those in contact with the stone, ached with a grinding ache; his throat was sore and the shivering to which he was now accustomed alternated with hot sweating fits. Fever.

331

And here, without medicine, lying in filth and untended, fever had one predictable end.

His thoughts no longer had clarity or coherence. Death came to all. Death was preferable to living in this way. He had done his best. People were ungrateful. A good thing the old man was deaf, fever patients raved. Nobody must know. Poor Caroline, poor darling. Let her off lightly. Pity those who never knew such joy. Water, I need water. I tried to arrange it so that no one should lack any necessity, now I have not so much as a cup of water. I shall die. Death is the only lasting cure.

So he died, not easily, but quite quickly; and presently was resurrected, in a bed, in a sunny room. Strange, he'd never believed in life after death, had flung that away with everything else that his old father preached — except love thy neighbour. However, here he was, and comfortable, but weak, weak like the newborn; perhaps born again. Sleep.

When next he woke he was in the same bed, the same room, but less weak. This time he could turn his head and see the soldier on guard by the door; and as he turned his head something rasped on the blanket. Feebly he moved a flaccid hand and felt the beard, quite long. And inside his head his wits and his senses, temporarily scattered, fell into line again. In the weak, old man's voice that went with the beard, he said,

"Where am I?"

The young guard jumped as though he had been stabbed.

"It is not permitted to talk, Excellency."

"Why not?"

"It is an order. Forty lashes for disobedience."

Amongst other things he had forbidden flogging in the army except for the most heinous offences such as striking a superior officer. Your law no longer runs in Denmark.

Muting a voice already almost inaudible, he said,

"How long have I been here?"

The boy — he was nothing more, probably one of the last victims of the compulsory conscription at twelve — said,

"Three weeks." Then he opened the door and looked out into a whitewashed corridor, and came back, slightly reassured.

"The Blue Tower?" Struensee asked.

"Yes; the hospital."

"You have been on duty all the time?"

"Eight hours each day, Excellency. To talk is forbidden. I am supposed to inform . . ."

"Just tell me one thing. Did I rave?"

The boy said, "Constantly"; and then, with the unlettered man's acute perception he answered the unasked question. "Nothing to be made head or tail of. Doctor's stuff. You were afraid you would not pass your examinations and once you tried to innoc . . . innoc . . . you know the word, everybody, to save them from smallpox."

He hoped that this was true. And now his most urgent question must be asked in sidelong fashion.

"Is His Majesty well?"

"He is sick in the head; Prince Frederick is Regent."

"And Her Majesty?"

"She is in the castle of Kronborg at Elsinore. It is now necessary Excellency, that I should report . . ."

He lay and thought, for the hundredth time, that if anyone had *known* anything, he would have come forward in July. Nobody knew; nobody could prove anything.

I shall deny it, completely and categorically, to the last; and so will she, so will she . . .

CHAPTER
SIX

Carlton House, London, February 1772

"It has been my death-blow," the Princess-Dowager said.

George looking down on the supine, frail body of the woman who had always been so strong and so resilient, knew that this was no exaggeration. The news from Denmark, killing Mamma's will to live, had killed Mamma.

It had been a severe shock to him, too; and deep inside himself he admitted, sadly, that he was not resilient, not equipped to withstand shocks, or even minor irritations. And there were so many; not only political: his brother Henry, Duke of Cumberland, cited as co-respondent in the Grosvenor divorce suit and told to pay £13,000 in damages and costs, and then deserting his partner-in-guilt and marrying — everyone said they were married — a widow, with eyelashes a yard long. Everyone said that Henry, Duke of Gloucester, was married to another widow with whom he had lived openly for years. And now this!

What is wrong with this family?

He had to find something to say to comfort Mamma.

"It may not be true. Struensee had many enemies and Caro had little sense. When everything is told, her name may be cleared."

She was past the point now where protecting George was a main aim.

She said weakly, "Caroline is guilty."

"That has not been proved."

"It will be. She is. I've known — ever since I met her in Luneberg. In order to live I made myself disbelieve."

It was impossible to say — Then why, in God's name, didn't you *do* something? Not to a dying woman.

"But she is your sister," Mamma said. "You mustn't let anything — awful — happen to her. You are King of England."

So I am; I wish I weren't. What am I expected to do? Make war on Denmark because they call my sister slut?

"Nothing will happen to Caroline, Mamma. At the worst, divorce; and nobody thinks much of that, these days."

"Death-in-life," Mamma said, her voice growing weaker. "Like Dorothea of Zell. Forty years. Caroline is twenty." She closed her eyes visualizing behind her closed lids a forty years' imprisonment; once a day a ride in a closed carriage, four miles out, four miles back, always the same road. And her hands remembered the warm, love-enhanced vitality of the daughter she had embraced at Luneberg. Death would be kinder.

"Get her home, George," she said, opening her eyes and focusing them with some difficulty on the face of her firstborn. "She is your sister. Bring her home."

"You may rely on me, Mamma, to do my best."

"I know," the Princess-Dowager said. She produced a smile, astonishingly sweet on her ravaged face. "I know. George, always my *good* boy . . ."

CHAPTER
SEVEN

Kronborg, January-April 1772

At Elsinore time lagged, too, though Caroline had her baby, some books, and a piano and the company of the people appointed to attend her. Not one of them was well-disposed towards her, and though on the day following her arrest there were comings and goings between the Castle and the capital nobody volunteered a crumb of information or seemed able to answer her questions about what was happening. She thought it unwise to inquire about Struensee by name and she was consumed with anxiety. Mantel tried to talk to the servants who knew, or pretended to know, nothing. Alice volunteered to go into Copenhagen and find out what was going on; but she was stopped at the gate and informed that though she was free to leave, if she did so she would not be allowed to come back.

On the third day, however, Sir Robert Keith, the new British Minister to Denmark arrived and was admitted and left alone with her. It was only by the exercise of severe self-control that she restrained herself from asking immediately what had happened to Count Struensee; but she managed it.

Sir Robert, prepared to sleep late on the morning after the ball, had been awakened and told the news and was horrified. He realized the delicacy of his position; the Queen, his master's sister, an English Princess, had been accused of a shocking crime; but until she was proved guilty she must be assumed to be innocent; and at the same time it was his duty to maintain diplomatic relationships with those who presumably thought her guilty and had locked her up in Kronborg. He had been in Denmark only a short time; he was aware of the rumours which he had discounted, having quickly realized that Struensee had enemies who would have accused him of cannibalism if they had thought of it. It was a very awkward situation and he was anxious to handle it well, for he had ambitions; he hoped, one day, to be Ambassador in Paris or Vienna.

It took him a little time to obtain an appointment with Prince Frederick, now Regent. By whom appointed, Sir Robert wondered. That poor crazy King who one day could sign anything and the next nothing? One day Struensee, quaintly calling himself Prime Minister, in complete power, backed by a Cabinet, a gang of his friends; the next day, a Regent backed by a Council, a gang of *his* friends. Very tricky.

But when at last he obtained audience with the new Regent, Sir Robert was favourably impressed; he was sensible and sympathetic.

"It *is* a grave charge," Frederick said, saying what he sincerely believed, "but against the Queen it will not be pressed."

"And against Struensee? Your Royal Highness, no man commits adultery alone."

"It was necessary to remove Struensee, quickly and for good. There are other charges against him, but the evidence takes some time to prepare. But it will be found. The charge of criminal communication with the Queen will then be dropped."

"And her reputation ruined forever?"

"Talk, far more damaging than any direct accusation, which after all, can be refuted, has been going on now for two years. Last spring . . . you may not realize this . . . nineteen out of twenty people believed that Struensee had fathered the child born in July. And so long as Struensee was free, and she blindly played his game, such talk would continue. This direct confrontation will end it. Struensee will certainly deny any charge that might take him to the block; her name will be cleared."

"And I shall be permitted to see her?"

"But of course. Her imprisonment is merely . . . symbolical."

"About communications," Sir Robert said. "Is her Majesty allowed to write letters?"

"But of course," the Prince Regent said again. "Why not? She would be well advised *not* to write to Count Struensee; words of sympathy are easily misread. And another thing — this would come well from you, Sir Robert, she is not, legally, bound to answer any question put to her by anyone but the King. Forgive me, you probably knew that and would have told her.

She is Queen, in Denmark she has but one superior, the King and he alone has the right to question her."

From this rather curious interview — what a devious inscrutable young man! Sir Robert went to Elsinore and Caroline cried,

"Oh, how glad I am to see you. Nobody here knows anything. What is happening in Copenhagen? This whole absurd thing . . . I was whisked away . . . nobody could tell me why, or by whose order. In the middle of the night. And my son left behind. He must have missed me. Tammi too, he looked on me as his mother . . . Sir Robert, tell me everything, *please*."

The jerky, quick, unfinished sentences were so like her brother's whenever anything upset him, that Sir Robert who had met her only a few times, in formal circumstances, was a little taken aback. He sought refuge in his most official manner.

He told her about the change of government; he told her that so far as he knew the King and the Crown Prince were well.

That, so far as he knew, was true. In actual fact, father and son, though in good health were suffering a very similar affliction. The loss of familiar faces. Christian missed Struensee and Brandt; Freddy missed Mamma, Struensee and Alice. Christian, muttering, retreated a little farther back into his cave; the Crown Prince, not yet suppled by experience, lashed about, yelled, sulked, refused his food. This was certain proof that Struensee's way of child-rearing was faulty, and they would have taken Tammi away, too, and put him

341

back into the orphanage but for the fact that he was the only one who could persuade the Crown Prince to eat.

Of this Sir Robert, knowing nothing, could make no report; he said that husband and son were well and then, perched astride the uncomfortable diplomatic fence, wondered whether he should mention Struensee, or whether to leave it to her.

She said, bluntly, "You know why I am here? You know of what I am accused. I am extremely concerned about the person accused with me. Count Struensee . . . what happened to him?"

Poor girl, he thought, poor child; guilty or not, the last forty-eight hours must have been an ordeal.

"He was arrested and is now in the Blue Tower."

She seemed to grow smaller, to collapse inwardly.

"I hoped that he might have got away," she said, and put her hand to her face for a moment. Then she lowered it, folded it with the other in her lap and straightened herself.

"It is a ridiculous charge. Purely political. Count Struensee has made enemies and they have concocted this tale to bring him and his government down. In that they have been successful . . . but Sir Robert, having accused him, they must try him. And I assure you, there is not, there cannot be, one crumb of evidence. He will be cleared."

"One hopes so. I ought, perhaps, to point out that your own conduct may well be subject to scrutiny."

"It will bear it. In fact, in view of the manner in which Count Struensee and I have been treated, investigation will be welcome."

342

Her confidence impressed him.

"I understand that other charges will be preferred against Count Struensee. Count Brandt is also in prison, concerned with these other charges."

"That in itself proves to me that the plot is directed against Count Struensee," she said with a surprising shrewdness.

"Yes," he said, remembering his conversation with the Prince Regent, "it is possible that the unfortunate . . . business which brings you here, Your Majesty may be heard no more of. But, if anyone attempts to question you, on any matter whatsoever, you are within your rights to refuse to say anything. As Queen of Denmark you are answerable to the King, and to him alone."

"I did not know that, and I thank you for pointing it out. I will remember. Now, there is another thing. I have written some letters, but the Governor of this Castle said he had received no orders about dispatching my mail. Could you undertake to send them for me?"

"Family letters only."

"I have written to my brother, my mother and my sister. I could hardly write to him — to Count Struensee — not knowing where he was."

Sir Robert found his mind divided. Face to face with her he found it impossible to believe her guilty of a sordid intrigue which would have involved, over a period of two years, connivance with menials, subterfuge, furtiveness; she had too much dignity, too much candour. Yet the news of Struensee's whereabouts had been a blow to her; and her last remark held

343

significance. He compromised; she was fond of, perhaps in love with, the fellow, but not an adulteress.

The letters had not been easy to write. George, Mamma and Augusta — if they wanted to hear from her at all — would want angry, downright rebuttals of the charge; she had not written vehemently enough. "I have committed no crime," she had written; love was not a crime; nor, in Denmark any longer, was adultery; one of Johann's new laws decreed it as a misdemeanour. "I have many enemies, eager to believe the worst." That was true enough. "I beg you to believe that infidelity and licentiousness are foreign to my nature." Again true; her fidelity to Johann had never wavered, and it had been love, not lust, that had motivated her. But even as she wrote she was aware of sophism and feared that the fundamental dishonesty would show through, especially to Mamma.

It was possible that Mamma never read the unsatisfactory letter. Next time Sir Robert came it was to tell her that her mother had died on February 8th. "Very peacefully, Your Majesty." *Would* Mamma have died peacefully knowing that her daughter was confined to Kronborg with such an accusation levelled against her? Had someone had the good sense to close the sickroom door against the poison? Had Mamma been too ill, perhaps unconscious.

She wept bitterly, thinking of their last meeting, deceit a barrier between them. "You must give him up." If only she had. But how, having once experienced such joy, could one deny, retract, opt for the old sterile loneliness?

She said, through her tears, "I wish she could have lived to see my name cleared."

Sir Robert, who in the intervening days had been in the capital, close to events and alert even for gossip, felt a little pang. There had been no whisper, no hint of the major charge against Struensee being dropped; somewhere someone in authority was determined to have his head. The revelations, it was rumoured, would be scandalous. Perhaps it was as well that the Dowager Princess had died when she did.

He applied what comfort he could.

"Her Royal Highness, your mother may never have known of your . . . involvement, Your Majesty. I reported immediately, as I was bound to do. Simply the facts. But westerly gales were blowing, the crossing would take longer than usual. And in January the roads . . ."

She acknowledged his attempt to console with a little watery smile, very touching, but disturbing, too. Such an emotional, responsive, *warm* creature; and married to that poor demented boy. All too easy to believe, but one must *not!*

"I have other news," he said presently. "Count Struensee has been unwell, but he has made a recovery and will soon be well enough to be examined."

Johann would deny everything, completely and categorically. And apart from themselves nobody knew.

Sir Robert was not sure what anyone knew, some fantastic stories were circulating; but he also was confident that Struensee would deny everything — he had his head to consider. But under and behind it all, Sir Robert's sharp diplomat's sixth sense was aware of something dangerous and infinitely malicious, something determined to ruin not Struensee only, but this poor child. Yet even he never suspected the form this rooted hostility would take. When he said "examined" he thought of interrogation, some tricky lawyer's questions. He was English and it was a very long time since physical means had been employed in English legal procedure. Even the rough usage of those suspected of witchcraft had been largely disapproved and finally forbidden.

The idea that Struensee might be tortured never once occurred to him. Nor, mercifully, did it to Caroline.

With renewed expressions of sympathy with her loss and the assurance that he would come again and keep her informed, he took his leave.

Cuddling the baby Louise-Augusta, now successfully weaned, Caroline was bound to think again about mother-daughter relationships. Suppose that sometime in the future she should be obliged to put out her own thin, brown-speckled hand and *plead*, and this child, grown to womanhood should, in her heart, grudge the time, anxious only to be back with her lover. For that was how it had been at Luneberg. But no! That pattern could never be repeated, since she would see to it that Louise-Augusta married the man she loved, for her love's table would be openly spread, she would not be forced to dangerous devices in order to have a crumb.

Alice said, "She was a good lady, very charitable. If there's a Heaven, she's in it now."

Caroline did not question Alice's use of the word "if" as she would at one time have done. Johann's atheism, seldom explicit, always there, part of him had affected her thinking, so that her own philosophy was now a matter of "if". She had never, however, cut adrift entirely, as he had done; and now she said, "I hope that there is a Heaven, and that Mamma is there and happy."

Alice once more congratulated herself on always being able to hit on the right thing to say.

CHAPTER EIGHT

Kronborg, February-April 1772

Caroline's next visitors were four members of the new Council; and although Baron Juel-Wind, Chief of the Judiciary was one of them they had chosen Baron Schack to be their spokesman. They were all men who, two months earlier, would have regarded it as an honour to be invited to her table; they were all men who had been opposed to Johann's reforms.

When they had greeted her, Baron Schack said,

"We are here to ask Your Majesty a few simple questions."

"On what authority?"

"That of the Regent and the Council. The government of Denmark."

"I am sorry, your Excellencies, but I can answer no questions except those put to me by His Majesty."

They looked at one another and shared a thought. That damned interfering British Minister; he put those words into her mouth; he should never have been allowed to visit her. They had all said so at the time; so had the Queen Mother. Juliana said that in permitting Sir Robert's visits the Prince Regent had acted unwisely; one must beware of plots. The Prince Regent had retorted that one must also beware of anything that looked like pre-judgment; not to allow the Queen a visit from her brother's appointed representative in the country would be a breach of international convention. The situation with regard to England was ticklish enough, anyway. To refuse the Queen a service available to any drunken sailor in any foreign port might have unpleasant repercussions. The English Government might recall the Minister, close the Ministry doors and thus declare its non-recognition of the new régime.

The Prince Regent presented his argument well; and it was soundly based.

But this was one result of his policy.

Baron Schack said, "But as Your Majesty must be well aware, His Majesty is in no condition to make an inquiry into anything."

His condition was indeed shocking; with no Struensee to manipulate the puppet, no Brandt to exercise tact, it had been fully exposed. Since the night of the Palace Plot the moon had twice been full. Juliana had offended Heer Reventil by treating him as a person of no importance — a hired keeper, as once he had been a hired tutor — and he had not thought it necessary to disclose to her the secret of the little black book. She, in a forked stick, anxious on the one hand that Christian should be thrust aside and a Regency established, equally anxious to show that the King, so far as he willed anything, was in agreement with the new régime, had taken him out in a carriage, to ride around the city and its suburbs, so that everyone might see that he was alive and well and on good terms with her. Half-way through the drive he had become violent and tried to throw himself out of the carriage.

Caroline said, "I understand my husband's condition. But he is still King of Denmark. I am Queen; answerable only to him."

"The questions we wished to ask Your Majesty are directly concerned with the conduct of Count Struensee," Baron Schack said.

Even spoken in that way, the mention of his name affected her; but she gave — she thought — no sign.

She said, "The conduct of Count Struensee? I can answer no questions — as I have explained — but about his conduct I am prepared to make a voluntary statement. It was, down to the smallest thing, concerned with the welfare of His Majesty — and of Denmark. His Majesty's health and happiness, the welfare of the country, of everybody in it down to the poorest peasant, they were his main concerns. That I can say; I was always there; I saw everything."

"Would Your Majesty be prepared to comment upon Count Struensee's behaviour towards you?"

"But of course. It was invariably kind, considerate, and respectful. There were times when His Majesty was unwell, or one of the children ailed when strict formality was impossible; even so he never once failed in respect."

On the way back to Copenhagen, Juel-Wind said,

"Her claim to be answerable to the King alone is valid. We shall get nothing useful from her."

Count von Thott said, "The Prince Regent may have been right in urging that this charge should be dropped. It is unsavoury, it is calculated to set England by the ears, and it may be unsuccessful. It might have been better to stick to forging the King's signature."

"I must repeat," Juel-Wind said irritably, "that Struensee did not *forge*. Let us have some exactitude in this. There was no attempt to imitate a signature."

"Undue assumption of power, then," Count von Hosten said.

"Too vague. And with the King in the state he is . . . Someone must govern. Undue assumption of power is a charge that could be brought against all of *us*. Some day. What we want now is proof of criminal communication; and she has been shown how to take advantage of a legal point."

"She is vulnerable," Schack said. "Press hard enough on Struensee and she will change her tune."

Three days later Schack returned to Kronborg, alone.

"I have not come to bother you with questions, Your Majesty," he said, producing a paper. "We thought this document deserving of your attention."

Out of all the close clerky writing his name leapt out, Johann Frederick Struensee; and before she read anything else her face betrayed her again. Struensee had persuaded her to abandon the thick pink-and-white applied complexion behind which a woman could blush or turn pale with impunity. He said the white lead which was its base was a poison, responsible for the death of many women. So Schack saw her colour flare and die away and flare again as she read the

351

terrible statement, signed in Johann's hand, shaky but unmistakable.

My dear one, my darling, what did they do to you to make you say and sign this? "Guilty relationship begun in spring 1770" . . . "Intimacy with the Queen as far as it is possible to go."

She said, "What this means I cannot know. I do know that Count Struensee would never have said such things."

"You deny the truth of this confession?"

"Absolutely. There is no truth in it at all."

"It was taken down as it was spoken, word for word; in the presence of six witnesses — I was there myself. It is signed, as you will have observed." Signed in an old man's quavering scrawl.

"He was ill when he wrote this," she said, "or in great distress."

Schack remembered every second of the examination. Struensee looked gaunt and ill, his eye-sockets and cheeks hollow, his clothes hanging loosely upon him; but he'd had an answer for everything, a refutal of all the suspicious-seeming circumstances which, given a centre, could be significant, and without a centre were trivial and meaningless. He had been stout in his denials, as stubborn as his paramour was now being; but the sight of the rack had unmanned him; two turns, inflicting some pain but no real damage, had set him babbling.

It was impossible to subject the Queen to a racking, but Schack was prepared to subject Caroline to some mental torture.

352

"He was under certain pressure," he admitted. "This is not the kind of statement that a man makes voluntarily. And as it is it is very imprecise and inconclusive. Spring 1770 is very vague. He will be obliged to amplify . . ." He noted with satisfaction that though one thought she could not have turned more pale, she did, as that shot went home. "And there is," he went on, "another way of looking at this whole affair. Your Majesty denies the truth of this statement. If this," he tapped the paper which she had dropped on to the table between them, "is a mere tissue of lies, invention, imagination, the man has violated Your Majesty, not in a way which any ordinary man could consider as human, and thus understandable, but in a particularly vicious and obscene way. *For such a man there could be no hope at all.* The utmost penalty would then be enacted, because otherwise any liar could claim to have been Your Majesty's lover. I trust I make myself clear."

She was beginning to look confused — always a good sign. But she had understood; there was a threat; a renewal of pressure whatever he meant by that, in order to oblige Johann to amplify. And the pressure must have been hideous to lead to this . . . betrayal. There was also in the baron's speech a hint of promise; if the confession were a lie there would be no hope, that implied that if it were true there might be.

Something rose in her mind and spread — she might save him yet. In doing so she would ruin her name forever, but it was already so damaged that it hardly mattered. What did matter was that Johann should be spared more of that pressure and saved from death.

She said, "Baron Schack, without admitting anything at all, may I ask you this? If I did; if I said it was all true and that the blame was wholly mine, that I took advantage of my superior position to instigate the affair — would that exonerate him?"

"It would go a long way towards it." Most fortunately she had used the word exonerate, not liberate or save. Nothing could save Struensee now, but exoneration was possible; any crime could be exonerated once it was expiated.

"Then I will do that. I will confirm the truth of this statement and take complete reponsibility."

They'd run her out of Copenhagen on a hurdle; but Johann spared, would join her; there would be life together in another country. She would make up to him somehow for the ambition which love had frustrated. She had never boiled an egg in her life, or made a cup of tea, but she now had a small bright vision of herself presenting Johann with a tasty meal, prepared by her own hands, in some cosy place like the Davies' kitchen, when he came back from seeing a lot of patients, all doing well.

"Will you write it, or shall I?" she asked, hoping that he would do so, for her heart was labouring and her hands as shaky as *his* must have been.

"I came prepared," Schack said, producing two papers. "This is a denial, this an admission — both in reference to what Count Struensee confessed. It is your wish that I should add to this one words to the effect that you and you alone were culpable. That you were, in fact, the seducer?"

354

"Yes," she said. "Add that."

He scribbled and handed her the pen and she wrote *Caro* ... and halted. Stupid. Caroline was her unofficial, family name. Here she was Matilda. She looked up, about to apologize for this slip. Something in Schack's face ran an alarm bell in her mind. I am giving all, and getting nothing!

She said, very breathlessly, "I think that ... before I sign ... away my good name ... for ever, I should have ... some assurance, in writing, that taking all the blame on myself means that Count Struensee will be liberated. And," she said, remembering the look, "we will have a witness. Lieutenant Colonel von Hauch, the Governor here. Would you ring that bell ..."

Schack said, "Your Majesty, that is an assurance that I cannot give. I am only one man. I have no power ..."

"Enough to come here and trick me. I see now. I have been shamefully deceived ..."

A violence in her, suppressed all these years, be pleasing to Mamma, to George, to Christian, to Johann, broke loose.

"I shan't sign," she said, and took the pen, a handsome gilded quill and threw it against the wall. Then, gasping and spent, whiter than chalk, she sagged in the chair.

Schack took stock of his position; what he wanted lay there half signed. Until that bell rang they would not be disturbed. She was a woman, already shocked and distraught, on the verge of collapse. He was a man. He retrieved the pen, its nib undamaged, redipped it and put it into her limp hand, closing his own over it. While she screamed "No no! Mantel!" the pen propelled by two hands, completed the signature ". . . line Matilda."

On his way back to Copenhagen Schack was conscious of triumph. He had judged her accurately; he had acted with decision. But under these satisfactory feelings something nagged; he couldn't help asking himself whether any of the women with whom he had consorted would have been willing — supposing him to be in Struensee's position — to have acted so . . . chivalrously. Not that he envied Struensee . . . He would die. But he had been loved.

CHAPTER
NINE

Copenhagen, March 1772

Everything had gone most disastrously wrong and the Prince Regent was appalled. The double confession completely changed the nature of the plot to which he had committed himself. He had been so certain in his own mind that even from Struensee no confession could be wrung. He knew about pain; he had lived with it as long as he could remember; his back had always ached; fearful attempts had been made to force the crooked shoulder into line; he had spent three years of his early boyhood in a kind of iron cage. And he knew, he *knew* that if Caroline had picked him, instead of that great lumbering oaf, to be her lover he would have let himself be torn in pieces between two frantic horses, burned alive, racked till every joint gave way, and never said a word. Struensee, not even injured, merely frightened, had told all. On top of everything else, a coward.

Of the trickery behind Caroline's own confession, he knew nothing; the four Commissioners had kept silent about that; the Prince Regent imagined that faced with Struensee's confession she had felt that further denial was useless. Her taking all blame upon herself was typical; he'd always known that she was gallant.

There were other troublesome aspects of the situation. He had not found it as easy as he had supposed to shake loose his mother's hold on the new administration. Because he was young and inexperienced they'd all taken the attitude that he was a figurehead, she the real power. What does Her Majesty the Queen Mother think, say, feel? We must wait for, consult with, be guided by Her Majesty the Queen Mother. They'd set him up as the driver of a clumsy coach, harnessed to an unruly tandem team, handed him the reins, threads of cotton, and given her the whip.

He feared even to make too open a stand in his attempt to shield Caroline; for one thing he had his own secret to preserve; for another, she was now being so vilified that one incautious move on his part would set people asking, *Why? Was he also one of her lovers?* Anybody really determined to do so could have made out a case in that respect; he had always sought her company, ridden with her, danced with her and when the child was at Fredericksborg had on more than one occasion gone with her on visits — he liked the little boy and a man had the right to visit his nephew. Now, when they were all willing, indeed eager, to believe that she was lecherous and indiscriminate as a cat, he had to be very careful.

But he had faced the four commissioners, and his mother, and said, "This has now gone far enough. The evidence appears to be incontrovertible and in my opinion it should be used to obtain a divorce and then shelved and forgotten."

358

Five blank and uncomprehending faces looked at him; then Juliana said,

"A divorce? What purpose would that serve."

"It would enable the King to marry again. As recent events have shown, a second son is sometimes a form of insurance . . ." He spoke in that flippant way that had lightened some tedious hours for Caroline. He was delighted to see his mother flinch. *That* was something she had not thought of.

She said, "In Christian's present condition that is unthinkable."

"What has been done once can be done again," Frederick said. Think on that.

Baron Juel-Wind said, "But, Your Royal Highness, are we to condone treason? Both these statements admit criminal communication and in the circumstances that is treason."

"True. But we must remember the little matter of treason being a thing apart — if I read rightly, judges are not considered competent to try cases of high treason."

"That is so. There will be no trial in the ordinary sense; a Tribunal of Notables will examine the evidence in private and reach a decision."

Frederick said, still almost casually, "I do not feel entirely comfortable about it. Struensee, you admit, was under pressure; Her Majesty was alone, without a legal adviser. The whole thing smacks of connivance. And we must remember that she is an English Princess."

"Who became Queen of Denmark and admits, openly admits that she indulged in an adulterous relationship with the King's physician."

To that there was no real answer; Struensee, weak evil man, had cut his own throat; Caroline, poor silly girl, had cut hers.

Juliana said thoughtfully, "The English would, I do not doubt, suspect evidence given, by Danes, and even the Queen's own statement, given without witness, to a Dane. You were wrong there, Baron Schack; some witness, preferably the castle Governor, should have been present. But no matter. We can bring evidence from an unsuspect source — the word of another Englishwoman."

"They've come to take me away," Alice said, "and they've got an order. But they were good enough to let me come and tell you."

"Oh Alice," Caroline said; she began to cry inside, the worst way of crying; not tears of salt water spilling down the face, tears of blood, leaching away inwardly. This was the projection of the threat, felt long ago, with Alice doing her hair and announcing that she, too, was coming to Denmark.

"What is the charge?" she asked.

"Count Struensee is accused, amongst other things of mishandling His Royal Highness, the Crown Prince. This person is not charged, but her evidence is needed."

"And I'll give it," Alice said. "He was well on his way to being an idiot; the doctor saved him, and I helped.

And that," she looked straight at Caroline, "is all I can say." The look said, Your secret is safe with me!

"Is it necessary for her to be taken away? Would her statement not suffice?" Mine did; and from the moment that my signature was forced, there has been a steady diminution in respect and consideration.

"We have our orders," one of the three soldiers said.

Caroline thought of Struensee, a strong man, her lover broken, abject. She said, in English,

"Alice, say anything. Tell them what they want to hear. Never mind me. I confessed and my reputation is gone. You mustn't suffer a moment's pain or ill-usage on my behalf. Nothing can help me now."

"We'll see about that," Alice said.

The soldier who had spoken before said, "This leave-taking has lasted long enough. We must go."

The Queen and the foundling girl embraced for the first time in their lives. Alice's kiss was timid and restrained, kisses were not a currency with which she was familiar; Caroline's was wild and passionate, with something in it of the quality that her mother had detected. Carrying the memory of it with her — she's fond of me, too, Alice knew that she could, if necessary, face lions.

"You are being extremely stupid," Baron Juel-Wind said. "Your mistress and her lover have both *confessed*. It is useless for you the one closest to her, and for two years occupying an adjoining apartment, to deny that these things went on."

"But I do. That is what I am saying. I was always there. I must have known. There was the door between her room and the nursery; it was never shut. I went in and out, all the time; often in the middle of the night, if one of the children was restless. I was there . . ."

Baron Juel-Wind, Chief Justice of the Supreme Court, knew a moment's regret that he had not agreed with the Prince Regent and let the thing go. Really, interrogating an ignorant serving girl was not his province. The Queen and Struensee through their lust had not only undermined the majesty of the throne, but also the dignity of the law!

In a voice sharp with irritation he said,

"Then may I ask how you account for these confessions? Listen!" He read out the salient sentences. "Yet *you*, in the next room, the door, you say, not closed, saw and heard nothing?"

"There was nothing to hear or see. Something happened to him to make him say what he did. They say he was off his head for three weeks. And she was tricked. That I do know. She's never been the same woman since she wrote her name — if she did write it, and that I doubt — on that bit of paper. Shamefully deceived, she said. I think myself there's been some funny business going on."

Too near the truth to be comfortable. He shifted his ground.

"We have here the deposition of one, Anna Peterson."

"A born liar," Alice said. "I've seen some liars in my time; but her, why if you asked her the time of day, she'd tell you wrong."

362

"I am not asking you for your opinion of Anna Peterson's character," Baron Juel-Wind said, a little wearily. "I do ask you to listen to her deposition. She says that, troubled by suspicion, on two occasions, she scattered a white powder by Her Majesty's bed and in the morning found, upon the treated surface, the imprint of footprints; large, male foot-prints."

"That'd be the pages," Alice said. "They always drew the bed curtains. They come small, but a year's good feeding and they're men, almost."

"Perhaps I should draw your attention to the fact that we have methods for extracting the truth from unwilling witnesses."

"I know," Alice said. She had seen it, a dreadful looking thing, blocks and ropes and pulleys, just inside the door, a little to one side but in clear view as you came in. "May I say something?"

"We are anxious to hear whatever you have to say."

"Hurt people enough," she said, "and they'll say anything. A rabbit in a trap'll make a noise like a baby, that isn't to say it is a baby. So far, as well as I can I've told you the truth. If I'm hurt I might say anything, but it wouldn't be the truth; it'd just be to stop being hurt any more."

Chilblains that festered and rubbed in the ill-fitting shoes, toothache, earache, slaps across the face, real beatings when Mrs. Brewster was in a bad temper, and terrible pains every month since she was fourteen. Alice knew what pain was and reckoned she could bear as much as most.

When it began she clamped her upper teeth into her lower and screamed, and screamed through her nose.

It was a mild racking; less even than Struensee had borne; but though Alice's muscles were stringy and tough, her bones were a foundling's bones. The beef pudding which she had remembered in Mrs. Davies' kitchen had been a treat all too rare. Bread, gruel and turnip stew had built her skeleton and it was frail. Under a turn that should not have dislocated a joint, one of her thigh bones broke and pierced an artery.

For Alice it was suddenly spring again; spring at Kew, flowers everywhere and birds singing. They were all young together, happy in the sunshine. Princess Caroline said, "Alice must have some too." Heaven.

The body was easily and quickly disposed of.

Once again, cut off from all communication, Caroline waited, certain that something dreadful must have happened to Alice. My fault, my fault.

"Sir Robert, will you *please* inquire? She was . . . is . . . English, too. They said she was wanted as a *witness*. I told her to say whatever would make things easy for her. She must be in prison . . . or dead."

"Or unable to re-enter the Castle, lacking a pass," Sir Robert said.

"You never knew Alice," said Caroline, beginning to cry again. "If she were alive and free, she would have got in somehow."

On the following day, William Smith, the non-marrying man, was back in Copenhagen, nose down on the track of Alice. At the Christiansborg he was told that the Queen was at Kronborg; he hired a horse and

364

set off. Without an official pass nobody was allowed to enter the castle and his attempts at bribery failed. He'd noticed in Copenhagen, and it was the same here, everybody seemed scared of something, all of a jump. He returned to the capital, intent on getting a pass but with no idea how to set about it or to whom to apply. However, as he had lounged about Count Bernstorff's stables and the riding school he had come in contact with several young officers and he patiently sought them out, one by one; "Sir, how do I go about getting a pass into Kronborg?" The question appeared to cause dismay, alarm, suspicion; but at last somebody pointed out that this was not a military matter; it was lawyer's stuff. And — "You're English, aren't you? You go about trying to get into Kronborg and you'll find yourself somewhere else in double quick time." As though he could save the Queen single-handed! She was doomed; they'd cut off her head. And then what would happen to Alice? Alone and without a job?

He found a lawyer in a dim office up two flights of stairs and put his question adding, "Just tell me *who* to ask. I can pay." That was true, he had a pocketful of money; Sir William had been delighted with Peppo and sent practical proof of his gratitude. But even the mention of money seemed not to serve here, and Smith said, his patience wearing thin, "Who's the head of the lot? Who's the top lawyer. Tell me that."

"Baron Juel-Wind is Chief Justice of the Supreme Court."

Then for a day and a half Smith hunted the Chief Justice who had more lackeys and they more insolent than any he had ever seen. He was told to stand back there, to get out of the way, to give his name, to state his business — and at the mention of a pass to Kronborg you'd think he had leprosy at the least. Both at his residence and at the Exchequer good care was taken that nobody who had not been sieved through several minor department's meshes ever got within spitting distance of the Chief Justice of the Supreme Court. So there was only one thing to do.

It was a risk. The two chestnut horses were coming along at a spanking pace, the light carriage bouncing behind them. Smith, like a man intent upon suicide, stepped out in front of them and gave the secret horseman's word. They checked as though confronted by a ten foot wall. The coachman, cursing, aimed a blow at Smith, which, if it had landed might have removed an ear. Missing him, he lashed the horses. Smith, alongside said,

"You'll only mar their hides. They'll stand till my business is done," and went to the carriage window, already rolled down so that the Chief Justice could see and ask what the devil was happening.

"It was," Smith said, "the only way I could get near you, your Excellency. I tried and tried. I just want a pass to go to Kronborg." And even on this aristocratic, well-fed face there was that same look.

"Nothing political," Smith said hastily. "It's just that there's a girl there, a girl I want to marry. And I can't tell her without a pass."

"You must be mad," the Chief Justice said, "accosting me . . ."

366

He put his head further out of the window and shouted,

"Drive on, man!"

"They're a nice pair!" Smith said, "it'd be a pity to break their nerve. And do no good. They'll stand till judgment day, or till I get my pass."

And it was true that the whip was whistling, and striking.

"I just want," Smith said, "leave to go and see Alice; that's all."

Oddly enough the Chief Justice remembered Alice, who had died with her upper teeth driven through her lower lip, mouth sealed, screaming through her nose. "A girl I want to marry."

"Alice is no longer at Kronborg," he said in his best judicial manner. "It would be a waste of time to look for her there."

"Then where is she?"

"That I cannot tell you. She was involved with this most unfortunate affair with her mistress. But she had nothing to add to the accumulating evidence, and my concern with her ended."

"Did she go back to England?"

"Probably. She is not at Kronborg; so you are wasting your time and mine."

"I'm sorry," Smith said, "but at least now I know."

He walked until he was level with the horses,

"Off you go, my beauties . . ."

Probably in England; a girl called Alice, with no other name, no roots. Go and get drunk, what else was there to do? But before he was even half drunk he was arrested, gaoled for two days and released, and given a line in the records, "William Smith, an English ostler — for obstruction on the public highway."

He never knew that he had been lucky. The authorities learned that he had left Denmark with his master in September 1770; he could, however severely racked, have contributed nothing. Let him go.

Let him go to England; and hunt and search and ask questions, and follow trails that led nowhere, look into the face of every woman and sometimes — very rarely — imagine that he saw . . . and quicken the pace that led him to the inevitable disappointment, and pass on. Begin again.

Alice, rotting in salt water, Smith tramping London streets; Struensee and Caroline, awaiting trial for treason — all victims of that universal, unpredictable thing called love.

And in the great palace of Christiansborg the four year old Crown Prince of Denmark, suffered unwittingly, the same complaint. Mamma; Alice, Tammi; they had made his world, they were gone and he wanted them back. He screamed, he stamped, he bit those who tried to control him. Everybody said that this behaviour was the result of Struensee's mishandling.

Prince Frederick, Regent of Denmark, asked the British Minister to wait upon him, and closeted together they had an earnest and uncomfortable talk. Both were reasonable men, and on one point they were of the

368

same mind; but the Regent found it necessary to take the Danish view of things, Sir Robert the English.

"It would brand Denmark as barbarous in the eyes of all the world," Sir Robert said. "At the moment I can think of no erring Queen being beheaded since Henry VIII had Catherine Howard's head off. The grounds for divorce are there, to our great grief. But execution . . . Am I supposed to take this seriously?"

"Very seriously. Her Majesty has committed treason, and admitted it. The trial can do nothing but expose a lot of unsavoury details. It cannot clear her — clever though Uldall is; he has undertaken her defence, had you heard? Public opinion has been affronted. I seriously think that the extreme penalty may be exacted. Unless His Majesty of England moves."

"In what direction, Your Royal Highness? Are we to provoke an international incident over one misguided woman?"

"If I remember rightly England once went to war over a pirate's ear. Not," he went on hastily, "that war would be likely, or even possible. But some show of firmness, of support for her, whatever she has done, must come from her own country, *and from her brother.*"

"My master," Sir Robert said, "is in an unprecedented situation. Devoted to his sister, imagine his distress. But he is anxious not to move hastily, or to seem to interfere in any way with the due process of law in Denmark. If only," his diplomatic voice and manner deserted him, "she had not signed that damnable document. If only I had been there — or anyone else capable of advising

369

her. There is the rub. With that signed the King of England cannot accuse her accusers; nor can he very well say — Yes, she is guilty, but she is a Princess of England and I forbid you to try her."

"I agree. But I hope, Excellency, that you will not conceal from him the extreme gravity of her situation and the possibility that her life may be in danger."

"I will write again," Sir Robert said. He sighed inwardly; the King had worries enough and he was not a man who bore worry well; despite his stolid appearance, his "Farmer George" interests and manner, he was a highly nervous man, liable when agitated to speak so quickly that no one could catch what he said, to repeat himself and to mutter irrelevancies. In fact, but this was a thing which Sir Robert kept locked within himself — there had been times when he had seriously thought about the blood relationship between the King of England and the King of Denmark; they shared one pair of grandparents and other less directly linked streams flowed in both their veins.

That thought must be pushed aside; he was His Majesty's representative, not his physician; and if, as this grave young man had hinted, events might take such a fantastic, ugly turn, it was better that His Majesty should be prepared.

"I will write again," he said.

Prince Frederick thought he had managed this well. What he, as the Regent chosen by the party which had brought Caroline down, could not do without arousing more gossip, more invidious suspicion, George of England could do under the banner of brotherly love.

She had hurt herself, that bright, shining girl; she had been frail and faulty and indiscreet; but beyond the harm she had brought herself, choosing the wrong man, a lowborn fellow who had betrayed her, and then, still doting, betraying herself, she should suffer nothing more than loss of reputation and position. Because he still had his reserve in reserve . . . But he hoped it would not come to that; for he knew that he would be, for some years, an excellent Regent.

Part Six

CHAPTER
ONE

Copenhagen; Kronborg,
March-April 1772

On a bleak day in the last week of March one hundred and thirty-five men, the "Notables" of Denmark, met in the Great Hall of the Exchequer to consider the evidence for and against the Queen.

England had made no move, so the decision of this tribunal might be a matter of life or death; but the procedure was singularly lifeless; a brooding over of depositions taken beforehand; a speech for the prosecution, a speech for the defence and more brooding.

As the dreary business dragged on Baron Juel-Wind regretted more and more that he had not paid heed to the Prince Regent's suggestion that Struensee's confession and the Queen's admission should be used as a cause for divorce and the whole thing left there, without all this business of prurient-minded ladies-in-waiting and coarse-minded serving girls. It was disgusting, much of it had little to do with law as he understood it and it was boring; he relieved the tedium by trying to frame sentences in which the evidence of

Fräulein von Ebehn and Anna Petersen for example, could be purged of indecency and made fit to go down in the records. As a variation he wondered what on earth Advocate Uldall could possibly say when it came to the defence.

Uldall was perhaps the best advocate in Denmark and it was the Prince Regent who had urged that he be employed. "It is necessary to remember that until she is found guilty and deposed, she *is* Queen of Denmark. She must have the best. What I mean is that there must be no grounds for criticism afterwards."

So Caroline had the best.

Uldall began by pointing out that as Danish law stood — as he hoped that it would always stand — a confession was not sufficient to condemn the person who made it. A confession in itself, unbacked by outside evidence had no value; a person might make a confession while temporarily insane, ill, intoxicated or activated by a wish to help another. Nor, he held, did Her Majesty's signature have any significance; in his experience he'd known women who had signed away their rights to money and property; given the right circumstances any woman would sign anything. And it may have been observed that Her Majesty's signature on this particular document varied somewhat from her usual one . . . Baron Schack moved in his chair and fixed his eyes on the sleet sliding down the window.

The confession meant nothing, the signature indicated some strain; and what of the independent evidence? If these things had been going on for two years, *for two years*, why had nothing been done, or said? Servants could hardly be expected to interfere, but all the ladies-in-waiting were well-connected women, capable of understanding that in a Queen adultery was treason; why had not one of them made a protest or a complaint?

Indeed one might ask what there was to complain of, to protest against. Not one of the depositions contained any evidence at all of the accused ever having been found in even a moderately compromising situation.

He begged his listeners to study again the depositions, so full of details, culled by such sharp eyes and ears; was it feasible that over a period of two years these same sharp eyes and ears had not seen or heard anything more positive, direct and convincing?

Bit by bit he demolished and ridiculed the so-called evidence; his defence was skilled and spirited; but the two confessions weighed more heavily than any argument and the squalid nature of some of the so-called evidence told against Caroline; a Queen who laid herself open to such suspicion was — whether guilty of the ultimate act or not — unfit to be first lady of the land. She must be deposed; and how could that be done unless the verdict were guilty?

Not all, but enough of the Notables were influenced by Juliana, who in her long undercover campaign against Christian had learned the effectiveness of the unfinished sentence, the sigh, the look of concern. She could say, "She is *still* very young . . ." in such a way that any man listening could visualize a young reckless creature who, having got away with this, would think she could get away with anything, and proceed, by indulging in further affairs to bring more disgrace upon herself and upon Denmark.

The verdict of guilty was necessary, and it was brought. Then began hot debate as to what was to happen to her. She was guilty of adultery, therefore of treason. The extreme penalty was legal; some believed that it should be exacted; others held that life imprisonment in some remote place would be sufficient punishment. And even some of these were not blind to the danger of plots; already Count von Bulow and Baron Schimmelmann had been so vociferous in the Queen's defence that it had been thought wise to arrest them.

On a day that all the signs indicated that Caroline might go to the block, the Prince Regent talked with his mother.

"It will be an atrocity," he said. "And you must stop it."

"I? My dear boy, what can I do against a hundred and thirty five men, backed up by the law?"

"They most of them eat out of your hand," he said sourly; "they regard you as the leader of the revolution, the one who saved Denmark from Struensee and anarchy. They will do what you indicate to be your wish. And it would be a not unpleasant rôle; your plea is ready made. A Queen yourself you have a natural aversion to the cutting off of Queen's heads."

He watched her carefully. George of England had let him down; the moderate opinion amongst the Notables had let him down. Would she?

378

She said, "Naturally I have an aversion. But to be honest I shrink from the responsibility. If she lives and there are plots . . . After all, people like von Bulow and Schimmelmann can't remain in custody forever . . . it could mean civil war."

"People who shrink from responsibility should not assume power."

"Power! I have no power, Frederick. Oh, they ask my opinion and sometimes take my advice; they know my devotion to Denmark and I am old, considered knowledgable. But I am only Mother of the Regent . . ."

He looked at her as though he were about to shoot her, taking careful aim.

"And that not for long, perhaps. If they pass sentence of death on the Queen they can look for another Regent."

Straight through the heart!

"You . . . you couldn't," she stammered.

"There is no law that I know of that compels me to be Regent. I refuse absolutely to be nominal head of a state that reverts to medieval barbarity. I have sedulously refrained from any interference in this business; I am not interested in whether sheets were soiled, or by whom. I *am* interested in my own reputation and I refuse to go down in history as the Regent who signed the death-warrant for an unfortunate girl who committed an error of taste."

Rage restored her; after all the work and the waiting; the hope, the despair, the devotion to his interest, and now with complete success within reach.

"Anyone would think you were in love with her too," she said with the utmost spite.

"The use of the word 'too' postulates the existence of others who loved her," he said, coolly. "Who did? Her mother, her brother who shipped her off to marry an idiot? Christian, infatuated with his page-boy? Struensee, who at the turn of the screw betrayed her? A sorry company; and I am to join them because, in the year 1772 I refuse to associate myself with something out of the Middle Ages? Believe what you like, so long as you also believe that I mean what I say. If that crowd of old muttonheads pass the death sentence, I resign."

Run and tell your minions that.

She did not run, but she made haste; she did not mention the threat. She spoke in her usual, sidelong way about the climate of opinion in these modern times, the quality of mercy, especially where the young and foolish were concerned, of her own natural feelings about the one who had been her daughter-in-law. Most of them were glad to be given so definite a lead; even those who from conviction or a backwash of disgust were willing to pass the death sentence, had recoiled a little when it came to the point of considering *how* a Queen should be beheaded. For Struensee, and for Brandt, his accomplice in all his doings, the axe would serve; but more than two hundred years earlier that old Bluebeard of England, Henry VIII, had thought it necessary to send to France for a swordsman to sever Anne Boleyn's little neck. Must they do likewise, or was there in Denmark . . . ? They were happy enough to concede.

On April 9th Baron Juel-Wind went to Kronborg and in the presence of the Castle's Governor, Lieutenant-Colonel von Hauch, informed Caroline of her sentence. She was to be divorced; her name was to be removed from the liturgy; and she was to spend the rest of her life in the castle of Aarbourg, in the Jutland peninsula.

It meant nothing to her. Struensee and Brandt had already been sentenced. From them the law was to exact the extreme penalty. First their right hands — those tools of treachery — were to be severed; then their heads were to be cut off; they were to be disembowelled, cut into four quarters and exposed to the gaze of the morbid crowd and the sharp beaks of birds.

It was too horrible to think of, yet it must be thought of day and night, night and day. This, this was the bloody, obscene end of the path she had chosen on a sunny afternoon; this the price of a love that harmed nobody. She was to blame for it all; Johann, Brandt — and Alice. She could neither eat nor sleep, she could not sit still; she could hardly bear to look on her baby, the child of love. Better a thousand times never to have been born than to have been brought into a world where such vile things could happen.

Only death, she knew, could relieve her the burden of guilt. When she thought of Johann, so unfailingly kind, that right hand, that head packed with knowledge, good sense and good intentions, the body that had taught her ecstasy ... Not to be borne. Let me die too! Twice, since those who, at the beginning had no news about

381

where he was, and later had no news of Alice, had been ready to tell her about the sentence passed on him, she had tried to kill herself, because this nagging torment, the burden of guilt was not to be borne.

Once, on the ramparts, where she was allowed to walk and where the wall was breast high, she had leaned over and seen far below the flagstones of the courtyard. One dive from the top of the rampart, no more decision needed than it took to put a horse to an unfamiliar fence, and her skull would crack like an egg and this misery would be ended. Mantel had come and taken her by the knees as she heaved herself up and pulled her back. "When the gods call," he said, "they send a messenger. You are not yet called." He'd given her a draught of one of the concoctions which he had learned to make from his old grandmother, he said. It made her sleep, and the next time, and the next time, presented with such a dose she pretended to drink, hid the glass, and when five doses were there, secret and hidden, had swallowed the lot. Go to sleep for ever; put an end to this. Whatever it was, it must have lost potency by being kept; she slept, but she woke and the torture went on.

When the Gods call they send a messenger; she had hoped that Baron Juel-Wind was that messenger, coming to tell her that on some day in this month of buds and flowers unfolding, she would follow, or precede Johann to the block. I am the guilty one . . .

"Your Majesty will be addressed ceremoniously," Baron Juel-Wind said, "and a proper suite will be in attendance."

382

He thought that she looked very ill and very old; in the little time since he had seen her last she had aged by twenty, thirty years. Beauty, youth, vigour all vanished; and who would plot to put such a completely discredited woman, prematurely aged, back into any position of power? Nobody, he thought, need fear plots on her behalf. Let it not be forgotten that she was the King's first cousin; the King was lunatic and lunacy ran in families. It could be, he thought, noting her apathy at the reception of what after all must seem momentous news for a woman who had lived for more than a week under the shadow of imminent, ignominious death, that she was demented too.

He had just thought that when she said,

"My daughter, the young Princess, will she be allowed to accompany me to Aarbourg?"

"No, Your Majesty. The Princess Louise-Augusta will join her brother, the Crown Prince."

Well, better so. It is an acknowledgment of her royal status. And better for her in the long run, to be thought of as the daughter of the King of Denmark, than as a bastard, father beheaded, mother dead of misery and shame.

Nevertheless she cried as she held the child for the last time. She cried a good deal now, making up for the time when, as a girl, she had cried little, Mamma had disapproved, Edward had been inclined to jeer and Louise had cried enough for two.

Taking his leave, his errand done, Baron Juel-Wind said,

383

"Her Majesty looks very ill. I doubt if her stay at Aalbourg will be long."

The Castle Governor, instantly on the defensive, for who, in these upset times, knew friend from foe? said,

"I assure you, Her Majesty has had every care and consideration; a well set table twice a day . . . what more can I do?"

"Oh, nothing, nothing," the Baron assured him, hastily. "I was merely remarking . . ."

Now, doomed not to die in a fashion that would have been some kind of expiation, she lived in an unending nightmare. Mantel still made the brews that he had learned from his grandmother, and sometimes she slept a little, saw Johann handless, headless and woke screaming. Mantel said that when the lime trees bloomed he would gather enough to stuff a pillow for her — nothing like a lime pillow as a cure for sleeplessness. He made little strips of toast, English fashion, and presented them to her, with fresh made tea; his eyes were like a spaniel's, pleased to retrieve — look-what-I-have-brought-you. To please him, poor faithful fellow she ate mouthfuls of toast and sipped the tea. All waste. Any day now, which day, what day she did not know, but soon, with the opening and flowering of the year, Johann would go to his terrible death. And then she would die, too . . .

CHAPTER
TWO

Copenhagen, April 28th 1772

Struensee had believed for a short time, immediately after his arrest, that the people would rise in his favour. They had not done so. The scandal had momentarily swamped what feelings of gratitude had been entertained and there had been shock and disapproval. Ordinary men had a living to make, busy all day and asleep all night they had no time for meddling in affairs; they were unaccustomed to taking action, even on their own behalf, and, perhaps most important, they had no leader. The new government had taken the precaution of temporarily arresting men like Count von Bulow, and Count Schimmelmann who believed in the Queen's innocence, and therefore, by implication, in the innocence of Struensee. So nothing was done.

But, when it came to the erection of the scaffold the authorities ran into a little trouble.

On its three landward boundaries the capital had broad *allees*, spread with gravel and bordered by trees. They were used by soldiers for exercises and parades, by citizens for walks and by itinerant entertainers and salesmen.

In mid-Apil the authorities commissioned a master carpenter to build, in the eastern *allee* a wooden structure, twenty-four feet long, twenty-four feet wide and twenty-seven feet high. It was to be soundly built and quickly built; if he and his apprentices could not complete it by the twenty-fifth of the month, he could sub-contract; expense did not matter; time did. Also needed, a mile away, in the westmost *allee* were two poles, each surrounded by four wheels.

By this time the sentence passed upon Struensee — and upon Count Brandt who was convicted of being his confederate, and of having laid disrespectful hands upon His Majesty — was known, and the carpenter suspected the purpose of the work he was asked to do. He remembered that Struensee, whatever else he had done, had passed the act that forced noblemen to pay their debts like anybody else. Several jobs the payment for which he had never hoped to see, had been promptly paid for and the carpenter did not intend to have any hand in the erection of what he judged to be a scaffold.

"It can't be done," he told the minor official who had been put in charge of the job. "All my boys have an annual holiday — in April. And I couldn't do it alone, not with my back as bad as it is."

The word had spread. In the whole city of Copenhagen, no carpenters, their journeymen or apprentices would work upon this simple structure. They all had excellent excuses; holidays, other urgent jobs, a remarkable number of crippling ailments. Wheelwrights were similarly unemployable. The minor official, intent upon promotion, sought further afield for labour, and said that the structure was to be the beginning of a pleasure house, a stage where puppet shows and other popular entertainments would take place in the coming summer. The scaffold, he saw, must be erected. The wheelwright's work was less essential. In almost every coachhouse some old vehicle stood rotting and it was easy enough to borrow eight wheels. Their condition was not important. What they were to bear was not heavy.

The execution was timed to take place so early in the morning, when it was hoped that the crowd would be small, that the soldiers and sailors who were to surround the scaffold moved into position by torchlight. But the word had gone round, and long before it was light enough to see the Town Commandant could sense the presence of a great multitude ominously quiet. When the sky in the east brightened and the dawn of a clear April day broke, he could see the massed faces, all pale in the new light. Even the weathered faces of soldiers and sailors looked pale; probably his own did. He feared a demonstration and was glad that he had insisted upon so large a force being called out — even the young cadets from the military academy. Between six and seven thousand men, all armed, some mounted, made a barrier between the scaffold and the crowd, but even so they were outnumbered, three, four, five to one. Best, he thought, to intimidate the people immediately; he had three hundred dragoons and he ordered them to make and keep clear a space between the outer rank of service men and the front rank of the crowd.

Daylight brightened; in the trees the birds stirred and began to call. A carriage brought Dean Hee, also looking pale. He had been on his knees most of the night praying for the souls of the men who, whatever their offences, must be reckoned amongst those for whom Christ died. The executioner and his assistants arrived and the crowd made a sighing sound, like wind blowing through a cornfield.

Then came the carriage in which the two condemned men sat, guarded and manacled.

Now, thought the Town Commandant, it will come if it comes at all. He gave a signal and the dragoons stopped pacing and each one swung his mount around to face the crowd.

Brandt was embittered, but resigned. He had invited trouble by throwing in his lot with an upstart with a head full of idealistic notions and absolutely no sense. He was believed to have been in Struensee's confidence in amorous as well as other spheres, and that was unjust, would presently be seen to be unjust. Not that that made any difference now. What did matter was that he should not disgrace himself, his family or his caste by showing the slightest fear at the crucial moment. It should not be too difficult. He came of a long line of brave men, many of them soldiers and any soldier, going into battle faced the possibility of being horribly wounded and left alive with the pain. This would be short and sharp; two blows, the last one final. There would be a great crowd and he would show them how a gentleman should die.

Struensee was not resigned, though, like Brandt, he was embittered, not by the injustice of his sentence but by the obvious ingratitude of the people for whom he had worked so hard. He had been the People's Friend and the people were prepared to see him butchered. Like Brandt he blamed himself; he'd been a fool, throwing off so many of the conventional, accepted ideas, but retaining one, a sentimental belief that one woman was preferable to others, that copulation was not in itself sufficient.

When he thought of his right hand and all the patient skill it had acquired and of the muscle, ligaments, bones and veins . . . when he thought of his head, all he knew, all he planned, all he had been, could have been, should have been, then he rebelled against the waste of it all. But worst was the fear. He'd never seen animals on the way to the shambles without a feeling of shuddering pity; he had for years been almost a vegetarian. When he thought of the block black horror engulfed him. When he thought of Caroline he saw her as his partner in folly, the instrument of his undoing. Two years ago, almost to the day, on just such a day as this promised to be, they had ridden together along the western *allee*, where tonight this body of his would lie, hacked into joints, meat on a butcher's slab.

He knew that he would have lived like a monk, lived on bread and water, slept on the bare earth for the rest of his life, in order to have had the rest of his life. He would have been happy to be stupid, ugly, poor, despised, so long as he could see the dawn, the dusk, the change of seasons. He knew — who could know better than a doctor? — that all men must die, but not like this: in the fullness of time, a life's work done, the bones weary; the mind ready for rest in oblivion.

Brandt went first, carrying his well-bred, insouciant arrogance to the end. When the shackles were struck from his wrists one of the executioner's assistants went to help him out of his jacket. Brandt said, "Stand off, do not presume to touch me." Dean Hee spoke to him and Brandt nodded and smiled, a gentleman agreeing to take wine, to participate in a game of cards. He rolled back the right sleeve of his shirt, laid his head on the block, his hand beside it, bore the two blows which his limited imagination had foreseen, and was dead. Not a tremor; not a flinch.

He'd died as a man should. God give me strength to do likewise.

But Johann Frederick Struensee, you cast away God years ago, when you were a pious little boy, shocked to learn that many of those who prayed "Give us this day our daily bread", seldom had bread at all, lived on seaweed, boiled nettles, goosegrass, Rousseau and Voltaire his priests, Reason his deity, the good of all men his aim; love his undoing. And nothing to lean upon now.

Fifteen steps up to the scaffold; Enevold's blood still steaming in the fresh morning air; the crowd watching, silent and passive. Dean Hee, futilely attempting to make a routine out of a massacre. "Are you very truly sorry for your actions?" "Do you leave this world without hatred or malice against any person whatsoever?"

Stamping the passport for admittance to a Paradise that did not exist.

Agree; get it over with.

He had to be helped out of his jacket; other hands rolled up his sleeve. When his right hand was severed he jerked so violently that his head moved and the last, merciful blow, though it severed his neck, went a little awry, leaving his chin on the block, glued down by Brandt's now coagulating blood.

The three hundred horses of the Dragoons, the horse of the Town Commandant and the humbler steeds between the shafts of the various vehicles, became restive, disliking the smell of spilt life. All the little birds took wing.

"Both died, truly repentant," Dean Hee said.

It went off without a hitch, the Town Commandant thought, with great relief.

The executioner decided that his assistants could deal with the disembowelling and the hewing into four quarters.

The crowd dispersed, peaceably.

The bits of what had once been men were heaved into a cart which trundled off to the western *allee*, along which, on just such an April day, two years ago but for two days, Struensee and Caroline had ridden to their doom. On each post a head, and a severed hand as the law decreed; on each wheel one quarter of a carcass. The little birds who greeted the morning spring with song stayed aloof, but the flesh eaters to whom there was but one season, that of hunger, swooped in and picked the bones as clean as those of the skeleton from which Johann Frederick Struensee had learned the principles of anatomy at the University of Heidelberg.

At Kronborg Caroline woke from a dreamless sleep induced by one of Mantel's brews. Light showed behind the curtain's edge and the birds were singing. Another day to be lived through with nothing but despair and remorse for company.

Then there was something new, a paralysing fear such as she had never known or imagined. The worst nightmare had not terrified her so. She was alone in the barely twilight room, shut in with something so unspeakably evil, so threatening and so real that she wanted to ward it off with her hands, but they could not move. She tried to call out and no sound came. She lay helpless, sweating and shivering, waiting for whatever it was to strike. It came close and fell upon her and as the fear had been all consuming, so was the pain; not in any one place, not with bruising or burning or the agony of childbirth, simply pain all over and all through.

Death; this was death; accept it, give way to it, be glad of it . . .

Mantel always came first, padding softly in case she should be asleep, poor lady; she never once had been on any morning since they had come here. He would draw the curtains, inquire if she had slept at all, regard her with grave concern, paler, thinner than yesterday?

make some remark about the weather and then go down and make a cup of tea.

This morning there was no sound from the bed and he withdrew quietly. The last draught had been effective and she was short of sleep. He took up a position outside the door so that he could guard her from the first clattering maid, the first dilatory lady. "Her Majesty is still sleeping." He was about the only person in the place who now used her title without hostility and a covert sneer. She was divorced, she was deposed, she was disgraced; why should she still be addressed as though she were Queen?

She was still asleep at ten o'clock and at eleven when the Castle Governor came to make his daily visit, to ask if she had any complaints. Today it was also his duty to tell her the news, brought from Copenhagen by courier, that the sentence upon Count Struensee had been carried out. Dry disciplinarian that he was Lieutenant-Colonel von Hauch was not an unkindly man and was not unwilling to defer this unpleasant task for an hour or two.

But Mantel was growing anxious; there was nothing noxious about the draught, an infusion of bruised willow bark and dandelion leaves with enough honey and rum to render it palatable. Nothing there to hurt anyone. Was there? Was there?

The lady-in-waiting whom he liked least came back for the third time and said crossly, "Unless Her Majesty wakes now we shall hardly have her dressed in time for dinner."

393

"Her Majesty has slept badly all these weeks," he said. It was only a half protest.

"That is no reason for delaying everybody and everything. Go in and draw the curtains."

However careful one was they rattled. The bright sunshine of a perfect spring morning made its way through the narrow, deepset window and fell upon the bed.

For a moment Mantel thought his mistress was dead, her face was so changed; all the marks of misery and hopelessness that had marred it and aged it by twenty years in three months were smoothed away; she looked peaceful and happy. All her woes over. Then he saw that the sheet — greyish-looking, wet-looking — rose and fell as she breathed.

He said to the lady-in-waiting at the doorway, "Her Majesty is sleeping peacefully."

High heels clattered on the stone between doorsill and carpet.

"Your Majesty! It is almost mid-day! It is time you were awake."

Caroline opened her eyes, seemed to be confused for a second or two and then said, as she said every morning, "Good morning, Mantel." She smiled, the first time he had seen her smile at Kronborg. He bowed and wished her good morning.

She looked towards the other side of the bed; one of her ladies; she'd been too sunk in apathy and despair to bother about their names; this was one of the most hostile; but in this awakening she, too must be smiled at.

394

"I shall be ready to be dressed in about half an hour," Caroline said.

"As Your Majesty wishes," the lady said; the flounce of her skirt, the click of her heels expressed displeasure.

"Your Majesty will take tea?" Mantel asked, watching for, apprehensive of the moment when she should come to her full senses and that old, troubled mask fall into place again.

"It's late, isn't it?" He thought she was referring to the difficulty — how could she know? — of getting a kettle boiled in a kitchen where bad-tempered cooks were preparing dinner.

"I'll manage," he said.

"I've been away a long time, Mantel. To a very far place. I wish I could tell you, but there are no words. I can tell you, though, that everything is all right. Nobody need be sad any more. Just a frontier to be crossed."

"Would Your Majesty eat a finger of toast?" He had occasionally coaxed her to eat that.

"Anything," she said. "You know, Mantel, Lazarus couldn't explain either; but you may take my word for it. What happened this morning made no difference. Everything is all right . . ."

Mantel knew nothing of Lazarus; the Bible had played no part in his upbringing. Years before he was born Germany had been torn by the religious wars; Catholic against Protestant and in the confusion a few people had slipped away, back to older gods, less controversial altars. His family had been amongst the renegades; every morning his old grandmother in her

395

little inn at the forest's edge, sanded her floor in a pattern that ignorant people thought pretty; it was a guard against evil spirits. She had methods of attracting the attention of the good ones, too, and they appeared to work satisfactorily. She had never heard of Lazarus, dead for three days and come back, able, if he could have found words, to tell all.

Running down the stairs to do battle with cross, flushed-face cooks for a hook on which to hang a kettle, for a place at the fire to toast a bit of bread, Mantel attributed all that the Queen had said to the fact that she had been abruptly wakened from some happy dream. He must get her to eat and drink before misery clamped down again. He heard, in the kitchen, what had happened at dawn in the capital.

Caroline knew that it was no dream. Dreams were communicable in a fashion, this was not. Dreams began to recede as the day opened and ordinary things displaced them. This was not a dream; it was an experience, part of her, forever. She knew. This world where everything seemed to matter so much, had no importance at all; it was a bridge to be crossed, a tunnel to be passed through.

CHAPTER
THREE

Copenhagen, April 28th 1772

The Prince Regent asked, "Sir Robert, have you been to Aarbourg?"

"No, Your Royal Highness. I have been busy here. But I did send one of my secretaries, a reliable and observant young man."

"And what did he report?"

How difficult! She had been found guilty, just escaped a death sentence. Could one legally, rationally, complain about the place to which she was to be confined? There had still been no move from England; the whole situation was tricky and without precedent.

"He is young," Sir Robert said, "perhaps a little sentimental . . . He said it was no place for a Queen, but that is only his opinion." The young secretary had said that it was a place hardly suitable to house pigs.

"I sent a man, too," the Prince Regent said surprisingly; "he is not young, he is not sentimental; his report disgusted me. There has been some attempt to render the place weather-proof, in part at least. What few drains there are run into an open cesspool, two hundred years old — it is two hundred years you know, since Aarbourg was lived in. The water supply is equally defective."

The situation is unbelievably remote and the aspect very bleak, so the young secretary's report had concluded. The Regent's man, blunter and briefer had said — fit for pigs, not horses.

"Do you believe, Sir Robert, that His Britannic Majesty would wish his sister to live out the rest of her life in such a place?"

"He may feel reluctant to interfere with the decision of the Tribunal."

"So am I. But she is not my sister."

Between them yawned the thing about which neither of them spoke. Aarbourg, disused for two hundred years, crumbling to ruin, had been repaired, in a limited way in February, before Struensee had confessed, before the Queen had signed that reckless statement. And nobody knew by whose order; some men had arrived, done some makeshift repairs and departed. Somebody knew; somebody had made provision, of a kind, foreseeing the verdict of guilty and its possible stopping short of the death sentence.

"His Majesty of England has many houses," the Regent said. She would be happy in England, roses, dogs, horses; other lovers?

"It is not a matter of accommodation," Sir Robert said, ashamed that this suggestion should come from the wrong side of the gulf.

"It is . . . as always . . . policy."

"With me, also. There is the law and the law must be upheld by those who are upheld by it. I think that

398

Aarbourg is completely unsuitable as a place of residence for a woman already in poor health, but for me to say so would seem a criticism of the Tribunal's order. I feel that her brother could be informed, and he could offer some alternative accommodation, without risking criticism. Would you not agree?"

Sir Robert agreed. "I will write to that effect," he said; but he was dubious as to the result. His master had remained curiously detached, even when, for a time, it looked as though the poor girl's life was in jeopardy.

"There would be no opposition to any proposal His Majesty cared to make," the Regent said. "Frankly . . ." Frankness was not a quality easily associated with this curious young man, Sir Robert reflected, but he was reasonable and not ill-natured; ". . . her removal would be welcome to almost everyone. Opinion is not unanimous; the Queen has some vehement partisans."

"Your Royal Highness would wish me to draw His Majesty's attention to that aspect of the suggestion?"

"It might help him to reach a decision."

When Sir Robert left the Regent eased his aching back in the tall chair and surveyed his performance with satisfaction. He had saved her from death, and he had saved her from incarceration at Aarbourg, and done it without revealing his hand. Once again he visualized her in England, the place for which, he had deduced from a chance remark or two, she had always been a little homesick.

However, when in May Sir Robert went to inform Caroline of the change in her future, it was not of

399

England that he spoke. It was of Zell in the Electorate of Hanover, not far from the city of Hanover.

"An ancient but beautiful castle," said Sir Robert who had never seen it. "And I understand that at the same time as my instructions were issued, orders were sent for urgent work to begin at Zell in order to make it fit a residence for Your Majesty."

Where and in what style she lived was no longer of any importance; but it would be a relief to be away from the disapproving Danish suite. And she felt grateful to George for this evidence of family loyalty. She well understood why he was unable to offer her a home in England.

"I shall be happy to go to Zell," she said.

"I hope that you will be also gratified to know that — after some negotiation — the matter of your dowry has been decided. It is to be returned, intact."

With pride and triumph Sir Robert laid these trophies of victory before her, and he wore the same spaniel look; see-what-I-have-brought-you. To the dowry she had never given a thought, but plainly he had worked on her behalf. Warm gratitude washed over her; on impulse she put her arms about him and kissed his cheek.

"All this I owe to you," she said. "You are my deliverer. Thank you. Thank you."

He went rigid with embarrassment; his worst doubts about her nature confirmed.

"It was my pleasure as well as my duty to protect your interests." But the warmth had touched him. "I am more than rewarded." He was angry with himself for sounding a little breathless. He went on to tell her that two or three English frigates would be sent to take her from Kronborg to Stadt.

Back in Copenhagen — all the way thinking so warm, so impulsive, so young, small wonder she had come to grief, but actions can be misconstrued, anyone watching this afternoon might think that I — he wrote to his sister, the one person in the world to whom he could express himself freely. "Can you figure to yourself," he wrote, "what I felt in passing through the vaulted entrance of Hamlet's Castle to carry to an injured and afflicted princess the welcome proofs of fraternal affection and liberty restored?"

"Zell?" Mantel said astounded. "My home. My birthplace. It is so beautiful! Your Majesty will be happy there." He knew that he had used the wrong word, or in the wrong sense; that kind of happiness for her was over. She was resigned and tranquil, free of distress, but he had known her in the days when she was happy and he knew the difference. To cover the slip he proceeded to describe the castle and its environs; the moat, the drawbridge, the pepperpot turrets which he remembered with enchantment. "Better than this, Your Majesty; better than Aarbourg." He had heard some doleful descriptions of Aarbourg; but he had been determined to go there, if the Queen went, and to mitigate so far as was in his power, the discomforts of the place.

"So, after all, England has remembered her prodigal daughter," Juliana said sourly. She had suffered another, she felt final, disappointment. On the morning of Struensee's execution she had stood by one window of her rooms in the Christianborg, and watched, through a seaman's glass, the whole gruesome business. There goes the last of my enemies! Frederick was Regent as she had always intended, and she had visualized the long happy years through which they would work in close accord. The enticing fruit of fulfilled ambition had hung for so long, almost, never quite, in reach; now, in her hand at last, it was a wasp-hollowed shell. The Prince Regent was not the loved and loving son for whom she had planned and schemed and worked. Instead of the slavish devotion to which she felt entitled, there was animosity; he seemed to be against her, to take a perverse delight in being awkward. That was bad enough, but worse was the realization that she no longer loved him; that his call to power gave her no delight now. She saw that she had not, in fact, been ambitious for him at all, but for herself. He seemed to know it, too; and he had inherited her skill at dealing verbal wounds. Too often he mentioned, in a casual tone, the possibility of Christian remarrying, the possibility of his own marriage; in other words saying that her time as first lady was limited. The barbed remarks she launched at him he parried with skill. She continued to make them. She made one now.

"For her a most advantageous move. The Hanoverians are amongst the most well-set-up and amorous men in the world. And a divorcee, with no reputation to lose . . ." One of her unfinished sentences.

"You are the first person I have ever heard hint that she was promiscuous," he said calmly. "Have you access to information denied the rest of us?" Have you been working behind my back?

"I only know what was brought out at the Tribunal."

"That surely pointed to the opposite of promiscuity."

"It indicated lack of opportunity. In her immediate circle the temptation was slight. She took as her lover the first proper, well-set-up man who entered it."

"Oh," he said, "were you also an admirer of Struensee?"

She knew nothing of how he felt; she would never know; nobody ever would. But, she had used the words "well-set-up" twice in two minutes. He'd heard and resented them; and in due course all such jibes would be paid for.

CHAPTER
FOUR

Kronborg,
May 27th-30th 1772

Captain John MacBride had the disciplined, cool, stolid exterior of a typical naval man and his appearance did not belie his nature; his hasty, even violent temper had been so disciplined that now few people guessed at its existence; he was cool in danger or emergency; nobody had ever seen him excited or unsure of himself. But in secret there had survived in him one tiny thread of boyish romanticism almost atrophied for lack of exercise, but still capable of seeing, in his latest errand, something of a crusade. He was, in effect, a knight going to the rescue of a damsel in distress.

That the distress was largely of her own making, he did not consider. Newspaper reading and tavern gossip were things with which sailors early in their careers, learned to do without; he had little knowledge and less interest in what the Queen of Denmark had done, or was said to have done. She was an English Princess in the hands of foreigners and he had been dispatched to rescue her. Foreigners, of whom the world was full, foreign parts being anything outside territorial waters,

404

were liable to do anything and the Danish foreigners had shut an English Princess in the Castle of Kronborg and he had orders to take her off, to make her as comfortable as possible aboard the *Southampton* and conduct her to Stadt.

The frigates arrived and anchored in the lingering light of a late May evening; and within an hour Captain MacBride's temper was aroused. In proper fashion he sent an officer ashore to ask four simple questions; first, if he fired a salute of guns, would it be civilly returned; second, was Sir Robert Keith at Kronborg; third, was Her Majesty being treated with respect; and fourth, could he call upon her.

The officer came back; a salute would be returned; Sir Robert was in Copenhagen; nobody could be allowed access to Her Majesty.

Captain MacBride put on his best uniform and had himself rowed ashore, as soon as the salute of seventeen guns had been fired, and returned. He also went through the vaulted entrance, but having profited little from his education, he did not think of Hamlet; he thought it a dreary place and chilly, even on this warm evening. The commandant of the castle, Lieutenant-General von Hauch and Count Holstein received him civilly enough. Conversation was difficult; Captain MacBride knew no German and his French had been learned in the wrong places and from the wrong people. Count Holstein's — he had had a French tutor — was so fluent and rapid that Captain MacBride was convinced that he was a Frenchman and in his report to the Admiralty referred to him as the "Compte De

405

Holstein". It was made quite clear however that no orders had come from Copenhagen to allow anyone, even Captain MacBride, access to Her Majesty. Most probably he would be allowed to see her in the morning. He would be informed.

Would he drink a glass of wine with them? His temper, rearing, dictated an impossible retort — that he had no orders from the Admiralty that obliged him to drink with a couple of old wooden figureheads, who could, he was convinced, have let him go to the Queen had they wished. However, temper had been mastered long ago, in his midshipman's days, and he thanked them, but he must get back to his ship; the loading of the Queen's baggage must begin first thing in the morning.

Nothing happened next day; no message, no baggage. By four o'clock in the afternoon he was furious; but he knew the rules. He was in charge of this expedition and it would be improper for him to expose himself to a further rebuff. He sent for Captain Davies of the *Seaford* and said, "Look here, Taffy, you talk Froggie. Go ashore and tell them from me that I'm waiting to know what's happening. Did the Queen get my message? Where's this Keith fellow? Where's the baggage? You can tell them I think they've been rude. Rude and worse. I don't even know how many people will be coming aboard. They're either bloody inefficient, or they're up to some trick."

Captain Davies came back, again with unsatisfactory replies. Sir Robert Keith had just arrived from Copenhagen and would receive Captain MacBride at noon the next day and present him to the Queen. About twenty people would be embarking with her. Twenty! Take all day to stow.

Without employing any arithmetic, in which he was expert, Captain MacBride had thought of the distressed damsel as young and pretty: he was not disappointed; nor had he been wrong in the matter of distress. She was calm, amiable, even smiling, speaking English with a slight hesitation and apologizing prettily, "Except with Sir Robert, it has been a long time . . ." When she smiled or spoke with animation she looked very young; at other times there was a look of settled sadness and resignation which made her seem older. He was convinced that the foreigners had not treated her well; and then, as he was leaving the Castle, he was not treated well himself. A Danish Commodore, plainly chosen for the job because he spoke English, came up and greeted him and said that he had been ordered to inspect the accommodation allotted to Her Majesty aboard the *Southampton*.

This was another of the sad little misunderstandings that bedevil good intentions. It was the Regent, Frederick, who was anxious that on a voyage lasting seven days Caroline should be as comfortable as possible; he had feared that "the prodigal daughter" might be received as such and put into cramped and inconvenient quarters. But he had, as always, moved under cover and the English-speaking Danish Commodore said to Captain MacBride that the inspection was to be made by the King's orders.

"And they," said Captain MacBride, "mean absolutely nothing to me. Unless you come as part of Her Majesty's suite you don't set foot on my deck. All you can do is to show me the exact place from which Her Majesty will embark. And when she crosses the high water mark she will be in my charge."

In his opinion they had all been, as he wrote in his report, with a capital letter, "Aukward", And he could be aukward too.

He had marked the spot around the point of land on which the castle stood to which he intended to take his frigates in order to make the Queen's embarkation easy; but he did not move to it in order to facilitate the loading of the baggage. Let the beggars sweat it out! He developed a fanatical tenderness and concern about the paintwork of his vessels. Teach the beggars to be careful!

Finally everything was stowed and the three frigates rounded the point, beautiful and precise as birds in flight. If all the Lords of the Admiralty, if the King himself had been expected aboard the vessels could not have been in better trim; everything that could be scrubbed and scoured had been scrubbed and scoured, every bit of metal polished to a blinding brightness; the sailors themselves were so clean and neat and wooden-faced that they looked like out-size children's toys. The Navy, at least a small bit of it, was here.

Caroline was ready. She was leaving, forever, the country where, amongst some miseries, she had known the happiness of love and this could have been an emotional moment. But though Johann's skull, picked clean, still stood, impaled upon its post and his larger bones lay on the wheels in the western *allee*, she did not feel that she was leaving him here. She was leaving her children, the son whom she had intended to bring up so well, the daughter whom she had meant to save from the kind of loveless marriage that she herself had known. This was sad, and she was sad, but not in the way that she would have been sad before. Everything would be all right in the end, when the life sentence, whatever shape it took, had been served. Of her own life sentence she had served almost twenty-one years, crammed with varying experiences; she hoped it would end soon. In the meantime there was nothing to do but to wait, to be amiable, calm, even cheerful — since all would be right in the end.

A temporary landing stage had been built out from the top of the grey stone sea wall against which the tides beat themselves in vain, to the point where the water was deep enough to bear a boat. At its end waited Captain MacBride's own barge. On to this landing stage she stepped, her hand on Count Holstein's stiffly bent arm. Then Captain MacBride had his great moment. *She* was English and would understand; there was no need to bother with Froggie talk. At the exact point where high water mark showed, he stepped forward and tapped the man whom he still thought of as Compte De Holstein, smartly on the shoulder and said,

"From now on Her Majesty is in *my* charge. Madam, permit me . . ." He offered his arm and Caroline laid her hand on it and gave him a smile that he

409

remembered to the end of his days. Moving as though he were walking on eggs he took her to the end of the little landing stage and in the scoured, furbished-up barge the biggest, best looking member of the *Southampton*'s crew — who never could understand what he had done to be selected for this tricky task, stood up and handed the Queen of Denmark down. She was nimbler than most women and the transfer from Danish soil to what Captain MacBride thought to be an extension of England was made neatly and without hitch. And the moment she was seated, safe in this bit of England, all the flags broke out on the frigates and the guns roared a royal salute.

Her departure in summer sunshine, banished, disgraced and bereft, was more spectacular than her arrival in Roskilde. Captain John MacBride was a better scene-setter than Christian.

She should have been delighted, and in a way she was, this was England, this was George, but it meant nothing, just another little scene, well-played; the actors in it to be thanked and congratulated. The great thing was, she now realized, that as one served one's life sentence, passed through this tunnel, crossed this bridge, one must try to make everybody happy, so far as one could.

Part Seven

CHAPTER
ONE

Zell, June 1772-October 1774

One of the difficulties about keeping everybody happy at Zell was the matter of boredom; her small suite was now composed of Hanoverians, some of them not ill-disposed towards her, but her Court was not really a Court, people became bored, and then because they were, they quarrelled; changes were frequent. The other problem was money, something she had never been obliged to think about before.

With her dowry and her jewels she looked upon herself as a rich woman. Other people thought so, too; the tradesmen exploited her, stewards cheated, mendicants at all levels begged. Count Seckerdorf, who was Comptroller of her Household, made unavailing attempts to explain to her the difference between capital and income and would point out if the former were drawn upon the latter would decrease. Then she would say, "I don't mind. I wouldn't mind being poor." Maybe not, he thought, but His Majesty of England would mind, and be compelled to supply you, and that he would not like. At the same time the Baron found it impossible to be strict enough with her; he thought she was charming and ill-used; when she suggested the construction of a little theatre so that the Court could have some entertainment, he sighed and gave in, merely remarking that it would be very expensive.

Hospitality was expensive, too, and during her first year she was called upon to supply a great deal of it. Visitors from every country in Europe were eager to see the woman who had been the cause of so much scandal. If their credentials were in order they had to be fed, sometimes lodged; and then, every other Wednesday Augusta came, and Caroline was always anxious that nothing should be lacking then.

Augusta's first, second, even third visit, had been very welcome to Caroline; another of the family lining up alongside, giving proof of family solidarity. Someone to whom she was Caro. But her pleasure in these visits steadily decreased. Augusta was very inquisitive, very critical, and much given to remarks which began, "Had you only . . ." or "Had you not . . ." She could even convey this phrase in a look, and she invariably did so when Caroline made any mention of her children. Augusta herself had a daughter — named Caroline — and was planning to marry her to George's eldest son; and that struck an odd echo. Not that it mattered.

What did matter was the steady lessening of affection; it seemed so sad that Augusta should travel between thirty and forty miles, once a fortnight, in good weather and bad, and then kill all sisterly fondness by criticism, advice that sounded like criticism, and questions. One day a very distasteful thought occurred to Caroline — Does she come to spy on me? It was not a thing one should think about one's

414

sister, but once the possibility had entered one's mind it refused to be dislodged.

Augusta, who was firm and businesslike, thought the household at Zell a very ramshackle affair and Caroline's whole attitude most unsatisfactory. She gave no sign of any real penitence for her outrageous behaviour, little interest in or curiosity about affairs in the outside world; no real concern about what she wore, what she ate, or how she was served. She'd say, "Yes I know," or "Well, does it matter so much?" And once she said, "I don't care."

"And that," Augusta said with asperity, "has always been your trouble. 'Don't care was made to care'" she said, quoting the old nursery rhyme.

"That was one of Alice's sayings," Caroline said. For a second her face assumed the wistful look that it took on when she mentioned her children. Then she said, "Dear Alice!" and smiled.

Over the matter of possessions the new government of Denmark had been extraordinarily generous — Caroline had never suspected to whom she owed this gesture. She had been allowed to bring away not only the things which she had taken from England but anything she wished from the gifts that had been presented to her while she was Queen. One of these was a beautiful centre-piece for a table, made in the Copenhagen factory which was rapidly expanding the range of its work. Four cherubs held a bowl in which fruit or flowers could be placed. Out of myriads of

415

things she had chosen it to bring away because she liked it.

One day, sitting down to dinner, Augusta said,

"Has the cherub bowl been broken?"

"Not so far as I know."

"You don't sound very *sure*. You should insist, Caro, that any damage to your personal belongings should be reported to you *at once*. That is a rule that I made, and held to; in a household larger than this. And far busier. With your permission I shall inquire about that bowl and I shall speak severely to anyone who has been careless."

"I sold it," Caroline said. "I needed some money and poor Seckerdorf sighs and sighs . . . So I picked out a few things with which I could dispense and Mantel took them into Hanover and sold them for me. They fetched far more than I dared hope."

"No wonder," Augusta said when she had recovered her breath. "Every fat, rich burgher's wife would be only too pleased to have in her house something that you, once a Queen, had been obliged to sell. How could you? Will you never learn? Selling things from your table. How does that reflect upon George, upon me?"

"In no way," Caroline said placidly. "Mantel is far too discreet. And his sense of what is seemly equals your own. He had some story, I forget now. Something about his grandmother — who keeps an inn and sometimes takes payment in kind."

"So now," Augusta said with intense bitterness, "you connive with servants!" She added irrelevantly, "And Mantel is too old and too big to be a page."

"I know," Caroline said placidly. "I promoted him. He is now my *valet-de-chambre*. I was," she said, "locked up in Kronborg for four months and apart from Alice he was my only friend there. Often I feel that apart from Baron Seckerdorf, he is my only friend here."

As she said this she looked at her sister. It was a look so candid, so — Augusta thought — witless — that the immediately following thought was — No wonder she came to grief! Absolutely no sense at all. And yet, of all the sisters, Caro had always been regarded as the clever one: which simply showed how mistaken governesses and tutors, and even Mamma had been.

Even in this slapdash establishment, enough of formality was preserved to require that anyone calling upon the Queen and wishing to be received by her, must step into a cold little cell to the right of the entry and sign his name in a big leather-bound book and give some information about his nationality and social standing. He would then go away and await an invitation. Whether he were merely received, invited to a Drawing-room, or the theatre, or to dinner, was later entered in a separate column. On each of her visits Augusta inspected this book, keeping a sharp lookout for the names of people — men especially — who came too frequently and also for anyone of Danish nationality; Caroline, having so little sense of self-preservation, must be protected.

Over her visitors — growing steadily fewer as time went on, Caroline was as vague as about everything else. Augusta would say, "And whom have you seen since I was here last?" and Caroline would try to remember, adding where possible, some comment. When she forgot, as she often did, to mention a name that Augusta had noticed, Augusta would mention it herself, at the same time giving Caroline a suspicious look — What are you trying to hide from me? You can hide nothing from me!

Spy was an ugly word, and even in the mind to be avoided; but the conviction that Augusta had been told to keep an eye on her grew steadily as time went on. And it seemed a pity that as the visits became less pleasurable, they became more prolonged. Augusta grumbled about the food, the bed clothes, the service, the temperature of the rooms, yet she came regularly on alternate Wednesdays and now stayed until Friday, or Saturday, even Sunday occasionally.

One day in September 1774, she arrived, studied the book and presently invited Caroline to account for her doings in the last eleven days. Caroline made no mention of one visitor, who had been received twice in a week, once to a Drawing-room and once to dinner. So, when nothing more seemed to be forthcoming, Augusta asked in a sharp tone, and with *that* look,

"And who is this Nicolas Wraxall?"

"Oh," Caroline said, "how could I have forgotten him? Such a pleasant young man. English: a great traveller and most interesting to talk to." It might be as well not to mention that he had promised to do his best to obtain a picture of her children whose portraits were being painted by someone whom he had known in

418

Florence and who would, if asked, as a favour to a friend, make some additional sketches; to mention Freddy and Louise-Augusta would only provoke another look.

"You received him twice in a week."

"That is true. I invited him first to a Drawing-room and he was most entertaining. And he is a very respectable young man — the Prince of Anhalt-Dessau entertained him; I could hardly do less. Also he undertook a little errand for me."

"What?"

"Augusta, we were always told that except as an exclamation of surprise, 'What' was not a word to be used alone."

Then — and this the sorry part of it — at this reminder of the upbringing which they had shared — Augusta smiled, almost in a shame-faced way. We are sisters, we could be friends, Caroline thought, if only she would take me as I am.

"He was going from here to Hamburg," she volunteered. "And he said he would see the British Minister there, Mr. Mathias, and ask him to arrange for a company of French comedians to come and perform here in my little theatre. If they come I hope it will be on an evening when you are here."

"If you inform me in time I will make a point of being here," Augusta promised. There was the absurdity of it: her visits to Zell, begun as a duty, had become a pleasure to her. The place was ill-run, the food often inferior, there were so many changes that often Augusta thought that only Baron Seckerdorf and Mantel were permanencies, disputes were frequent, visitors growing rare; and yet there was something lively about it, informal, warm, almost happy that made it compare favourably with her own establishment. After all, Augusta too, had spent her formative years at Kew.

Part Eight

CHAPTER ONE

Hamburg; Zell, October 1774

Nicholas Wraxall had friends and acquaintances in almost every major city in Europe. Young, presentable, rich, restless, he was typical of the English gentlemen who went about, spending freely and by their demands greatly improving the service in inns and the quality of post horses. He was more amusing than most, endlessly inquisitive, a confirmed gossip; he was also romantic and completely intrepid.

In Hamburg, as soon as he had installed himself at the inn where he was remembered and warmly greeted, he washed, changed from his travelling clothes and strolled along to make his presence in the city known to his friend, Hans Loesel, a ship owner who lived like a prince. He hoped to be invited to supper, and he was. "It will be quite a party," Hans said; "I have eight or nine other guests, all men. Two or three Danes from Altona across the river. And a sucking pig is cooking."

Wraxall's last meal under a private roof had been with Queen Caroline, in Zell, and a very bad dinner it had been; since then he had been on the road, served with the ubiquitous veal of German inns. A supper party, with sucking pig and the chance of making fresh acquaintances opened out a most engaging prospect.

He was a gossip, but he was a man of breeding, and he decided not to mention his visit to the ex-Queen of Denmark. With Danes it might well be a sore subject: but he could, and did mention that he had dined with the Prince of Anhalt-Dessau, and that he had seen and talked to the Princess Royal of Prussia who was confined in Stettin, in much the same circumstances and for exactly the same alleged offence as Caroline was at Zell.

A man on the opposite side of the table, leaned a little forward and said,

"Mr. Wraxall; you are English, I understand. Zell was no great distance. Why did you not visit your own Princess, so similarly immured?"

"I did," Wraxall said, slightly irked by the implied reproach. "I attended one of Her Majesty's Drawing-rooms and on another day had the honour of being asked to dine." He spoke with some emphasis; after all, he had not tactlessly volunteered this information; he had been challenged to give it, and he managed to put into the words *Her Majesty* and *honoured* the feeling which he had experienced as soon as he had actually seen the Queen; she was innocent and she had been treated disgracefully. It would be rather shocking to offend anyone at the supper table of a mutual friend; perhaps it would have been better, in the circumstances, to have refused to sit down at table with Danes at all. Now that the rift was made, he might as well be explicit.

424

"I chose not to mention Queen Caroline alongside the Princess Christina because it is my opinion that the two cases are in no way comparable," he said, looking about him defiantly. Nobody spoke. But silence could convey dissent as well as consent. He said, almost fiercely because once a thing was started one might as well make a good job of it, "I think Her Majesty innocent, and very ill-used." He looked towards the head of the table where his friend, Hans sat, and said, "Hans, I am sorry. So controversial a subject is out of place at table. But that is the way I feel and nothing can alter it."

The man opposite who had provoked the outburst said, with something of cool rebuke in his voice,

"It is possible that you are not alone in your opinion, Mr. Wraxall. You are a great traveller; tell us, have you visited Pompeii?"

It was a smooth, gentlemanly change of subject and Wraxall responded to it in smooth, gentlemanly fashion. Nobody else at the table had visited the excavations of the city that had lain under a sealing crust of lava for seventeen hundred years, a seal so airtight that loaves of bread, placed in an oven on the day of the eruption, were still recognizable as loaves. Wraxall, eagerly and meticulously describing what he had seen on his three visits, held the table entranced and hoped that he had made up to his host for the near contretemps.

It seemed so, for as he took his leave, Hans said, "For how long are you in Hamburg, my friend?"

"Two days; perhaps three." He never knew; he moved as the whim, the itching foot took him. "I have a small commission. Perhaps three."

"Then you must come again when I can have you to myself. If that is agreeable to you."

"It would be most agreeable."

The inn where he was lodging and the house where he had supped were within walking distance, and both in a quiet, respectable part of the city. Responsible and obedient residents in this quarter hung lanterns over their doors at sunset, so there was no need to hire linkboys or to go attended by a servant armed with a cudgel. Wraxall set out alone; and in no time at all knew the spine-creeping feeling of being followed. He heard nothing; no dogging footsteps; glancing back over his shoulder he saw nothing; but he was being followed. He felt no fear; his pistols were locked in his valise; but he had his heavy silver-knobbed stick in his hand and he did not doubt his ability to defend himself. He rounded a corner, took ten paces and backed into a dark, yawning doorway. The corner was lighted and for a second as the follower rounded it, he was illumined; a tall man, with, it seemed no face; the collar of his cloak held so high, his hat so far drawn down. And under the light *he* paused, looking over *his* shoulder as though he feared that he might be followed; or as though he were looking for a confederate.

He passed from the lighted corner into the gloom between them, and then he said, quietly, "Mr. Wraxall?"

"I'm here," Wraxall said, stepping out of the doorway, reassured by the diffident, cultivated tone of voice and the use of his name. "What do you want with me?"

"A few words," the man said. "Forgive me; it is better for the moment that I do not tell my name or show my face. Will you cross the road with me?"

The other side of the road was unlighted; it was the boundary of the little square, dusty laurels, gravelled paths and a fountain, visible from Wraxall's window at the inn. The unknown man was more familiar with it; in complete darkness he found a seat and said,

"It is better to sit while talking. And I apologize, we apologize for this approach. There is no other way. The business is secret; it could be dangerous."

Excitement tingled in Wraxall's blood. This unknown spoke good English, with a faint foreign accent; the last Jacobite attempt to seize the English throne for the Stuarts was less than thirty years away. Secret. Possibly dangerous. Was it possible that Nicolas Wraxall was about to be asked to connive with the hopeful exiles, scattered all over Europe and the diehards in England who toasting the King, were always careful to have a glass of water handy over which the wineglass could be passed so that they drank to the *King over the water*? As to all romantics, a lost cause appealed to Nicolas Wraxall, though as a man of the world he had no rigid political affiliations.

Bumping rather clumsily on to the stone seat that he could not see and feeling the chill through his best satin breeches he said,

"What is the business?"

"It seemed that you were in favour of Queen Caroline-Matilda. That you believed her innocent and ill-used."

"I said that; as clearly as I could, in mixed company."

"Not mixed, Mr. Wraxall. Every Dane who was there this evening shared your sentiments and because of that can no longer live in Copenhagen on account of persecution and the threat of worse. They are Danes, loyal Danes, but they live in Altona so that, if the worst happens they can cross the river and be safe."

"They believe her to be innocent?"

"That is why they are in Altona."

"Then why don't they do something about it?"

"But they are, Mr. Wraxall, they are. Ready and willing, eager and not ill-prepared. The difficulty is the lack of communication. The Queen has many friends whose one wish is to restore her. But they cannot move until they have ascertained her wishes. Access to her is made impossible for those who most wish it. And she is surrounded by spies."

"I got in easily enough."

"Ah yes. That is why we are here. The Queen's friends are anxious to know whether you would be willing to use this ease of access in order to sound her out. To discover whether, if her friends took action it would be welcome to her. The circumstances under which she left Denmark were not exactly conducive to goodwill . . ."

"Are you a Dane?"

"My nationality does not matter, Mr. Wraxall."

"Then it seems that I am supposed to ask that poor unfortunate woman a question calculated to raise the highest hopes, and on no better authority than a few words spoken to me in the dark by a man whose name I don't know, whose face I have never seen. Preposterous!"

"You are hasty," the man said. "In coalmines men often take a little bird in a cage, to test for foul air. I am that little bird. I was sent to test your feeling. Naturally before a word was said to her, you would be given proof of the integrity — and of the importance of the men who move in this matter. You will see their faces, and know their names. But first we must know whether you are willing to act as go-between. Will you think it over and perhaps meet me here on the evening after tomorrow?"

"I have no need to think it over. Of course I will do it." He was all agog, all afire. An errand after his own heart. An adventure; something dramatic to enter in the Memoirs he intended to write one day.

"It could be dangerous," the man said. "If you were suspected . . . For you a stab in the back: for her a poisoned dish. She has friends; but enemies, too, who would stop at nothing. Her own sister is one of the most active of the spies. I think it would be as well to think it over."

"I have said that I will undertake it. If I thought for a year I should be of the same mind."

"Very well. Then if you will give me your word of honour, as an English gentleman, to hold their

429

identities secret, I will arrange a meeting between you and those most involved."

"I can only give you Nicolas Wraxall's word. It has never yet been questioned."

"You will be visited," the man said. "Tomorrow morning, at eleven o'clock, if that is a convenient hour for you."

"I will make it convenient."

"Then I will say good night, Mr. Wraxall; and I beg you, be careful. There is rather more risk involved than you realize."

Next morning Wraxall was called upon by two gentlemen, Herr Hutten and Herr Bucer the serving boy said. In the privacy of his room, with the door closed, they revealed themselves; one was Count von Bulow, formerly Her Majesty's Master of Horse; the other was young Baron Schimmelmann. They talked for two hours — of their own imprisonment during the crisis, the treatment that had made them take refuge in Altona, the growing discontent in Denmark where people were beginning to realize what Struensee had given them and the new government taken away, the situation between the Prince Regent and his mother which amounted to nothing less than civil war, being fought out within the walls of the Council Chamber. Nine out of ten people in Denmark, they said, would be heartily glad to welcome back the Queen and see her installed as Regent, the King being incompetent and the Crown Prince a minor.

The time had come, they both said, ripe for action; but before any action could be taken the Queen must be consulted. And also her brother, George of England. There had been no open breach with England, but trade had suffered. If the King of England would give his blessing to the plot to restore his sister to the throne from which she should never have been removed, the hands of the conspirators would be enormously strengthened.

"I will return to Zell immediately and sound out Her Majesty," Wraxall said, eager to be on his way. "A simple word, yes or no, initialled by me and sent to this inn, addressed to Herr Hutton, will serve? Good. Then I will speed back to England and test the ground there."

Count von Bulow, glad of the wholehearted co-operation, nonetheless felt a little uneasy. English; hasty; rash. But Wraxall's next words gave evidence of something behind the apparent carelessness.

"I shall need," he said, "something in writing. Something to prove to her that this is not a silly jape."

They were both silent for a moment. Then Schimmelmann said,

"At this point, Mr. Wraxall, it would be wise not to commit anything to paper. If you met with an accident . . . It would be far better if between here and Zell, all was in the head. When you are safely there you could write, or even convey by word of mouth, what we have discussed."

"I know what you mean," von Bulow said. He went to the writing table, worked the flint and tinder and lighted the thin candle. He held the sealing wax to the flame until it was bubbling and dripping and then dropped a great blob of it into the palm of his left hand, stamping it down with the sealed ring which he wore on the third finger of his right. Then he peeled it off, bringing the scalded skin with it.

"Show her that," he said. "She will know it."

Wraxall took the frail wafer and placed it carefully between the pages of the book he had carried about with him for some time and never made much headway with, Sterne's "Sentimental Journey". Suddenly the title struck him as being profoundly apt. He was about to set out on a sentimental journey; more! he was about to take a hand in the making of history. He was elated; but at the back of his mind the ferrety curiosity twitched its nose.

"The man," he said, "who followed me last night and arranged this meeting. Who is he?"

Count von Bulow said, "A reliable man; like us, entirely devoted to the Queen."

"He chooses to remain anonymous," Baron Schimmelmann added. "But his warning about spies, about the Princess Augusta, about the danger to yourself and to Her Majesty if one word leaks, they come from the very source. He *knows*."

Mr. Wraxall looked at the gold watch, a present from all his father's tenants upon his coming of age. Almost one o'clock.

"I'll be on my way," he said. He'd miss dinner, but no matter, he could eat the flannelly veal for supper, somewhere thirty, with luck even forty miles along the road that would take him back to Zell. He thought what a pity it was that this had cropped up when the evenings were beginning to draw in.

As on former occasions he wrote his name in the book, and in the next column the nature of his business, "To present a letter". He had not delayed in Hamburg to speak to Mr. Mathias about the French comedians, but Her Majesty would forgive him when she knew what he had come to tell her.

He lingered for a moment, in his friendly, gossipy way, to exchange a few words with the official who kept the book, and learned, to his consternation that Princess Augusta had arrived, unexpectedly that morning and intended to stay for three days.

Communication could not be by word of mouth; it must be written down. He returned to his inn and devoted his undoubted literary talent to compressing a two-hour conversation into a few succinct sentences. He then, with fresh wax, attached Count von Bulow's seal to the page. He was about to fold it when he realized that this was intended for a woman's perusal. And it might be opened in the presence of other people since the Queen was expecting a letter concerning French Comedians; the contents would be a shock to her; she might exclaim, change colour, even faint. So he took another sheet of paper and wrote on it that the contents of the other were so important and so secret that she must postpone reading it until she was alone.

"It is particularly necessary to conceal it from H.R.H. the Princess Augusta."

He folded the two sheets in such a way that the warning would meet her eye as soon as the letter was opened.

Next morning he received the expected invitation to dinner.

When he was shown into the drawing-room there were ten people there, awaiting the entrance of the Queen and the Princess. When they came Caroline, having said a few words of general greeting, went straight towards him and said, "Mr. Wraxall, I am glad to see you here again. You have a letter from Mr. Mathias."

He bowed and handed it to her, excitement tingling again in his blood. Caroline turned a little aside; read the top sheet, put the letter in her pocket and said, without looking at him, "Very satisfactory"; and in the most natural manner started a conversation with one of the company.

At dinner the Queen and her sister sat together in two tall chairs midway along one side of the table; Wraxall was placed opposite. As the meal progressed he congratulated himself on having managed well. And the Queen, he thought, was a splendid conspirator. Then he realized that those who had said that she was indiscreet had not misjudged her. As the cloth was drawn and the dessert brought in, she took the letter from her pocket, and holding it in her lap, read it carefully. He was so horrified that he lost track of what his neighbour was saying. But the Queen, reading words of such an explosive nature paused several times and looked up and contributed some words to the conversation. Agonized he judged the proximity of those two chairs; about a foot between them, but both were large, with out-curving arms, so that there was considerable distance between the sisters. The Princess was getting on in years; some people grew long sighted as they aged. Had she? What a risk to take! What a witlessly rash thing to do! The pear with which Wraxall was rounding off another not very sumptuous meal tasted like turnip.

Afterwards everyone retired to the drawing-room and stood about drinking coffee; then the royal ladies retired and Wraxall, still shaken, went back to his inn, prepared to wait for the Queen to make the next move. He imagined that she would send for him on some pretext the next day, and see him alone. And he would *warn* her, personally and very firmly. He removed his jacket and his neckcloth — damp as a result of his agitation — put on his dressing gown, poured himself a glass of brandy and made another assault on his book.

He was soon disturbed, however. His room was just at the head of the stairs and he heard his own name, "Mr. Wraxall, an English gentleman . . ." a voice said. Abandoning Sterne for the twentieth time, Wraxall opened his door and saw at the foot of the stairs Baron Seckerdorf whom he had lately seen in the castle drawing-room.

"I will dress, your Excellency, and come down," he said. He was agitated again. Discovered already?

"No, no Mr. Wraxall. I must apologize for disturbing you. We spoke so much about the pedigree and performance of this horse that I forgot to ask the price. May I come up?"

"If you don't object to my room as well as my person being in some disarray . . ."

Not surely the stab in the back. Not openly like this. Nevertheless, Wraxall was aware that from the moment when he agreed to act as go-between, he had stepped on to unknown, potentially dangerous territory. Having admitted his visitor he slammed the door and stood with his back to it, wary, ready for anything.

"Her Majesty sent me," Baron Seckerdorf said in a low voice. "Move from the door, Mr. Wraxall, there is an ear at every keyhole. She sent you this, her own, personal seal." He held it out, a pretty trinket: but that might be a device to distract attention: without taking his eyes from Baron Seckerdorf, Wraxall reached out his left hand.

"You are cautious; rightly so. I assure you that Her Majesty trusts me absolutely. I must be brief. She bids me tell you that she has read your letter with great emotion and wishes you to inform Count von Bulow that she is in full agreement and willing to co-operate in every way. She begs that, having communicated with him you should go to England and endeavour to enlist her brother to her cause. She trusts you to keep her informed. But do not return openly to Zell. Go to the *Sand Krug*, a little posting inn on the edge of the forest. Present yourself as a French merchant; order roast duck for supper and pay for it with an English

436

guinea. Her Majesty is grateful for the service you are doing her and begs you not to take any avoidable risk."

"To serve her is my pleasure," Wraxall said.

"We have talked long enough," the Baron moved to the door, said in a low voice, "God speed you," and then opening the door, changed his tone.

"No horse is worth it. I'm sorry to have troubled you."

"A horse is worth what it will fetch. In my opinion you have missed a bargain."

"Augusta, excuse me for a short time. Baron Seckerdorf is waiting for me in the library."

"Business? What a time to choose." It was almost ten o'clock. Having made her comment upon the dilatory way this place was run, Augusta was disposed to be helpful. "If it concerns money, perhaps I could be of assistance." She would dearly have loved to get her hands on the Castle's accounts and see where the money *went*. Not on food certainly; nor on clothes. The red silk dress which Caroline was wearing was one of those she had brought from Denmark.

"I think it might embarrass Baron Seckerdorf, Augusta. Poor man, he hates some of the things he has to say to me; he would find it more difficult in the presence of a third person."

"Wait a minute," Augusta said. "Are you quite well? You look . . . feverish."

"It is nothing. A touch, no more, of my silly old complaint. Look . . ." She lifted the lace that bordered her sleeve and showed her arm, striped and blotched.

437

"It may last a day, it may go off in an hour." She knew the cause of this attack. Excitement and shock; the really astounding news from Denmark; the confirmation of her suspicion about Augusta; the need for haste, the need for cunning. "I shan't be long," she said and sped into the library where the baron waited.

"Did you find him?" she asked breathlessly.

"I did, Your Majesty. I think he is a reliable man and will do his best for you."

"I am sure of it. I liked him from the first. Now how long do you think? Shall I be back in Denmark by Christmas?"

This was a Caroline that he had never seen before; even the pace of her speech had changed. He said, reluctantly, because it was like dashing a child's hopes.

"That would be quite impossible. May I speak frankly?"

"I thought you were always frank."

"Oh, about money? Yes indeed. But this a business of such magnitude ... I wonder if Your Majesty quite realizes what is involved. You took your decision instantly. Others will be more cautious. Revolutions take time. I feel that Mr. Wraxall will make many journeys before His Majesty of England and your friends in Altona come to terms. It will take months, perhaps a year even.

"I was thinking of the children. Baron Seckerdorf, I *thought* I was resigned; that all I needed was patience — and faith, to sit out my time here. But when I read that letter and understood that I still had friends who believed in me; that I might see the children again and bring them up . . ." She had almost given herself away, about to say, "as he would have wished," ". . . according to my own ideas; something seemed to snap, here," she smacked her hand to her collar bone behind which her heart was thudding. "How I sat there at the table and then talked to you over the coffee, I shall never know. Never."

For although the world was a bridge to be crossed, not built upon, a tunnel to be passed through, and although she still believed that all was one, all was right in the end, when such a call sounded so clearly, so almost miraculously one saw that, in crossing the bridge, trudging through the tunnel one might make repairs, shoulder burdens. She would return to Denmark, educate, or re-educate her children, and rule as *he* would have done.

She was still intensely aware of him; not as a dead man, some shamed bones, but as part of the experience of which she could never speak. On the day of his death, drowning in despair, she had been saved; and now, rotting away in idleness, she had been called back to service. To say — even to think — that this was his doing was silly, a putting into human terms something that could never be so expressed; but she had no doubt of whose hand had drawn the curtain aside, just a little, so that she might see and be comforted by a glimpse of what was beyond; and she had no doubt about this later revelation. Tilting the page in her lap, guarding it against Augusta's sharp eye, she had read, and understood, her orders.

And even on an earthly level, where words were available; everything fitted in. Mr. Wraxall, truly a gift from God; Mantel's old grandmother at the Sand Krug, Mantel, Baron Seckerdorf.

Baron Seckerdorf said, "Your Majesty must be very careful and always remember that there are those who would sooner see you dead than restored."

She said, "Oh, I know. I know my enemies by name. I shall be *extremely* careful."

He had asked permission to be frank; now he had to be brutal.

"Your Majesty's demeanour . . . forgive me . . . it shows a certain excitability; any really watchful eye . . ."

"My face," she said, putting her hands to it. "This is something that happens in my family, from time to time. My sister understands . . ."

CHAPTER
TWO

Zell; London; Zell, February-May 1775

The little post house at the forest's edge, was a humble place which made no pretensions to catering for the "carriage trade". But on this bleak February afternoon, with the candles lighted within and the shutters not yet closed it was a welcome sight to Nicolas Wraxall who for the sake of caution had made the final stage of his journey on a slow, jolting post wagon. It had been an uncomfortable day and more tedious than it might otherwise have been, for now travelling in the guise of a Frenchman he had thought it advisable not to use more German than was necessary to get along with, so he refrained from chatter. His fellow travellers were not talkative, except about the weather; such steady rain had not fallen, day after day, within living memory. Every river and stream flooded, houses washed away, people and animals drowned. Nicolas Wraxall could have told them that in all his journeys, from Naples to the borders of Lapland he had never experienced such weather or such discomfort. He was soaked to the skin and somewhat regretted that in his anxiety to look and play his part properly he had abandoned his heavy English topcoat with its three-tiered cape off which even this rain would have shed as from a duck's back. But he was being thorough, and in a way he was enjoying himself, though even before becoming one of the proletariat, he had had vicissitudes; he had crossed one swollen stream on the back of a carthorse, another by boat, and then, on a quagmire of a road his hired carriage had overturned.

All the other post-wagon passengers save one had alighted, generally at some cross-roads with flooded fields on all sides. When the wagon lumbered into the yard behind the *Sand Krug* Wraxall forcibly restrained himself from bustling ahead of the other man, from entering the place as though he owned it and setting everybody and everything astir by his demands, as in the ordinary way he would have done. For him this night no private room, no cans of steaming hot water, no jugs of rum punch.

The mercy of a room to himself was granted him; and in it he rubbed himself down with an inadequate towel and opened his valise himself and dressed in dry clothes and then, since his room had no stove in it, carried down his soaked ones and approached the fierce-looking old woman who seemed to own the place, with the request that they might be put somewhere to dry. She said grudgingly that it might be possible when supper had been served. He ignored the surly manner, bowed and smiled, and told her in what he sincerely hoped was German spoken in a French way that she was very gracious.

"I am from France," he said. "My name is Rolland. And I hope you have a duck on the spit."

"No duck," she said. "Stuffed cabbage tonight. You understand me? No duck. Unless Monsieur wishes to give a special order and pay for it. *Canard, Monsieur Rolland? Montrez votre monnaie!*"

He took out a handful of mixed coins, selected a guinea and held it out.

She also was skilled in her part. Grumbling about people who made unreasonable demands, and telling him he would have to wait, you understand, wait, because the duck must be killed and dressed, you understand, she retired towards the kitchen quarters, taking the guinea with her.

He waited; by now he was almost accustomed to the exercise. When the duck was finally placed before him it was beautifully roasted, stuffed with apple and onion: and with it came a bottle of Burgundy wine, as good as he had ever sampled, something he would never have dreamed of ordering in such a humble hostelry.

"To compensate," she said, "you understand me, for the waiting. The waiting is necessary."

His fellow traveller and the two men who had been there when he arrived, had eaten their stuffed cabbage with every evidence of satisfaction, and gone to bed.

The waiting was necessary; so he waited, and so did the old woman and the formidable-looking dog that had never left her side and had backed away from Wraxall's advances. But at last the dog rose, ran to the door and wagged his tail and made whining noises.

"The waiting is done, you understand," the old woman said. She rose and opened the door and admitted the young man whom Wraxall vaguely remembered having seen at Zell. He wore one cloak, carried another on his arm, and as he entered closed and shook in the doorway a large umbrella. He then closed the door, bowed to Wraxall and embraced the old woman, calling her grandmother.

"This was right?" she asked.

"You were right. Now, sir, if you will come. It still rains, but by the short cut it is not far." He held the second cloak for Wraxall and the old woman fetched his hat, already half dried.

"I smell stuffed cabbage," Mantel said. "We shall be back in an hour."

"It will be hot," the old woman said.

Outside, Mantel opened the umbrella which was a large one, and side by side they plodded through the rain and the sucking mud. To one accustomed to it the distance might not seem far, to Wraxall it was a long way. At last they reached a gateway set in a wall, entered, crossed a cobbled yard and came to a high, arched doorway, beyond which was a passage, dimly lighted and a short flight of stone stairs. At the top of these Mantel removed Wraxall's cloak and took his hat; then he opened another door and stood back.

It was a pleasant room with an open fire, some shabby comfortable-looking chairs and enough books to justify it being called a library. Wraxall regretted the muddy state of his boots.

444

Caroline came in and greeted him with a warmth that was almost affectionate.

"Pray be seated, Mr. Wraxall; no, take the chair nearer the fire. This is vile weather for travelling. I'm afraid you had a most uncomfortable journey. I cannot possibly express my gratitude. If things go well, I shall immediately restore the Order of Matilda and you shall be the first to receive it. Do things go well?"

His observant, gossip's eye detected a change in her appearance — though she wore the same red silk dress — and in her manner and in her speech. She was thinner, more animated and spoke quickly.

"Well enough, but slowly. His Majesty needs more time to make a decision, and more information."

"Did you see him? How did he look? Is he well?"

"He is well. I was unfortunately unable to obtain an audience with him. I tried to make an approach through Lord Suffolk, but he was laid up with gout; so I went to Baron von Lichtenstein to whom Count von Bulow had recommended me. He is certainly in His Majesty's confidence too, for the next instruction I received was to avoid Lord Suffolk entirely and communicate only with Baron von Lichtenstein."

"So we are no farther forward."

"Oh yes, we are indeed. Revolutions are not made in a day, Your Majesty. His Majesty himself enjoins you to be patient. This is the situation, now. He feels that he cannot risk a breach between England and Denmark by giving you his open support. Nor, for various reasons can he give financial aid; but this is his promise. The moment you are restored his government will recognize the government set up by you as the legal government of Denmark. That, Your Majesty, is a great step forward."

"A very half-hearted step," she said almost violently. And immediately she regretted the words. They were critical of — and therefore disloyal to — George, and they sounded ungrateful to this man who had taken so much trouble and was now looking at her with a spaniel's eyes, look-what-I-lay-at-your-feet.

"I'm sorry, Mr. Wraxall. Of course it is a step, a great step. I am not sufficiently patient. Or political."

"I am of the opinion that you will find in the end, far more support from England than this message indicates. His Majesty is anxious to have more particulars. If he could be convinced that the majority of the *people* was in favour of your restoration he would move sooner and more positively. England is, after all," Wraxall said, smiling, "a constitutional country, dedicated to the belief in majority rule. Vox populi, vox Dei."

"In Denmark the people have no voice," she said bitterly. "That was to have been the next thing. The autocrats saw it coming; so they murdered him — and me."

The little note-taking machine at the back of his mind registered her avoidance of the dead man's name; very significant. Happy lovers could not keep the loved name off their tongues, unhappy ones could not speak it.

"They murdered your reputation, Madam, and your heart — by separating you from your children. But you

446

are alive, and if I may be permitted to say so, looking better and younger than I have yet seen you."

Men always confused health with prettiness and said one looked well when they meant handsome, and better when they meant less plain.

"Thank you Mr. Wraxall. I will admit that the thought of seeing my children again, of continuing the programme of reform, and of rewarding my friends, has rejuvenated me. And the exertions of men like you and Count von Bulow and Baron Schimmelmann are very . . . heartening to one in my position."

He noted that she made no mention of being revenged on her enemies. A truly noble person.

"My exertions have so far been small and few; but I assure Your Majesty that my time and my labour and what ingenuity I possess are completely at your service." He would have added, under the impact of a novel emotion, that he would have died for her, gladly. But English gentlemen did not make melodramatic statements.

"So far," she said, "everything has been tentative and done by word of mouth. If I wrote to my brother, urging him to be . . . to have a little more faith in my popularity with the ordinary people, could you undertake to deliver it?"

He put his I-will-die-for-you feeling into his assurance,

"I will deliver it, Your Majesty."

She went quickly to a table, sat down and began to scribble, very rapidly, but with pauses during which she gnawed the quill and once or twice snapped the fingers of her left hand.

Like most other communities strictly supervised, the family of the Princess Dowager had evolved secret means of communication, based on a simple code. Unused for ten years or more it came back to her now, easy as the alphabet, but phrases like, "the poor oppressed people" had not figured in the game played at Kew; the business of translation hindered her, made her slow where she wanted to be quick; and the need for speed was always at the back of her mind these days. She thought of her son, seven years old now; her daughter three and a half; how were they shaping? Once, from the beginning of her exile until the moment when she read, in her lap, the secret letter, she had been resigned to the fact that they would not be reared as she wished; when this world was nothing, and everything was bound to come right in the end, detachment was possible. But that letter had changed everything and she no longer saw herself as something discarded, making a slow progress to the grave; she had not yet played out her part; the world was only a tunnel, but as one went through it one must bear any burden laid upon one's shoulder; the world was only a bridge, but as one crossed it one must make any repair within one's power to make.

She was anxious, excited, impatient and always aware that time was short. Why short she did not know.

"This letter," she said, handing it to Wraxall, "could never, whatever the circumstances, compromise you,

Mr. Wraxall. Only my brothers could understand a word of it. Where do you go from here?"

"To Hamburg, Your Majesty. I must acquaint Count von Bulow and Baron Schimmelmann with His Majesty's decision and receive from them the proof which His Majesty requires that the restoration is the wish of the people. They will, I am sure, be encouraged by His Majesty's promise to acknowledge the new government, once it is established. But all these negotiations take time. A little might be saved if I could assure their Excellencies that Your Majesty would be willing to return to Copenhagen at any time that they deemed appropriate."

Her first impulse was to say — I will come at any time. But immediately she thought of George.

"I cannot move from Zell without my brother's permission. I live here under his protection, in his castle, in his dominion; I cannot leave without his consent and approbation. I have made that clear in my letter . . . Mr. Wraxall, I must leave you now; my absence may be noticed. Please believe that I know and fully appreciate what you have done and are about to do for me." She gave him her hand and smiled. For one wild moment Wraxall thought that she was about to kiss him — in which case he would never again wash the place on his face where her lips had rested. But she did not. She opened the door for him, and outside Mantel stood, the cloak and hat in his hands.

"God speed you," she said, "and guard you."

She leaned against the edge of the door feeling, inexplicably, that she would never see him again, never

449

hang around his neck the rose-and-silver striped ribbon bearing the glittering Order of Matilda. This, after all, was a risky business. If the implacable people now in power in Denmark ever even guessed, something horrible would happen to this delightful, high-hearted young man.

She stepped out to the head of the stairs and called sharply,

"Mr. Wraxall!"

"Your Majesty?" he said, halting, turning, looking up to where she stood.

"Whatever happens, don't set foot in Denmark. I will send for you as soon as it is safe."

Spoken loudly like that, in the open; enough to ruin all. The English gentleman and the German page made identical gestures to silence her.

Unheeding, she said, "Promise me."

"I promise," Wraxall said. Seckerdorf had said *an ear at every keyhole*; and in the passage that led away from the library there were many doors. Mantel cocked his head and listened; had one of the doors closed softly? Had he heard an indrawn breath?

Wraxall, half-way down the stairs, bowed again. Mantel said, "Come, we must not be seen," and hurried him away.

It was still raining, and huddled together under the umbrella, plodding back through the mud to the Sand Krug, Mantel said,

"That, sir, was a pity; but she spoke from concern for you. She is a lady whose heart has always ruled her head."

450

"When next you see her, assure her that nothing could possibly happen to me. It is for her own sake that she must be more careful."

"I am careful for her," Mantel said. He was now the only one in her confidence at Zell; Baron Seckerdorf had felt that he could serve her better by joining the conspirators in Hamburg-Altona.

Mantel's old grandmother and her dog were both awake and watchful and the stuffed cabbage was hot. Wraxall was invited to share this late supper and did so, and to his surprise enjoyed a dish of which he had formerly fought shy. The dog remained unfriendly, and it was the first one, in all his travels, that he had known to be inimical after five minutes. He'd been so successful with dogs, everywhere, that he had evolved the theory that all dogs understood English.

Mantel sat at the place where his grandmother wished him to sit for the next forty, fifty years; at the head of the white-scrubbed table. He was home and she intended that he should stay there. She had been kept in ignorance; she had simply been told to look out for a French merchant, demanding roast duck and paying for it with an English guinea and when he arrived, to let her grandson know. But she had guessed a great deal and suspected more. She resented her grandson's attachment to the Queen in the castle, an attachment that had prevented him from coming home when a boy's curiosity about the outer world had been satisfied; she resented the idea, engendered by suspicion, that something was afoot that would take Wolfgang away again. You let them go when they were young and restive, but you wanted them back. They were loaned, not given to the world. The amiable, good looking young man who pretended to be a French merchant, but seemed to her far more like a English milord, was, she concluded, merely a messenger; do away with him and there would be another and another. But the dog hated him, and this confirmed her suspicion that the young man's errand, whatever it was, was inimical to her. And she thought, watching the two men eat cabbage, that cutting twigs and branches was a wasteful business; it was at the root that one must strike. She prepared herself, with all the skill and experience acquired in seven decades, to strike at the root.

"Go to the gentleman, then," she tested the dog, as Wraxall held out on the palm of his hand a little of the meat and liver with which the cabbage had been stuffed. The dog growled and backed away.

Wraxall said he must go to bed, he would be leaving early in the morning. He saw a delicious, busy time ahead of him. He would shuttle between Hamburg, London and Zell. The least that the conspirators would ask would be that, whatever happened, even civil war, the British Minister would stay at his post and the ministry's doors remain open. The least that George III would ask would be a list of the names of the nobles prepared to rise in his sister's cause and some assurance that the main body of popular opinion was behind them. A lot of running to and fro; this time with a purpose, devotion to the woman who had stood at the

452

stairtop in her worn red silk dress and urged him to be careful.

He rather regretted that he had promised not to set foot in Denmark; he felt that, reverting to his role of simple English traveller, he could have gathered useful information, tested public opinion, but he had given his promise.

"They eat so well in the castle kitchen?" the old woman asked dryly.

"Nobody makes stuffed cabbage as you do," Mantel said.

"So!" she said, and smiled at the compliment while discontent seethed in her. The boy, through associating with fools, had become foolish, willing to occupy a menial position in another's house while his own place stood empty. He must be brought home.

For Caroline waiting became harder and patience more difficult to maintain. She realized that George did nothing in a hurry and that even her urgent appeal in the childish code would not change him. He would collect information and brood over it; he would ask advice, accept this, discard that, brood again. In the first flush of hope she had hoped to be back with her children by Christmas; now she thought Easter, perhaps, Whitsun, Midsummer . . . The small flowers of spring bloomed and faded; the daffodils flowered and after them the stately Dutch tulips with their ponderous, commemorative names, Admiral von Enkyen, General van Eyck, and while they still lined the garden paths the lilac broke into flower. Her sense of urgency quickened; she felt that if something were not done quickly it would never be done at all. Baron Seckerdorf sent her the kind of letters suitable to the circumstances, missives anyone could read. Invariably he mentioned the weather. "The weather is improving," meant that things were progressing well. "A storm yesterday," meant a set-back. With such snippets she must be content; and wait and wait.

It was May again.

She liked to walk alone in the garden before breakfast, marking the changes that had come overnight. On the first Thursday of the month she went out into a perfect morning, the counterpart of the one on which, in Kew, she had tried to be one with the lilac bush. And suddenly she knew that this would be a momentous day; another turning point in her life. That delightful Mr. Wraxall would arrive today and bring news that would end the waiting. She was so sure of it that as she walked she planned to give him a good dinner. Beef; somebody must go into the town and procure a sirloin of beef. There would be asparagus too, the young bed was, this year, for the first time, in full bearing. I shan't be here to see the last of it; somebody else will eat the apricots, small green things the size of hazel-nuts against the sunny wall. I shall be in Copenhagen, with Freddy and Louise — and Tammi. They would have parted Freddy and Tammi, *his* ideas were all in disrepute, but wherever Tammi was she'd seek him out; all together again.

Mentally she took leave of the garden which she loved; she reckoned that at this season, in such good weather, travelling as she would travel, unwearying and eager, she could be in Denmark in five days. By this time next week she would have her children in her arms.

It was a dizzying thought and it dizzied her. She was accustomed to such little spells when everything blurred and tilted; they lasted only a few seconds; one had only to wait. She waited, clutching for support at the sun-dial upon whose worn face the words "Tempus edax rerum," were still just discernible. Time devours all.

It devoured the dizzy spell; but it had lasted longer than any she had known and left her feeling strangely weak. The tulip-lined path from here to the door she must make for was a mile, was infinity.

But here was Mantel.

"Your Majesty, what is the matter?"

"Nothing. A dizzy turn. Your arm."

He gave it and said, "I have told Your Majesty that to walk out without breaking fast is unwise."

"You were right." She sagged against his arm so that they seemed to make no progress. The tulip-lined path was a mile long, was infinity.

"Excuse me, Your Majesty; we should do better if you would put your arm around my neck and allow me to put my arm around you. So, is that not better?"

Half dragging, half carrying her he reached the door, the cool dim space behind it, and he steered for the stairs.

She said, "No."

"I think you should go to bed."

"Not on this day. I shall be all right. Help me to a sofa."

Seated, her feet up and a cushion behind her, she felt better. She said, "Mantel, I must not give way now. News will come today."

"We are ready for it," he said, thinking of his good old grandmother, alert for Mr. Wraxall's return.

She said, "Mantel, when all is settled, I shall restore the Order of Matilda, but I shall call it the Order of Caroline. And you shall be one of the first . . ."

Mantel said, "Don't worry about such things now. May I bring Your Majesty some tea?"

"I should like that. And Mantel, while you are in the kitchen, order beef for dinner; the best beef. And the asparagus can be cut. Mr. Wraxall will like that . . ."

"I think I should also send for Doctor Leyfer."

"There is no need. I am better now."

But she spent the morning on the sofa. Her ladies fluttered around, suggesting a glass of wine, a loosening of stay laces — though hers were never tight, a sniff at a bottle of smelling salts. She said thank you, and thank you, and said she was feeling better, would be well by dinner time.

Dinner time brought the asparagus, heaped high, and a splendid sirloin, but no Mr. Wraxall. She dragged herself to the table, but could eat nothing, was faintly nauseated by seeing others eat. When Mantel suggested for the second time that she should go to bed, she said, "Yes. Perhaps that would be as well." Her ladies undressed her and when she was in bed she dismissed them. "I shall do, now. Go to your cards."

Doctor Leyfer came. Five days earlier he had been sent for to attend a sick page in the castle. A few questions had made him reasonably certain that the symptoms indicated putrid fever, so he had sent one of his assistants. An assistant could not be sent to Her Majesty, so, cherishing his preconceived idea, he came, in some fear, and feeling her racing pulse said to himself, oh, dear dear!

"Does Your Majesty feel a soreness of the throat?"

"I feel ill all over." On this day of all days; she still expected Mr. Wraxall to arrive before nightfall.

"The page, recently dead," Doctor Leyfer said, making himself small, drawing little cautious breaths, "did Your Majesty come into close contact with him?"

Stop pestering me; suggest some cure or go away!

"Her Majesty visited him. She visits anyone who is sick," Mantel said.

So there was no doubt about it Dr. Leyfer thought, drawing himself smaller, breathing more shallowly. Putrid fever was most contagious; there was no cure and no palliative except laudanum. The mechanics of contagion were not understood, but its results were plain; with some diseases one victim meant another and another and putrid fever moved fast. Doctor Leyfer, who did not share Struensee's cheerful belief that a doctor who lived to be thirty was immune, could hardly get himself out of the sick room quickly enough.

The Queen would die. He was her doctor, so he must make the hopelessness of her case clear from the start, thus forestalling criticism afterwards. The words *putrid fever* ran around the castle like a cold draught. It

457

seemed sensible to leave Mantel, who had helped her indoors and spent most of the day by her side, to continue to attend her. It was remembered with dismay that she had been present at the dinner table, but the thought that precaution might now be too late made nobody bold.

Mantel did not accept Doctor Leyfer's diagnosis. No other page had sickened — though they had shared sleeping quarters with the dead boy; Her Majesty's visit had been short, just long enough for her to see that he was comfortably bedded, to say, "Be of good heart, Erich; you will soon be better," and to order the window to be opened. Why should she be smitten?

Under the impact of the fever, and the laudanum, faithfully administered because it eased the pains, Caroline's mind was blurred most of the time, but she had sharp sudden intervals of clarity. It seemed to her that whenever she woke Mantel was there. "Mantel, you must go to bed," she said: and "Mantel you must rest." But she had lost all count of time and had no idea of how long his vigil lasted. "Mantel, this is no job for you. Where are the women?"

"I happen to be here, Your Majesty. Don't fret about such things."

On the first day he had sent a message to the *Sand Krug* demanding of his grandmother some anti-fever draught, and something to combat weakness. They came and were administered alongside the laudanum, but they were useless, too.

"Mantel, I am going to die."

"No," he said stoutly. "Your Majesty must not say that. It is now the fourth day. Doctor Leyfer was wrong."

She could not bother to ask what the doctor had said.

"I shall never see my children again. But Mantel you must not grieve."

He would grieve for her and mourn for her as long as he lived.

"You must not lose heart. Would you drink some tea?"

"Did you say four days? Have you slept at all?"

"Oh yes. In the chair."

"I shall never be able to reward you properly; but it will be all right, in the end."

She had drifted away again before the tea could be made and brought; Mantel could no longer spare the time, nor was he welcome in the kitchen. Of the page who brought the tea he asked his invariable question, "Has anyone else sickened?" Nobody had. Sometimes, between sleeping and waking, Mantel entertained fantastic suspicions. Those incautious words in an open corridor with many doors. Poisoned? But how? The only thing she took that was not shared by others was the tea; and he, having developed a taste for it, more often than not drank what was left in the pot.

Then she woke, and seemed better, well enough to write. Her conscience was uneasy about George; she knew that to love was not a crime, but George was still firmly in this world; an assertion of innocence from her death-bed would comfort him.

Red-eyed and half stupefied from lack of sleep, but greatly cheered by the demand for writing materials, Mantel collected them and she forced herself to the final effort. "I die innocent . . . I did not deserve any of the frightful accusations by which the calumnies of my enemies stained my character. In the most solemn hour of my life, I turn to you, my royal brother, to express my heart's thanks for all the kindness you have shown me during my whole life, and especially in my misfortune. I die willingly; for the unhappy bless the tomb."

She wondered whether to mention Mantel and commend him to George's attention, ask some reward for this faithful servant. But that might be misconstrued. Once one's good name was lost every action was suspect; and even she admitted that for a Queen to die, attended only by her valet-de-chambre, was quite extraordinary. Also, even if George refuted so vile a suspicion, his idea of properly rewarding Mantel would be to give him some job on the farm at Windsor — poor George's idea of earthly happiness. The boy would be better here.

She signed the letter, leaving it for Mantel to fold and seal. Then she pulled from her finger the ring that had never been removed since Mamma placed it there. Ten years' wear had not blunted the clarity of the inscription. Read against the background of what had happened to her, the wish might seem ironic, and yet . . . she had known happiness of a kind denied to most people.

460

"Give me your hand," she said. The ring was just large enough for the little finger of his left hand. "May it work for you, too. I thank you for all you have done for me, Mantel; and I tell you again, not to grieve." If she could she would have revealed to him the secret, but it was one that could not be told. All she could say was, "Nothing ends, dear Mantel. There is no end. All is one."

This assurance did not prevent him from weeping when he realized that she was dead.

She was dead, there was nothing more that he could do here. He went down, saying brusquely, "Her Majesty is dead," and pushing his way through all these finely dressed, high-officed people who had eaten and slept and played cards, and feared for their lives. He went to the *Sand Krug* where the old woman said, "So! You have come home."

Mr. Wraxall walked with his brisk, light step back to his lodging in Jermyn Street. Everything was going superbly. He had just learned that His Majesty had written directly to his sister and sent the letter by special Hanoverian courier. Nobody could know what the letter said, but everyone *knew*. Even Baron Lichtenstein, a cautious man, said that His Majesty had convinced himself, at last, that his sister's restoration was the best thing that could happen to Denmark. "His Majesty's letter will inform and prepare the Queen; and to you, Mr. Wraxall, because of your singular service to Her Majesty, will fall the honour of conducting Her

461

Majesty from exile to the country waiting to welcome her."

Could any man ask more?

His servant took his hat and the silver knobbed stick and said, "Sir, have you heard, the Queen is dead?"

The world was full of Queens and it was typical of a serving man to be so inexplicit.

"What Queen?"

"The Queen of Denmark, sir."

That troublesome old woman in Denmark. It couldn't have happened more fortunately! Quite astonishing how once luck turned it ran full spate. It was from Juliana, not from the Regent, that opposition was expected.

"The Queen Mother, Tomkin," Wraxall said, anxious to get things straight; otherwise Tomkin, communicating with his ilk, would spread the most misleading rumours.

"The Queen, sir. The one put away. Zell was it?"

"Great God Almighty," said Wraxall, usually sparing of expletives. "My hat!" However much perturbed a gentleman could not appear in the street without a hat. Hatted, he rushed out in search of a refutal of this rumour.

But it was true. She was dead.

The King of England, reading her letter and knowing that she had never read his, blamed himself for dilatoriness and took another little step along the road at the end of which melancholia waited.

In Copenhagen the Queen Mother and the Regent jostled for power and quarrelled incessantly: the Crown

Prince grew more handsome and more headstrong day by day; the King, sometimes emerging from his cave, enjoyed papercutting; fold here and here, cut there and there and pleasant patterns emerged.

The conspirators, who in the very week of Caroline's death had decided to wait for George no longer, but to move, even without his support, went their ways; some to compound with authority, some to live, self-exiled in Germany.

Caroline lay in a vault in the church at Zell, close to her great-grandmother whose story had been so similar to her own, and yet so different.

Nicolas Wraxall, though he had now no errand, decided to spend the summer in Europe; his father was beginning to show signs of age and when he succeeded to the baronetcy and had responsibility for the estate his free-footed days would end. On his way to Berlin he would visit Zell, seek out Mantel who was said to have been with her in her last hours and who might have some light to throw upon the mystery of her death.

The *Sand Krug* where, for sentimental reasons, he chose to lodge, had changed; Mantel, who had been about the world and lived in places, knew what sophisticated travellers looked for. The old woman and the unfriendly dog had retired into the background; the floor was no longer sanded in curious patterns and the large scrubbed table had been replaced by separate, smaller ones, with stiff white cloths.

"I am not hungry, Mantel," Wraxall said, after they had greeted one another. He had not dined, and a pleasant odour came from the kitchen, but he had no appetite.

"Perhaps, sir, you would take a glass of wine with me?"

"That would be very agreeable. Thank you."

Mantel brought the wine, a good Rhenish, cool from the cellar, poured it and sat down.

"You wish to hear about . . . the end?" Mantel asked.

"I admit to a certain curiosity. Some strange and conflicting rumours are going the rounds. There is even talk of poison; and it is a fact that for some the death was most opportune."

"In Zell," Mantel said, "they are as sure that she was poisoned as though they had seen the poison administered; but they blame an Italian cook who was dismissed more than a year ago. I have considered the matter myself; I was there . . ." He described how near he had been. "It was not putrid fever, nobody else sickened and so far as I could see there was no evidence of poison. I think her course was run."

"That is one way of looking at it," Wraxall said. But so young, so eager, so much alive, calling to him from the stairtop. He'd hoped to see the crown back on that pretty head.

"The Castle," Mantel said, "is deserted again; her rooms just as she left them. The keys were entrusted to me; if you would care to see . . ."

"I think not," Wraxall said, remembering the drawing room where she had greeted him so warmly, the great table where she had re-read the letter under his horrified eyes, the library and the stairs. "What I wish to do, Mantel, is to go to her grave." The word rang hollow; the grave, end of all youth, of beauty, of hope. Now that it had come to the point he was not sure that he could bear it. But company would help, would force composure upon him. "Would you care, Mantel, to accompany me?"

"No," Mantel said, twisting the ring upon his little finger. "I have never . . . I never shall. *I cannot think of her as being there.*"

So alone, with no observer to brace or to criticize, Wraxall, thinking of the girl in the shabby red dress, shed some English tears over the place where the exile lay.

Also available in ISIS Large Print:

A Calf for Venus

Norah Lofts

The Coffee House was a warm, brightly-lit place. The serving girls were pretty and the men who visited the rooms seemed polite enough. But still there were whispers, ugly disquieting rumours about what happened at night when the big oak door was closed.

The young doctor had never been inside the Coffee House — and indeed had no wish to — until he met the frail, shabbily-dressed girl on the Newmarket coach. And when he learned she was joining the girls who worked in the serving rooms, he decided it was time to visit the strange, secretive house on the other side of the square . . .

ISBN 978-0-7531-7944-4 (hb)
ISBN 978-0-7531-7945-1 (pb)

Gad's Hall

Norah Lofts

There were no screams in the night, no objects flying through the air, no murderous, disembodied voices — but Gad's Hall was haunted just the same.

For the Spender family, the ancient, beautifully kept house had seemed a godsend, an incredible bargain, almost a gift from its owner — a kindly man who merely wanted someone to protect the family homestead, to make Gad's come alive again.

And it did. Soon a strong-willed, sensible woman would be overtaken by irrational feelings she could not control, all because of the unspeakable secret kept by the women who had lived at Gad's Hall more than a century ago . . .

Rich in historical detail, suspense and romance, Gad's Hall subtly entices us into the realm of the supernatural with the tale of a house forever doomed by a young girl's powerful obsession.

ISBN 978-0-7531-7942-0 (hb)
ISBN 978-0-7531-7943-7 (pb)

Out of this Nettle

Norah Lofts

His name was Colin Lowrie. A tall, red-haired Scot; a man at 16, whose pride was the ancient clan pride of the Lowries.

And when the clans were broken — massacred in a brutal revenge at Culloden Field — Colin Lowrie was forced to take flight on a journey half-way round the world. A journey to a barbaric slave plantation in the West Indies, then on to New Orleans and a life of lust and debauchery — and to a strange eerie love affair with an eccentric heiress . . .

And always, wherever destiny or chance took the young Scottish rebel, he carried with him the dream of Braidlowrie — Braidlowrie, the home of the Lowries — the home from which he was forever exiled . . .

ISBN 978-0-7531-7940-6 (hb)
ISBN 978-0-7531-7941-3 (pb)

Charlotte

Norah Lofts

When young John Vincent died, the outward respectability of the Cornwall household was undermined. Strangers pried, asked too many questions and pointed accusing fingers at Charlotte — herself eager to escape from the oppressive atmosphere of her father's home.

She fled deep into the countryside and there taught at a school run by the untrusting and untrustworthy Mrs Armitage, who was prepared to keep quiet about Charlotte's past — but only up to a point. When the events come to be recreated, some questions naturally arise. Had Charlotte been responsible for the death of the little pupil she loved? And has that crime been repeated?

In darker moments, even Charlotte herself cannot be sure.

ISBN 978-0-7531-7880-5 (hb)
ISBN 978-0-7531-7881-2 (pb)

Hester Roon

Norah Lofts

The Fleece Inn stood where the three roads joined —
the roads to London, to Norwich and to the sea. Its
trade was prosperous, its hospitality famous and the
host was jolly and generous.

To his servants he was cruel and menacing, and to Ellie
Roon, the most menial servant at the Fleece, he was a
figure of terror. Ellie was used to being bullied, but
when her illegitimate daughter was born — in a
rat-ridden attic of the Fleece — she decided that Hester
must have a different kind of life.

And so, Hester Roon began her eventful progress in the
harsh world of 18th century England. After fleeing
from the inn, and the attentions of the owner, she
became involved in the London underworld. From
there she found herself in a world far beyond her
imaginings . . .

ISBN 978-0-7531-7734-1 (hb)
ISBN 978-0-7531-7735-8 (pb)

ISIS publish a wide range of books in large print, from fiction to biography. Any suggestions for books you would like to see in large print or audio are always welcome. Please send to the Editorial Department at:

ISIS Publishing Limited
7 Centremead
Osney Mead
Oxford OX2 0ES

A full list of titles is available free of charge from:

Ulverscroft Large Print Books Limited

(UK)
The Green
Bradgate Road, Anstey
Leicester LE7 7FU
Tel: (0116) 236 4325

(Australia)
P.O. Box 314
St Leonards
NSW 1590
Tel: (02) 9436 2622

(USA)
P.O. Box 1230
West Seneca
N.Y. 14224-1230
Tel: (716) 674 4270

(Canada)
P.O. Box 80038
Burlington
Ontario L7L 6B1
Tel: (905) 637 8734

(New Zealand)
P.O. Box 456
Feilding
Tel: (06) 323 6828

Details of **ISIS** complete and unabridged audio books are also available from these offices. Alternatively, contact your local library for details of their collection of **ISIS** large print and unabridged audio books.